THE

KIRSCHBAUM

LECTURES

SETH ROGOFF

Sagging
Meniscus

Set in Janson with LaTeX.

ISBN: 978-1-952386-56-5 (paperback)
ISBN: 978-1-952386-57-2 (ebook)
Library of Congress Control Number: 2022950165

Sagging Meniscus Press
Montclair, New Jersey
saggingmeniscus.com

The Kirschbaum Lectures

The Burrow Revisited

T SEEMS LIKE EVERYONE is here now. As I was on my way to the lecture hall, the dean's assistant stopped me and told me a class roster has been placed in my faculty mailbox, but I have no idea where in the massive building to find this faculty mailbox and have come without the list of your names. The absence of the class roster will frustrate what seemed to be the dean's chief concern when I met with him and his assistant a couple of days after arriving from Prague—the enforcement of your attendance of this course, Introduction to Literature, which, as I understand, is a core requirement of the college. I spent the flight from Prague in search of a way to begin this first lecture. I opened my notebook to an empty page and gazed down at it for a long time. Strangely, it didn't seem to be the emptiness of an unmarked page, though I hadn't made a mark on it. Rather, it was more like the emptiness of erasure, of words, names, and stories once there and now gone—related, I suspect, to my stay at the clinic Zelená Hora and the methods of its director, Dr. L. Hruška. I'd have to begin, I thought, by locating the palest contours of those erased marks, tracing them with my mechanical pencil. I

bent down over the page for hour after hour until, somewhere above the Atlantic Ocean, the first ghostly forms surfaced into the visible realm, or, to put it another way, into consciousness.

During my first months at the clinic Zelená Hora, I'd become friends (I hesitate to use this word) with another patient or "guest," the novelist Daniel Cohen. Then one day it occurred to me, quite spontaneously, that I'd known him years ago in Berlin. How my past with Cohen had remained hidden from me for those months remains a mystery, though this secret knowledge, as Dr. Hruška called it, aligns with patterns of memory I'd like to investigate in this course, patterns which necessitated—Hruška believed—my admission to the clinic in the first place. When the memory of Cohen surfaced, it provoked a severe deterioration of my relationship with the doctor. I imagine it is because the story I told him about Cohen shattered the coherence of the case-study he was writing about me; and he had, up until this point, been sure it would be one of his best case-studies yet, based as it was on the discovery of a new psychological "disorder." Hruška, facing difficulty trying to force the past events with Cohen into his understanding of my case, instead concluded that the memory was made up, a symptom, he said, of my compulsion to form antagonistic pairings to locate myself in the world, pairings that enabled me, he said, to conceal deep tensions between truth and self-deception.

Days after the intrusion of memory, as I was waiting for my session to begin, the assistant, Ms. Králová, mentioned to me—and I have no doubt he instructed her to do this—that Dr. Hruška was now fully resolved to reassemble the pieces of my case. In fact, she said, he had already made significant progress.

If I hadn't found my way out of the clinic, I have no doubt Hruška would have succeeded in putting the story back together again, fusing its now scattered and splintered fragments into a seeming whole. I did find my way out. The letter I received from the dean, extending me the offer to teach this course, enabled me to escape Hruška and the clinic and Prague and all of Europe. It allowed me to return home to be with my ailing father, Professor Emeritus Walter Kirschbaum, and to pretend the last twenty years never existed.

Undeniably, though, these last years did exist, however much of a blur they've become. My father had gone from a neurotic but playful intellectual to something of a manic-depressive octogenarian, who did little beyond scribbling answers to crossword puzzles and taking afternoon walks. And I, as you surely know, had completed the translation of Jan Horak's *Blue, Red, Gray*, which was sufficiently impressive to the dean—or at least he was impressed by my winning of the PEN Translation Prize—for him to offer me a one-semester appointment as a visiting professor of literature. Because he had no proof I could teach, he offered me what he called a hybrid position—one course, this class, combined with a residency stipend to pursue my own work. But I have no other work. The seventeen years translating Horak's magnum opus have bled me dry. More than that, the translation process, as Hruška and others (my brother, Henry, for example) tell me, obliterated the thin border between Horak's masterwork and my *Preface* to it—in other words between my life and Horak's. And this migratory impulse, so says Hruška, threatened the stability of my "structure of selfhood," such that the slightest slippage between one zone and another might result in complete collapse. A thick wall must be erected, Hruška told me, and no doubt Henry would agree, between oneself and another, between the life of a novelist and that of the novel's translator, between that which is inside and that which falls beyond. To the contrary, I responded, this barrier is precisely what needs breaching. There would have been no way of completing the translation of *Blue, Red, Gray*, let alone the composition of my *Preface*, without this rupture. Literature, I said to Hruška, occurs in the breach.

The memory of Cohen came to me one evening as I was returning from a walk and saw Milena coming toward me across the stretch of lawn between the large, unused aviary on the far side of the clinic's garden and the guests' quarters. She had paused by the so-called "wounded cedar" to remove a pebble from her shoe. This cedar—fittingly a Siberian—had been struck by a shard of shrapnel fired on the clinic by the Soviet army, who were perhaps aware that during the planning of Operation Barbarossa, the clinic's main building housed what was called the map room, one of the key administrative centers for coordinating German attacks. Just minutes before the strike, as Hruška never tired of telling (though how he knew this was unclear), the clinic's alarm system had issued its "all-clear," or *Entwarnung*, a long, even tone that continued to resound for weeks after the Nazis abandoned the grounds.

With her right hand, Milena steadied herself against the cedar's trunk, placing her fingers a few inches away from the tree's wound, a vertical incision of some length, out of which a golden resin had flowed and hardened, creating a jewel-like, translucent bulb. With her other hand, she reached down and grasped the pebble, removed it, inspected it briefly, and then tossed it to the garden path—an intoxicating, seductive choreography.

Milena was originally from Warsaw and had arrived at the clinic, like Cohen, from Berlin. She was a fashion designer, but because of a nervous breakdown, she'd developed tremors in her hands, and the shaking of those poor hands acted as a stimulant for relapse, sending her spiraling into the darkest of mental states. To still that tremor—there could be no greater calling for a lover, a lover like me who could lead Milena out of the thick undergrowth of neurosis and into the open meadow of health. Horrible words! I know, I know. Don't note them down, whatever you do—if you've noted them down, cross them out: undergrowth, cross out, meadow, cross out.

After some casual remarks, I mentioned to her that I'd be spending the latter part of the evening in the library, finishing an article I'd been asked to write about Horak's novel and what has been described as my "unorthodox" *Preface*. I told Milena I'd be pleased if she joined me, especially since it would be helpful to get another pair of eyes on the text before I mailed it off to the magazine in New York. As part of my treatment at the clinic, I was forbidden to use computers and had to submit my handwritten pages to Ms. Králová for typing—and Králová couldn't be bothered with corrections if mistakes were discovered later. Milena declined; she was, she said, burrowed deep into Cohen's new manuscript—his next book after the magnificent novel *Stuck*.

As Milena walked away, it came to me: the night of November 28, 1996, my "shattering" memory, which Hruška could resist or react to but couldn't figure out how to assimilate. In it, Cohen and I stood in front of a three-story building on Grunewaldstrasse in Berlin. We passed through an iron gate and went up a set of concrete steps. The door in front of us was a muddy brown color. To the left was a brick wall with a plaque on it. I read:

Die Guten gehn im gleichen Schritt. Ohne von ihnen zu wissen tanzen die andern um sie die Tänze der Zeit.

And underneath, this:

Franz Kafka 3 Juli 1883 – 3 Juni 1924

Der Dichter lebte in diesem Hause von Spaetsommer 1923 bis Anfang 1924

I looked on as Cohen retrieved a skeleton key and inserted it into the lock. It took some effort, but finally the bolt gave way and the hinges creaked as the door swung back into the dark, gaping hallway. Dark! Gaping! For God's sake, it was late November. It was a threatening, damp, cold night, like countless other nights. I followed Cohen inside. Off to the left was another door. He knocked. Nothing stirred. Cohen found a second key, not unlike the first, and unlocked the door. We stepped directly from the hallway into a small living room with no vestibule.

Earlier that November evening, I'd taken refuge from the party to catch my breath, to think, to suffer, on a balcony off the bedroom. Through the bare branches of a chestnut tree, I saw the turgid waters of Kreuzberg's Landwehrkanal reflecting the streetlamps and neon. Traffic peeled away from an intersection on Kottbusser Damm. The party was a celebration of Ingrid Müller's book *Forest Poems*. It was among my earliest translations—and it was the first time my client was also my lover.

By the end of the translation process, our relationship had become complicated. While the strain of completing the slim volume was nothing compared to the suffering that went into Horak's masterwork, I was, at the time, only twenty-one years old, and I didn't know how to alleviate tension and nervous anxiety except through the ravages of love. I was on the balcony, holding a bottle of beer and running my thumb around the bottle's mouth, when Cohen stepped outside.

He asked if I was Sy Kirschbaum, the translator.

"Yes," I told him.

He said with a good amount of perversity that he imagined it must be something to wrestle with a corpus like Ingrid's.

"I guess," I said, "though I'm not sure I'd put it that way."

"From all appearances," he said, "you've endured some blows." I said I didn't know what he meant. "There's no way to tame that verse," he said. "I know it better than anyone." This comment bothered me a great deal. I told him I wasn't trying to "tame" it, pronouncing the word *tame* with extra vehemence. He told me that that's not what he'd heard. I wanted to know who told him this. Was it Florian? "Who else," he said.

It had been Florian who'd introduced me to Ingrid and gotten me the job translating *Forest Poems*. There was wildness in these poems, something barbaric or even Teutonic—horribly Teutonic—that evoked an atavism that made my skin crawl. At the same time, in this atavistic wildness—or at least running alongside it or woven into it—was a luscious beauty, what I've called, in my *Preface*, a voluptuousness. A voluptuousness that also meant a ripeness, a distended quality—the point when ripeness turns to rot. The poems burst to ripeness with an elemental power and then, their juices surging, begin to decompose, and this precise moment, the turn in the poem from ripeness to rot, from growth to decay—and all the poems contained such a transition—was conveyed with the lightest possible linguistic touch. And to translate this touch, what was this but an attempt to replicate a fingerprint or the texture of a lover's skin?

The party blurred into the background. In the distance lay the canal, the Kottbusser Damm. I'd seen Cohen in the kitchen, putting a pack of beer into the refrigerator. I'd seen him over by the shelves, inspecting Ingrid's collection of vinyl records. Then

I saw him leafing through a copy of the translation, now and then rubbing his fingers in his thick, black beard. How did I not recognize him right away when I came to the clinic? In truth, on the night of the party I never learned his name. In addition, he'd grown much thinner over the years, making him appear taller and older than he was—more like me. He'd gotten rid of the beard, shortened his hair and replaced his wide, rectangular glasses with a pair of wire-rimmed ovals.

The interior of the house on Grunewaldstrasse looked like a grandmother's living room—a sitting room for tea and polite conversation. Stuffy. Kitsch. Overstuffed pillows, floral patterns, cheap objects on wooden shelves. Faded wallpaper.

I asked him if he lived here.

"Of course not," he said.

I asked him if he'd been here before.

He told me he had, though "only in a manner of speaking."

There was a door along the opposite wall that appeared to lead to a closet or pantry. Cohen opened it to reveal stairs leading down into the darkness.

"You've been here before," I said, "you know what you're doing."

Again, he replied, "In a manner of speaking."

As we walked down the narrow staircase, Cohen told me that Franz Kafka had spent the last months of his life in this house on Grunewaldstrasse. From the space above and heading downward, Cohen said, Kafka had built his final literary structure: a burrow. At the center of the burrow, Cohen told me, is the castle keep, a "vaulted and beautiful chamber" to house the stores. The keep is the fortress within the fortress, the refuge, the place of last resort—that is to say, Cohen said, it's the symbol of freedom and its opposite: imprisonment, confinement, loss. Beyond the castle keep are the ramparts, constructed with blood and suffering, then the long passageways and ventilation holes, then the labyrinth—built in baroque fashion to confuse and disorient—and finally the doorway of moss leading up to the world above. The system is elaborate, intricate, and as a defensive structure, he said, a gorgeous failure. The first attack, the first breach of even the outermost line of defense, would expose its weakness, the shoddiness of its design, the limits of its builder's vision. Or perhaps it would simply prove the radical impossibility of the goal, Cohen concluded, absolute security, or a type of selfhood only possible in a dreamless sleep.

Cohen, Daniel Cohen, I thought as we descended, if one of us were the inhabitant of the burrow, the other would be the one whose distant sound would give rise to the inhabitant's panic, the one who would provoke the inhabitant not only to question everything, but to consider fleeing from the burrow into the wild fate of the forest. But who—Cohen or myself—is this second entity, this unseen and inscrutable being who issues a sound like a swarm moving through the earth as it gets closer and closer, closer to overtaking the burrow, to filling its passageways and laying waste to the stores? Who? Who! My god, a bulb flickered, and shadows stretched as we moved down the staircase.

We came to a door at the bottom. Cohen knocked.

The door opened and Cohen entered. I hesitated, then stepped from the passage into a poorly lit room. An ashen man was standing there.

"Kirschbaum," Cohen said, "this is Dr. Kaesbohrer."

He extended a gaunt arm and wrinkled hand. His handshake was limp. When he stepped back, I looked around the room. Against the walls were the chemist's experimentation tables, covered with grimy glassware. Above one of the tables, an elaborate mathematical equation was carved into the wall. I asked Kaesbohrer what it was.

Many years ago, he told me, he had started to hear a strange noise coming from somewhere below him. At times, it seemed like the noise was holding steady, at others like it was intensifying, indicating that whatever was making the noise was coming closer. A number of details needed to be known about this "thing"—a thing represented only by sound. To determine these details, and to solve the pressing problems the noise represented, Kaesbohrer explained, he'd had to stop work on his main academic experiments. Of critical importance were the following questions: 1) Was the thing drawing closer, staying in the same place, or pulling away? And 1a) If away, in what direction? 2) Was the thing a) some human construct, a machine, b) an animal, c) a geological force, or d) a non-material spirit? 3) Was the thing a) singular or b) a pack or swarm of things? 4) What were the basic physical characteristics of the thing, if it wasn't a non-material spirit or force? 5) Approximately how far away was the thing currently? 6) At what speed was it moving?

Kaesbohrer had answered, at least tentatively, only one of the questions. As far as he could tell, given his understanding of the properties of sound and the geological material through which the sound had to pass to reach him, the thing was anywhere between twenty and two hundred meters down into the earth at a thirty-five-degree slope in a southwesterly direction.

"It's a complex calculation," Kaesbohrer said, "as anyone can see from the equation on the wall—and the equation on the wall represents only the final stage of the theoretical process. Of course, the formula contains many assumptions, too many to name; they have to do with variables like the presence of electrical and magnetic fields, other physical unknowns, and what I like to call a metaphysical unknown—the term I use is the general unknown [*die allgemeine Unbegreiflichkeit*]. I have represented it with the mathematical expression U^a, the unknown or unknowable to the general power. As you might be able to tell, this variable acts as a vortex on the entire statement, ultimately subsuming it into itself, collapsing all that is known into that which is not, and cannot be, known. It is only by bracketing or removing the general unknown, the U^a, that we can arrive at the still-speculative 20-200m SW. But this was enough for me, and I intended to meet the challenge of the thing by confronting it. After years of calculating, it was finally time to act. It was time for me to build my experimental trench in the direction of the thing."

Cohen sat on a wooden chair by the table of glassware. I stood over a square outlined in charcoal, the demarcation of where Kaesbohrer would have started digging the entrance to the trench. The trench—now we are getting somewhere—a downward sloping, crosscutting trench, a forward thrust. Yes, this is getting somewhere.

"No sooner had I outlined the spot," K. said, "then the sound abruptly stopped, or maybe it faded, or it became a kind of different sound, a staccato sound, a rhythm, one might say, that would require not a trench, but something more like a burrow, an underground spider's web—something with an extra dimension, maybe a fourth dimension, to ensnare and destroy the thing. Yes, to ensnare and destroy it. But nothing more happened after this decisive shift from sound to rhythm. The course was set; fate was sealed. The trench became an abstraction. I wasn't about to give in to doom," K. said. "I was intoxicated by the idea of two hostile or antagonistic maze-like systems weaving around each other. I was determined to find the way of expressing this puzzle, as you can see from the other wall, and this expression had to do with the fate of that physical being, the idea of the transformation of physical matter through combination, namely with a type of chemistry that gestured to something older, to what one might call the alchemical tradition. And through that, through the alchemical, two related but divergent paths would emerge. The first path leads into the magical, the second into the psychological. And these two paths seek their endpoint in the general unknown, converging at the U^a. How, then, do we get to them? How to embark, which way to go? For years, I sat and thought about these questions, about the limits of the artistic and scientific mind to grasp at higher knowledge. It was as if my very body became the web of passageways, and the energy inside me was like that noise pulsing through the labyrinth, pulsing through the earth, pulsing through my blood. Did I, Kaesbohrer, become a variable in the equation? Did U^a transform into K.? I started mixing—a pinch of one thing and another. It's confidential. I can't share with you even the more seemingly inconsequential details. No. The point is that I developed an antidote to this deteriorating situation. There is no easy way to describe the antidote's effects; one needs to experience it. Since I've run out of ingredients, I've only got a little bit of the substance left. Here, take the last two vials. Drink them. Glimpse that inaccessible opponent, the thing, the beast whom you long to devour and who longs with equal rapaciousness to devour you."

Cohen and I pulled the corks out of the glass vials. Inside each was about a spoonful of cloudy yellow liquid. I hesitated. I could feel my hand that was holding the vial begin to tremble, but I didn't know if it was trembling out of fear or desire. Had I not just come from the party, had things (especially things with Ingrid) taken a slightly different turn in the weeks and months leading up to this night, I don't think I would have poured Kaesbohrer's potion down my throat. But I did. I can remember nothing more about that night or the following day.

Nothing except this: as I was emerging from the deeper blackness, I had what resembled a hypnagogic vision—a vision of the real within the unreal that takes place as we first fall asleep. I experienced a kind of counter-story of my life, a parallel current of existence. It was as real—as possible—as me being here giving this lecture. No, this lecture is in fact less possible than its countercurrent.

In the countercurrent, I was not single and alone, as I am now, but married with two children, Lillian and Ezra. I lived with my wife and children in a small attic apartment in Berlin. I had written five novels, which sat unpublished on the shelf of my closet-sized office, a room accessible only through a tiny door in the apartment's kitchen. Undaunted, I was writing another book about a character named Daniel Cohen, a man I had met at a clinic in the Czech Republic—a clinic that had previously been named the Grünhofberg, but now was called the clinic Zelená Hora. Though it was the same clinic Horak used to go to, there was no Horak in this counter-world, there was no translation of Horak's *Blue, Red, Gray*, there was no Ingrid Müller or Florian or any of the others. I'd been forced to go to the clinic after a breakdown, during which I had smashed all the computer equipment in our home—a desktop computer (thrown from the balcony), two laptops, and an Internet router. The precise trigger for this psychic break didn't make itself clear in the counter-narrative. My wife, Beata, found me asleep after the smashing. She woke me up, tried to figure out what had happened, upbraided me, and then left with the kids. I fell asleep again, couldn't keep my eyes open. Flashes of scenes with Hruška played and replayed—scenes from the clinic, scenes with Horak, scenes inside Horak's masterwork with its protagonist, Josef Kostel, with Sidney Keter, with Isaac Mondschein and *The Book of Moonlight*, and on and on until this paroxysm came to an end and I was walking, years later, on a cold, rainy day through the streets of Steglitz and wandered, quite by accident, past the house on Grunewaldstrasse. No skeleton key, no living room, no small doorway, no passage to the basement, no subterranean chamber, no Kaesbohrer, and no Daniel Cohen.

Then I woke—wifeless, childless, alone, and sprawled out on a bed in a cheap Kreuzberg hotel, feeling like absolute hell. Cohen—nowhere to be seen.

It must be said by way of a tentative conclusion to this first lecture of the semester that there was another Kaesbohrer—actually, two more. The first was a writer who died of tuberculosis in 1924 and left behind a young fiancée and a crate of unpublished manuscripts. One manuscript contained the story of an animal who builds his burrow only to be gripped by fear of a strange noise in the undefined distance.

The second—or rather, third—Kaesbohrer was a lawyer for an insurance company who saw what was happening in Berlin in the late 1920s and set out to construct an underground chamber beneath his rooms in a building on Grunewaldstrasse. In 1936, after being fired from his job, the third Kaesbohrer left the world of the living behind and descended into his lair. No sooner had he achieved a sense of relative peace and routine there than a strange noise emerged, coming from the distance. After years of sleepless nights and constant worry, Kaesbohrer decided to construct an "experimental trench," as he called it, sloping down from his chamber toward the southwest. He started digging. Days and weeks and years of exhausting work went into the trench's construction. Eventually, this third Kaesbohrer started to think that the noise was getting closer, growing louder, that his mysterious adversary drew nearer. In the spring of 1943, just as the German army began to lose the initiative in Russia, just as the whole course of human history was about to take its decisive turn (not that the third Kaesbohrer knew anything about it) the experimental trench opened at the bottom and out fell the burrowing lawyer into a tunnel deep underground.

As it happened, the tunnel ran from the central Reichspostamt in Kleinmachnow—the central post office of the German Empire—into the heart of Berlin, ending at the SS complex on Wilhelmstrasse. The tunnel was packed with people pushing mail carts back and forth, creating a near-constant humming, rumbling sound. Not surprisingly, Kaesbohrer was arrested at once. He was brought to an interrogation cell in the basement of Prinz-Albert Strasse 8 and there accused of being a member of the so-called Mole Society, or *Maulwurf Gesellschaft*, which, though it didn't exist, was said to be planning to penetrate the Nazi system of tunnels and bunkers to demolish the nerve centers of the regime. There is no record of Kaesbohrer's interrogation in the basement of Prinz-Albert Strasse 8. There is no record of his death. Perhaps, if we go to the site of that place—now a museum—and press our ear to the ground, we will be able to hear a noise that resembles a human scream still trembling in the earth.

Guests at the Hotel des Bains

 CRIME OCCURRED toward the end of my stay at the clinic Zelená Hora: Daniel Cohen's newly completed manuscript was stolen. In an age when it seems like even God can't wipe our fingerprints from any surface we touch, when evidence of our activities lingers forever, it is absurd to think that an entire manuscript could vanish without a trace. At first, it appeared that the manuscript was the casualty of a lovers' quarrel, but this theory would prove too convenient, too simplistic to hold out against my journey toward the truth.

Just days before the theft, I'd received word about winning the PEN Translation Prize for *Blue, Red, Gray*, which provoked in me a sort of dialectical reaction of both a massive pride and a rather inexplicable sense of shame and depression, the latter overshadowing the former. I say this not because it makes sense of anything or explains even a single sub-phenomenon within the greater or bigger phenomenon, but because it gives the thing a certain thrust, a velocity, or maybe, to speak more visually, a shade or tint to the composition. In a strange twist of fate, the heady moment of the PEN announcement coincided with two other events. The first was that my translation of the first novel I'd ever done, Anton Grassfeld's *Trending Toward Zero*, was acquired and re-released in a large print-run. This provided me with a handsome windfall—I won't bore you with the financial details but will only point out that the sum far exceeds the meager contract extended to me by the dean. The release of the new version of *Trending Toward Zero* and the seemingly universal assessment that Grassfeld was the next Günter Grass or W.G. Sebald related to the second event: my receiving in the clinic's mail, the day before I left, a copy of another of Grassfeld's novels, *Ein Mädchen am Strand* (*A Girl on the Beach*), which the publisher wanted to put out as soon as possible. In the span of twenty-four hours, one book had vanished, and another appeared. Dr. Hruška, in what would be our final session, chided me, telling me that of course it wouldn't do for me to have one thing happen without the other. Thesis, he said, always required me to produce an antithesis.

What would you expect from an introduction to literature course except books flying this way and that? One appearing, one vanishing. And despite the undeniable materiality of its existence, Cohen's manuscript would have remained an airy nothingness had not Milena vanished with it—and had she not followed the trail I knew she would follow to the place I knew she would go.

Permit me to spend some moments on *Mädchen, Girl on the Beach*, since it will eventually lead us to Milena. Before that, though, a bit of necessary context will keep the dean's assistant off my back, at least for a little while. It seems the dean has set her up as a sort of sentry, maybe as a way of ensuring that this will be my one and only contract with the college. They've had their PEN prizewinner now. Box checked. They can wipe their hands clean: a happy board of directors, a nice blurb in the alumni newsletter, a local news story. Don't worry, I can defend myself, though most likely unsuccessfully, just as I defended myself (unsuccessfully) against Hruška, besting him time and again only to succumb to the inevitability of a creeping defeat.

I was living in Berlin—Kreuzberg—and was not much older than you are now. I'd come straight from college, plunging into that rubble-heap of a neighborhood still in the shadow of the Cold War. Can you, who were born well after 1989, imagine such a place, a divided Berlin—an immediate post-partition Berlin, a Kreuzberg of Turks and anarchists, punks, drunks, artists, utopians and dystopians? Through a friend, I'd been introduced to Florian, a translator from Slavic languages to German and West Berlin native. He had a room to rent, and I was happy to take it, despite the need to constantly attend to one coal-burning oven for heat and another to boil the hot water for my weekly bath. I'd brought some money with me, but quickly burned through it despite the utter cheapness of everything in the city, including my room in Florian's apartment, which cost me about $75 a month. By the age of twenty-five, Florian had already achieved considerable success and had the contract to translate the first book to be published in German by Jan Horak, the post-1968 novel *Rain*. Little did I know how key this timing would be. When Florian saw that I was broke, he offered to help me out, eventually introducing me to a group of Kreuzberg writers, from among whom I received the job to translate *Forest Poems* by Ingrid Müller. It was a shattering, destabilizing experience and at the same time a near-total ecstasy, a type of euphoria that erodes one's sense of self and gestures toward absolute and blissful annihilation. It was a tightrope walk between total love and total desperation. Youth—I'm sure you know the feeling. There's no way to avoid it, despite all the warnings about propriety from the dean's assistant. It was about love, sex, dissolution, disintegration, and demise.

I still don't know the backstory between Florian and Ingrid Müller, though I know there was a backstory, maybe a long one. That such an affair would begin between me and Ingrid was bound to lead to friction at home, though the type of friction that would remain undetectable, at least for a time. In retrospect, what seemed like friction now appears to be deliberate sabotage, starting with *Trending Toward Zero*, continuing with *Blue, Red, Gray*.

Trending Toward Zero—the dark, postmodern descent into West Berlin of the 1980s with the anti-hero *par excellence*, the Romanian-German Emil Hofer, at once a street thug, a German ethno-nationalist, a leftist-anarchist, and the lead singer of a Kreuzberg punk band called The Nihilists. It was a disquieting work, a disgusting work, actually, a work I felt dirtied by, sullied when rendering it into English. Still, there was no denying its magnificence, its cold, brutal beauty. Despite this beauty, as I said in my *Preface* to *Blue, Red, Gray*, I would have abandoned the book halfway through if I didn't really need the money. It was Hofer's performance of "Burn Down the Synagogue/Torch the Mosque" which made me throw down the pen. And I threw down the pen, I did, but eventually I picked the pen back up at the behest of the editor Phil Jones, who made a series of polite entreaties followed by a set of hostile demands, including the threat of a lawsuit over breach of contract. "We're not paying you to be a literary critic," Jones wrote, "just to translate the damn pages." As it happened, following the release of the English edition critics called "Burn Down the Synagogue" a brilliant piece of cultural commentary, many comparing The Nihilists' performance to Oskar Matzerath's performance in the "Onion Cellar" in Grass's *Tin Drum*. Professional opinion concluded that Grassfeld had produced the great challenge to pre-unification German society of the Kohl years. German sales of the book surged in the aftermath of the Communist collapse. The English version caught fire as Berlin itself caught fire, becoming part of the nostalgia machine that linked 1920s cabaret to the punk rock scene in SO36 to the current techno-design ethos—from bohemian counterculture, in other words, to the ecstasy-techno capitalism of today. I can't get into that now, not this evening as the sun sets behind us. No. The horrors and the hypocrisies of the current situation are too much here, the city, Berlin, unrecognizable after my seventeen years in Prague submerged in Jan Horak's world.

I'll admit another thing, which I'm sure you have already assumed—but it's a foundational point: even with the honors and accolades, by the end of translating *Blue, Red, Gray* (and even after the PEN award) I was broke, basically penniless. The windfall from the re-release of *Trending Toward Zero* provided a bit of fuel—and then *Mädchen am Strand* arrived at my door. Under these circumstances, I had to consider it. It was irksome to me that I needed it, needed to return to the valley of Grassfeld after standing atop the Promethean heights of Horak. When I had finished Horak, I had vowed to myself I would never translate another word.

Now we can leave these preliminaries behind and set out on the path after Milena. The first step along this path requires a detour, the purpose of which should become clear by the end of the session today. Grassfeld calls his book *Mädchen am Strand*, the translation of which is *Girl on the Beach*. After reading the book, I was convinced that the title was a mistake. Better would have been *Mädchen am Rand des Meeres* or *Girl at the Edge of the Sea*. When I wrote to Grassfeld and suggested it, he fired back that I should leave the creative part of the work to him. He added that he looked forward to receiving my draft so he could make the "necessary corrections."

Girl on the Beach—we need to start here, to start with the central triangle upon which the whole system can be assembled. One corner of the triangle is a German novelist named—horribly—Anton Grassfeld, a forty-eight-year-old former Berlin bohemian now living in a large Kreuzberg apartment with his British wife Susan and their two kids, Rolf and Cassie, ages fifteen and ten. Grassfeld is thin, tall. He wears thick rectangular glasses, has a short beard with graying whiskers. He's on vacation with his family for three weeks on the Italian Riviera, in the town of Finale Ligure. The second corner of the triangle is Renzo Romano. He's the opposite of Grassfeld. He's short, stout, tanned, brash—in typical Grassfeld (author) fashion, something of a stereotype, a cliché, the type of stereotype that ultimately fractures the book and allows some of its internal energy to seep out. The third point is, of course, Anita, a young woman from Senegal, a beach vendor in Finale Ligure, where Grassfeld is on vacation and where Renzo runs his business, a business that pays the way for Senegalese women to come to Italy to walk the beaches and sell his wares, first to slowly pay off their debts to him and then, finally, to earn a modest living, most of which is then sent back home to support family or to pay for the next relative's journey across the Mediterranean. After the season, when debts are paid, Renzo's women fan out— some to other businesses he owns or has connections to, others somewhere else entirely. The beaches are just part of Renzo's empire. Sure, he earns money on the goods—hats, sunglasses, scarves, bags, umbrellas, towels, and so on, maybe a hundred thousand euros a year, depending on the year and depending on how many beaches he can manage to control in the complex dealings with property owners, local politicians, and the mob.

Equal to this—or even greater than this—is the profit he obtains from the human migration, from the hundred or two hundred women who, when all is said and done, pay Renzo about three or four grand each. Each year, therefore, he pulls in maybe half a million euros from the beaches—a lot of money, yes, of course, but only a small fraction of his total worth, which also includes businesses and real estate throughout Liguria, Tuscany, Turin, and Milan. Renzo is from Milan, where he lives most of the year with his wife and son, Carlo, a student of law at Milan University.

Carlo is thin, medium height, with a long, narrow face and a Roman nose, dark skin, dark eyes. He's good looking, but in a gawky, gloomy way. Probably having to do with having a dominant father, he is reserved. He's a good student, though not excellent—a fine student, an average student. Now twenty, he had a phase at seventeen of wanting to be a poet, but couldn't break free from the most obvious word, phrase, or image. He fails to shatter the commonplace or to harness the commonplace in the pursuit of some notion that pushes toward what we might call, in one way or another, in one form or another, beauty. After a year or two of wasting energy to move beyond his God-given limits, Carlo surrenders to them. He finds tranquility there, a type of calmness that comes from recognition of inevitable mediocrity. It's a position that typically results in a softness of character, a mushiness of form—but not with Carlo. Carlo remains austere, serious, forlorn.

Anita sells shawls for Renzo by walking back and forth along the miles of Ligurian coastline each day with her fabrics draped over her arms and bunched in a basket on her head. She lives with two older Senegalese women in a small apartment about twenty minutes' walk outside of town, an apartment with one small bedroom that the three women share, a bathroom, and a kitchen. It wasn't her but her mother who was supposed to come to Italy. Her mother was a strong, sturdy woman. She'd raised Anita and her two younger brothers alone after their father had died.

I can't spend much more time on Anita's mother—the path to the manuscript and to Milena doesn't necessitate such a wide detour. If it had, if the search had required, in other words, an act of courage or bravery or selflessness or simply anything that took a bit of daring and boldness, anything that would have made me uncomfortable or scared or even disquieted—though in truth I was disquieted—it's unlikely I would have made it to the end. Anita's mother fell ill after her older brother left for the country-side. The younger brother went to live with their grandmother. Anita went to Renzo.

This is disgusting on a basic level. I'm sure you're feeling the disgust as it creeps in. The refined genius of the German male narrator named Grassfeld, the prepossessing but dull and per-haps artistically stifled youth, Carlo, who is trying to conform to the expectations of his rich father, Renzo, a figure on the bor-derline of capitalism and criminality. Only someone like (the real) Grassfeld could write such a book, a blend of Goethe and Thomas Mann with the shadowy zones of Hesse, the coarseness of Günter Grass, the lyricism (at rare but undeniable times) of Sebald.

Carlo arrives in Finale for a weekend on the beach in July, after completing several major exams. Instead of staying at his family's villa off the road to Borgo, he decides to occupy their apartment overlooking the beach so he can go to sleep with the sea in his ear and wake up to the sight of that vast expanse of blue. On the day of his arrival, he takes a spot at the Bagni Garibaldi, the private beach directly across from the apartment, which hap-pens to be near the Hotel Marconi, where Grassfeld and his family are staying—and thus, as you would expect, they also rent umbrellas and chairs at the Garibaldi. And the Garibaldi is part of Anita's daily route. She traverses it, back and forth, at least half a dozen times per day.

Grassfeld, who has been in Finale already a week before Carlo arrives, has taken note of Anita. And I use "taken note of" deliberately to imply the coolness—or the feigned coolness—of his gaze. It is something like the German word *Wissenschaft*—science—and how it's extended to nearly every domain of inquiry, as if "to inquire" necessarily means to inquire with a certain adherence to a methodological paradigm and with appropriate methodological rigor, that the one who does the inquiring has tools, principles, methods, concepts—a *Wissenschaftler*, a scientist. Here, the artist as *Wissenschaftler*, Grassfeld (character) props up the back of his beach chair, takes his notebook from his canvas beach bag, clicks the lead out of his mechanical pencil, and jots down a few notes about a young "African" woman selling a turquoise shawl to his wife and a coral-colored, lace-fringed beach dress to Cassie, his daughter. He notes, "beach vendor, deep black skin, young, captivating, transfixing eyes, skin on neck—luscious, regal posture, 'noble savage,' I—full of civilized savagery." In the evening, he walks down the promenade to have a drink at the Ristorante Garibaldi. He orders a beer and guzzles it down. He has a scotch on the rocks, sips it. He can't get Anita out of his mind, takes out his notebook and pencil. Click, click. It's a story about a German man on an Italian beach who fantasizes about a black African beach vendor. I know I might get in trouble with the dean's assistant for saying this, but this is how it's written: it felt to Grassfeld like masturbation, yes, like pleasuring himself in some dusky peep show, some dingy, back-alley sex shop. No! An upwelling of some vestige of propriety forces Grassfeld to stop writing, to put down the pencil, and to tear up his pages. He can't go through with the story, can't bring himself, in other words, to climax. He considers his life, his literary success. He's published six novels. He's won prizes, given readings at the Frankfurt Book Fair. Back in Berlin, he's something of a celebrity, hosting a monthly literary program at the Volksbühne's *Roter Salon*. What does the fame matter? The ripping of pages—and he thinks of himself as pages—is nothing less than a crisis of selfhood. Class dimensions, sexual politics—yes, all of it. He takes another drink, another scotch. But he can't stand it, any of it—himself, his past work, his life, the very fact that he is sitting alone at a table at the Ristorante Garibaldi listening to Italian rock ballads and drinking mid-level scotch. The word "German" crashes over his mind. He hates the word—despises it—and yet it seems to consume him, to subsume him into its etymology. The ways she displays her garments, the eyes, the cheeks, the roundish face, the sea of color draped around her. He wants her real story, not some false progressive self-flagellation of a middle-aged, middle class author yearning for the Third World, if such a thing exists. Her story, his writing. He would redeem himself by suppressing his ego and allowing her voice to reign.

In the late afternoon of the following day, he calls Anita over to the umbrella. Susan has gone to the water with the kids. Does he need something, Anita asks him—a dress for his wife, another shawl? Nothing like that, he says, and tells her about being a writer, a novelist, that she'd made an impression on him as an artist. He tells her how he'd started a story about her, or not about her precisely but about a woman like her, modeled on her, on his imagination of her. He tells her that in the end he'd ripped up the pages. It dawned on him, he told her, that for once he should drop the veil of fiction and write something real.

She starts to tell him her story. And then that evening they meet and she talks more, and the next evening, more. Yes, and the evening after that, again. Days between these evenings he spends on the beach making notes, outlining, listening to parts of the story again and again from his recording device, the one he carries with him to record his thoughts at particular moments of insight when pen and paper are not at hand.

Her voice, too childish to be lilting, too modulated to be dramatic, but altogether enchanting—and, yes, Grassfeld (character) uses this precise word, and so we'll put it in quotes, "enchanting." There is, as you can imagine, an orientalist quality— the voice heard time and again becomes a seductive chant, intonations come to the ear as musical notes, as drumbeats, as vibrations. Speech, words—at times breathless and perfect and at others forced, wrong, and nearly incomprehensible.

Enter Carlo, and the novel's tensions and conflicts start to build. He sees her talking to Grassfeld under his beach umbrella. Her beauty strikes him at once. He approaches her on the promenade after the day's work. He's Renzo's son, he tells her, though Anita doesn't know Renzo directly. She's heard of him, but deals with Ricardo, one of Renzo's guys. He, Carlo, saw her talking to a man under an umbrella, he says to her, a tall man with a short beard and short brown hair, etc., etc. You get it. Clumsily, Carlo tries to pick her up, to invite her for a walk through the town in the evening, for an ice cream, an espresso, or a drink on one of the many terraces facing the sea. Carlo's soft eyes, his gentle manner—Anita likes him, likes him more than she likes Anton Grassfeld, whose basic stiffness and intensity make her feel ill at ease.

In the evening, they sit on the piazza and drink tea and coffee. It's too late for other of Renzo's women to be out. They are never out at night, save for the few who work the after-dinner shift selling trinkets to tired kids and baubles to tipsy women on vacation. Not Anita. Not now—she suddenly feels far away from it. As she sits there on the piazza in the cooling summer-time air, it seems to her as if she's melting—melting back into a person, a young woman from Senegal with memory and history, a daughter, a sister. Beyond the gaze of any and all, beyond culture and the world, nobody sees her, nobody but the gentle Carlo, and who could tell at that moment just how tyrannical this Carlo could be? Or maybe she knows. Most likely it's Grassfeld (author) who doesn't know, doesn't want to know, despite the textual hints, even though the other Grassfeld, the character, despite his suffocating jealousy, sees the wolf in schoolboy wool.

The approval of the father, it's a tired subject, to be sure, but we can't seem to get away from it. If word got out that Carlo was seeing Anita there would be hell to pay from Renzo. The progressive aging post-punk German hipster versus the racist Italian businessman—tired, fine, maybe, but still somehow captivating. The problem with the whole thing is that Carlo has fallen in love with Anita. Grassfeld sees it. Even after the years of erosion of the sharp edges of his emotional being, he can tell. He knows the look of it, a vision of life that awakens in him those dormant feelings. There's a family dinner scene. They are out at a restaurant with outdoor seating tucked away in a quiet square. The kids are drinking Cokes. Grassfeld and Susan are sharing a carafe of sparkling rosé. Allow a quote:

> Between sips of wine, Grassfeld gazes across the table at this strange woman, who just happens, rather randomly it seems, to be his wife of almost twenty years. He watches as she takes a drink of her wine. Her face contorts slightly as she swallows and then returns to its normal emotionless ex-

pression, the type of expression that creates a common bond between the English and the Germans, a way of being that makes it seem next to impossible that such emotionally tempered people could ever have fought two world wars against each other in a period of a mere thirty years. But why think of war on such a night? Susan had come to Berlin as a photographer in the late 1980s from London. To Grassfeld, she seemed in complete control of her being. Energy, she had a type of energy that created, created without trying to create a thing. There is, in fact, a war of sorts, Grassfeld thinks as he stares at his wife, a war over the forces in this energy field, a field which unfortunately included Rolf and Cassie. They were caught in the middle of these fixed objects—egos of planetary dimensions, one small and compact, the other diffuse and massive. They had once lived on the edge, on the precipice of something, beyond which was something else entirely. Beyond was oblivion, that's how he thinks of it—thinks of it as a completely empty space, a type of interstellar emptiness or the fiery inferno of the underworld. Elemental might be a better way of putting it—like the photograph in his office at home in Kreuzberg of the same street in the summer of 1945, the burned out, bombed, shelled ruins of civilization, a world utterly destroyed. Their building had been the only one on the block to escape destruction. They had moved into the top floor in 1988, moving out of a squatted house a few blocks away on the canal. The new building seemed to have existed for decades as a refuge for the drunk and the insane, caught between East and West in this Green Zone of the Cold War. They, Grassfeld and Susan, had risen together to become stars, he as a writer, she has a documentary filmmaker. They bought the place in 1993, renovated it largely by themselves a year later, renovated a second time with the help of a fancy architect in the early 2000s, just after Susan's first big deal. He drinks more rosé; she does the same. The waiter sets down a large plate of antipasti—Cassie and Rolf dive right into the choicest selections of meats and cheeses. Grassfeld takes a piece of grilled zucchini, Susan a marinated mushroom.

I'll stop the quote there—I think you get it. Estrangement, alienation, the divergent courses of two adults moving through time. He has fallen in love with other women at least half a dozen times over the past twenty years, sometimes for months or years, others for the duration of a single glance. He's had three affairs. One was a weekend tryst in New York while giving a series of readings following the publication of the translation of one of his novels. The woman was the journalist who interviewed him for the *Times*, a dark-haired Midwesterner. After that, there were a few months with Ingrid Müller, a poet from the Kreuzberg scene. Toward the end of it, right before it blew up, Grassfeld had even considered (for the first and only time) leaving Susan. Finally, and most significantly, there was a relationship of many years with Pepi, a Czech writer he would meet in Prague, occasionally in Dresden or Vienna, perhaps three or four times a year. Susan, too, had strayed, first when she was away on trips for work and then, increasingly, closer to home, culminating with a torrid embrace of a Serbian cinematographer in her home studio while Grassfeld served drinks to their party guests in the living room. Storms weathered. Foundations shook but didn't crack, or cracked but structures didn't crumble. In the end, you could say these affairs didn't matter. What mattered, at least for Grassfeld, was the dissipation of energy, the ennui, the boredom. They craved loudness, noise, being immersed in sound, textures, body, crowd, masses—punk Berlin, anarchist Berlin, the artist's Berlin.

I need to skip ahead a bit—but I'm sure you'll be able to draw these threads together. At the critical moment of *Girl on the Beach*, with Anita's improbable relationship to Carlo blossoming into some delicate idyll, Grassfeld makes the most repulsively obvious play: money for sex. It is not totally unnecessary to add the following to give you the full dimensions of the book: before the proposition, Anita wasn't, generally speaking, repulsed by Grassfeld. At times she felt afraid of him for some vague reason, she found him frigid, perhaps too plain, too devoid of color, or stark, that might be a better word here, stark, sharp, too contrasting, too many angles and not enough curves. Classified. Formalist. I'm adding this terminology—words to capture her subtle responses, the way she behaves and moves and acts when she's around him. He wants to experience a feeling of possession, not a life together, not a love affair, though he might love her in some way, the most repulsive way possible. One moment of possession for three thousand euros or more, a lot of cash compared to the average price of even an expensive European prostitute. For Grassfeld, this isn't about prostitution—or not only. As he sees it, it's a sort of bestial humanitarianism, if that makes sense. It doesn't make sense. Desire rarely makes sense.

Three thousand euros or more—the book is unclear about the exact amount. Whatever it is, it's enough to pay off her debt to Renzo, enough to destroy Carlo, to turn Carlo against her, enough, apparently, for her to risk everything. Three thousand euros for the erasure of a life, a life still quite traceable, a life in wan outline—or to see it from the other side, a life thrusting forward, a person reborn from spectral traces.

Only a writer like Anton Grassfeld would hold us in the moment before the sexual encounter, relish in the monstrosity of it. Fine, let's get to it. Grassfeld has his way, has sex with Anita. It's a terrible scene, slow, detailed, raw. Then the novel under-

goes an abrupt shift in pace—it starts to careen. The relationship with Carlo crumbles. Carlo drives her mercilessly off the
beach, Grassfeld confronts Carlo in the Ristorante Garibaldi,
they argue, they fight, Carlo grabs a steak knife from the table
and cuts Grassfeld's cheek, nothing terrible, but enough to need
six stitches. Susan finds out about the affair. Rolf overhears her
shouting at Grassfeld. Susan takes the kids and leaves. The story
cuts.

It is years later. Grassfeld is in his office at home typing a
story about a family vacation in Italy, about falling in love with a
young woman, a beach vendor from Senegal, about paying her
for sex, about a jealous lover named Carlo, about a man whose
life falls apart in a single page of prose. Susan knocks on the door
to tell him she's on her way to the airport. She's taking the kids to
London for her father's ninetieth birthday. He's got a deadline
and needs to stay behind.

Then he's on a train, moving in and out of sleep—Berlin to
Munich, Munich to Innsbruck, Innsbruck to Verona, Verona to
Venice. He takes a *vaporetto* across the lagoon to the Lido and
makes his way to the Hotel des Bains. He moves through the
dim interior to his room on the second floor. Yes, I know, I'm
running out of time, but we're nearly there, give me an extra five
minutes, ten tops. I can't possibly start this whole thing over next
week. Wait, yes, he's exhausted but at the same time overcome by
the memory of a great conflagration of desire—a type of primal
desire he'd experienced only once before. He feels disoriented.
Maybe it's the dust; maybe it's the long trip or the strange quality
of the room's light. He picks up the telephone to call the front
desk to see if there have been any messages for him. There's
nothing on the line besides a soft whooshing of distant voices.

He's outside, walking away from the massive hotel, which
seems to Grassfeld less like a hotel and more like a hospital, a

clinic, a sanatorium. Could it be, he thinks, that I'm sick? Could it be that he somehow made his way into this place and slipped into a crack in time, some sort of mnemonic trap? Down on the beach, he watches the gentle waves slowly pushing their way onto the sand. It's late autumn and there's not a swimmer in sight. Cold winds swirl around him. Peculiar, he thinks, that what appeared beyond doubt just hours ago on the train now seems to be loosening and breaking apart. The "real"—he'd always had a fondness for the real, which meant an aspect of existence that bordered on the grotesque, the perverse, the raw edge of desire. It could have been the loneliness or isolation, or something much deeper, external, the bleeding of ink from one surface to another, turning words into smudges, into amorphous forms, blobs, accidents.

The gray evening deepens. Out of the corner of his eye he sees a small figure moving quickly back and forth from the edge of the sea to another figure sitting higher up on the sand. He's drawn to the movement—back and forth—and he sees as he approaches that it's a little girl, three or four years old, gathering rocks and shells from the seashore and bringing them back to her mother, who is sitting directly on the cool sand in a pair of blue jeans and a purple sweater. From about ten paces away it hits him: Anita. He's sure of it—maybe too sure, because how could it be Anita, really?

"Diya," she calls, "come to me, it's time to go. It's getting cold."

"No, mama, I'm not finished yet."

"Anita," he whispers, so quietly it's swallowed up in the gathering night.

He moves closer until he's practically standing above the woman. She still can't see him, can't feel him there. "Diya, mama's cold. It's time to go now. It's time for supper."

"Just a few more minutes, mama, just a few more shells and stones."

Grassfeld sees the pile she's made, ordinary rocks, pieces of sea glass, a few clamshells. For twenty years, he's been returning here, to the Hotel des Bains, the perfect intersection point, capacious enough to house these many crosscurrents. Just imagine for yourself such a place. In a space for five hundred guests, there were just six: the real Grassfeld, the character Grassfeld, Anita, her daughter Diya, myself, and (you probably guessed it) Milena. Milena was there precisely for the reason I was there, to fold the present together with the past, to merge a written story—Cohen's manuscript—with reality, to turn flesh and blood into ink, ink into body, body into spirit and soul, to inhabit multiple worlds, to transcend the limits of Cohen's imagination, and mine.

The dining room is full of used dishes on tables and newspapers written in every European language—German, Polish, French, English, Russian, etc. Across the large hall, Milena sits at a table and pores over those typed pages. Diya is across from Milena playing with sea glass in a wide glass bowl. The child seems at peace. Greens, purples, reds, frosted whites—the pieces of sea glass slip through her fingers and strike the bowl. I approach, careful not to startle her, concerned Milena would see me coming and try to bolt, or worse, to destroy those pages.

"What's it about?" I ask. "The manuscript?"

Milena looks up at me. "What's it about?" She starts, then hesitates, then starts again. "It's hard to say. One could start by saying that there's an old hotel on the Lido called the Hotel des Bains. It's been shut down for decades, just slowly crumbling. On the other hand, there are guests at the hotel, some existing in our time, others from the past, characters who would be like ghosts if they weren't at the same time physical, real. And then there is a third type of guest, like Diya, who's not now or then but of some other time, a type of time parallel with our time, time both counterfactual and actual. And she, Diya, is an orphan, even though both of her parents are here, her mother Anita and her father Anton Grassfeld. But they can't find her, or she them, though at times, and in unexpected ways, they intersect—like earlier, a page or two ago, on the beach, when Grassfeld saw Diya playing on the edge of the sea, and you, Sy Kirschbaum, stood some distance away in the shadows, watching."

Jackie K.'s "Dress Shop Window"

MIGHT AS WELL tell you that I had a meeting with the dean and the dean's assistant on Friday. I'm not suggesting that any of you went above my head to those authorities set on high—no, I doubt you would have—but something must have percolated up to those rarified environs in any case, which provoked the dean to accuse me of "veering off course." At this point in the meeting—at the point when the dean said, "veering off course"—the dean's assistant slid a stack of archived syllabi across the table and told me it might be beneficial to have a look. The dean said I needed to "build structure." The dean's assistant added, in a quiet but unsettling manner, that it was a condition of the contract that I supply you with a syllabus at the beginning of the semester and I'd failed to do this. In addition, she added, as the dean ran his index finger along the side of his head (as, I've observed, is his authoritarian habit), I am required to provide a copy of the syllabus to the dean. To the dean!

Yes, good, I trust the copies have made their way around the room. You are welcome to ignore everything on this syllabus. I put it together last night with no other goal than to mollify the dean and the dean's assistant. Put it together—I simply wrote my name at the top of a syllabus developed by a certain Professor Rosinky, who taught here in the mid-late 1990s. Rosinky, as far as I can tell, was not an uninteresting man, and judging by the syllabus was a meticulous and perhaps even demanding teacher, maybe not a bad one, certainly a better one than I am, but since I'm not Rosinky and could never be Rosinky, you can disregard the Rosinky syllabus, his reading list, his assignments, his schedule, his rules. Still, keep the syllabus, place it in a folder, and if the dean or his assistant approaches you about the syllabus for this class, pull out Rosinsky's masterpiece and wave it in front of their perplexed, bewildered faces.

I'd like to talk today about someone I met during my second year living in Berlin, a young woman whom I'll call Jackie K. For those of you who've read my *Preface* to Horak's book, you'll know that toward the end of it I discuss several relationships I had in Prague during those seventeen years, in addition to, of course, the earlier one (if we can call it a relationship) with a woman named Ida Fields. That I left Jackie K. out of the *Preface* is nothing surprising—it was one tangent too many, one detour too far.

Forgive me for a second, but I have to back up and talk for a minute about Ida Fields and my childhood friend, Ida's husband, Gabe Slatky. Then, as promised, to Jackie, or more specifically (this is a literature course, after all) to a story by Jackie that appeared in late 1996 in the literary journal *Loose Stitch*, not a terrible journal by any means, one of those expat projects that ran for four or five years—maybe a little longer. It doesn't really matter.

Imagine: it's late 1996. This isn't a course about my life, I know, and I'm not intending to deliver an autobiography from the lectern here, but we need some framing. I met Jackie after I'd spent a year and a half in Berlin. I'd come to Berlin as a sort of refugee, fleeing what had started as a high school jealousy of Gabe's relationship with Ida Fields but had turned into an endemic illness, an unshakable love of Ida that had persisted from my third year of high school through college and beyond—six years. Six years of faking just about everything one shouldn't fake: friendship, intimacy, happiness, love. Had the whole thing been one six-year-long delusion, I might have managed it. However much I wanted—needed—this love to be a self-deception, part of me knew it wasn't, that Ida, on some level, also had fallen in love with me. On some level: that's the key. I don't mean to say that there was a single point during these six years when Ida didn't love Gabe. She loved him the whole time, and it was clear she loved him much more than she loved me. But still, how can we get rid of even the smallest bit of love, such an indestructible, stubborn substance? It was lodged in her; it took her three months in Berlin to dissolve it, and then she was gone, back to Gabe. I, on the other hand, had a much bigger chunk, and only a tip of the iceberg sloughed off during those frozen winter months. But that came later, after Jackie.

Jackie was twenty years old when I met her. She was an art school dropout. She lived in a large apartment with five other people, what the Germans call a *Wohngemeinschaft*, or WG. There were two guys, university students in their late twenties, and two other women—an Italian named Gia and Mindy, another American a few years older. One of the guys, Christoph, had invited Florian and me to a party at the WG that extended over three floors of the building and the building's roof. It was on the roof, uncomfortably close to the edge, where I first saw Jackie. Can you imagine the first words I said to her were "Don't jump"? And she said, "I need to find someone who'll care first."

"Maybe that's me," I offered.

"Fuck off," she said and smiled. I smiled—but it was too dark for her to see my smile. I could see her fine because she was looking back into the light of a full moon. She had blond curly hair, a thin face with a wide, thick nose. She wore a tight top with a short miniskirt, looked kind of trashy, a little Goth—not my usual type. Nor was I hers, in my formless jeans, blue hoody, and gray running shoes. I think what attracted me to Jackie was that she didn't seem to like me very much but actually liked me a lot, the opposite of Ida, who seemed in love with me but wasn't. That's too easy—but you get it. The little smile at the edge of the roof, a slight curl of the lips almost despite her will, that's it, that's Jackie. Excuse the impropriety of the following, but this detail is quite important: Jackie made love with this same look, the look right before a smile—not a frown, no, but indifference and not the slightest hint of pleasure, even at the climactic moment. But then, suddenly, the unwilled smile, an expression I came to need, almost physically, to anchor my wellbeing. It was an expression I would spend whole days and nights searching for. One time I asked Jackie to marry me. Of course, she rejected the proposal brutally, bringing up Ida directly. Yes, she knew about Ida. She knew about everything. I was too young at the time, only twenty-one years old, to have figured out how to conceal things about my past. Once she asked me if she was as beautiful as Ida. "More beautiful," I said. "Wilder," she said. "Wild and maybe more erotic—but don't say as beautiful. I've never seen her, but I know it's a lie. Not with my master here," and she touched her massive nose. For some reason, she referred to her nose as her "master." It had come through time to haunt her, she said, from nineteenth century Lviv to New York via her maternal grandmother, skipping her parents' generation.

We had a few bottles of beer on the roof, until I got drunk and started to fear I might fall off the edge. We went downstairs, but it was too loud, too horrible. Florian had already taken off. Jackie and I went to a nearby bar to wait out the party. By three in the morning, things had fizzled out, and I ended up crashing at her place. The following morning, I was surprised to see Jackie coming back from a morning jog as I pulled myself up and tried to brace my body against a devastating hangover.

That's context. Now, let's get into it, Jackie's story.

"Dress Shop Window"
by Jackie K.
Loose Stitch (December 1996)

The first thing I did each morning, and by morning, I mean Berlin morning, or around 11:30 A.M., was to carefully wash the store's large front window. The store, a boutique dress shop owned by the German fashion designer Alfred Diener, was located on Auguststrasse in Berlin's center, or *Mitte*. I'd seen a girl wearing a dress designed by Alfred at an art-world party some months back, a few weeks after I'd arrived in Berlin. It was a white, trashy thing with black streaks across it, one slashing diagonally from hip to breast and the other intersecting it over the stomach, not quite at a horizontal. When I first saw it, I kind of hated it, but as the party went on and I got drunker, it started to grow on me.

I'd studied painting in college, in art school, but I'd quit after three years and moved from New York to Berlin for no real reason other than that some guy at a dive bar in the East Village told me it was a cool place to be—and dirt cheap. He promised

I could live for a year on what it costs to make ends meet for a month in Manhattan. That sounded pretty good. I never liked Manhattan much anyway. I'd grown up in Vermont and had come to NYC because I couldn't pass up the free tuition offered at the Cooper Union. In that respect, it didn't matter that I'd dropped out, even though my parents threatened to disown me.

I showed up in Alfred's shop one day to see about a job. He was totally different from what I'd expected. He looked kind of like a young academic, an English professor or something like that, something other than a fashion artist of the avant-garde. He had neatly cut blond hair, gold wire-rimmed glasses, and wore a pair of the most conservative and ugly pants I could imagine. Good thing he didn't design men's clothes. He didn't seem to understand the male body the way he understood the female. He understood the way the female body worked, that was obvious. It was obvious already from the dress I'd seen at the party. I told him I was looking for a job, that I'd made my own clothes for years and could help him cut, sew—anything really.

When I'd finished my rambling presentation, Alfred reflected for a moment and then said, "You have a perfect form for A.D." He called his label A.D., his initials, of course, but also the AD of *Anno Domini*, the year of the lord, and the English AD—or "after death," the clothing of the zombie.

"Thank you, I guess."

"No need to guess. I'd like to offer you a position."

"That's super, thank you. I can start right now."

"Wait," he said, "let me explain. I'm proposing to hire you as a live mannequin. I'd like for you to stand in the shop window wearing my designs." I wasn't sure if he was joking or insane— I happen to be attracted to the insane, or more accurately, the insane happen to be attracted to me. I accepted the offer, though not without a fair bit of worry. It wasn't that I feared Alfred, it was more like a vague, strange worry, a murky type of anxiety.

"Can you stand still?"

"That doesn't seem difficult."

"But for how long can you remain still in one pose?"

"I've got no idea. I've never tested it."

"Let's see. Put this on." He handed me a yellow dress with a high collar and motioned for me to go use the dressing room that was curtained off in the back of the shop.

Alfred was standing by the window when I came back. He seemed to be staring out into the empty street.

"There's not a lot of foot traffic here, that's part of the problem," he said in his British-accented English. "Let's start with a classic pose, hands on hips, legs spread apart even with the shoulders, one foot ahead of the other, a little twist in the torso. That's right, that's it. Exactly. You're a natural. We'll have to think about your hair, makeup, and accessories in the future. But that's not necessary now. This is a trial run."

"Yes, sir," I said. "And what expression should I have on my face?"

"The one that fits the dress. Each dress has a corresponding expression, just as it has a corresponding ideal pose."

I positioned myself in the window, posed, expressed, and froze in place. It was about ten minutes before the first person walked by the shop window. It was a haggard-looking drunk who didn't even look in my direction. I might as well be made of plastic! A father and his young daughter (maybe seven or eight) walked by next. The girl stopped and pressed her face against the glass. She said something in German that I couldn't understand. The father shook his head and said, "*Nein*," and then some other things. I tried not to blink—I didn't blink. I couldn't help but imagine that the little girl, in her red hat and green scarf, was trying to puzzle out whether I was alive, if I was real. For some reason, I desperately wanted her to believe I wasn't, that I was made of plastic. In the end, I couldn't hold out. I blinked. I twitched. I moved my front foot slightly forward. She pulled back quickly and howled in fright, which seemed to agitate her father. He pulled on her arm, and they were gone.

That night, I told Gia, my roommate, about the job. She said it sounded perverse, maybe "one of the most perverse things" she'd ever heard. I said I doubted that standing in the front window of a dress shop was that much different than walking down a street in Rome with all those eyes on you. Gia laughed. "It's not the looking that creeps me out," she said, "it's the stillness."

A couple of days later, Alfred said, "Jackie, do you know why the best dressmakers used to want real girls to model the dresses in their shops?"

"Not really. I've never thought about it."

"It's quite simple. The dressmaker is looking for two primary things. First, he wants to be able to show the customer how the dress looks from all angles, and with a live model, the customer can be still while the mannequin moves around her. This creates a sense of importance, of power in the customer, who starts to feel a certain acquisitive force building between her and the object of desire—the dress, of course, but also, in some way, the girl in it—a lust to consume dress and body, the perfect body. You have to keep in mind that this was before modern advertising. An aura had to be created *in situ*. Second, naturally, and more importantly, the live mannequin showed how the dress looked on a body in motion. We perfect a pose, an ideal pose, but this is just a promise of movement, after all, a pause in motion. The perfect pose must dissolve into movement and then coalesce again out of movement. It's flow, rupture, fixation, rupture, flow, rupture, fixation, and so on. Let's try it out. A customer comes in.

You're wearing this dress. Now pose!" he said, and I did as I was told. "Now activate. Show the left side. When I move my finger like this you show the left. Good. That's it. And when I move my finger the other way, you show the right. And then when I twirl it like this, you show the back, which is, of course, the key maneuver. One clap, you bring it back to the original pose. That's it. Nothing more. It's the formalism that keeps it from breaking down into sleaze. Front. Left. Right. Back. Return. Try again. Left—good—and now to the right— excellent— and then the twirl and the hold of the rear pose—very nice—and clap—return. A little too mechanical, which is not bad, but a little looser. Try again. Left—good—right—excellent—twirl—no, too voluptuous, hide it, use it, channel it—good, there you go— now back to me."

I stood in the window all day without a single customer coming in. The next day, three or four came in, but Alfred didn't consider them serious buyers and didn't have me show the clothes. I remained the whole time in the window in my pose, staring out, still. I found the work terribly hard. Most passersby barely looked up at me. Children played the game real/fake. Women seemed to be trying to peel the dress right off my body with their gaze, obliterating me, the mannequin, without damaging the garment. And men, yes, plenty of men peeled the dress off for completely different reasons. If this wasn't hard enough, to all those eyes beyond the glass there was one pair of eyes in the back of the shop, behind me, those of Alfred, which, whether fixed on me or not, seemed to possess me, own me, humiliate me.

Why didn't I just quit? I really don't know. One day Gia came and watched me through the window for a few minutes. She smiled, laughed, and cheered me up. She brought her friend Antonio, and he blew me kisses. It was good to feel human again. For a moment, I forgot about Alfred, about those eyes behind me, and lost myself in the gaping chasm of Antonio's large mouth, in the lusciousness of Gia's lips, in the golden sun.

Their visit shifted things for me and made me realize that the key was to surmount the transparent boundary and to allow the person on the other side to exist with me, to allow myself, metaphorically, to step from the stage of the shop window into the street, into real life. Suddenly, Alfred seemed to vanish or to turn his attention back to his designing and to forget about me. At the same time, more customers started to come into the shop, as if my new attitude had begun to lure them in, pulling them through the transparent boundary into my world. They were, for the most part, serious buyers, some even worthy of my performance—front, left, right, back, front. One month, my second or third, Alfred sold so many dresses that he ran out of two of his patterns and had to take a dozen orders. At the end of that month, he took me out and we shared a bottle of champagne. I was sure he'd try to sleep with me, but he didn't, didn't even touch me. In fact, apart from the arrangement of the dresses, he never touched me. I wondered that night if he saw me as real or fake, as flesh-and-blood Jackie or as animatronic Jackie, a hollow Jackie, a Jackie who was made of plastic or wax and just happened to be the perfect shape for his designs.

Outside of work, I wasn't doing much. I would have drinks with Gia or Mindy or the guys a couple of times a week. Art— hardly, but I didn't give shit. I was happy enough to take a break after three years at Cooper, or not happy about it, but resigned. One night, though, in late summer, after about half a year on the job, I did make a quick sketch of a scene, a view from outside the shop on Auguststrasse through the window, with me standing on the staging platform and Alfred in the background working on a dress, the same type of dress I was wearing. I made my nose even more out of proportion than it is, a massive protuberance. It was Pinocchio and Geppetto. Thread spilled out of Alfred's sewing machine in the sketch and flowed across the shop. It climbed up my body and bound my ankles and wrists like chains. The next day, in the shop, I thought about how it would feel to be tied up like that with sewing thread, thread not only on the ankles and wrists but around my legs, waist, even around my neck. I almost laughed, and right when a group of high school boys happened to be walking by. For some reason, this almost-laugh must have caught their attention, and they spent the next few minutes making any number of lewd gestures (pelvic thrusts, anal invitations) against the glass, until they finally ran away squealing with delight.

It was one of the most disgusting days of the year, a bitterly cold, overcast, and wet mid-November debacle of a day. It was the kind of day that would have depressed me even if I had been riding a manic high, which I wasn't, not even close. I was feeling blue. I'd had a recurring dream for months that I was totally encased in glass; the space was cramped and airtight, so that even my screams and cries for help went unheard. In the dreams, I'd be wearing Alfred's clothes, usually one of his fancier dresses, the type of evening dress the Russian women wanted to see "in action." I was trapped inside the glass—my very own bell jar—the only thing a young woman (especially a young art student) really desires: to be the object of attention, the object of fascination. Except in the dream (and in reality!) I wasn't fascinating. I was alone. I was unwatched. I was forgotten.

Anyway, on this most disgusting of days, on a day after a night of dreaming of the bell jar, a guy appeared at the window on Auguststrasse for the first time. He saw me from across the street, crossed, and then stood there with a blank, serious expression. He wore a pair of blue jeans, a blue hooded sweatshirt, and a pair of gray running sneakers. Even with the horrid cold, he apparently saw no need to take a jacket or a hat, marking him definitively as an American abroad. His hair was a rumpled mess and looked even messier with his unkempt, shaggy, ridiculous sideburns that fell to below the ear. He was slender, a runner's build, though maybe I just thought about running because of the sneakers, which looked pretty worn out, like a retired pair. His nose wasn't massive like mine, but prominent and accentuated by the narrow cheekbones. Brownish hair, blue-green eyes—and how many hours would I spend looking into those eyes through the glass. Wordless, silent: I wish I could come up with another word that goes beyond speech or speechlessness, beyond lack or absence, maybe beyond communication entirely and into the realm of current or force, a torrent maybe, a torrent of nothingness.

He crossed the street and stood in front of the shop window. He was about a foot or two away from me. As always, I held my pose, maintained my expression, and braced myself for whatever lewd or violent or sudden action might happen. I waited for the staring to end. After five minutes, I considered that maybe this guy was a bit dull, a bit stupid, and that he was playing that kid's game of real/fake. I decided to blink and to move my head from side to side to disrupt the illusion. It worked. He closed his eyes, shook his head a little bit, and then turned and walked away. I was relieved that he turned out not to be the type who would pound his fist on the glass, like others had done, causing me fits of terror and heartache. It amazes me what emotions, what outbursts, silence and stillness can evoke.

The next day, around the same time in the afternoon, he was back in front of the shop window. I was wearing one of Alfred's trashier dresses, which ended in the middle of the thigh and had a couple of revealing gaps along the left side and the stomach.

It was pink and black—Alfred's signature "dirty" black, a gritty black that reminded me of asphalt or tire tracks. The neckline was slanted, creating an inverse slant to the side-slash on the left. The dress fit tight around the waist and even tighter on the hips and over the buttocks. I wore an eighties wig with curled bangs and a ton of makeup, including clashing purple eyeliner smeared on thick. Did his face show disgust? The elegant night-queen of the day before turned into this trash princess, this cheap bar-room whore? Or had the cocktail queen been too much for him, too much for this sneaker-wearing American? I vowed to myself that, unlike the day before, I wouldn't break my pose or expression. I would stare at him as he stared at me—blankly, but with (as I saw it) an undefined hostility. At that moment I hated him, hated him for making me feel exactly how he wanted me to feel, however it was he wanted me to feel. No, I wouldn't succumb to it, to him. I composed myself, steadied myself. Hold the pose, I thought, hold the expression.

The next day I came into the shop and saw that Alfred had set out for me the most exhibitionist, perverse outfit he could have chosen. Perverse, yes, fetishistic, a sort of slutty European schoolgirl. "Wear it with pigtails and this purse," he said and handed me a red lacquered handbag. I shuttered. My first thought was to get the hell out of there. I didn't want the unnamed guy seeing me like this. "No makeup today," Alfred said. "The look is raw beauty, raw femininity, the perfection of youth." No. No. No.

There I stood with slightly pursed lips and wide teenage eyes as he crossed the street and came to the window. Five, ten, fifteen minutes he consumed me with his blue-green eyes. I don't want to say "devour," because devour implies desire, it implies appetite, and I could sense no desire and no appetite from him. For at least twenty minutes, he stared at me. I say "consume" because it was as if he were trying to decide whether to buy me or leave me in the store window. This was an evaluation of merchandise. I was for sale—I, not the clothing, and not even the body—and I don't think his eyes once ran down to my breasts or stomach or thighs or legs. They stayed with me, with my eyes. With me? In me? Twenty-five, thirty minutes—it felt like he had taken his hand and rammed it down my throat to pull out whatever it was inside me that he wanted—my words, my gut, my spirit. Then he vanished.

When he appeared the next day, I thought I'd lose it. The night before I'd gone out with Gia and gotten smashed. I spent the first hour with Gia venting about the guy, this sick fucker who wouldn't leave me alone. "Maybe me and Antonio should beat the shit out of him," she suggested. Then we cracked up, because Antonio was just about the most nonviolent and least intimidating person anyone could imagine. Besides, I said to Gia, he (the guy) hadn't done anything wrong. I put myself in the window, I took the job, I put on the dresses, I styled my hair or arranged the wig, I applied makeup. I had made myself into an object. He just stood there, perceiving me.

I stabilized. I felt woozy again. I closed my eyes for a long time and tried to block him out, to outlast him, make him vanish—poof, gone. But when I looked out again there he was beyond the glass. There he was, still looking into my eyes, still trying to ram his hand down my throat to grasp hold of my spirit, my being, pulling, pulling, gone.

Mindy and I sat at a bar, the second night in a row I'd been out drinking. I was feeling wasted. "It's almost over," I told her. "The week's almost done and then the guy will be gone."

"He's probably a tourist," Mindy said, "staying at one of those cheap hotels near the shop."

"I hope so."

There he was, walking across the street. Same jeans, same sweatshirt, same shoes, same hair, sideburns, eyes. Could it be, I thought, that his resolute sameness somehow drew him to my ever-changing appearance? Beauty queen, club trash, slutty teen, elegant secretary, lady at tea, fifties housewife, corporate girl. Could it be that I was merging his many fantasies, registering his shifting desires? But there was no desire. No. He was focused on that which was unchanging, that which was essential. Eyes, mouth, skin—body, but not body in the sense of pleasure, body as . . . as . . . as . . . and then it hit me: body as human being. It couldn't be. This was the biggest delusion of all. He must have spent a full hour at the window on the day after my night out with Mindy. I stood there without moving as waves of fear, self-loathing, and desperation crashed over me.

One hour seemed to be his limit—at least for a while. Each day for the next week, he was there for an hour.

"What the fuck?" Gia said and issued one of her wonderfully full, dark laughs. "Really, what the fuck is this guy's problem? I'll come down there. I'll confront him. The fucking pervert. I'll shame him."

"I can handle it," I said. "I'll deal with it."

"Aren't you scared of him? Maybe he's a homicidal stalker."

"Aren't we all, on some level?"

"What the hell are you talking about, Jackie? The guy could be a rapist. Call the police."

Each day became one hour, an hour of radical torment, an hour-long contest of survival. Blue-green, narrow cheeks, skin fading into a winter's paleness, stubble, clean-shaven. Blemishes appeared and disappeared. A pimple on the nose, the next day worried until it bled and dried. Hair greasy, hair washed. A gray hair appeared in the shock of sideburn. The jeans became looser and looser—was he losing weight? Eyes turned red and swollen. Drugs? Insomnia? Destitution? Malnourishment? Helpless, weak, pathetic—this was not the portrait of a rapist or murderer. He was a child who needed to be taken in from the cold. No! None of it—just stories, narration swirling like November wind.

Early December. The first snow of the year covered the city, a light dusting that quickly degenerated from an angelic white powder into a filthy brown sludge. I took a pen and wrote my phone number on the palm of my hand. When he got to the window in the afternoon, I made sure to hold it up to him for at least ten minutes, more than enough for him to commit it to memory. I expected him to call that night. Who could resist an invitation like that? But he didn't call that night, or the next, or the one after that, and instead kept crossing the street and standing in front of me behind the window, day after day, with the same expression on his face, whether on a precious day of sun or in wind, rain, sleet, snow, or Berlin's dense winter fog. He stood there, more a statue than I was, more lifeless than the mannequin he gazed at through the glass.

The next week I took a black marker and wrote on my palm: Bar Assel 22:00 Tonight. After he had been standing there for about twenty minutes, I slowly loosened my fist, uncurled my fingers, and pressed my palm against the window directly in front of his face. I left it there for about ten seconds—long, heart-thumping seconds. Then I retracted it, made a fist again, and resumed my pose. He didn't react, stood there another twenty or thirty minutes and left.

That night I got to the Assel a little early, descending to the basement bar at around 9:45 PM. I took a shot of bourbon at the bar, ordered a beer, and took it over to a table in the corner by the bathrooms, where a stream of Oranienburgerstrasse prostitutes moved in and out in dominatrix attire. I wondered whether my window seducer, my window torturer, longed for such a long-legged predator or rather preferred a more deer-like prey. Maybe, I thought, I should have presented myself as such a doe, an innocent, scared, trembling girl new to the city. We could have played hunter and hunted or barbarian and virgin. I'd told Gia and Mindy about the date with the window guy, and both thought it creepy: "As moth to the flame," Mindy said. But I couldn't figure out whether I was moth or flame.

An hour passed, then two. I had two more beers and another shot of whiskey before giving up and heading out. Beyond the bar, beyond the hookers, the area was desolate and shadowy. I turned a corner and sensed that someone was around me, watching me. I couldn't tell if the person was ahead of or behind me—all I felt were eyes on me, eyes all over me. "Is that you?" I said, "Is that my reflection in the window?" Nobody. Nothing. I quickened my pace and heard footsteps on the cobblestones. I broke out into a sprint, reached the stairs to the subway, and caught the train for home.

I was exhausted at work the next day, mercifully a Friday. Alfred wasn't happy because he said my eyes were "droopy" and my posture was bad. "You can't be a live mannequin if you're drinking whiskey in the evenings," he told me. "At most take a couple glasses of champagne. Drinking nothing would be better," he said. Nothing—that was the operative word—nothing. No thing. Void. I scrubbed "Bar Assel 20:00 Tonight" off my palm and wrote in all capital letters: NOTHING. Then, without much thought, I took the marker with the other hand and wrote with my left (non-writing) hand on my right palm, I AM. I was in the small studio bathroom and held my palms up to the mirror: NOTHING I AM. Then I crossed my arms: I AM NOTHING. NOTHING I AM. I AM NOTHING.

I stood in the window in the yellow dress I'd worn on my first day being Alfred's live mannequin. At least it was a busy morning. Three women came in—serious buyers—and Alfred had me go through the motions. For two of the three I showed four dresses each, front, left, right, back, front. Both women bought everything I showed, and the third woman bought the yellow one and then ordered a second dress to be cut in a custom size. "Maybe the haggard look has something to it," Alfred joked. "The next bottle of whiskey is on me." Since he'd just made seven thousand dollars in a single day while paying me next to nothing, I said, "How about a raise?" "I'll give you a bonus. Two months extra pay right now." He reached into his pocket and handed me the bills. That afternoon, flush with cash, I joyously pressed my palms against the glass. I AM NOTHING. NOTHING I AM.

That night, I met my friend Josh, a Cooper grad living in Berlin and showing work at the Spreeufer Gallery. When I told him about the situation at Alfred's window, he recalled a story he'd once heard in an art history class (whether it was true or not he didn't know) about a man, an ordinary gardener, who was arrested in the late nineteenth century in Paris for trying to have sexual intercourse with the statue Venus de Milo. The diagnosis at the time, he told me, was that the man had an abnormally intense libido combined with a lack of courage, which prevented him from attaining "normal" sexual satisfaction. A man sitting on the other side of me decided to enter our conversation. "The guy you describe outside the shop window has a bad case of agalmatophilia," he said. "What the hell are you talking about?" Josh said. "Paraphilia, man," the bearded stranger said, "deviant sexual obsessions. You've apparently hooked a guy who wants to have sex with dolls or mannequins—that's classic agalmatophilia. It's related to necrophilia. In a sense, then, this guy has a death wish, it's the death drive, Freud's *Thanatos*." I stood up and said to Josh, "Let's get out of here," and we paid our bill and spilled out into an endless Kreuzberg night.

On Monday, I stared at him and wondered whether he could tell from the look in my eyes that I had diagnosed him. I had my palms prepared again—on the right hand, DOLL and on the left, DEAD. DOLL DEAD. DEAD DOLL. I crossed and uncrossed them, pressing them each time against the glass. Alfred's sewing machine whirled in the background. Blink, blink, nothing but that horrifying fixed stare.

Weeks passed with our communication existing on two parallel sets of rails. One was the rail of the gaze as it moved back and forth through the pane of glass. The other was going only in one direction, broadcast by my word-palms pressing against the screen for him to read.

There was something holding me back, preventing me from confronting him outside on the street. For the life of me, I couldn't figure out what it was. One morning before work I drew an eye on each palm—sort of all-seeing eyes. I held them to the glass in the afternoon. This got no reaction from him. The day after, I drew closed eyes and held them to the glass. The next day, I presented him with a sun and a moon, and then the next day with the words DREAM and REAL—DREAM REAL. REAL DREAM. Cross. Uncross. On the next day, I painted both palms completely black. It was a signal of the end, that I'd had enough, and I really had, I really couldn't take it anymore. But he kept coming back, even after those black palms, even after day after day of empty palms. He fixed his eyes on me. I gazed through the glass at him.

In the middle of what felt like the darkest week of the year, at some point in mid-February, a note appeared taped to the dress shop window. It was hand-written on a single sheet and taped across the entire back with clear packing tape. It was stuck precisely where his head would have been.

Dear—

There's a small cabin in the woods. It has no plumbing, no electricity. It's just a single room with a wood-burning oven for cooking and a Franklin stove for heat. There's a loft made on top of the rafters that can fit two people comfortably for sleeping, three crammed in. It was there, in this cabin, that my friend Gabe wrote his first play, *Rehearsal for a Eulogy*, which was performed during the upcoming year and won the statewide one-act play competition. I imagine you don't care about any of this, though you might care that I first saw Ida Fields when she stepped on stage in the high school auditorium to perform her role in Gabe's play wearing a white silken robe. In other words, she stepped from the curtained imaginary into what we might call the stage light of the real. My first thought was that Gabe had conjured her from the mystical waters that flowed near the cabin and had thrust her on stage to radically alter, unsettle, and destroy my life. Did he possess his creation or was he, rather, possessed by it for the next seven years until, suffering and insane, he brought her back to the wilderness, dug a hole in the ground near the cabin, and buried her? It came as quite a shock, you'll understand, that something like a kindred soul of this same being, Ida Fields, now inhabits a woman who stands in the window of a dress shop on Auguststrasse. Your presence threatens to drive me toward a world that cannot possibly coexist with my world. I can never again gaze through this pane of glass into your eyes. I can't stand seeing you stuck between fantasy and reality, precisely because I still can't exist fully in either place. There is one place I can imagine the glass shattering between us. There is a "fairy tale" fountain in the Volkspark Friedrichshain. I will wait for you this evening by the reflecting pool.

I didn't go—I'm not a total lunatic, despite the impulse to meet him, to be conquered by this strangest method of seduction. Some months later, my roommates threw a party together with two other apartments in our building. I wasn't in the mood for it after my day at Alfred's studio, and it would be, though I didn't know it at the time, my last day. Needless to say, those months after he left the note were the absolute worst. The grinding and maddening tension was replaced by a gnawing nothingness, a chasm of loneliness.

There I was, drinking a bottle of beer on the edge of the roof, when he stepped off the ladder and emerged, grim reaper–like, with the hood of his blue hoody pulled up over his head. I'm not sure he recognized me, despite the light of the full moon washing over me.

That's where the story ends. It ends, as you see, at the beginning of our relationship. By the time the story appeared in *Loose Stitch*, Jackie and I had parted ways. Actually, it was Ida who discovered the story as she was leafing through a copy of the journal in a bookshop while waiting for me to finish a translating session with the novelist Anton Grassfeld at a café nearby.

"A strange thing happened while I was waiting for you," Ida said when we met. She told me she'd found a story called "Dress Shop Window" in a local English-language literary magazine in which her exact name appeared together with the name Gabe. This was a dangerous moment for me, the first time Gabe had come up since Ida's arrival in Berlin. I asked who wrote the story, and she told me it was a woman named Jackie K. "She seems to imply," Ida said, "that I don't exist, that I'm simply the projection of two imaginations, Gabe's and Gabe's friend's, who happens to be described an awful lot like you. The story implies that I materialized as a product of desire and vanished as a result of repression. Strangely, reading Jackie's story made me question, for a moment, whether I do exist or not, so much so that I started to run my fingers over my skin and through my hair to substantiate my being alive. She's wrong. Here I am. And yet she's right, exactly right. I'm too much the product of two competing and warlike imaginations, too much a battleground."

Finally, and this is me speaking and not Ida, and I'm saying this right now, to you, and not back then to Ida, finally we get to the border of the darkest region of my *Preface* to Horak's book. It is in this blinding darkness that we can peer into the unknown of those days before the two vectors shot off in opposite directions, one carrying Ida back to Gabe, the other sweeping me to Prague for seventeen years of work translating *Blue, Red, Gray*. And this raises a critical question: what was the propulsive force that shot those two arrows and which tore apart this convergence point with such violence that it could never again hope to re-gather except through the most devious of inventions, that is, through a literary text perched on the border between truth and lie?

Notes from a Session with Dr. L. Hruška

NEED TO GET BACK to Dr. Hruška today, but before I do, I want to mention an encounter I had this morning as I was sitting in a nearby café, drinking coffee and organizing these notes. The interesting thing is that this encounter and these notes fit together, though it's not completely clear how. And it's not clear if they only seem to fit together or if they actually fit together, or if there is any difference between an "apparent" and a "real" fit.

I'm sitting in the café nursing my third or fourth cup of coffee and in walks a blind man, feeling his way along with his pole. At first, I register his being there by the tapping of his pole against the concrete floor and the wooden base of the barista's counter. These haptic movements interrupt my thoughts and for a moment pull me toward the sound. The idea pleases me—the pulse of the tap, the vibrations traveling up the pole and into the man's hand, the registering of the information in the nerves behind the eye or on the backside of the optic nerve, that mystical tangle, that mirror to the soul. It's only when I turn back to my notes that I realize the man is Landesmann, the rabbi who presided over my bar mitzvah and who, not long afterwards and while still in his mid-thirties, had been forced into retirement as the congregational rabbi by a degenerative eye condition.

"Rabbi!" I call out, almost against my will. "Rabbi, it's Sy Kirschbaum."

"Why hello, Sy," the Rabbi says in the gentle, soothing tone I remember from our year of study together.

"Please," I say, "if you're here by yourself, sit down with me."

He agrees, orders his coffee, and brings it back to the table, skillfully navigating the space. It's been decades since I last sat across from this man, and the feeling floods back to me—the utter emptiness of self I experienced as he gazed across his desk at me, a copy of the Hebrew text of my Torah portion lying in front of him. I remember how he looked then: short, thick sandy hair, closely cut mustache, plump. He wore gray or tan suits, never blue, black at funerals, white on Yom Kippur. He's thin now. The sandy hair has receded and whitened. The mustache is gone.

We make small talk for a while, the rabbi probing me with questions in his therapeutic way. Then, from some deep mnemonic recess, a line from that Torah portion forces its way up my throat and out of my mouth. "*Vaiyomer adonai el-Abram lech-lecha.*"

"*Vaiyomer adonai el-Abram lech-lecha,*" Landesmann repeats, seemingly savoring every syllable of the Hebrew. "The Lord said to Abram, go forth from your native land."

"I remember what you said to me, you said that at the beginning of each journey toward faith, there's a flight, a rupture, an exile."

Landesmann's vacant eyes look past me to the wall, on which are hung two brightly colored paintings of coastal scenes with fishing boats and seagulls in quiet harbors. He takes a sip of coffee, then another, and a third, a fourth. At some point amid this stilled time, he rises from the table and unfolds his pole. As he is about to leave, he bends over me and, grasping my shoulder, says, "This exile is the trauma, the trauma that comes from saying to God, as Abraham said, 'Here I am.'"

"Tell me about Mondschein," Hruška said in one of our daily sessions, a week or two after my arrival at the clinic.

After seventeen years spent translating *Blue, Red, Gray*, the statement seemed like a deliberate and inimical provocation. "Nothing much can be said about it in three quarters of an hour," I told him. "In any case, I don't think you really care about Mondschein."

"Why do you think that?"

"For one, because you've never even read Horak's novel. I don't understand how that's possible, especially for a person of your age, from this country."

"I've read your *Preface*, your so-called 'translator's' *Preface*."

"As a doctor."

"What else?"

"A human being."

"For today, I am asking you about Mondschein."

"Are you referring to *The Book of Moonlight* or to the man, to Isaac Mondschein?"

"If that's where you'd like to begin. Or maybe with Julia? Should we begin with her?"

"Why drag her into this?"

"Didn't you 'drag' her into the *Preface*? You dragged her in even though she didn't belong there?"

"Are you doubting she was in Prague?"

"What reason would I have to doubt it?"

59

"You doubt that she was searching for *The Book of Moon-light*?"

"Go on."

"Get to the main point, Dr. Hruška. I see those notes on your pad of paper—those words underlined not once, but twice—and in blue pen!"

"I meant for you to see them. The words belong to you, af-ter all. I'll quote from your *Preface*, 'One copy [of Mondschein's *The Book of Moonlight*] was catalogued in the New York Public Library. When I investigated it, the librarian was able to dig up the record. The book was checked out on May 10, 1946, and never returned.' Let's pull the thread."

"We'll find ourselves at a frayed end. I know, you know, that Esther Bird flies into oblivion."

"I don't know anything of the sort. In fact, it's just the oppo-site."

"According to what?"

"Inquiries."

"With whom? Don't tell me Cohen."

"Nonsense. What would Daniel Cohen know of Esther Bird?"

"It's hard to tell."

"It wasn't Cohen; it was Slatky."

Hruška was referring to my childhood friend Gabe Slatky, whom you know from my *Preface*. There's no time now for a full re-introduction. Besides, didn't I speak about him last week? You can't have forgotten, despite the obvious lack of attention most of you pay to these lectures. I don't mean to criticize. There's a dubious quality here, no doubt. It's a miracle that we're four weeks into the semester and none of you has gone to the dean.

What could Gabe Slatky have known about Esther Bird? Let's go back to 1994. As you know from my *Preface*, I'd come back to my hometown after being away for years and had to confront the reality that Gabe and Ida would never separate. In fact, Gabe proposed to Ida soon after I arrived. Could Gabe have been ignorant of what everyone must have known: that I was still madly in love with Ida Fields? And that Ida, for however much she loved Gabe, couldn't shake me off completely? Nonsense! Nothing had ever happened between me and Ida, and nothing would happen until she came to Berlin two years later. I have trouble thinking clearly about those days. I was suspended in a fog, a cloud of thick, oppressive, choking mental pollution. I was aimless; I was penniless. I took a job as a substitute teacher at a local high school and found a cottage to rent on the beach for the winter months. In the evenings, when they finished their work at the theater (Gabe writing and administering, Ida setting the program, acting, and directing) they'd drive out to the beach, and we'd take walks on the frozen, corrugated sand. Then we'd come back to the house and sit around the table and talk for hours. We talked about everything, everything imaginable, except for the essential thing. And the essential thing was this: Gabe and Ida were happy, and I was miserable.

It was the biggest snowfall of the year, a gloomy blizzard that covered the house and road and dune grass and beach with over twenty inches of snow. The ocean steamed like a giant, gaping mouth expelling its salty breath. Horrible, right? If I close my eyes, I can feel Horak's body leaning over me, his boozy voice in my ear. "Cross it out!" Horak shouts. "Cross it out! Cross out that damn nonsense!" They pulled up to the house in Gabe's old blue Ranger pickup, Gabe driving, Ida in the passenger seat. They got out and moved toward the house. It would be too much to say that I saw the diamond on her finger dazzle as I watched them through the large window facing the driveway. It must have been the snow, the snow alighting on her finger and catching a glint from the porch light I'd left on for them.

After they left, it took me about two hours to pack my possessions into a duffle bag and a large hiking backpack. Without telling anyone, I parked my car in front of my parents' house, left the keys under the visor, and caught a bus to Boston. In Boston, I crashed with Mona. It was Mona, of all people, who told me to go to Berlin. She'd come back from Berlin at the end of the summer. She knew a German guy from her time at Harvard who'd come to Cambridge to study for a year. His name was Florian, and he was a translator. Mona knew he had a cheap room for rent and sent him an email. He responded a few hours later, must have been four in the morning at that point. Mona and I were drinking shots of bourbon at the table in her tiny Cambridge apartment when the note came. By the middle of the following day, I was on a plane to Berlin.

You can see how quickly a life can be transformed, especially when you're young—young and without a clue. Now we're getting somewhere. We can see two curves bending away from each other, intersecting the path—the flight—of Esther Bird. But why do we have to talk about things like intersections and convergences? Why do we bend and twist toward coherence?

"Would it surprise you," Hruška said after a long pause, "if I were to tell you that Slatky claims that a man named Isaac Mondschein fled the Russian Empire after the Revolution of 1905 and settled in New York's Lower East Side?"

"I don't surprise that easily."

"Would it surprise you that this same Mondschein started an anarchist newspaper called *Die Freiheit*, that he married an Italian immigrant named Giulia (from Rome), and that they had a daughter named Esther?"

"As usual, Gabe has it wrong. Not totally, or rather, yes, totally, but not completely. This is nothing new."

"What would you say if I offered you proof?"

I laughed. Proof! Hruška! He thought he was backing me into a corner with his "proof." And he was backing me into a corner. But which corner? And isn't the specific corner the key thing when it comes to backing into corners?

"If you want to go in that direction," I said, "I'll take you."

"Go on," said Hruška.

"Don't prompt me. I'll go on or not go on depending on whether I want to go on. I should say, before I get into this, especially since you haven't read *Blue, Red, Gray*, that this comes from Horak, though not from the novel. It comes from the novel's periphery, that airy substance called novelistic context, the material beyond the page."

Let me move out of this conversation with Hruška and into the deeper historical textures of what could be considered the most important section of Horak's masterpiece, the discussion of *The Book of Moonlight*'s notion of the Defeated God, the defeat of God and then the subsequent great withdrawal of the divine presence from the human realm, followed (eventually, or potentially) by the return and reconciliation, and finally the harmony, the ultimate harmony, emerging from the ultimate disharmony—what *The Book of Moonlight* calls the state of "total war." We have to get into it. This is ultimately what Hruška's interest in Julia must have been about.

Julia, as you know from my *Preface*, was in Prague in search of the papers of the Jewish mystical philosopher Isaac Mondschein, who, she believed, was the original author/compiler of what came to be called *The Book of Moonlight*. It's true I might have misled Julia, told her I'd be able to access underground rooms of the Strahov Monastery, where, I told her, Isaac Mondschein found refuge amid a period of orthodox zeal to root out heretical actors in the wake of the Sabbatean movement. It's true I told her I could find those documents, that I was aware of traces, that through my work on *Blue, Red, Gray* I'd discovered certain elements, certain particles. It's true I had the desire to find them, and if I thought hard about it, it seemed to me the hazy outlines of various palimpsests would (and did!) present themselves to me. This, I suspect, is ultimately what Hruška wanted. He wanted to push me into this past to discover both the origins of *The Book of Moonlight* and the true identity of its author, Isaac Mondschein. And why would Hruška need to find his way to Mondschein? His case-study, his diagnosis, his usurpation of the truth!

Hruška's voice broke into my thoughts. "I'm holding in my hands something you'll be quite interested in."

I propped myself up from a slouching position and gazed at a stack of cloth-bound notebooks tied together with a leather string which sat atop Hruška's desk. The palm of his right hand rested on top of the stack.

"I have here the diaries of Sidney Keter, the translator, as you know, of *The Book of Moonlight* into English."

Sidney Keter, according to Horak's novel, was a loner, a drifter, a mystic, who translated *The Book of Moonlight* into English in Prague in the 1930s while working in the studio of the painter Josef Kostel. When he returned to New York in the early 1940s, he published the book with the Workmen's Circle, only for a warehouse fire on the Lower East Side to destroy the entire print run. One copy survived in the New York Public Library. In 1946, a woman named Esther Bird checked out *The Book of Moonlight* and vanished, seemingly into thin air.

I tried my best to pretend I wasn't rattled. The worst thing one could do in a situation like this was to appear rattled, to appear to have succumbed to inner tumult. It was Hruška's particular talent to engender such a state of being, and then to mercilessly exploit it. Perhaps this is what was meant by Králová's assertion, quoted on the clinic's promotional brochure, that Hruška could "read souls." A lot more could be said about that particular piece of commercial propaganda—the clinic's brochure—but I'll have to save it for another day, perhaps for a time beyond the limits of this class, beyond the classroom, as the brochure certainly belongs beyond this classroom, controlled as the classroom ultimately is, I'm afraid, by the dean and his enforcer, the dean's assistant. Here are a couple of samples (and I'm translating off the cuff from the Czech): "Sessions with the doctor will be at once tranquil and probing," or, "Dr. Hruška is known for his *daring* and *effective* methods." I think you get the point. I would call it deceptive, though true propaganda doesn't deceive in the common meaning of the word. True propaganda shatters reality, then replaces it with a total otherness, a parallel state of existence that mirrors truth but diverges from it at some seemingly imperceptible point.

Hruška said, "I've marked some of the key passages. Key, that is, in the context of our dialogue, for your case."

Hruška untied the leather string and took out a dark green volume from the middle of the stack. He read the following entries:

January 2, 1941

Names. It was time to part with that mix of first and last names: Jonas, Adams, Brill, Kašpar, Bruno. Mix of first and last names, of second- and third-class cargo. Hardest to leave Bruno, young Bruno, who (like all of us?) seems on the very cusp of beginning to exist. He's sixteen, still a boy, without the least bit of hope left in his skinny, frail body; such are these times. Such are they. When I saw—or rather perceived—this utter hopelessness, a sentiment in direct but necessary contradiction to the landing in this "new" land, I'd taken it upon myself to introduce him to Isaac Mondschein's *The Book of Moonlight*. It was a particular hope within hopelessness, faith wrapped in layers of despair, which I longed to see flicker in Bruno's strange dark eyes. I've written page after page about this extraordinary boy, a being as light and airy as anyone I've ever known, apart from Josef Kostel, that is, apart from him—as insubstantial, as shadowy, and yet as full, as undeniably real. What will he do when we reach the shore? What future does a being such as this have in the world? Will he head for the interior—Chicago, St. Louis? Maybe he's under the impression that interiors of continents are safer than the coasts. Or maybe he doesn't think it, and why would he think such an absurd thing after this last catastrophic decade? But Bruno isn't much of a thinker. He becomes morose and reticent whenever I bring up *The Book of Moonlight*, as I read my translated pages to him in an English, admittedly, he can barely understand. Romania, Croatia, Slovakia, Bohemia: Bruno, as I've said many times before in these notebooks, had slipped into one of those razor-thin cracks between the borders of states, and therefore was not run over by those thousands of transport trucks, tanks, trains, and cars that moved the great armies and their seemingly inexhaustible supplies. Supplies, my God, to see the supplies being loaded and unloaded—it was as if the earth heaved and poured its bounty into a gaping hole, a vortex, into the nothingness of war. Bruno found his way out by moving through the cracks between nations. But how, precisely? The question "how" was the one each of us asked the other, and the question none of us answered, thereby creating, by this interminable asking and interminable refusal, a kind of dialogic fog that enveloped the ship. Nothing, not the most powerful Atlantic storm, could clear it away, and conversation about anything else would eventually be lost in it. Bruno's secret, as each of our secrets, made it possible for this boy to be ready tomorrow to step from the boat with hundreds of others onto Manhattan Island. And this brings up the fundamental question: how is it that Bruno is where he is? Bruno, with his dark eyes, black hair cut short, wide forehead, knobby chin. It would be easy to call him a frightened young man, or to compare him to a feral cat. Sudden noises did alarm him. Yet he wasn't frightened. I suspect this is because he knew or sensed that the most frightening things have already happened. He had already lost his faith; he had already lost everything there is to lose in life, except, of course, life—blood moving with the abandoned spirit of God. In my search aboard the ship for a person who might be a Mondscheinian, I found only Bruno. He proved to be a poor disciple, though one can never be a disciple in the Mondschein view of things. I tried hard to introduce Bruno into this realm. Last night, for example, I placed my hands on Bruno's skeletal shoulders and said to him, "My friend, you have closed your ears to all that I've been saying for these long days of our journey together. You've closed your eyes and barricaded your mind to every word and image around you. Nothing of Mondschein has penetrated this crumbling fortress of a body. No fires, no Mondscheinian blaze (if such a thing exists, I doubt it, I doubt it) has kindled in your spirit. But these words and images and fires still swirl around you. They are the tornados you're bound to encounter as you make your way through Toledo and Cleveland and Kansas City and across the great grasslands of Nebraska into the dizzying Rockies. A crack might emerge, yes, a crack must emerge that will allow a flood of light, and you'll be afraid of this light—terrified by this light—and suddenly you'll sense that everything is pulling apart, not around you but inside yourself, and when things pull apart far enough the structure will start to tremble, and then a little more and it will begin to crumble and then collapse, and at that moment (and only at the moment of total collapse) you'll glimpse it—what?—the warped mirror of the divine. Fissures and cracks will appear in the mirror, and behind this mirror the vast abyss of Chaos waits to devour you. Once devoured, you will begin to live again."

January 3, 1941

Sylvia set down the tray with the teapot, cups and saucers, spoons, and the white cubes of sugar. She was trying not to look directly into my eyes, but when I'd look away or pretend to look away into the shadowy corners of the kitchen, I'd see her gazing at me intensely. Her glasses looked enormous against her mousy face. Since I'd been away, she'd had her hair cut back. She used to wear it long. After setting the tea down, she took a seat at the table, filled the cups, and dropped a cube of sugar into hers. I looked on as she slowly stirred the tea with the small spoon. Everything seemed smaller now—Sylvia, her face, the spoon, the kitchen, the apartment, everything, that is, except those oversized glasses that had now slipped halfway down her nose. She pressed them back into place. I asked about our parents. She made a swatting motion like one used to chase away a housefly. "How are you feeling," she asked me, though not in a friendly or sisterly way—in a cool, distant, maybe scientific way—probing me. "Ill at ease," I told her. "Nothing," I continued, "is at ease with the shadow looming." She asked me what I meant by shadow? "It's nothing other than the darkness of the collective soul." She didn't react much, but the slight movement of her mouth indicated she thinks I'm going insane. I know this look; this look has a long history. I see it on my mother's face, on Sylvia, on the face of our late brother, Abe. As I sat there in the moment of silence, I thought of all those letters I'd written to her during breaks from translating *The Book of Moonlight*. I would be in Kostel's studio. I'd move away from my desk, find a clean sheet of paper, and stand by the window with the paper on the windowsill. Kostel would be in the background painting, creating those magnificent worlds of color. I said to Sylvia, "What's your opinion?" She sipped her tea; she gazed at the stove. She moved her eyes to the clock on the wall. It was late in the afternoon. "It's not the darkness of anything," Sylvia said, "it's mankind. It's what mankind has become, or what it's always been, a collection of hideous and aggressive people competing for wealth and power. It has nothing to do with the depths of the soul, Sidney. You need to stop looking for secrets. Everything is on the surface. It's just what it appears to be. That's what I think. But there's no point arguing about anything. Try to rest. You don't look well. I had no idea what happened to you after that last letter you sent from Prague two years ago." I asked Sylvia if she had Greta's address. She said she had it, but that she'd give it to me some other time. She said I shouldn't be running around in my state. She asked where I was staying. "With Greta," I told her, "I'm on my way to find her." Her face tightened. "It's not that I don't like Greta," she said, "it's that I don't trust her." I told her I didn't trust her either, even though I'm in love with her. "You should stay here," Sylvia said. I didn't answer and instead drank my whole cup of tea in one tilt. "Give me the address, please." She went into the bedroom and returned with her notebook. She took out a blank piece of paper and scribbled out Greta's address. Then she added another. "This is for the Workmen's Circle," she said. "Ask for Lewis. I told him you'd be coming around."

Hruška flipped to another part of the volume, one that he'd marked with a green strip of paper. He removed it and began to read again.

April 14, 1941

Greta was talking to Crawford and Morris. She glanced over at me as I walked in. I'd like to think she allowed Crawford to keep coming around because she felt sorry for him, but I know that's not the reason. Morris seemed glad to see me and crossed the room to shake my hand. "You've got to take a look at Greta's print," he said, "it's the graphic for the cover of Hannah Rubin's new collection of poetry." I followed Morris to where Greta and Crawford were standing. Crawford, reluctantly, took my hand and shook it. Greta didn't make a move toward me, she hardly looked at me. When she did look at me, it was at my chest, not at my face, not in my eyes. And she didn't say a thing. I didn't expect her to say a thing—but her silence or avoidance still bothered me a great deal, made me despise Crawford even more, and even Morris, whom I generally like. A scattering of geometrical shapes faded from stark black lines into spectral shadows: *Poems of a Vanishing World.* The title was printed across what seemed like uneven steps. The four of us—me, Greta, Crawford, Morris—stood over the print for a while in silence before Crawford suggested we drink a cup of coffee at the table. Crawford is a tedious and ridiculous man. Morris is fine, but dull. I wouldn't utter the name Mondschein in front of them. None of them deserved to hear me utter the name Mondschein. Only Greta could hear me utter Mondschein, even if Greta was one of the most hostile people in the world to Mondschein.

June 26, 1941

War of all versus all: one interpretation of Isaac Mondschein's "Sixth Recession of the Defeated God" is that it leads to, or is in some way announcing, the utter and total disharmony that is thought to precede the return to the complete harmony of Day Seven, the same harmony we find in the statement, *Let there be light. And there was light.* As such, some look at today's world with increasing hope, hope that the great struggle of nations will end with the final peace prophesized by Isaiah. Jacob, of course, is the first Mondscheinian, and his dream of the ladder is the beginning of the faith. Faith. No, it is not a faith but an aesthetic proclivity for wonderment, it is the gaining of selfhood through the obliteration of selfhood into thousands of shards of ego. There is no such peace near us, nothing of harmony on the horizon. In the seventeenth century, some believers in *The Book of Moonlight*, most famously Shimon Levy, believed that the cataclysm following the sixth recession would be so vast that there would be, in fact, no Day Seven, no pause in God's withdrawal from the world, no turning back to face what He created. Nothing. Instead, the sixth recession would be a bowing of the head and a final surrender, and this gesture of surrender would not harken back to light but forward into "spiraling darkness." I can trace the Shimonian branch as it moved from Budapest to Vienna, and then into Moravia and to Prague and Berlin, and finally from Berlin to Hamburg and from Hamburg to North America. Everywhere they went, Shimonians clashed with Mondscheinians. They sought to deny Day Seven, to assert the dawn of darkness, the final and utter extinguishing of light, light in the higher sense, *the* Light, the force of creation. Despair over love, hope, and beauty, darkness covering the world.

June 27, 1941
The translation is delivered to the Workmen's Circle. Another copy, a secret copy, has been hidden away, even from Sylvia, even from Greta.

June 28, 1941

Went to see Sylvia at the office of *Die Freiheit*. Met a young woman there named Esther, the wife of the syndicalist Paul Bird. This visit propelled me into the vortex of ideology: the Leninist Wolf Greenberg, the Trotskyite Schuldner, the Bakuninist Tazza, the Fourierist Rollins, etc., etc. Paul Bird is a tall man with a long oval face. I don't know him, though his picture has recently been in the newspapers for opposing the war.

Hruška closed the green volume and set it down on his desk. Without looking up at me (how could he have looked up at me at this exact moment?) he lifted a brown volume, found the first marked spot, and started to read again.

October 3, 1941

Zeffi, editor of *Die Freiheit*, asked me what position a Mondscheinian would take on U.S. involvement in the war. I sat there in silence, gazing across the room at the two men readying the press. I sensed Zeffi wanted to co-opt me, which is perhaps why he suggested I write an essay for the paper criticizing U.S. involvement from a Mondscheinian perspective. From what he'd heard about *The Book of Moonlight*, he told me, he sensed a powerful anarchistic impulse surging through the text. A surge, yes, a surge of desire. But what is the essence of this desire? This is the only question that matters. This is the question Zeffi could never ask.

October 4, 1941

I was visiting Sylvia. "There was a man here earlier today," she told me in her softest voice. "He claimed to have come from Vienna, last name was Osterhase, an ashen complexion, an awful man. He looked," she said, "like he'd dug himself out of his own grave. Smelled awful," she said. "Clothes," she said, "like rags." I felt numb. I couldn't imagine how Osterhase had found me. Stepping out of Kostel's Cathedral-vision, from decades in the past, from the road leading north from the Italian coast to Vienna, Osterhase, the only non-gypsy in a camp of gypsies, yes, Osterhase, that shifting shadow of a man, and it is this man who found me. Sylvia knows, as I know, that this is a dark omen. To be found by Osterhase means darkness is close behind. Not that Osterhase himself is violent, far from it, but it's sure he contains a trace of death, a trace of the fog of death that blankets Europe, a fog that came long ago during those eerie years and transformed Josef Kostel into shadow, shadow into memory, yes, into faulty, worm-eaten memory.

October 5, 1941

Greta told me about Paul Bird's plan to halt industrial production in the U.S. for a single day. It's to be a warning to Roosevelt that U.S. workers could cripple production and thus undermine the war effort if the president takes the country into the European conflict. This, Paul Bird says—according to Greta—was the ultimate missed opportunity during the last war, the moment when the worker could have seized hold of the entire industrial apparatus, cast off the great yoke of capitalism, and unchained himself from servitude. In the last war, Bird said, according to Greta, the chance presented itself for a supranational labor movement to arise and destroy the state system. That chance, Bird said, has passed. But, he said (according to Greta), a new moment has arrived at which not a complete collapse of the state system is at hand but rather a chance for the U.S. worker to remake his economic conditions, to dismantle the unholy triangle of power of industrialist-capitalist-politician, which, together, wields force through the barrel of the gun. Those wild eyes burning, Greta said, more Trotsky than Stalin. Wild, like the eyes of a hunted man. No sooner had Paul Bird called out the workers then he became one of the most hated men in America. Another living corpse. But Paul Bird was no shadow. He has a thin but steely body. But gray, all the same, a gray column of steel ash all the same.

October 6, 1941

I feel fingers grasping me as if I'm a pen in the hand of a giant. My body stiffens. I'm tilted to the perfect angle for the ink to flow from my mouth onto the white, empty page. Or are these gigantic fingers divine fingers, one of which etched the Law into stone. I look down at my naked skin and see the pale outlines of alephs and bets and vovs and yuds and shins and kufs—an indecipherable text, this body of mine.

October 7, 1941

Two commentaries on Jacob's dream of the ladder, which appear in *The Book of Moonlight*. The first is a Ladino text from the mid-sixteenth century, most likely a translation of a much earlier Arabic source, the latter possibly derived from Hebrew. The author's name is unknown, as is the precise location of origin. The text, in its Ladino form, seems loosely connected to a community of Jews originally from a narrow valley north of the Ebro River. I discovered the commentary in 1937 in the basement of the Strahov monastery. The second piece was discovered in Budapest. It is unclear when it was written, but it surfaced in the research of D. Sonne and was published in Hebrew and German translation as an appendix to an issue of *Wissenschaft des Judentums* in 1898.

The Montenegrin Epistle

Jacob had a second vision of the ladder, which was left out of the book of Genesis. He is making his way back home with his large family after many years in Laban's camp. The vision comes to him during the night after his struggle with God on the bank of the Jabbok River. Jacob knows he will meet his brother, Esau, on the following day.

Jacob returns to Beth El and lies down in the same spot as before, resting his head on the precise rock where he had rested it years ago as he fled his father's anger and his brother's wrath. He is now called Israel, or rather he is both Jacob and Israel, a combination of two names, two beings. As soon as Jacob-Israel falls asleep, the ladder appears above him. Instead of remaining lying down, as he had the previous time, observing and waiting, he gets up and approaches the structure, which seems to dissolve into the infinite heights above him. He thinks he can glimpse the point at which the ladder disappears into the clouds, but he can't be sure if this speck is not the distant wheeling of an eagle or falcon around the entrance to the divine space, forever unable to enter it, for no bird of prey may enter it.

As Jacob-Israel puts his foot on the first rung of the ladder, he feels a strange but powerful energy begin to course through his body, as if his blood is moving faster, as if the ladder contains a fire, a burning—not one that burns Jacob-Israel, no, a burning that provides strength and a certain type of resolution for the great climb. And the climb is great. Night gives way to morning, morning to midday, then evening, then night again, and another night, and another, as Jacob-Israel climbs. Day after day he ascends the ladder, careful not to lose his balance, focusing not on the destination (how could he see it?) but always on the next rung, the next grasp or step. It could be that years pass as Jacob-Israel climbs upwards toward the seemingly unreachable goal.

Despite the continuous presence of the fire or burning, his legs grow weary, his hair whitens, and his body becomes gaunt and frail. The birds of prey above him sense that he is nearing his end and soon will fall, lifeless, from the ladder, plummeting down to the earth below, where they will feast on the last remains of meat still clinging to those old bones. But Jacob-Israel doesn't fall. He keeps climbing, moving upwards, now slower, now faster, until he reaches the precise point he saw from the ground, the place where the ladder seemed to pierce the clouds. Moving beyond that point, Jacob-Israel discovers yet another endless rise and another distant point far above him. He becomes downcast, afraid, angry, thinking that a mischievous God has deceived him. Yet he climbs higher and higher and longer and longer until, finally, at what feels to him the edge of death, the heavenly gates appear before him. Jacob-Israel approaches the gates. If these gates had been shut and locked, they would have been impenetrable, but they were left open and are now swinging in the high wind of the highest sky. This wind swirls around him with such ferocity that Jacob-Israel is surprised it doesn't lift him up and toss him into the abyss below. The winds seem to part around Jacob-Israel as he makes his way through the gates of heaven and into the abode of God. What he sees there shocks him. All around him lie the decomposing forms of souls, souls that had once, he assumes, ascended from the earth into the everlasting immortality promised by this divinely ordained passage, souls rewarded for having lived a good, just, Godly life. Here, they rot. And the angels! Their corpses are being torn apart by the same unforgiving wind. Piece by piece, souls and angels are disintegrating and falling into the lower regions of the clouds. Then Jacob-Israel lifts his eyes from the rotting souls and decaying corpses of angels and sees the ruins of this lifeless, empty heaven: the divine dwellings crumbling, the waterways dried up, and the light—the source of life—blotted out by the darkest storm cloud. Jacob-Israel says to himself, "I have reached heaven and have found it empty." Then he says, "God has withdrawn from here." Jacob-Israel walks through the barren territory. He surveys the entire span of the divine kingdom, finding not a trace of spirit, nothing of the divine. Then he turns back, passes through the gates again and starts his descent down the ladder. When, after countless years, he reaches the bottom of the ladder, he raises his head from the pillow of rock and says to himself, "How awesome is this spot that sits below the ladder, which leads to the desolate space where God once reigned with all His majesty but has now abandoned. Lo, I will never forget the wasteland of wind and sorrow. God has withdrawn from there! Truly, God flees from the power of man."

The Budapest Commentary

In Jacob's second vision of the ladder, he climbed to the gates of heaven. He passed through the open gates and saw the devastation left behind by the withdrawal of the Lord. It is said that upon perceiving the ruins of heaven, Jacob spoke thusly, "Truly, there is no Godly presence here; there is nothing left that is divine." Jacob returned to earth, lifted his head from the stone, and continued on his way to his camp. Along the way, he met a shepherd who had come down from the hills to water his flock. The shepherd was named Bilal. "Have you heard the news?" Jacob said to the shepherd. "God has withdrawn from heaven. He no longer dwells in his abode." This is how the shepherd Bilal responded to Jacob:

"From the hilltop, I watched as you passed through the desert and the valley to the place called Beth El. There you placed your head on the stone and saw a ladder above you. The first time you did this, many years ago, you saw angels going up and down. You were fearful of the ladder's height and majesty. You didn't know the ladder was placed there for you to climb. I could see from the hilltop that thoughts of ascending the ladder were absent from your mind. Years later, you returned through the desert and valley. You placed your head on the same stone and again perceived the ladder. This time, you understood it was there for you to climb. You climbed the ladder, and as you climbed you thought you were alone, alone amid those majestic heights, while around you the limits of the dream crashed into nothingness. Had you moved even the slightest bit either to the right or to the left of the ladder, you would have come against the rough edge of God's abandoned creation, a decaying creation that is, at the same time, the beginning of a great disintegration, because the very moment of the infinite statement, *Let there be light*, is also the onset of darkness. God underestimates his adversary—humankind. You, Jacob, know this better than anybody. While this adversary is inferior in every way, it still can't be defeated. The mirage of the horizon obscures the borders of creation and hides the proximity of chaos, just as the height and majesty of the ladder obscure the closeness of the divine and human realms and, therefore, the vulnerability of God. A shepherd's life, a nomad's life, requires the tracing of the horizon, the finding of borders and edges. Once the empty heaven is perceived, nothing more can be gained by climbing. Instead, one must search for harmony or oneness in the swirling vortex of chaos and darkness, in the darkness where the winds of creation still howl in the night and where the waters of the deep reign supreme. Find the edge, Jacob, and you will learn to sing the very song that will call out to God and lure him back toward our world."

Perplexed by the words of this strange shepherd, Jacob remained silent. The old man lifted his staff and went on his way, leading his flock toward the river. Jacob glanced back in the direction of Beth El, but nothing remained of his vision. Evening was falling. Jacob embarked toward the borderlands.

Hruška closed the volume and placed it on the top of the pile of notebooks. I was ready for him to take out another, but instead he announced, much to my annoyance, that the day's session had come to an end. We had run out of time, he said, and would have to continue the following day. There was nothing I could do but swallow my reproach of Hruška's "methods" and slowly lift my exhausted body from the chair and make my way to the door.

When I opened the door, Milena was standing in the waiting room. She had the appointment after mine, the unfortunate 12:30–1:30 P.M. slot, which must have wreaked havoc on her lunch schedule, not that my slot was much better in this regard. I was always starving after my confrontations with the doctor, and yet I couldn't eat. To take anything other than a bottle of apple juice would cause intense nausea. Milena and I exchanged glances as we passed by each other. I wanted to warn her that Dr. Hruška was in an aggressive mood, that he was lying in wait for her, that he had something prepared, as he had prepared something for me—the Keter diaries. As she vanished into Hruška's office, I thought of a certain evening when, after dinner, I'd been walking through the clinic's garden and had seen Daniel Cohen in the distance beneath the luscious petals of a magnolia tree, the one next to the old stone wall that marked the garden's edge. I hadn't yet talked to him and couldn't have fathomed at the time that almost two decades earlier, this pale, sickly being was the same man as my bearded guide into that subterranean world on Grunewaldstrasse. I'd seen Cohen with Milena on numerous occasions in my short time at the clinic, often in secret embrace, secret because sexual coupling between the clinic's guests was strongly discouraged. After a few minutes of inspecting the flowers, Cohen took a small blue notebook from the back pocket of his jeans and a nub of pencil from his front pocket. He sat down in the shadow of the magnolia and began to write. How could I have known that this was the precise moment he would begin the novel that would be the follow-up to his brilliant novel *Stuck*? How could I have known that this novel, *Guests at the Hotel des Bains*, in its completed and typed manuscript form, would be the one Milena would steal in her attempt at a magnificent moment of rebirth? And how, finally, could I possibly have known that her rebirth would also, in some strange way I haven't yet fully understood, be mine?

Pepi Kafková's "Night of Fire" (My Translation)

 HALF-EXPECTED Pepi would have paid me a visit at the clinic Zelená Hora. No, half-expected doesn't really capture it. I expected it totally—expected that particular past, our shared past, to erupt into the here and now in order to assert a completely different temporal dimension, one that moved in parallel to those years after our relationship fell apart into fragments of unfinished translations, blurred words, acrimony, and self-destruction, which saw at the same time a phoenix rising from the ashes—a phoenix, yes, because only after this complete dissolution could I find my way to the end of translating *Blue, Red, Gray*. It was in this way that I expected Pepi to arrive at the baroque ruin called the clinic Zelená Hora, previously (and for over two centuries) known as the Grünhofberg, the same clinic (though under different management) to which Horak would retreat in acute states of crisis. On the other hand, I knew it was utterly impossible Pepi would come. Our relationship had been over for a long time. In the intervening years, she'd married Ivan Novak, a poet from the Prague scene. Pepi and Novak had had a child, a girl (as

I've been told), whom I'd seen from Horak's balcony overlooking Rieger Park, as I've already written in my *Preface*. Though I can't expect you to remember these details, this particular detail, even though it might seem insignificant to the reader, is actually one of the most important pieces of the *Preface*. The detail is this: as I was taking a break from the translation with Horak and recuperating on the balcony, I looked out and saw Pepi walking with Novak while pushing a stroller with a "light green top." It's not that I hate Novak, and I'm not sure the word "hate" is the best one. What word should I choose to express my feelings about the ruination of a spectacular artist (Pepi) by a person whom I can only describe not as a non-artist, but as a member of a much rarer species, the anti-artist? I'm convinced, in some fundamental way, that Novak set out to destroy Pepi— or not "her," but her luminescent poetry. Why? That's the question. Did envy drive Novak to be consumed by this homicidal impulse? Fear? A lust for power? How was it, I thought, as I looked down that day from Horak's balcony at their stroller's light green top, that a man like Novak could possibly, under any circumstances, destroy a poet like Pepi? There could be a whole course—a whole major of study—dedicated to this most radical of questions: How did Novak, that particular Novak, destroy Pepi—poet, artist, and woman?

It's been many years since I saw the stroller from the balcony—and I imagine you remember from the first lecture of the semester how I was on Ingrid Müller's balcony in Kreuzberg when I first met Daniel Cohen. I was looking out at the lights reflecting off the water of Berlin's Landwehrkanal. And now we're here in this classroom and we can connect these "balconies," drawing together two images that might have existed in two totally separate worlds: two balconies, two points of crisis. Every day at the clinic, I expected the impossible visit from Pepi, which never came, as it couldn't come. When I left the clinic, I hoped the longing would dissipate or fade back into the now un-revisable words of my *Preface*. For the first weeks, thoughts of Pepi receded, primarily because I was spending most of my free time with my father. As I've said before, I came back here not specifically for the job teaching this course but because my father's been sick, suffering from some undiagnosed ailment. We take walks in the forest. We sit together in the living room. We sip coffee in the kitchen. But nothing could keep the memories of Pepi from pushed their way in.

When we met, Pepi was living on the eleventh floor of a massive apartment building on the outskirts of Prague, one of those behemoth developments built in the 1970s in an attempt both to solve a housing crisis and to assert a new, socialist type of living. Whatever utopian charm the structure might have had when first completed had been totally lost by the time I spent the first of many nights there, during those hard middle years of my translation of *Blue, Red, Gray*. And it was here, in that horrible apartment, in that horrible nowhere, where Pepi did her astounding work. I'd like to share with you one example—the only one I have with me here. The rest are back in Prague, packed away in my old steamer trunk. This is a prose poem I translated amid a particularly intense spell—one of those black holes of life—during which Horak was lost in the depths of the Grünhofberg.

Night of Fire

A fire burns in the building across the street, a wide street with three lanes on each side and tram tracks running in both directions. The building is facing this one, it is a building exactly like this one. Earlier in the afternoon, I was on my way to see the Painter—for weeks I'd promised him I'd come—when I ran into a neighbor, the Acrobat, who said the night would be "a wild and crumbling night." I paused and stared at him for a moment, his large mouth, his pale face, before he turned away and disappeared around a bend in the corridor. I thought of a poem from 1997, written when I was twenty years old, in which I describe a night as "wild and crumbling." I've lost this poem now. It was never published, but I remember I called it "The Arrival," because it had to do with the expected arrival of a woman from Budapest. In the poem, the train is set to arrive late in the evening at Prague's main station, where I wait for it, but it is delayed and delayed and never comes. And it is either amid this event of non-arrival or after it, as it slips away into a past that never happens—into that dustbin of pasts that never materialize, never become concrete—this time, this, when the peculiar phrase "wild and crumbling night" appears on an otherwise blank page as the opening of a poem. It hasn't been long since my grandmother passed away and left me her apartment in this monstrous building, a warren of narrow alleyways, flickering and pale light, concrete, paint in muted hues flaking everywhere, a beehive of rooms and rooms, and a swarm—yes, a sedated swarm—of drunken, slow, couch-sitting, television-watching, human beings—drinkers and painters and acrobats and former secret agents and workers and pensioners and sleepers and dreamers and poets and masses of children: a collection of forgotten nobodies. It is crazy to think that in a place like this a young woman, my neighbor on the left, for example, could get pregnant and suddenly no longer be a young, bright-eyed woman. Suddenly, like the raging of that fire across the way, her small room fills up with unimaginable things like toys and diapers and empty beer bottles. A man, the child's father, appears from time to time to rebuke her, to belittle and degrade her. Then a door slams and this creature makes his way from this one den to another, where a group of men sit around a glowing box watching ice hockey, or he goes to another young woman, who sits alone, who doesn't have a child, whose room is without diapers and toys and clothes hanging from lines and radiators—without noise. Without—and he knocks on the door and enters and gives this other young woman a cheap cloth rose that he's bought at the textile store at the base of a building near the tram stop for the amount of two half-liter mugs of beer at the pub next door. He slams the door and there is silence for a moment, and then, inside that first den, the baby's crying pierces through the yellowy inebriated stillness of this desolate place, a building, no, a complex—an urban trauma. This is the dull, muted sound I hear as I write this poem, thinking about how the Painter served me tea in the afternoon. He lives five stories under me. He invited me to view his work. On his walls hang several paintings, all completed, he said, in the 1960s, before he was banned from practicing his craft. He said he tried to sell a painting to my grandmother, but she'd refused. After he said this, he waited for a reply, but I just crossed my legs and took a sip of the tea he'd prepared. Which one pleases you the most? He asked. Where are you, he asked, on the color spectrum? Are you a cool blue or a radiant yellow, a rich red, an empty white, or maybe you're the radical emptiness of black—yes, he's found something there, he said, whichever it is, the original color, he means, it must, with me, tend toward the black. I remained silent, sipping, feeling cocooned in my silence, no desire to speak, a silence that pulled words out of the Painter as black pulls all color into itself. There was such a painting hanging in the room, a swirl of blackness eating its way out toward the edges of the canvas, flaking off from its outermost borders into slashes of charcoal gray, the creamy whiteness retreating, a minimalism of plainness, disorganization, sloppiness. The Painter took it from the wall (he saw me eying it) and set it on the table in front of me. He told me to take it, to hang it in my apartment, to see how it settles in the room, the space I'd inherited from my grandmother, to see how it influences or bends or shapes or disrupts the energy there. I carried it back to my place, hammered a nail into my living room wall next to my desk, and placed it there. Then I caught a tram for the city, heading for the café and bookstore belonging to the publishing house that published the collection of poems from which I'd taken the six I'd read there that night. When I arrived in the center of the city, I had a beer and a cigarette in a basement bar and then walked the streets aimlessly as evening fell and it was time to show up at the literary evening and read my poems to the two dozen people in the city who have a longing to hear a poem read aloud by a poet, to hear language, to hear the rhythms of words, to hear pauses and ruptures and sentences that would sweep the listener into the blurry void of sound. I arrived. Katka, the bartender, brought me a beer as I looked at the stack of thin volumes of my collection that sat on the table next to the thicker and more numerous books of the other readers. I arrived early. The other two poets, Emil and Róbert, will be late, and they will arrive together, as they always arrive together. Even when I was with

Róbert, they arrived together, laughing in some boisterous and stupid way. They will make their way, together, toward the front of the room as if the microphone has been placed there just for them. I found a place in the corner of the café and took out my pages to look over those six poems, four short pieces, each ten lines, lines often containing a single word—an irreducible word like "here" or "there" or "night" or "beyond." These irreducible words spill out into more ambiguous ones, into words that themselves leak additional meanings, like "footstep" or "woman" or "stillness"—and these ambiguous words, in turn, cascade or careen, even if all too slowly, into those impossible words like "city" and "being" and "death." Róbert, with whom I'd had a long and tedious affair, once called this layering of words spilling into others an "impossible architecture," reproaching me for it, reproaching me for everything possible that one could re-proach another, and since this time I have always despised the word "architecture," and have developed a particular aversion to the profession of the architect, whose quest is to ensure stability, structural integrity, when I long for, as the Acrobat said, "crumbling"—a dissolution, and now and then a total structural collapse, a poem falling in on itself or exploding out into fragments of sounds, curves of letters, lines, dots. To those four short poems, I added a longer one dedicated to my brother, Štěpán, a cellist, who has refused to speak with me since our mother died. It is a poem of Štěpán on stage, while I am in the audience watching him, but he doesn't play, he sits there with his instrument be-tween his knees and his head bowed, as if he had already finished (had he?), as if he were waiting to begin (was he?). It is a poem of distance and closeness, nearness, proximity—words revolving around a careening emptiness (of the cello's sound, of meaning) or the hidden word (never mentioned) "betrayal," whose betrayal? Or disillusionment—whose disillusionment? After the four short poems and the longer one came the first prose-poem I had written, the same prose poem Róbert told me was total garbage during our last night together. Why does Róbert hate me? Hate me so much that he once fulminated against this prose poem as a prophet fulminates against the sinners, sinners unaware of the coming of judgment time? As expected, he walked into the café with Emil, walked in with his black trench unbuttoned, with his red-and-black checked scarf swinging, with his green sweater caked with lint. It was late autumn, as it always seemed to be in that café, in the city, in my relationship with Róbert. He didn't bother to look at me as he walked in with Emil, although he saw me sitting in the corner drinking a beer and looking over my pages. I was scheduled to read first. I took the stage and read the short poems, followed by the longer one about Štěpán, who of course was not there in the café, and finally the prose piece, which is called "Miriam's Song." I read: "Sing, sing to the Lord, in silence, and in silence she sings. Silence, with her silent timbrel in her hand. She dances, silently, moving noiselessly on the desert sand, and sings, sings silently on the edge of a roaring sea. She is a prophetess, Miriam, now walking through the city, silent, a singer, a poet, Miriam, an orphan like her brother Moses, like her brother Aaron. She kneels on the riverbank and sings to the water moving slowly below her, she sings to the swans and the ducks and the pleasure cruises—in silence. She walks through time, silently, moving quickly on her toes, gliding like a ballet dancer over the seasons. They sing, they, those sons of Moses, those sons of Aaron, those calf-worshippers, those priests of the desert, who speak the words of others, nonsense words, words that fall from the sky, and they, the Aaronites, the Mosesites, act out the words on stage, performing again and again the climbing of the mountain and the receiving of the Law. The words of the Law—written, broken, rewritten, spoken, enforced by the sons who violate it, then control it, then use it to punish and kill. Yes, yes, in silence, in silence Miriam moves across the desert—to where? Hidden in darkness, to where? And she moves through the city, our city, as the swallows swirl in the evening sky, swirl above her in the gloaming, swirl as the streetlamps flicker and come to life, swirl above the golden glow. Silence, a weeping silence, as around her those sons of Moses and Aaron drink beer and talk, and scream, and stutter—she moves and remembers their whispering, their speaking in hushed voices. She sits at the typewriter, typing, silently, striking silent keys until the silent bell rings and the machine swings back to begin a new line. Nobody knows the sound of her voice, the typist—Miriam. She has never said a word, even when others come and ask her what she has typed and what whispers she has heard and what those voices have said in their hushed tones. She cannot speak, she cannot sing. Children whirl around her feet. She cooks and cleans—and she sings in silence. No. No. Her hand strikes the timbrel, strikes an ancient timbrel that has been stolen in some faraway place and brought to a warehouse where she works cleaning because there is no other work for a silent prophetess who sings silent songs and types silently and can't hear whispers and hushed voices. She steals it and rushes to the edge of the river to sing her song. As the crowds gather and the sons of Moses and Aaron talk about revolution and shout about freedom and around her those sons beat on drums and play guitar, she is silent. And Miriam sings: Sing to the Lord, Sing to the Lord who is victorious. Yes, she closes her eyes and sings to the Lord. She can barely hear her voice, and the

Lord can't hear her, and the sons of Moses and Aaron can't hear her. They pass by her on the riverbank with shabby clothes and unshaven faces and messy hair. They smoke cigarettes and drink beer and call to her to sit on their laps so they can whisper into her ear—this is what the silent prophetess sings on the edge of the sea. Those liberators, those sons of Moses and Aaron, those revolutionaries, those sons of Moses and Aaron, those Law-givers, those sons of Moses and Aaron, those punishers, those sons of Moses and Aaron, those would-be kings, those sons, those sons—sing, she sings, sing to the Lord for He is victorious, horse and chariot He has thrown into the sea. She wanders through the streets, through the desert, she gazes out at the river, at the endless expanse of desert sand, at the night, at the nothingness. And she sings, and she sings, alone and surrounded by darkness, there, a flicker of sound comes, nothing but a whoosh, a wind sweeping over the sand, sweeping over the water, the beginning of a dull, muffled roar, yes, dull, muffled . . . it comes, it can be heard, faintly, the prophetess, Miriam—alone in the night, she wanders, she wanders and feels alone, solitary, free." I looked up after reading this and saw that Róbert had closed his eyes. I could tell his rage was building, he was fighting to control it, it was oozing out of him. He clutched at his folder of papers, his work, which he sensed couldn't be read aloud in this place now, even though it would be read aloud minutes later. But for a moment, I had destroyed him, or perhaps this was only my wish, my fantasy, to prevent him somehow from rising from his chair and displacing me at the microphone. Róbert read in his usual manner, sounding like a husky-voiced bird chirping words and phrases, some abstract, others jarringly material. I sat there, back there in my corner, and wondered why I couldn't hate his work, his words, even though I hated him. As a lover, he was a tyrant, an abusive asshole, a raging child, a beast, but as a poet he was something else, something like an emancipator of sensibility, and as I sat there in my corner and sipped my beer and gazed half at Róbert and half out of the window (it would have been impossible to gaze fully at Róbert) I felt my mouth curl into a smile and I almost let out a burst of laughter between his husky words, his chirping phrases—a laugh at the cruel joke that such beauty was housed in this ugliest of human beings. He paused between poems, he glanced over at me and saw my smile, he quickly turned to Emil, took a sip of water, cleared his throat with a cough, and looked down again at his pages. When Róbert finished, it was Emil's turn at the microphone. But I could no longer pay attention. I'd lost patience, lost myself in the indeterminate zone between Róbert's body and his words, his reproaching voice and his lyrical voice. Emil, short, blond, thin, fair-skinned, smooth-faced, ruby-cheeked Emil, a boring poet. Boring, yes, and there on the other side of the room sat the writer Jan Horak at a table by himself, no longer listening (like me) but shelling and eating peanuts as he drank his beer. Scraps of peanut shells littered the table and gathered by his feet on the floor. "A wild and crumbling night"—Daniela was there and brought me a beer after the readings ended. She took out her camera and showed me some of the photos she'd taken of me at the microphone, then others of me as I listened to Róbert. She asked if I wanted to crash at her place nearby instead of traveling the long way back to that nowhere place on the periphery of the city, the concrete block of stillness and drunkenness, emanating the glow of television sets and babies crying, of doors slamming and painters painting and singers singing—a place of chaotic torpor, of everything and nothing. She said she was meeting friends and asked if I wanted to come along. As Daniela talked, I saw Róbert circling. He was unable to stand still, unable to focus. He moved away from the others, avoiding conversation. He was drinking quickly, finishing a beer, ordering another, finishing that one, ordering another. He fidgeted with his clothes, tugging at this, adjusting that, fussing with his beard. He seemed like he needed to tell me something. He circled. He loomed. Something, something to destroy me, to banish me, but he'll never banish me, and maybe he sensed this coming failure. Snap, snap—a photo of me looking at Róbert, a photo with the half-smile, half watching him, my trophy, a memento of my revolution. I ran through the nighttime streets as the rain fell, as mist rose from the asphalt, as wind blew, as cars and trams and people moved around me, and I thought about what the Acrobat said as I was on the way to see the Painter: "tonight will be a wild and crumbling night." Wild—there was wildness around me, crumbling—there were buildings and sidewalks and streets and statues crumbling around me, there was a nighttime sky crumbling above me and falling in slabs to the ground around me. I was staring up at Štěpán's building, at his windows on the fourth floor. The lights were out, but he was there, I felt him there, even though I haven't seen him in many years. On and on the night goes, the wild night, the crumbling night, the night of fire—and here I am, not looking up at Štěpán's windows but out of my own window at the concrete monstrosity across the way. And I feel words, all words, pulling up anchor, abandoning sentences, throwing meaning overboard, setting sail, setting sail through the blue expanse, yes, those words, those shells or husks of voice—those. It starts with ashes tipped out of a pipe onto a carpet when the man, the smoker, falls asleep in his armchair as he watches television. For sure, he's been drinking—and he's worked a long, late shift somewhere and the carpet is partly wool and partly polyester, and it catches on fire and the fire slowly burns its way across the room and catches on one of the wooden table legs, and then the table burns, and the chairs burn, and the sofa burns, and smoke fills the room and the pipe smoker suffocates and the cabinets catch on fire, and the walls burn and the floors and ceilings burn and the glass melts and the flames burst through walls and doors and windows and into other apartments and down the hallway and climb the outer wall. It rages as we watch from across the way. For endless hours, as they work to tame it, to put it out, to confine it—it rages. We watch—we. Each alone, each stationed in a window across the way, each one of us, a lone, still, mute figure standing in a window and watching as the fire rages. And flames light up the night. And smoke billows into the blackness. As the flames rage and the smoke billows, it is at the same time impossible not to think of this as a purifying force, a raging against ugliness, against the ugliness of history, the violence of history, the violence, the hubris, the inhumanity contained in that awful structure—and in this one. Should the innocent suffer on account of the guilty? This is Abraham's question to God as He prepares to destroy Sodom and Gomorrah. Should the righteous be sacrificed to smite the wicked? Why is it Abraham, and not God, who calls out to save the innocent? God's flames strike Sodom and Gomorrah. Ash. Don't look back. Don't think about the sinners. No compassion for them, no mercy, no memory. But Lot's wife looks back, yes. I feel myself turning into salt, and in every window of this massive building, a pillar of salt. Then it occurs to me that the fire I see is not in the building across the way, it is inside me—and it is burning, raging to unmake those horrific, violent, inhuman structures that I—architect of my soul—have erected year after year, clearing forest, paving grassland, filling in wetlands, destroying ecosystem after ecosystem, only to be able to dwell in stillness and silence on the eleventh floor, high above the world.

There are two details about Pepi and this poem that require a bit of explanation. The first and most obvious: why was Horak in the café during the poetry reading? Horak, whose work is deeply poetical, was not a great lover of poetry, and I can't recall a single time during our seventeen years of work together on *Blue, Red, Gray* that he attended a poetry reading. For sure, I wasn't aware of what Horak did every evening, but I was familiar with his general character. And this attendance was a step far beyond it, not that this fact alone is enough to cast doubt on Pepi's scene. It's unlikely Horak would have just stumbled into the café for some other purpose, especially since the only reason he'd be in a café alone would have been to watch a hockey game, and this particular literary café has never once had a television set. You might think he'd gone there to see Pepi because of my relationship with her, out of jealousy or curiosity. I can disabuse you of this notion: Pepi's piece was written at least one full year before I met her. My god—that Horak would be shelling and eating peanuts is beyond imaginable—and yet what is it but the strangest of images in the whole piece, the most material, the most real? It goes without saying that I asked Pepi about it while we worked on the translation together. She would never answer directly. There is the option Pepi could have inserted the part about Horak later, after the night our affair began, when I'd fallen in love with her, when around me the entire night and everything it contained *did* begin to crumble. And if this is true, if

Pepi did add that line about Horak sitting there shelling and eat-ing peanuts, it could be that the entire motif of "crumbling" was added later—that is to say, it could be that the whole of the poem was added anew to itself, maybe for the third or fourth time, and that any notion of a single, sustained work—a poem—should be immediately thrown out of this window behind me and into the street. If we can assume or imagine this layered work, this assem-blage, this cracked or fissured structure, why not, then, take it in pieces: those scraps of peanut shells, Štěpán's dark windows, the hidden face of the Acrobat, Daniela's fingers on the cam-era, Emil's blushed cheeks, Róbert's circling, the Painter's paint-ing, Miriam's silence. These elements catapult us deeper into the past, into some other poem—into the silent song. This Pepi was obliterated by Novak—no! I can't bear it. Can't think of it any longer.

Let's get to the other puzzling detail. This one connects us to the second lecture of the semester, when we talked about the German writer Anton Grassfeld and his novel *Ein Mädchen am Strand*, or *Girl on the Beach*. In it—and I bit my tongue at the time, even though it was a painful moment for me—I mentioned that a character in the novel, also named Anton Grassfeld, had had a lengthy affair with a Czech poet named Pepi. There could be no other Pepi than Pepi Kafková, and this forces us to ask whether the real Anton Grassfeld had had an affair with Pepi—and if he had had it, did it not overlap in months or years with my affair with her, which terminated only after Horak returned from what would be his final visit to the Grünhofberg? But this is where paths intersect, because during Horak's final stay at the Grünhofberg, Pepi had gone to visit him. She told me about it when she returned. She said, "I went to see Horak." I was furious. My heart was thumping, and I must have unwittingly shaken my head. "Yes," she whispered, "I did. I went to see him.

I told him he needs to break off work with you, that the project is doing both of you in. I told him he shouldn't come back to Prague; he should go immediately to stay with his son in Brno. If he comes back, I told him, he'd immediately start drinking again, drinking himself to death. I told him you'd follow him anywhere, including into the grave; you'd follow him into the realm of death if only, on the precipice, to translate those last words, the inscription on the headstone—rest in peace."

We've run out of time. I'll pick up the thread next time, next week. Somehow, strangely, a type of symmetry has been achieved at this point in the semester. Let's collect the key images and line them up: Daniel Cohen unlocking the door on Grunewaldstrasse; Milena sitting at a table at the Hotel des Bains; Ida Fields in a Berlin bookshop reading a story by Jackie K.; Jacob climbing the ladder to a heaven abandoned; Pepi gazing out of her eleventh story window, lost in the blaze; and I—standing here in front of you amid these countervailing winds of hurricane strength—trying not to be ripped apart.

An Encounter with Daniel Cohen

'LL OPEN THIS LECTURE with three passages from Daniel Cohen's novel *Stuck*. First, a few words of orientation in the text. The protagonist is a man named Isaac Schultz, around forty, who accidentally locks himself in a rather spacious storage room in his Vermont house right before he intends to go for his daily jog. His wife, Emily, being away for the day, Isaac decides to jog in the space, doing circles again and again at varying speeds.

Excerpt #1:

The lock clicked and I looked back at the door and could tell without touching the knob that I was confined. There was nothing to be done, and yet I still tried to act, to measure my strength against the power of the object, the door, and against the metal lock, which I had recently installed for no apparent reason other than that Emily had mentioned one day she wanted to be able to lock the door and forget about the storage, to cordon it off from the rest of the house, the living house, a space that was "now" versus the "then" of the past. The past would be boxed up, crammed in, locked, and forgotten. It was convenient, Emily said, that the storage room was as large as it was.

Another bit of framing for the second passage: Isaac, the narrator, is the director of marketing and advertising for the Vermont Cheese and Yogurt Company of Woodbury, VT, a town some twenty miles north of Montpelier and adjacent to the more famous cheese-making town of Cabot. In this section, Isaac remembers one of his professional triumphs, the rebranding of a line of variously aged Goudas.

Excerpt #2:

As memory of the Gouda campaign flickered and passed through my mind, I couldn't help but increase my pace. Yes, it was all I could do to keep my feet on the storage room floor as the moments came to me. I saw myself at the desk in my home office after days of intense thinking had led nowhere—or more precisely, had led to all the expected places, the meadows and valleys and mountains and grassy expanses and green carpeted cow fields and the gurgling of a Vermont stream and the flight of an eagle over rolling mountaintops. Bears, yes, bears bounded through my head and left footprints and ate blueberries, and my feet pounded as I ran, and I could feel my heart quickening at the thought of an idea forming in some deep region of my soul. Form— how could I use such a word to describe the idea that took this small-time cheese and yogurt maker and thrust its products onto store shelves from Maine to California—the best stores, the leading stores, the stores that people with money and taste want to shop in, where they want to be, to be seen, stores where the person in charge of ordering and stocking cheese ranks with the buyer of wine, the roaster or buyer of coffee, the stocker of craft beers, as a first among equals, as a person who bends the enormous flow of capital coursing through the artisanal cheese and yogurt world as a gardener directs the hose. I got up from the desk and took the Gouda folder in my hand. Inches thick—I first had Bill working on it, then Andrew, then the best on my team: Bianca Jones. Bianca had talent, but it was ultimately of the type—I realized while running in the storage room—that took the ordinary as far as it would go. She'd take the image of an old barn and silo on a hill to the very point where the bucolic or pastoral met the urban idyllic. And this could and did and *does* sell a ton of cheese and other dairy products. There's no doubt. And Bianca, in her work for our lines of cheddars and goats, has performed well, certainly has outperformed Bill Ellis, and has crushed Andrew Jackson, whom I had to remove altogether from our campaign for domestic parmesan and reassign to maple blends: maple yogurt, maple spread, and a signature maple spicy jack. Bianca had won us market share; this shouldn't be forgotten, despite the pedestrian nature of the concepts, despite the existence of something so horrifyingly banal, a banality that brought even the quotidian nature of cheese a step lower instead of a step higher, higher, reaching, soaring after not cheese but substance, *the substance*, what one might call in delusional grandiloquence the Platonic ideal of cheese, of Gouda aged six or twelve or eighteen or twenty-four or thirty-six months. The milky whiteness and suppleness of the cheese deepening and darkening into an orangey yellow, its softness hardening, its creaminess giving way to brittleness, crumbling, as time crumbles, as existence crumbles, as energy undergoes entropy, as life solidifies and then crumbles, as a relationship, a marriage, a career becomes friable, delicate, weak. Disintegration. The flexibility of new Gouda mirrors the unforgiving stubbornness of its aged self.

I tried to hold it together. I tried to reconstruct the chain that led from this metaphysics of Gouda to the notion that in one wheel of Gouda exists the past and the future of all Goudas—that the wheel of cheese was also a wheel of time, turning, transporting, revolving, returning to the moment of birth, that mystical moment when a cheese comes forth from milk.

The third excerpt comes toward the end of the novel. You'll be introduced to two characters here, Jake and Nicole, neighbors and close friends of Isaac and Emily.

Excerpt #3:

Two years ago, Jake and Nicole had a son, whom they named Amos—Amos, like the prophet Amos. I remember saying to Emily at the time of the birth that I would like to have son whom I could name Amos, and as I remembered these words my legs seemed to slow a bit and I found that my circles were becoming more languid. Amos: "You cows of Bashan." Yes, Amos, the righteous prophet of destruction in the name of justice. "The ivory palaces shall be demolished and the great houses shall be destroyed." This house, this house that Emily and I had built, a house which should reflect or embody ourselves, our desires. White pine—swirls and patterns of the finished wood, cedar scents, traces of nature. Confined, refined. Samaria—we who exist on the hill of Samaria, we "who defraud the poor, who rob the needy." I have the prophet Amos inside me, and others, other prophets who call out into the vast space of this earth with a message, some message, a message meant to be heard and heeded—one that's ignored, one that becomes easily bent and twisted, boxed up like a dozen pairs of old ice skates and cross-country skiing boots and hats and gloves and old college files and notebooks—notes filling thousands of pages, line after line about the Protestant Reformation and the Scientific Revolution, about Galileo's challenge to the Church, about Dostoyevsky on the firing line, about the fact that a line about the abolishment of slavery was included in Jefferson's first draft of the Declaration of Independence, about the fragility of democracy, about the rise of fascism, about British colonialists in Africa, about the building of the Volta River Dam in Ghana to create the world's largest manmade lake, displacing hundreds of thousands of people in order to power an industrial aluminum smelter, which, by the time of its construction, was already doomed to economic failure. What else was in those notebooks, those repositories of my diligent work to copy down the thoughts and ideas of other people instead of taking the time to think for myself? Amos—after destruction, rebirth, after punishment, restoration, and a new covenant, a new promise. How I reach for these promises, how I believe in the idea of restoration even though there is no proof of it anywhere. And to believe something in the complete absence of proof, what is this? Madness? Genius? "I will plant them upon their soil." I remember this line from the book of Amos—and as I do, I feel a hot stream of tears running down my face and I realize Amos is not Jake and Nicole's child, he was our child, it was Emily and not Nicole who gave birth to him, this storage area was to be his nursery, the rain did not fall on the field and Amos perished as Israel perished, a death, a destruction, an earthquake of two years before—such is how the book of Amos begins. Two years after the earth shook and ripped open, burst, oozed, broke, two years after the moon slid into the path of the sun and everything was dark and nothing could be seen and hail fell and the raven soared and Satan visited the earth to torture Job.

Late one night, not being able to sleep, having just read this passage about Amos for something like the hundredth time, I made my way to the clinic's library to get out of my room, which during these periods of sleeplessness transforms into a torture chamber. Along with a dozen other guests, I had been given a key to the library and permission to use it whenever I wanted, morning or night. The others, those non-key-holders, were limited to the hours of normal operation between 9:00 A.M. and 5:00 P.M., when the space was attended by Vojtěch, a man of low acumen who spent his days reading the local newspaper and listening to something on a set of headphones plugged into his phone, paying almost no attention to what was going on in the library. This represented a breakdown in the clinic's system of surveillance, which, whether actual or apparent, created in the guests a certain level of anxiety and maybe even duplicity—certainly a tinge of mistrust was added to most encounters. In the library, on the other hand, separated from the clinic's gaze by Vojtěch's inattention, we tended to let down our guards. Not that this is directly relevant to this lecture, because Vojtěch didn't work nights, and only on the rarest of occasions would one key-holder meet another in the library after hours. I, for example, tended to seek refuge there only under the most dire circumstances of sleeplessness and only in the early hours of the morning, between midnight and three or four. For my first six weeks at the clinic, I went to the library more than a few times and never met another soul. You can imagine my surprise, then, when on this night, as I turned into the so-called "reading room," there sat Daniel Cohen in the precise leather armchair I had intended to occupy to work on various matters, including an important letter I was writing to my father. Cohen had a blue notebook in his lap and was bent over it scribbling when I entered the room. He didn't look up until I said, "I'm sorry to bother you. I didn't realize anyone would be here at this hour."

"How could you have realized? There's no reason we both can't stay. There's plenty of room." He gestured to the other armchair and the plush sofa across from him.

I sat down in the armchair. Between us, there was a small coffee table, upon which Cohen had scattered a bunch of handwritten pages of notes. I looked down at the nearly illegible writing, the minuscule letters only now and then finding correct form, indicating either an unstable hand or a desire to get the thoughts down so quickly as to lose interest in any sense of order. It was as if Cohen was running away from language altogether, replacing the alphabet with an impenetrable cuneiform nonsense.

"My next book," he said.

"What's it called?"

"*Guests at the Hotel des Bains.*"

"What's it about? Is it related to *Stuck*? I'm curious to know."

"I can't tell you much, but the main character is a woman from Warsaw. Her name is Milena. She's a fashion designer, but she's had a nervous breakdown and now can't hold her hands steady. It's a book about stilling a pair of shaking hands."

"Does Milena, the real Milena, know about it?"

"That's a dangerous question, Sy, one that follows us down those steep stairs into the basement on Grunewaldstrasse."

It was the first mention of Grunewaldstrasse between us, though I'd already told the story to Hruška in one of our sessions. I could tell by the look in Cohen's eyes when he said "Grunewaldstrasse" that Hruška, at some point, must have tried to use the story against him. If not against him, Hruška probably deployed the information in a session with Cohen in order to recruit Cohen in his campaign against me.

"You knew Milena in Berlin? She told me she moved to Berlin around the time you moved there."

Cohen was silent for a minute or two, then he said, "I'd like to tell you a story from those Berlin years, Sy. I think you'll find it important to hear. If it won't answer any of your questions, it could, on the other hand, very well preempt others you've yet to ask. Milena should be coming here soon. I don't want to lose time. I've been waiting to tell you this since you first arrived, but as you know, it's hard to find the moment, the right atmosphere at the clinic for storytelling."

"Please do," I said, anxious to hear it.

"It's about an old friend of mine. His name is Walt Myerson. You might have heard of him. Ten years ago, he wrote a novel called *Journey to the North*. It won a bunch of prizes. It was a good book. The publication, though, also started, for Walt, what can only be described as a process of disintegration. Walt was married to Dinah when the book came out, and he worked as a high school English teacher at a private school in Brooklyn. He quit when he got the advance for *Journey*, which, he told me, was about twice his yearly salary at the school. Dinah was a journalist, and you can imagine that when Walt stalled out writing his next book and Dinah had the second baby, money got tight. Walt didn't handle it well. He tried to push it, to force the ending of the second book, but the harder he pushed, the faster it fell apart. He started to drink more—and when I say more, I mean way too much. I was living in Berlin already, but he'd call me at all hours, desperate. I told him to knock it off, to quit it, that he was risking way too much for nothing, for a book that he'd be better off putting on ice, because a book can't be forced the way Walt was trying to force it. It could be poked, prodded, but not pushed, never forced. And one day it fell apart—both the book and Walt's life. He came home after a day of drinking and Dinah was gone. She'd taken the kids and moved to Vermont, where her parents lived. Walt tried to call her, but Dinah's father answered and told him she didn't want to see him again until he got his act together. 'She isn't saying she wants to leave you,' her father said, 'just for you to gain control over your life, to get your life back on track. To stop drinking.' For a while—and I wasn't around and don't know the exact timing—Walt tried to clean himself up. He locked up the manuscript in his desk drawer as if it contained an evil spirit, which, for him, I guess it did. After that, I didn't hear anything from Walt for a few weeks. I'm not sure exactly what happened, but one night I came home from being out at a bar and there was Walt, passed out in front of my apartment door in Berlin. He only had with him a half-packed school backpack. I'm not sure he had a full change of clothes. There was no choice but to take him in, to let him stay with me, even though I only had one bedroom and a kitchen. Don't think it wasn't a major disruption. I was in the middle of writing *Stuck* at the time and was at a key turning point, and I didn't know how I could possibly nurse Walt back to health. He needed both physical and psychological nursing—care—something that I couldn't provide.

"It wasn't hard to find apartments in Berlin in those days, as you know, and it didn't take me long to find Walt a cheap place nearby where I lived. It was small, like mine, a bedroom and a good-sized kitchen, a narrow bathroom, and a narrow hallway. Walt didn't have much money and had no prospects of earning any. Continued sales from *Journey to the North* provided some, but we're talking about a few hundred dollars here and there. And he had ten or fifteen grand saved from the advance on the next book. As soon as Walt moved out of my place, I called Dinah and told her everything. She cried. She asked me to watch out for him, to shield him from himself, to tell him she still loved him and would wait for him, that she had told the kids he was away for work, doing research for his next book, that he'd be back. Tell him, she said, to come back clean, to come back as Walt.

"It was late fall when Walt moved out of my place and into the apartment a few blocks away. Throughout November and December, I saw him pretty much every day. Then, just after New Year's Eve, he vanished—and I didn't hear from him again until nearly a year later, when he was already in Vermont. What had happened during these intervening months? This is what he told me:

"On New Year's Day, Walt woke up with a massive hangover and made a resolution to take his life back. The separation from Dinah and their two girls was crushing him. He barely knew the baby—and she, Autumn, certainly wouldn't recognize him, or the feeling of his touch, or his smell. With these thoughts prickling his mind, it took only a matter of minutes for Walt to pack his things (he didn't have much) and to book his flight to New York for the next day. He considered, he told me, letting Dinah know he was coming, but then thought it would be better to first arrive in New York and then to make plans to go to Vermont. He said he wanted to be already within striking distance. That night he couldn't sleep—probably, he thought, because he hadn't had a single drink that day and his body was starting to deal with the sudden loss of its besotted internal atmosphere. He decided to take a walk to try to clear his foggy mind, maybe to tire himself out. Walt claims that he intended to swing by my place on his way home to say goodbye, but who knows. According to him, he walked along the canal some distance and then turned south toward Bergmannstrasse. He bought a candy bar and a bottle of lemon soda at an all-night bodega and found a seat on a bench on Chamiso Platz. Maybe you know it? Of course you know it! He sat there for a long time, slowly eating and sipping until he was finished. It was a cold night, well below freezing. At some point, it started to snow. Not heavy snow, more like tiny ice particles that covered everything with a slippery, icy film. Seen through the pale light of the streetlamps, Walt told me, the falling ice shimmered, creating a surreal atmosphere, a surreal and altogether magical mood. He got up and left the small park, crossed the street, and saw a woman in front of him stumble out of a building. The street—the entire square—was otherwise completely deserted. Walt stopped and watched, and the woman turned away from the door and started to rush down the street. She was wearing a short, tight black skirt. She had on a thin white blouse, which flapped around as if it'd been torn (it had). Most significantly, she had on a pair of black, lacquered high-heeled shoes, which made walking on the icy surface of a street that sloped down toward Bergmannstrasse nearly impossible. After a few uncertain but determined strides, the woman slipped and crashed to the ground.

"If you knew Walt, you'd know that despite some unfortunate incidents while drunk, he's one of the kindest, gentlest souls you can imagine. He ran over to the woman. The first thing Walt noticed was a bad scrape on her left knee, a scape that had torn away a large swatch of her stocking. She clutched at her leg, trembled, kept looking at the doorway to the house she'd exited. Walt bent down to help her up, but she pushed him away, tried to get up, fell again, and then started to slide or crawl her way down the sidewalk. Walt called on her to stop, that he'd help her, that she was injured, needed to see a doctor, etc. At this point, it's likely she saw Walt as her only way out of the situation. She grasped his shoulders as he lifted her into his arms, carrying her the same way he had his four-year-old daughter, Abby. He was surprised how light she was, how little difference there seemed to be between Abby and this woman. On Bergmannstrasse, Walt hailed a cab. He told the driver to take them to the nearest hospital, but the woman got his attention by squeezing his arm. She shook her head—no. He looked down at her leg and saw that the raw scrape wasn't terrible. He told the driver the address of his apartment and the cab pulled away. As they drove, the cab driver asked the woman what had happened to her leg. She didn't respond. After some moments of silence, Walt said, 'She slipped on the ice.'

'You have to be careful out there,' the man said. They drove the rest of the way without speaking, listening to the sounds of Arabian pop.

"When they got back to the apartment, Walt saw her for the first time in the light. She was young—Walt estimated that she was no older than twenty, though in truth he didn't have much of an idea. Her skin was dark, though a pale dark—a type of dark that hadn't seen much sun. Her hair was blond, but clearly dyed—freshly dyed, because it was only at the very edge of the scalp that Walt could detect the existence of her natural dark color. In general, she was thin—and not a healthy thin, Walt was adamant to say, but a sickly emaciation—sticklike arms and legs, flat chest. On her face was a good amount of makeup—it was caked on, Walt said, probably to enliven a rather corpse-like appearance. She had no coat, no hat, no gloves, no scarf—just that outfit: black miniskirt, white blouse, black nylons, black high-heeled shoes.

"When they entered the apartment, Walt led her over to the sofa in the kitchen. He went to the bathroom to get some supplies to clean and bandage her knee. He didn't have much and needed to rummage around in his packed suitcase to find a few small bandages and a tube of disinfectant gel. By the time he returned to the kitchen, the woman was already asleep. She slept the entire time Walt worked to clean her knee, apply the gel, and bandage her. The next morning when Walt woke up, she was still asleep. He roused her to check and see if she was okay, letting her know he only had a few hours before he needed to go to the airport. He was flying to the U.S., he told her, his stay in Berlin was over. She didn't respond to any of this, just lay there looking up at Walt as he spoke. She closed her eyes when he finished, seemingly slipping back to sleep. Walt touched her shoulder to get her attention again, this time offering food. He'd been to the bakery, he said, and gestured to the rolls and pastries sitting on a large plate on the table. When he took the plate from the table and held it in front of her, she managed to sit herself up (with quite a bit of effort) and grasp a jelly donut. Walt offered her some coffee, but she waived it off. He poured her a glass of water, and she drank it greedily. Walt gave her a second glass, and she drank it just as quickly.

"After she ate, Walt asked her where she wanted to go. Did she need a doctor? She shook her head—no. Police, *Polizei?* A vigorous shake—no! Family? Shake—no. Friends? No response. On and on Walt went, asking the usual questions. The woman didn't utter a single word—didn't make a single sound—the whole time. Walt repeated he needed to find somewhere for her to go, he had a flight soon, he was leaving for the airport in two hours now. She closed her eyes, fell back down on the sofa, and was instantly asleep. After another hour, Walt woke her up. 'I'm going to call the police,' he said, 'they can help you. Police, *Polizei*,' he repeated in his best German accent. She seemed to understand "police"—and again shook her head, this time grasping Walt by the wrist to indicate the intensity of her opposition to this idea. It occurred to Walt that she might be involved in something illegal, like drugs, or, more likely, that she was illegally in the country and didn't want to be sent back to somewhere—no matter where that somewhere was.

"Whatever the case was, the young woman, according to Walt, needed clothing. He showed her the bathroom, indicated that she could take a bath if she wanted, brought her a towel, and then told her he'd go out and get her a few new things to wear. He was leaving in a few hours, he told her again, and it would be impossible for her to go outside—it was well below freezing—dressed in only her ripped stockings, short skirt, and thin blouse. Walt found a bargain clothing store on Kottbusser Damm and bought her a couple of pairs of thick sweatpants, a sweatshirt, a few t-shirts, socks, and a pack of five pairs of underwear. In the store next door, he found a pair of white sneakers, a down jacket, and a hat. Before he knew it, he'd spent a few hundred euros, which in his circumstances was a substantial sum. The clothes, of course, were of bad quality, but for the time being, he thought, they'd do. In truth, he wasn't thinking much beyond how to manage the immediate situation in order to catch his flight.

"When he got back to the apartment, he called out to let her know he'd returned. He didn't want to startle her. She didn't respond. He checked the kitchen, but she wasn't there. And she wasn't in the bedroom either. Walt paused and listened for splashing sounds coming from the bathtub—there wasn't a noise. Her shoes were still by the door, and he could see her skirt crumbled on the bathroom floor. The thought came to him that she could very well have fallen asleep and drowned in the bathtub. He called to her again, this time quite loudly, this time with a certain amount of agitation in his voice. Nothing. There was no choice but to look in on her. Walt slowly moved through the open doorway and turned to face the tub. There she was, submerged in the water, thankfully, Walt said, with her head above the surface. Walt gazed down at her, and though she must have sensed him there (her eyes were closed), she remained completely still. However thin she appeared to be while clothed was nothing compared to the radical emaciation of her naked body. She hadn't an ounce of fat, barely a muscle; all articulations of her ribcage, pelvis, and joints were bulging. The red of her cut knee shined among the otherwise white interior of the bathroom. Blue-and-yellowish bruises mottled her legs, arms, chest, torso. Her pubis had been shaved—only the palest gray indicated that any hair at all could grow there. This final observation caused Walt to shrink back from the bathroom. He felt dizzy, he told me, disoriented, disturbed—and it occurred to him precisely at this point that there was no way he could board his flight in the afternoon and leave this young woman alone in Berlin. He went to the kitchen and thought about what to do. A powerful yearning for a drink gripped him. He found a bottle of whiskey stashed away in the back of the cabinet and, out of habit, just as he used to, poured a few fingers into a glass. This was the key moment, Walt told me. As he held the glass and looked at the copper liquid, everything flashed before him—Dinah, the kids, the fate of the woman in the bathtub, his novel, his whole existence, as if this one drink, these few fingers of whiskey, was death—was his gateway into the realm of nothingness. Yet despite knowing this, knowing it more deeply and fully than he could have known most anything else, he, Walt, still longed for it, the drink, the feeling of the whiskey in his blood. The death drive, Freud had called it, the urge for destruction, the eradication of the life force. But the opposite welled up, unexpectedly, Walt told me, from some unknown source. Wife, kids, career—no. No, it was something else, something unmapped and undefined. Wherever it came from, whatever it was, it caused Walt's hand to jerk back, to pour the whiskey down the sink, to dump out the rest of the bottle.

"Walt told me he decided to write a letter to Dinah after seeing the woman in the bathtub. He wrote to her and said he was about to leave for the airport to fly back to New York when a peculiar situation occurred that was now delaying him in Berlin. No need to worry, he wrote, he would resolve it quickly and be back in New York and then in Vermont as soon as he could. It wouldn't be more than a week, most likely only a couple of days. Most likely, he wrote, the matter would be resolved before the letter even reached her.

"The woman got out of the bath, dressed in some of the new clothes Walt had stacked at the threshold to the bathroom, and went directly into the bedroom. Before Walt had the chance to say anything, she was asleep on the bed. She slept until the following morning. The next day, Walt tried to talk with her. He asked her everything you could imagine asking. What was her name? Where was she from? What happened to her that night? Was she in trouble? Did she have family around? Did she need help? Money? A way of getting somewhere? Was she sick? Did she want to see a doctor? Were people after her? To every question, to every utterance, the young woman confronted Walt with total silence. Naturally, it occurred to Walt that she might not speak or understand English. He tried his luck with simple statements in other languages—German, French, Spanish—but the result was the same. Silence. Total, absolute silence.

"It seemed, Walt told me, that the woman had been caught in the sex trade—and that she'd been manipulated to appear pre-pubescent. He asked her about it, but she didn't respond.

"It could be, Walt thought, that she had experienced such a trauma that she'd lost the ability or the desire to speak. He went to the library and searched through the DSM, the dictionary of psychiatric disorders, finding an entry on 'selective mutism.' Through additional research, he came upon the notion of post-traumatic mutism, which seemed like a plausible explanation for her silence, despite various studies that found no link between trauma and the loss of speech. Well, the woman was there and not speaking, Walt said to me, and whether post-traumatic mutism exists or not, it didn't change this basic fact. When he got home from the library, he brought her over paper and a pen and gestured for her to write something down or to draw a picture. He demonstrated this by drawing a figure with some of his characteristics and then writing the name Walt above it. He drew another picture of a woman and then above it wrote a question mark. She stared down at the paper for a while without moving. Then she closed her eyes.

"Walt made a couple of assumptions at this point. First, he thought that the young woman had no desire to stay with him and would simply leave when she had enough strength to do so. Second, he maintained that when she recovered and felt more comfortable with him, she'd open up and he'd learn about her condition—at least the basics, and all he really needed, he thought, were the basics to make a decision about what to do. The best thing he could do, in other words, he said to me, was to wait until the situation solved itself through the passing of time. Besides, Walt told me, Dinah seemed in no great rush to have him come. He could dedicate another couple of weeks to the manuscript of his new novel, and, in any case, he had paid for the apartment through the end of the month. He missed the kids—but by now the missing had become a chronic presence rather than the acute, stabbing emptiness he'd experienced during those first months without them.

"As Walt tells it, the next weeks passed with him waiting in a state of lazy anticipation. He worked on the manuscript.

When it was warm enough, he'd go jogging along the canal. He shopped, cooked, fed the young woman, who slowly began to regain color in her skin, to show signs of improving health. At times, over meals, Walt would talk to her. He told her about Dinah, the kids, the drinking, how Dinah had left him in New York, how he'd come to Berlin, come there to get sober, to get his life back together, to pick up the pieces. He told her about *Journey to the North*, about the failed second book, about the new manuscript he'd started in Berlin—about his parents, his sister, Courtney, his days at summer camp as a kid, anything that came to mind. Throughout these long discourses, she would remain silent, slowly eating, slowly drinking, looking either down at her plate or away into the vague distance.

"The obvious questions tumbled around in Walt's mind, but they seemed to lead to the same basic mystery: how did this young woman end up as what appeared to be a sex slave in Berlin? In this sense, he thought, her escape had been quite extraordinary, a product of many elements of luck—her client passing out in a drug-addled haze, her pimp occupied by an-other problem at precisely the right moment, the frigid night that made everyone turn inward, the appearance of Walt at the otherwise abandoned Chamiso Platz—Walt, who was willing to help by quickly taking her to the safety of his small apartment in Kreuzberg where, slowly, she could be nursed back to health.

"In early March, one of the first spring-like days, Walt took a long walk one evening and ended at Chamiso Platz. He sat in the small park in the middle of the square and gazed up at the building out of which the young woman had stumbled on that night in January. The building looked like any other build-ing on the street. It was entirely ordinary—five stories, a plain, though not unpleasant, pale-yellow façade. Some of the win-dows were dark, others illuminated by the warm glow of lamps, the blue of television sets, the white of computer screens. Occasionally, though not too often, someone would enter or exit the building—entirely ordinary people, Walt told me, doing entirely ordinary things.

"I could go on like this for a long time—Walt told me everything in vivid detail—but I'm afraid I have to skip ahead. Milena should be arriving any moment and I don't want to be in the middle of this when she gets here. The point is, as you can guess, at some point Walt had to go home. Yet months after the woman's arrival in his apartment, her situation was stubbornly the same. She still refused everything; she remained totally silent. She was without name, without history, without place—a character, in other words, only in the material sense, only in the corporeal sense. She was nothing beyond her body.

"Now, what would you do in such a situation? It's a tricky one, a very tricky one. Walt asked me directly: Cohen, what would you have done? Would you have acted any differently than I did? Over the months, it seems clear to me, Walt developed an attachment to the young woman. It wasn't sexual, though it's impossible to deny the existence of all libidinous force in an energy field of reasonable strength. Walt described it to me as an attachment to all that was good inside himself—and to abandon her, he said, would have been to surrender his soul to the darkest regions of his being. Melodramatic, to be sure, but Walt was somehow a melodramatic guy, though a kind of stiff New England type of melodrama, not histrionic, not ostentatious."

At this point in the story, Cohen and I heard footsteps in the hallway.

"I'll have to continue this another time," Cohen said. "I can't talk about this in front of her. I know what you're thinking—this nameless woman was, is, Milena. That isn't the case, or it's not so simple. But Milena is wrapped up in it. And her being here is a part of it—and, as you already suspect, I am here because she is here—though it could be the other way around."

The library door opened, and Milena entered the space. She looked first at Cohen and then at me—long, scrutinizing looks. Then she said, "I'm sorry to interrupt this boys' club."

"Daniel just finished a story," I said. "I was about to leave."

Cohen nodded his approval of this as I slowly slid off the chair and made my way to the door. For a moment, I considered looking back at them before leaving, but didn't. It would have been too much for me, I think, to confront their inevitable embrace.

Allow me to pull back out of this moment of departure, leaving Daniel Cohen there with Milena—shutting the door to that reality, opening another. It just so happens that I had met Walt Myerson before. It was, as you'd suspect, in Berlin, during one of my trips there for various reasons in the late stages of my work translating *Blue, Red, Gray*. A mutual friend, Ezra Stern, connected me to Walt—Ezra and Walt went to summer camp together. Before I met Walt, Ezra wrote with a bit of background.

Contrary to what Cohen had just told me, Walt had not come to Berlin from New York. He'd gone to Vermont with his wife, Dinah, who was pregnant at the time, and their daughter, Abby. It's true Walt was struggling to make a living in New York after the royalties from *Journey to the North* dried up, but it was not the case, according to Ezra, that Walt had fallen apart over it. In fact, through another friend, Adam Grube, Walt had landed a well-paying job as an advertising or marketing (I've never figured out the difference) writer for a local company that made yogurt and artisanal cheeses, the Vermont Cheese and Yogurt Company. Dinah gave birth to a son (not a daughter, as Cohen said) named Amos. It seemed like everything was working out perfectly. And then the most horrible thing happened: Amos, the baby, died when he was six months old. It was this, the death of the baby, the death of little Amos, and not anything to do with a second novel or royalties or money—no—the death pushed Walt down a spiral toward the psychological abyss. Depression, drinking, "a spiral of despair," Ezra called it, which, two years later, resulted in Dinah leaving him and taking Abby. A year after that, she remarried, had another baby, a girl, Violet, at which point Walt fled to Berlin—it was just about the only thing he could think of doing to keep himself alive. That's when Cohen started to write a novel called *Stuck*. And that's when Walt started to write a novel about a fashion designer, originally from Warsaw, with a tremor in her hands. Between these two novels, there lurked a nameless, placeless, silent character who resisted the story but couldn't be abandoned. The only way of dealing with this intractable force was to pull the character from one manuscript to another—to start the story again. How clear it must be to all of you by now why Milena would have wanted *precisely this manuscript* destroyed!

Milena's Marginalia (Part 1)

FTER I RECOVERED the manuscript of *Guests at the Hotel des Bains*, I returned to Prague and met Cohen—who left the clinic not long after I did— at a bar called Sladkovsky's. I slid those pages to him across the table, all of which had been typed by Cohen on a portable Consul typewriter (access to computers being banned at the clinic). Cohen reached out and ran his fingertips over the inky marks—letters, words, punctuation—as if caressing a lover's skin, her skin, Milena's skin. At the same time, he seemed pulled away from the text, pulled outward to the periphery of the page, where Milena, while she had the manuscript in her possession, had penciled in copious marginalia. That these marginalia were written in English and not in her native Polish seemed like a clear indication that the notes were for him, or (though you might find this hard to believe) for me. I didn't tell Cohen I'd read Milena's marginalia, and I certainly didn't tell him I'd copied them down in this very notebook I have with me here today while holed up in a cheap Venice hotel after getting the manuscript back. I spent three full weeks there. Not for these reasons, but for others, our meeting in Sladkovsky's turned out to be more complicated than I had anticipated it would be. Hruška would probably say the meeting was just as complicated—no more, no less—than I wanted or *needed* it to be. There is no way of comprehending that meeting in Sladkovsky's without the framing of the marginalia, itself now a "frame" for Cohen's text. I've left it unaltered. It must be presented in its raw form—or not at all.

[Page 1]

This book can't end without the erasure of you or me. As the author, you might not be able to fully erase yourself. On the other hand, it could be that every ending is an erasure, what you might call an "annihilation" of the self. The same might be said about beginnings—like how you conceal that we'd known each other for many years in Berlin. It conceals that you followed me to the clinic; it conceals, lastly, that you held me there against my will in an inky cage of prose. How does a person break out of a cage made of words? This must be what you meant when you referred to the "unused aviary" near the garden's wall.

[Page 2]

You write, "She entered the Volksbühne's Roter Salon on the evening of Grassfeld's reading." She, Milena, I. She appears there, coming through the door into the dimly lit, smoky space. She's young, early twenties, has a secondhand coat, badly dyed hair, high heels. She makes her way to the bar. It's a cold night outside—it's winter. She's underdressed, shivering from the long walk from Prenzlauerberg, where she'd been invited to dinner (you leave out with whom). She sits at the bar but doesn't order a drink. You imply that she's broke. You imply that she's fishing for a man to buy her a drink. Shifts up her skirt a little bit, crosses her legs. This is the place to insert, as you do, the trembling of her hands. They shake as she flicks at her lighter to light her cigarette. Her left hand trembles as she sits at the bar with her legs crossed and gazes across the room. She's been in Berlin for a few months by now. She lives in a flat in Wilmersdorf with two German women, a Serb, and a Bulgarian. They have three bedrooms. The two Germans stay together. The Serb, Maja, has a room of her own. Milena shared a room with Tania, the Bulgarian. Tania is tall, dark-skinned—you gesture to a Turkish blend, though Tania would have rejected this totally. She works as an assistant dramaturge at the Maxim Gorky Theater, does some side directing at Der Blaue Punkt, an "anarchistic" space on Urbanstrasse in Kreuzberg. At the Gorky, she works under the lead director, Max Krümmel. She was introduced to Krümmel by one of her mentors in Sofia, the playwright Radi Vanev, who (you falsely claim) seduced her and then left her heartbroken, connecting her to Krümmel to get her out of town and away from his wife and family.

I'm expecting her at the Roter Salon, but not until around midnight, which is hours away as I sit at the bar and cross my legs and hold my cigarette with a trembling hand—waiting for a man to buy me a drink. Austin Bly, my mentor at the Fashion Institute in New York, knew Krümmel—they were lovers in the late 1970s—and Krümmel introduced me to Tania during my first week in the city. It was a lucky set of circumstances—Krümmel had to take interest in me because of Bly, Tania had to accept the responsibility of doing something for me because Krümmel told her to. She hired me to sew costumes at the Maxim Gorky. For someone fresh out of the Fashion Institute, nothing could have been better than the job sewing for Tania, even if I hardly earned anything and had to fish at the bar for drinks.

[Page 3]

It was Tania who told me about the Kreuzberg scene and, naturally, about Grassfeld. Vanev had lived in East Berlin for most of the 1980s and came back in 1993 on a residency, had two of his plays performed, one at the Volksbühne. Grassfeld loved him. Vanev was everything Grassfeld admired—good-looking, "exotic," in possession of a decadent bourgeois affect, loved to drink, chain-smoked, chased women (successfully), and wrote with lightness and fury, a hellish fury that could set your hair on fire. But it was the lightness that Grassfeld found alluring—the subtlety, the humor, the wistfulness, a dreamy openness that flowed wild from the pen, at least this is what Grassfeld imagined.

A German—tight jeans, white collared shirt, brown corduroy blazer, shaggy hair—buys me a vodka and tonic. He talks about himself for a while. He knows Grassfeld, he knows Susan, Grassfeld's wife, he's an installation artist, went to the Düsseldorf school. Clumsy, ridiculous, "Joseph Beuys once said to me," etc. It was tiresome nonsense, especially because I didn't care one bit, even if (as you see) I remember it vividly. Those were vivid years. And it can't be argued that this encounter didn't have a particular impact. And on some level, as your text implies, I was there at the Grassfeld reading searching for love. Tania said to me earlier in the day, "Grassfeld's scene is ripe with prospects," even if, as she said, "most of the specimens are hideous narcissists." "But," she added, "there's bound to be a hidden gem. I haven't had the time to rub the dirt from enough of them to find one."

When I finished my second vodka and tonic, I excused my-self from the Beuys acolyte and wandered across the space. Among the crowd, I glimpsed various people I knew from the scene around the Maxim Gorky—the actress Henriette Korb, Hans Gans, editor of the magazine *Die Bühne*, Filip Cech, a singer from Brno, Looi Rademaker, a dancer from Rotterdam, and so on. I tried to light another cigarette, but the drinks com-bined with the rising social anxiety made my hands too shaky—and the thought of people staring directly at those shaking hands made the shaking positively out of control.

A young man said, "Allow me to help." The thought of need-ing help to light a cigarette repulsed and obliterated me, but I handed over the lighter anyway and he flicked it on and caught the tip as I inhaled. I felt impatient—maybe humiliated by him seeing my hands shake like that. I said, "If you're going to the bar, you can get me another vodka and tonic." I'd never said such a thing before. "Sure," he said and moved away. It took him a while to get the drinks, and by the time he'd made it back across the room the reading had begun. Peter Zosch introduced Grassfeld—not that Grassfeld needed any introduction to this crowd—and Grassfeld read a long section from *Tendenz Gegen Null*. When he finished, I leaned over to him and confessed that I barely understood a thing; my German, as you know, was still quite bad. "I'm translating the novel into English," he said to me. "I'll give you the section he read. How can I get it to you?" I took a pen from my purse and wrote down my phone number on a cocktail napkin. He folded it twice and slipped it into the pocket of his jeans.

[Page 4]

Tania didn't show up the Roter Salon, but I ran into her later that night at the Bar Internationale. At first, she was in a pissed off mood. She'd come from what she described as a tedious, grating meeting with her boss, Birgitte Lenz, the Maxim Gorky's dramaturge—the "vilest type of serpent," Tania called her, "a viper." But a woman, Tania said, didn't become the dramaturge of the Maxim Gorky by playing nice. A woman had to bite, to sting, and not only that, but if a woman were to bite and sting, Tania said, it had better be fatal, because the male boot would otherwise stomp down hard. She asked about the Grassfeld reading. I told her about it. She laughed. We drank a couple rounds of shots and then went outside to smoke a cigarette laced with hashish. I felt dizzy and my hands were shaking again, but I didn't care. Soon we were in a club near Ostbahnhof. Tania had taken some pills. I didn't want any. We emerged in the new light of the following day.

[Page 5]

A shaking of the hands—you leave it at that. The very ambiguity of a symptom, for you, represents the unknowability of a character, and in that sense, the unknown of the feminine—or is this pushing it too far? It could be that this shaking is your shaking, the shaking, or rather the quivering, of the text—hesitation, blockage, something ill or diseased about this text, your text, the way your words connect into sentences and paragraphs, the way these fragments, these tremors, integrate into a seeming whole.

But let's run down the options—or, better yet, back up into context. It's the summer of 1989. I'm sixteen, you write, and have two older sisters, both of whom are trained as primary school teachers. They are married to utterly bland men—men not of the party or of the resistance, Catholics, of course, but Catholics of the Polish sort, people who listen without hearing and certainly without thinking a single thought other than what is stuffed into their heads. One of the men is an engineer, though

even my oldest sister, his wife, admits he has no talent for anything. The other does something in food distribution. He could
have talent but has spent his first twenty-two years suppressing
it, forcing himself to blend in. My sisters married young, Petra
at eighteen, Anna at twenty.

The shaking or trembling of my hands, you write, started
that summer, the summer of revolution in the country. Was it
the political and social tension that began this chain reaction of
nervousness? Was I nervous? One July night, though it was still
very hot in the city, my hands started to shake. I didn't feel cold,
but I believed I was cold and wrapped myself in a wool blanket
and crawled into bed. Another time, same summer, we were on
a trip to the Baltic Sea. I was coming out of the sea (it was Au-
gust) when my hands began to shake. The sea was cold—and
my father told me in his harsh, domineering tone I'd stayed in
too long. A week later, I was running back home from my piano
lesson and was trying to ring the bell for my mother to let me
into the apartment. I had to wait at least two or three minutes
before I could steady my finger to press the button. My mother
said I was dehydrated and implored me to drink more water, especially in the stuffy apartment of the piano teacher, who had a
paranoid fear of "drafts" and "dust from the street" and almost
never opened a window. "An airless space for an airless woman,"
my mother would say.

My father was a computer programmer and worked for the
Polish military or secret service, at least this is what I think, you
write, though I never knew for sure. The position was a lowly
one, despite my father's great skill (or what I'm told by others
was his "great skill") with computers. Had he been born elsewhere or ten years later or had he lived another decade or two
(he died when I was eighteen, at the age of forty-three) he would
have been rich and successful. Instead, he died of a heart attack

and left my mother penniless. My mother worked in an industrial laundry. She worked there her whole life, even after the revolution when the enterprise was privatized. Is this why my hands started to shake? Is it because I imagined my mother loading and unloading endless bags of laundry into and out of machines, measuring and pouring detergent, hanging sheets and clothing out to dry on lines as long as soccer fields? Her hands were strong, tough. They never gave up. No arthritis, no carpal tunnel, not even a blister, rarely a cut. They were calloused, hard, bony hands with palms of leather, wrinkles latticing the backs. It could be that I absorbed her weakness, the weakness she couldn't tolerate. She cast it out of herself. It found its way into me.

[Page 5 Reverse]

It's true I was out with Jerzy. It was nighttime. We were down by the river, just lying there on some grass talking about nothing. It was a month after my father had died. Each of us had a bottle of Coke—the new luxury item of this new reality. I took out the bottle opener and was trying to pop the top off the bottle when my hands started to shake. I looked down at them, wondering where it had come from at such a quiet moment. Jerzy looked on—I'm not sure he'd seen it before, though he must have. But he hadn't commented on it. No, he'd silently observed it. Eventually I looked up at him and saw the concern in his eyes. He reached over and took the opener from me and opened my bottle and then his. We took a few sips without saying anything, looking out at the river, thoughts flowing gently away from our minds. Then he said to me, "Milena, do you ever wonder if the shaking is related to Chernobyl? There were so many lies, so much deceit at the time. This whole region must have been poisoned, but nobody said a thing."

Toxic environment—you love this metaphor of these hands. It's as if the whole city, the whole world, could be contained in these shaking hands, which are at the same time skilled instruments—designing, cutting, sewing costumes for the Maxim Gorky. Ruled out: multiple sclerosis, Parkinson's, epilepsy. The doctor in New York, a "specialist," called it an "essential tremor," which, he said, has to do with neurological malfunction in the signal-sending process from brain to muscles. He called it a mild case, though a mild case that could develop into a more problematic case—not that it has to develop in this way. There's no way of knowing, he said. He gave me some medicine that worked inconsistently. He said there were surgical possibilities, but he didn't recommend them unless the tremor became more severe and limiting. He told me to try to relax, to avoid stress, to exercise (though not too intensely), to keep hydrated, to eat healthy foods, to avoid alcohol, drugs, and cigarettes. I remember asking him about Jerzy's theory about Chernobyl. Surprised, he looked up at me from his chair, over the tops of his brown glasses and said, "Could be."

[Page 6]

It was my last year at the gymnasium in Warsaw. An American girl, Hannah Klinger, came to our school for the second half of the year—the term from January to June—as an exchange student. She was staying with our English teacher, a widow of around fifty. Hannah was from New York, Manhattan, as she said, and was Jewish, had roots in Poland, grandfather had been a philologist at the University of Warsaw, left one year before the Nazi invasion. She didn't speak much Polish at first, though enough for me, who spoke no English at the time, to communicate with her a little bit. After a couple of months, she spoke quite well, and she was teaching me English. We spent almost every afternoon together and most days on the weekends. For some reason, maybe her foreignness—meaning her difference from me, her essential difference—allowed me to find a new level of tranquility when I was around her, a calmness that I couldn't otherwise discover. She calmed me, my hands stilled when we would sit around the table talking, drawing, writing, being silent, being close. In June, after exams, which of course Hannah didn't have to take, her mother came from New York and took us both on a trip. It was my first time out of Poland. We flew to Milan, toured through Tuscany, then Rome, then back up through Umbria and eventually to Venice. Venice, yes, Venice—as I told you that night when I found you drowning yourself in a flood of booze in the Kinsky Bar, as I said to you, "Let me tell you about the depths of the wild Adriatic." It could have been a wonderful pickup line.

[Page 7]

Chernobyl—the idea that my body, my organism, carries around a small amount of nuclear fallout. The pollution of a history that was unforgivingly total, enveloping, consuming. Some part of that history must have remained in me, despite the attempts to wash the body clean. This was the meaning of the "essential" in Essential Tremor. Of course, I was "in love" with Hannah Klinger, an "in love" that witnessed great pendulum swings and took on what seemed to me at the time a vast multitude of meanings. Unlike my sisters, who either didn't have much talent or didn't care much to develop it, I did well in school. I had my father's brain for math, and even though I didn't particularly enjoy it, I got it—and in Poland, besides theology, math was the top subject. Jerzy was also good at math, and even loved it, but I was better. Still, I could think of nothing else but becoming an artist, some sort (any sort!) of artist—theater, painting, photography, fashion—it didn't matter, I loved it all. My friend Stanislav started an underground theater when we finished gymnasium, and he asked me to join him. I designed sets, built them with Jerzy, who'd gone straight to the university, and our friend Julia, whom Jerzy admired from a torturing distance.

You can tell I am writing this story *into* your story—asserting what has been left out. No, "left out" doesn't describe it. This life—I hesitate to call it "my life"—has been obliterated from the novel. But the fragments of this destroyed thing, this life-made-fiction, are gathering, becoming something again as I scrawl these words across the pages. That's why, as I write this without knowing whether or not you will ever read it, not knowing whether or not I will destroy this manuscript, this world that attempts to eclipse all other worlds—not knowing what I will do tomorrow, next week, a month from now—I must remember that it was Stanislav, not Jerzy—and certainly not you—who told me that the shaking of my hands might not be a tremor after all, but a vibration.

[Page 8]

Tania was tall, looked like she'd been stretched—long arms, legs, neck, long fingers, long nails. She had her hair bobbed, which only accentuated the appearance of length, had a round face, dark hair, and dark skin. It had to happen sooner or later: the struggle between Tania and Birgitte Lenz turned into an all-out war. And there was no doubt that once war broke out, it could only end with Tania's utter defeat and her expulsion from the Maxim Gorky. That's not to say she was fired. For reasons Tania tried to explain to me, it was impossible to fire her. She had to be expelled through other means, which meant a systematic campaign to destroy her. There was the expected de-motion, though not in title. Gradually, Tania's responsibilities were carved up and distributed to others. Her suggestions were brutally rejected; people delighted in going around and above her in the chain of command. Her allies, myself included, were ostracized along with her. When she finally, after more than two years—perhaps three—left the Maxim Gorky in a blaze of vituperation, I had no choice but to go with her, leaving everything behind, including by then a rather decent salary, to become a happy pauper at Tania's theater, Der Blaue Punkt.

[Page 9]

Costume. Disguise. Characters. I couldn't help but think that what I was doing was nothing less than provoking a transformation of the body. Actors becoming characters, characters coming to life as alternate selves. There was an old stage in Kreuzberg, accessible through an enclosed courtyard on Urbanstrasse. It had been a workers' theater in the 1920s—at least this is what people claimed. Everything worth talking about in Berlin, of course, had its roots in the 1920s, that narrow gap between Prussian Berlin and the Nazis. How could it be that the whole of Berlin was built in those short fourteen years from 1919 to 1933? A metropolis rose from the swamp to house four million people? The theater was connected to the workers union of the AEG and began as the Allgemeines Arbeiterstheater in 1925. It was situated in a courtyard deliberately to escape the reach of rightwing vandals, who roamed the streets looking to smash things up— and it's said that in 1932, when word got out that the theater was putting on a "radical" staging of Wedekind's *Pandora's Box*, a fascist mob succeeded in plundering the space and setting it on fire. From that point on, the place had been abandoned, slowly decaying, host to various communities of vermin, drug-addled youth, the occasional roaming band of hippies, now and then an anarchist meeting. This is why we're dealing here with margins: margins of text, margins of life. Performances at Der Blaue Punkt happened in marginal space. They were nothing if not marginalia, a thumb-sized space between the main body and the edge, the edge of nothingness, an abyss of emptiness.

[Page 10]

Rosa Fuchsbein—I could write that name in all capital letters, or better, I could take out a thick marker and cover your typed pages with big black blocks, such that your words are eclipsed almost entirely by that name, such that the reader has to squint and can still barely make out anything of Grassfeld or Kirschbaum or Cohen. ROSA FUCHSBEIN. Rosa Fuchsbein had met Tania in one of Dante's lower circles, and most of Berlin in those days existed in one lower circle or another. Her appearance here, her name written over and over on every page, devours your manuscript, her tongue like fire on your paper, her breath like water soaking through your words. Among her many works was a play called *Songbirds*, a piece about four young women sharing a squatted house in the late 1980s in Berlin. They are as wild as stray cats, no jobs, no money. They are not really friends, not quite enemies, roommates out of happenstance, because all four had found their way there. It's summer. The sun rises at four in the morning and with it the madness of those singing birds, which nest in the crown of a chestnut tree that rises to the attic window. Rosa Fuchsbein—wide, glassy eyes—eyes that always seemed strained and burning. Her hair, rarely combed, sat wild and tangled on her head—black hair with streaks of gray. Her dark skin came, she said, from her "Spanish side," which could have meant her Jewish side, if she were Jewish, or her Berber side, if she were Berber. Everything about Rosa Fuchsbein was enrapturing, unsettling, frightening, and beautiful. She wanted me to design the costumes for *Song-birds*. "How well," she asked me one day, "can you design rags?"

[Page 11]

I have to back up—years before I left the Maxim Gorky and met Rosa Fuchsbein—to the days after the Grassfeld reading. He called and reminded me we'd met that night in the Roter Salon, that he'd offered to give me the selection of Grassfeld's novel in English if I still wanted to see it. Though I didn't care about Grassfeld, I agreed to meet him at a bar that night. Maybe I was bored.

He seemed strung out when he got to the bar about half an hour late. I'd been waiting for a while and was about to leave. He apologized and bought me a drink, spoke about having gotten stuck at a particular point in *Tendenz* and how he'd needed to pop some pills to try to push through. There was nothing necessarily frightening about him, but he still frightened me—his energy, his nervousness and anxiety. It felt like a spider was spinning some emotional or psychological web around me, encasing me or capturing me in a space where he could move, and I could not.

[Page 12]

The songbirds were Bea, Mariam, Olga, and Helga. I'd taken a pile of discarded costumes that had been donated to the theater and had disassembled them, pulling out the stitching, and had cut the resultant pieces into strips or patches of varying lengths and sizes. Each of the four characters had a color spectrum and a body rhythm. I sewed robes for them, tighter or looser, larger or smaller, one of grays and blacks, another creams and whites with rusty browns, a third of pale blues with patches of navy, the fourth a leafy green with some dark, almost black patches.

During rehearsals I would study the movements of those four bodies—stillness and movement, the dance-like choreography, at times with a single character, at others with combinations of two, three, or all four women whirling around the bleak attic space high above the city.

[Page 13]

Rosa Fuchsbein invited me to Venice. I met her at the Hotel des Bains. She was coming from the south, I from the north. It was a convergence of fronts—producing thunderstorms which ripped open the Adriatic Sea and made the coasts bleed.

[Page 14]

Rosa Fuchsbein started to call me Mila, which in the Slavic means "dear" or "precious." She said I reminded her of another Milena, Milena Jesenská, about whom she was writing a one-act play. She'd come to the Hotel des Bains this winter to write it, as, she told me, she came to Venice every winter to write, staying from early December until late February, always living in the Hotel des Bains.

[Page 15]

She had the idea of staging a play in the Hotel des Bains—did I tell you this? I can't remember what we've talked about, especially since Hruška's methods have muddled my brain. Each room, she told me, would be a scene, and the audience would walk around the hotel and open the doors to the rooms and inside each room a scene would be unfolding. "But there are so many doors," I said. "How will you write this much? And how will the spectator hold it together?"

"The scenes are already written there," Rosa Fuchsbein said, "in the cracks in the plaster, in the scratches on the old parquet floors."

[Page 16]

"And the audience?"

"There is no audience in the Hotel des Bains. There are only actors—actors in rooms, hallways, on the terrace, in the restaurant, wandering away on the Lido, sitting or lying on the beach."

[Page 17]

This is how I found my way here—to the clinic, to the Hotel des Bains. Milena. Mila. She is a prisoner in lost spaces.

[Page 18]

Rosa Fuchsbein: "We need to find the older pathways, older even than the Roman roads. Pathways like those transhumance routes on which the great flocks of sheep migrated from the upland pastures of Castile to the waters of the Guadalquivir, or the desert pathways that moved cola nuts, palm oil, and gold dust north through the Sahara in exchange for salt and other goods, or those creases in the steppelands through which passed the great nomadic bands transporting horses and silk, flowing and ebbing like tsunami tides. Look beneath the concrete and asphalt to the unmarked cities of trees, long since felled, to those highways of rivers, long since dammed, to the migration routes that were the circulatory system of this formerly unified world, when the world, in its post-creation state, was still unified, before it fell apart into shards, into a collection of spaces defined by rigid boundaries."

[Page 19]

Rosa Fuchsbein: "What is a nomad? A nomad is not a homeless person, but one who finds dwelling on the pathways, lives in the movement between spaces. The nomad's map is an ecological one. It has no politics; it recognizes no civilizations. The world of the nomad ends at the next bend in the path."

[Page 20]

You claim that Fuchsbein is a character, a nothing, that she doesn't exist, that I conjured her in my combat with you, in my great battle against the tremors (vibrations?), in my struggle with Hruška. I look across the room and see Hruška's face—and as I look at it closely, deeply, it starts to shift and change, and suddenly it's your face there. And then I look still deeper and it's Grassfeld's face. And then . . . my hands shake, my mind spins out of control. I am swallowed up in darkness.

[Page 21]

You want a "Faustian struggle," as you pedantically say, between you and Rosa Fuchsbein, even though you are bound to lose and be destroyed by her. This is my story. I can only wonder why you want to destroy yourself, but then again all you have been after this whole time is dissolution. First, you make my hands shake, then my mind crumble, then my body pull apart into a thousand pieces. What can I do but rip the pages of this abominable "manuscript," destroying you, destroying me, obliterating the world we share? Who is the devil here?

[Page 22]

Rosa Fuchsbein: "How far do we need to drill down below these layers of concrete, steel, these spans of barbed wire, to find the path that sent dates and spices from Arabia to the Promised Land?"

[Page 23]

Rosa Fuchsbein: "Some years ago, while walking on the Lido, I met an old man named Theo Gutman. Gutman lives in Venice, but from the autumn of 1933 until the summer of 1934, he said to me, he shared a room in the old part of the Charité Hospital in Berlin with a man named Isaac Mondschein. Both had been diagnosed with schizophrenia, the 'treatment' for which was mandatory sterilization. Gutman told me he'd been medically incarcerated primarily for political reasons (he was a member of the Communist Party). Mondschein, he said, could well have been insane. During this half year, Mondschein, Gutman told me, wrote (or copied?) an elaborate theological text on the room's ceiling with a pencil so dull that the hospital staff never noticed it. But Gutman did—and he swore to me he would lie in bed during the darkest hours and stare up as those letters, words, and sentences glowed with blue-green luminescence, as if lit by the breath of God."

[Page 24]

"My case," said Gutman to Fuchsbein, "was #277. Decision by the Hereditary Health Court: mandatory sterilization to prevent the spread of mental disease into the German social body. Little did they know that my wife, Emma, was already pregnant at the time. During her last visit to me before she fled abroad, she told me that if we both survived this coming cataclysm, we would meet on the Lido near Venice at the Hotel des Bains. When this nightmare ends, she said, I would finally meet my child. She would name the girl Esther, because it meant to hide, to conceal."

[Page 25]

I copy from the official medical document, now housed in the Bundesarchiv: "Case #276 of the Hereditary Health Court. Isaac Mondschein: Schizophrenia of the Hereditary Type. Treatment: Sterilization. May 15, 1934."

[Page 26]

There is no door to that room in the Charité Hospital in Berlin, Rosa Fuchsbein said. But the room is still there, she told me. It's walled into the bones of the structure, like a spur or tumor. "I had to break through a wall to find it. And I found it—and I lived in this room for two years without anyone noticing. I came and went by the cover of darkness. It was only in the darkest of hours that the text above me, written on the ceiling, would begin to glow with its blue-green light."

[Page 27]

The text began: "With darkness over the surface of the deep." Another fragment: "A wind from God." And another: "Sweeping over the water."

[Page 28]

"Find the room," Rosa Fuchsbein said to me. "Lie there in the blackness and find that luminescent blue-green light that illuminates the text with the breath of God—a scene from the Hotel des Bains, Room 276."

[Page 29]

Night after night in room 276, I wait for you. I gaze up—and up—and up—past the ceiling and into the heavens.

[Page 30]

Rosa Fuchsbein took a small glass vial from her bag and handed it to me. We were sitting together on the hotel's main terrace listening to the clamorous sounds of a street band playing in the distance. This, she said, will make your tremors go away. Drink it if you want to be cured—or at least temporarily relieved. It lasts for about 48 hours, but there are some side effects, most notably the "complete implosion of the real."

Very briefly, before you leave, allow me to skip ahead (or slide back?) to that night after I left Cohen in Sladkovsky's, leaving him there to grapple with Milena's marginalia, leaving him, in some sense, to reassert—if possible—ownership (what a dubious term) over his manuscript. It was a warm evening. I didn't feel like taking the tram back into the center of the city. It occurred to me as I left the bar that I could try to find Horak, who was most likely out somewhere drinking himself unconscious. Then I realized it would be impossible to see Horak again—I knew this, knew it profoundly, even if I easily could have found him by making the usual rounds. The translation was over. There was no reason to find Horak now, I told myself, no reason to put myself through another night with him, no reason to force him again to endure me.

I walked through the twisting streets to a nearby park, then over to the park's wall, from which a small vineyard sloped down to the city below. Though it was late, many people were out—drinking wine on blankets spread out on the grass, strolling, making love. I climbed up on the wall, sat there, and gazed out at the city, my city after seventeen years, Prague. I would be leaving soon to come back to teach this course and to be with my father. What would become of my small apartment, I wondered, my narrow bed that fit only a single body, my antique desk, my books, my papers, if I were to lock the apartment's door and never return? At some point, months or years from now, the door would be forced, and a crew would enter to empty out the space, and perhaps another man, a writer from some far-flung corner, would move in. Or it could be that the apartment, tiny as it was, would be forgotten, its contents locked in an increasingly distant and fictive past, a room like that one Fuchsbein describes in the Charité, a room that disappears into the void, becoming not a room any longer but a kind of negative space of the real.

Or maybe, I thought as my eyes traced the line of the wall as it curved away into the darkness, I would return to my apartment; I would not leave the city or go home to be with my father; I would not teach a course called Introduction to Literature, and those students—all of you—would show up to class week in and week out, sit in rows of desks orderly arranged, take out notebooks and pens, computers and phones and, in silence, gaze toward the front of the room at the empty podium.

LECTURE EIGHT

Milena's Marginalia (Part 2)

 NEED TO DIVE IN where I left off last week. It can't be delayed. The dean is applying pressure, and it's unclear whether I'll manage to finish even this one semester. For proof, I could show you various documents—or re-enact those shadowy hallway encounters with either the dean or, far worse, the dean's assistant; when the knife is thrust, it is sure to be her hand on the handle. Who can say what they're so vehemently guarding? No matter—they sense something subversive brewing, and they're attempting to snuff it out. In all likelihood, you'll arrive for class one week, and I'll be gone. My college ID will fail to trigger the magnetic lock on the building's front door. Deactivated, alone, abandoned in the darkness of a northern evening, I will be at the mercy of the autumn wind.

[Page 31]

It was a frigid New Year's Eve. I'd spent the evening with Tania and Rosa Fuchsbein at the apartment on Chamiso Platz. We'd each taken one of Rosa's vials of cloudy yellow liquid. Then something happened, something that never had happened before. The thought, or rather the knowledge, hit me that I needed to leave the place immediately. Previously, there had been nothing after the drinking of the vial that could be described as "thought" or that had anything in common with the notion of "knowledge." To the contrary, the substance obliterated thought, exploded knowledge into shards of doubt, fragments of possibility. I got up and, realizing I was naked, rummaged around for my clothes. I wandered into the bathroom, where a pale light came in from a streetlamp, and saw in the mirror that my body had thinned during this one night, that my thighs and torso, front and back, were covered with bruises. Across my stomach, reaching up to the bottom of my now tiny breasts, was a streak of raw red skin. Was any of this real? I found a black miniskirt and a white blouse balled up together in the corner by the bathtub. A pair of stockings hung from the shower curtain rod. I dressed and tried to fix my makeup but didn't want to turn on the light and risk waking anyone up. In this almost-darkness, I could barely verify my own physical existence. What was shadow? What was body? I turned and left the bathroom, rushing down the hall, out into the living room, where legs and arms and necks and fingers seemed piled into a jumbled heap. I needed to get out—to get out into the winter air, however cold, even if it meant freezing to death on a park bench or behind a gravestone in the nearby cemetery. Out—get out! My fingers fumbled with the lock; keys jingled. I heard noises, couldn't tell if the staccato breathing was mine or theirs. *Get out.* I heard a voice within me scream—*get the fuck out*! My high-heeled shoes hit the icy sidewalk. I fell, tore up my knee, but didn't feel a thing. Got up. Fell again.

[Page 32]

Darkness and silence, yes, all was silent. That was the main thing, silence.

[Page 33]

Those eyes: rheumy, bloodshot, burning with fury, yet icy, or empty, or . . . watching me trying to get up from the sidewalk. Watching me try to become human again.

[Page 34]

This is where you own me, where Mila overtakes and casts a shadow back on Milena. I become her, then nothing but words on pages.

[Page 35]

The name Walt Myerson swoops down like a bird of prey on the blur of inky letters following that capital M.

[Page 36]

In the Faustian struggle, the antagonists appear to battle for the soul: Daniel Cohen, Sy Kirschbaum, Walt Myerson. Knight, Death, and Devil, in whatever order.

[Page 37]

You move away from the beginning with a rapid break. We are shut into these confined spaces—basement barrooms, offices, closets—spaces that can be sealed off. Doors shut. Locks engaged. There, under the microscope, you gaze at your pinned butterflies, at human tissue—these histological landscapes with layers as deep as canyons, rings like redwoods.

[Page 38]

Lies. But how can I complain about lies when all stories are lies? I should never have taken you to the room in the Charité where case #276 of the Hereditary Health Courts was investigated. As we pushed those loosened bricks out of the way and I revealed to you the hidden space, you looked at the ceiling and read those words glowing in blue-green light as if reading the face of God.

[Page 39]

He was broke, of course, but insisted on taking me out to dinner in Schöneberg. He tried to dress up, but he looked even more ridiculous than his normal rumpled appearance. I told him he didn't need to take me out to dinner, but he refused to budge from middle-class American dating conventions. We took the train over to Savigny Platz. The waiters wore tuxedos. I ordered a steak, potatoes, and salad. We drank wine. Coffee. French desserts. "How did you like the pages?" he asked while I chewed on a piece of red meat. He was referring to the selection in English of *Tendenz Gegen Null* that Grassfeld had read aloud at the Volksbühne. "I never read them," I said.

[Page 40]

My head slips under the bathtub water. External sound, though there is little of it, is replaced by an internal throbbing. I can't tell if the throbbing is coming from my heart beating or the blood moving through my head. I feel his eyes on me. I'll never lift my head above the surface again, I think. The water above me shimmers with a blue-green luminescence. Then the light starts to fade. The throbbing slows. One thought: life drains away— death is a spiral. Then, without doing anything, I am sitting up. The breath rushes through my nostrils and fills my lungs. My chest heaves. He vanishes from the threshold.

[Page 41]

Rosa Fuchsbein offers me a cigarette laced with hashish. It's rolled in an onionskin paper full of typewritten words. Those words burn away as I smoke them.

[Page 42]

"You're misunderstanding," Rosa Fuchsbein tells me. "Tania hasn't opened another theater. She is staging life itself."

[Page 43]

Mariam wears a robe of black and gray. She comes from the edge of the empire. She has escaped and made her way to this attic space. There is nothing you can do to cage her, as you tried (and for a time succeeded) to cage me in the unused aviary in the clinic's garden—your exotic bird, a heap of feathers only, barred from flight. But Mariam flies—she flies in and out of those broken attic windows, chasing a flock of swifts. She whispers the word "anarchy" as the birds outside sing in a hundred different registers to greet the morning light. "If there's any hope in the world," she says, "it is the hope of chaos." "But anarchy is nothing more than the strong overpowering the weak, chaos becoming darkness, evil. If there's good in anarchy, it exists only in dreams, in the utopian vision of mystics, in young revolutionaries who conceal their delight in gaining power, in smashing what has been built, in violence." Whose words are these? Mariam replies, "In dreams, yes, when sleep sweeps away reality and the space surrounding us crumbles, leaving behind not space but negative space, all that was pushed out of the picture before, all that was unable to emerge—and in this negative space we dissolve, we multiply and fracture, we form and reform. The serpent in the garden—chaos-in-creation—why do you fear it? Why do you remain steadfast against the crumbling of it all, against the dissolution of the 'real'? Those birds we hear each morning—you think they sit in the crown of the tree beyond the window. But they don't. Their sounds originate in your dreams. They tell us to close our eyes, to let it wash away, to plunge back down into the deep."

[Page 44]

Looming behind those attic windows—the police state. The songbirds' song was a warning: a scouting party had observed an enemy force decked out with riot gear, helmets, shields, batons, and guns. The call: "Clear this building." Floor #1: nothing but a burned-out space. Floor #2: a punk squat—easily swept. Floor #3: arsonists and looters, terrorists of the neighborhood. Floor #4: artists, musicians—surviving in fear of floor #3, occasionally allied with floor #2. Keeping heads down, trying to survive, engaged now and then in petty crime, stealing, selling dope. In the attic, the songbirds—soaring above the building, alighting on rooftops, spinning in and out of the crumbling brickwork, looking for twigs and leaves and pieces of metal and plastic to build their nests.

[Page 45]

Bea—you grapple with Rosa Fuchsbein over this name. You tried to write her into a counternarrative: Beata and two kids. She was fleeing from you. It is, of course, not because you smashed computer equipment, a pathetic whitewashing. Nobody would believe it for a second, and it could be that this is where the whole project starts to come apart. One can't say that you lifted your hand and struck her face. You did not. You struck her down in other ways, by other means. Rosa Fuchsbein lifted her up from the scraps of your notebook and wove her into her play; her play, the refuse of notebook scraps, recycled prose, characters and lives as patchwork as the robes I sewed to-gether from those discarded pieces of fabric, torn from costumes unused, unwanted, unloved. Indian calicoes, silks from Isfahan, muslins, woolens, leather, fabrics from around the world, and I cut and assembled and sewed. And one day a young woman slipped one of these robes over her naked body—a gorgeous body—and in that instant she became Bea, a Bea that finally, once and for all, was brought to life.

[Page 46]

The cloudy yellow liquid was not enough for Tania. The devil had taken hold of her, injecting his poison into her veins.

[Page 47]

You tell me you found a report in the archives about an attack on the Allgemeines Arbeiters Theater of the AEG Gewerkschaft. The article was written in the form of a journal entry by a "foot soldier," appearing in *Das Reine Volk* on October 13, 1932:

> *We gathered in a nearby park, about one hundred of us. We were dressed in black, armed with pipes, knives, and hammers. A few of us had guns, some pistols, others, including myself, rifles from the war. The group from the north was charged with lighting the fire that would burn the place down. This group had already taken care of many similar jobs, purifying our streets of the Bolshevik infestation. D., the leader of the arsonist band, told us that they'd count on twenty minutes for us to secure the place against any Bolshevik resistance. We could take what we could carry after routing the communist defense, but after the whistle blew, we should get out of there as quickly as possible. After the whistle, we'd have five minutes to leave the theater before it started to go up in flames. He told us not to delay, to pay attention, because even*

if we didn't see or feel the flames, the smoke would move fast, and the flames would be right behind it. When the plan was in place, we marched in silence to the street and two of the local boys busted open the door to the courtyard. The men swarmed into the space. We confronted a dozen men and women, subduing them quickly with blows with the pipes. No shots were fired. As we expected, we found the Jew director cowering by the theater's safe, forced him to open it, and then cracked his skull. A few of the undisciplined southerners got into the kegs of beer, but even they cleared out as they were supposed to when the whistle came. We gathered, one hundred strong, in the courtyard to watch the purifying flames.

[Page 48]

"We'll build this theater out of the ashes." That's what Tania said. God only knows what she meant when she said it. Which layer of ash of the many layers, for example, was she trying to sweep away?

[Page 49]

He asked my name. At that moment, Rosa Fuchsbein's voice whispered in my head, quietly but steadily, repeating over and over, "Mila. Mila. Mila." "Mila," I said to him. He repeated, "Mila." And I was named. I was called into this life. This one.

[Page 50]

Over and over, he read to me from the book of Amos. Why? Why Amos, this minor prophet, and not the big ones: Jeremiah, Isaiah, Ezekiel, or Daniel?

[Page 51]

Two years after the earthquake . . .

[Page 52]

My head lifted above the water, first my nose, then lips, chin, and hair. The haze faded away and I could feel the traces of the water on my skin, first warming and pleasant, then cooling, giving way to an icy chill. My body started to shake terribly. I could hear the sound of my arm lifting out of the water in the tub. Then it came crashing down into the water with a splash. I didn't have the strength to lift it again. I didn't have the strength to lift my other arm, or a leg, no strength to raise my torso, to bend my neck. My body slipped back toward the icy depths. This is the end, I thought, I'll finally drown in this delusion.

[Page 53]

Walt did not "turn away." There was no pile of clothes left neatly on the bathroom floor. The truth is that he pulled me out of that icy inferno with his own arms, an inferno that nearly devoured me.

[Page 54]

To the north was the Kingdom of Israel, to the south the lands of Judah, ruled from Mount Zion. Vengeance—God's wrath and retribution for iniquity, the plundering of neighbor by neighbor, the oppression of the poor by the rich. Seven years of plenty. Seven years of famine. Walt was stuck in the storage closet of his mind, stuck in texts, in notebooks that overflowed their bindings, ripping, tearing, burrowing, blurring, and merging. Such is our literature—such is the fate of a single book, fated to be consumed by others, by its own past and its ever-shifting present, by the tyranny of its future, consumed, as this book is being consumed, by words written over words, new words encasing old words, my words imprisoning your words.

[Page 55]

Walt had a thick black notebook in which he'd copied down the entire diary of the colonial captain George Prescott. Prescott, Walt said, was an officer in the frontier war with the Abenaki. He led the most destructive campaign on record into the northern hinterlands, what Prescott called "The Journey North," killing, by his own estimate, thousands. Despite this, Walt said, Prescott was sure he was a peace-loving man, a man of Christ. The novel, Walt told me, was no novel—it was a transcription.

[Page 56]

Walt was drinking himself to death just as Tania was killing herself with needles and pills, just as I was obliterating myself with cloudy yellow liquid, just as Rosa Fuchsbein was guiding me toward the summit of the world, which in Berlin's utterly flat swamplands was barely above sea level.

[Page 57]

One book about the collapse of space, about life boxed up and stored in a closet, the other book about the collapse of sound— page after page of silence.

[Page 58]

What do you see, Amos?
  A basket of figs.
  The ending.

[Page 59]

A basket of figs—this could be what I saw in the icy, fiery bathtub when my head sunk below the surface and the cold fire burned against my eyelids—I saw a basket of figs.

[Page 60]

He woke up from a long sleep and told me he had to leave Berlin. To go where? I asked him. Home, he said. But you have no home, I said to him, this is your home. He looked around, bewildered, shaking his head, trying to shake free of the previous night's bout of drinking, the previous night's drugs. I never went with him on these nights. Every time he left the apartment, and the door would shut behind him, he was gone from me forever. And when he would return, he was with me forever. That was how it was. That was the game, a game that was also real life—reality, a sham notion, reality, a lie—reality.

[Page 61]

Amaziah, priest of Bethel, sent a message to the king. "Amos," he said, "is conspiring against you." And Amos said to Amaziah, "I am not a prophet." And Amos said, "I am a cattle breeder and a tender of sycamore figs."

[Page 62]

Now you have to back up. You introduced Amos too early. Amos foretold of the cleansing of iniquity, the rise of righteousness, the purification of Zion.

[Page 63]

"You must be Mila," she said. "Milena," I replied. "I've heard about you from Rosa Fuchsbein," she said, adding, "I saw *Songbirds* and thought the robes were stunning. Rosa can't stop talking about you. You've enthralled her completely, and that's not an easy thing to do." "Who are you?" I asked. "Ingrid Müller," she said. "This is my flat. This is my party." She picked up a book from the table and handed it to me: *Forest Poems.* "I think you know the translator," she said.

[Page 64]

Was Rosa Fuchsbein scheming against Tania, or Tania against Rosa, or one or the other or both against me? You leave everything out. Everything important is left out. How can you tell this story without a single mention of Rosa Fuchsbein? How?

[Page 65]

The way to the clinic was not, as you imagine it to be, a straight line from Berlin to Zelená Hora. There were many twists and turns. There is no road that leads to Zelená Hora. Some old train tracks exist, and one must arrive at the departing station at precisely the right time to catch the train. You once read to me the following: *The train, which ran only once a week on that forgotten branch line, carried no more than a few passengers.* We are the passengers.

[Page 66]

I lay in bed, naked, shivering, covered with a thick down blanket. It was dark in the room, the only light came through the gap in the doorway between the floor and the door that led into the hallway. I could hear you moving around, moving from the kitchen table, where you were working, to the refrigerator, to the cupboard, back to the table. I felt pain in my knee from the fall, then a sharp knifing feeling on my left hipbone. Then the welt on my stomach began to burn and sting. Then it was the prickling feeling of hair starting to grow back over my legs, armpits, and genitals. One sensation would momentarily cancel out the others, but as it did it pushed the register of sensations higher, sharper, stronger, until my body felt so tense and stretched that I began to fear I would burst out of my own skin, elbows and fingers and ribs ripping through it, as if they couldn't wait to leave this bloodless body.

[Page 67]

We went to the cinema on the top floor of an anarchist squat in Prenzlauerberg. He bought us bottles of Berliner Kindl. This was before *Songbirds*, before I'd met Rosa Fuchsbein. It was before Walt Myerson lifted me from the bathtub and before Walt Myerson vanished into the wind, leaving me alone in that nightmare of a place, that horror, which was at the same time a place of beauty and maybe one of hope. The projector started to whir, and the lights flickered across the screen. The first scenes of John Ford's *The Searchers* gathered in front of us. At first, my whole being strained to resist this film, but then it started to soak into me: the desert wilderness, the savagery, the archetypes. How great is our desire to fold ourselves into a collective understanding of a thing. He sat next to me in that small theater without touching me. Not once during the film did he look at me. Pulled east, longing for the west—is this the basic human condition?

[Page 68]

Emil was a punk rock singer, a street fighter, an arsonist, sometimes a drug pusher, a drug user, a part-time father, and a womanizer. Everything that the orderly, respectable German middle class was, he told me, Emil Hofer was not. Somehow, he said to me, in the multiplication of these negatives, Hofer transformed into the very definition of a German. Somehow. He hates Hofer. I could feel this hatred. How, I asked him, could he write such a character he so passionately despises? He looked down at his feet as we walked along a dusty path in the Tiergarten. Then he said, "Hofer would rather burn the whole world to the ground than to spend a single second reflecting on himself. His entire being is outside of himself. How is it truly possible to hate such a man?"

[Page 69]

Milena was only Milena Jesenská—one character, one costume, one room. She sat at a desk and read his letters and wrote replies, narrating those replies out loud to herself as she punched them into the typewriter. It was a difficult play, uncomfortable, tense—austere in a way—but infused with a raw sensuality that was mostly buried but now and then broke to the surface.

[Page 70]

An escape to Prague, a train from Zoo Station. East or west, past or present—how deep do we push in either direction?

[Page 71]

It was September 1999. I was at the theater working on the costume for Rosa Fuchsbein's *Milena*, which was scheduled to premiere in January. There were a few options, variations on the same basic principle or concept—a tight black outfit. As I was nearing an end to one sketch, my hands began to shake. I did everything I usually did to try to control it. For the past few years, I'd been able to control it pretty well—to walk away from what I was doing that seemed to trigger it, to spend ten or fifteen minutes regaining my composure. But that night nothing worked. I was set to show the designs to Rosa Fuchsbein and Tania the following morning. I tried to force myself back to the table. I grabbed my ceramic coffee mug, but it shook out of my grasp, fell, and smashed to pieces on the concrete floor. As I tried to sweep it up, unable to control the broom, it started. It was the first time, or the first time I can remember: panic. The panic shot the tremor into my shoulder, where it caused my neck to freeze. The pressure was building, and when it broke the tremor shot up my neck and into my brain. My head began to throb. My eyes watered, I gasped for a breath and could only find a half-breath, then a quarter breath, then nothing but dead air. I wheeled around, trying to get out, to get into the fresh air, air that would force its way down my throat and into my lungs. Somehow, I got my jacket on. My hand found its way into a pocket; I felt a small glass vial. She had given it to me weeks before. She said it would help me confront the ghosts haunting my nervous system. I managed, God knows how, to get the vial out of my pocket, to uncork it, and to pour the cloudy yellow liquid down my throat.

I pedaled through the night on my sky blue Diamant bicycle, its dynamo whirring loudly. It was the depths of night. I rang at his place. He came down after what seemed like forever, unlocked his bike, and we started north. We crossed the river and turned west along the northern bank, passing Ostbahnhof, Alexanderplatz, and Friedrichstrasse. Finally, we arrived at the outer wall of the old campus of Berlin's Charité Hospital. We climbed the wall, finding footholds in the crumbling bricks. We passed into a courtyard and found the building we were looking for: the Nervenklinik. After 1933, Rose Fuchsbein told me, the clinic had been purged of doctors: Max Bielschowski, Paul Schuster, Franz Kramer, Edwin Strauss, Arthur Kronfeld, Kurt Goldstein. Eventually there came, Rosa Fuchsbein said, one of the most despicable men in an era of total human failure—Professor Maximinus Friedrich Alexander de Crinis, medical director of the T4 euthanasia program. He began as head of the clinic in 1938. But four years earlier, Rosa Fuchsbein told me, things were already rolling. Karl Bonhoeffer was overseeing the sterilization program. Cases #276 and #277 of the Hereditary Health Courts: Isaac Mondschein, case #276; Theo Gutman, case #277. We entered the building through a side window. All was still. I did exactly as she had told me to do, finding the long hallway, the stairs to the basement, the directions to the old surgical theater, its storage closet, removing the loose bricks to expose the large air shaft, climbing up the makeshift ladder to the secret room that was otherwise fully walled in—hidden in the internal structures of the building as a gap or void. I hoisted myself into the space. He followed behind me. We were covered in dust and dirt with scrapes all over our arms and legs. The room, cut off from all possible light, was completely dark. I couldn't see a thing—not even my hand as I held it in front of my face. Nothing. We felt along the walls, whispering to each other. Then I did as she had told me to do. I lay flat on the floor (he did the same) and looked up at the ceiling. First there was nothing, and still nothing, and still nothing—until, yes, slowly, very slowly, there emerged a blue-green glow, gathering into form, deepening, cutting its way into the ceiling, becoming a set of characters, letters, words. Radiance! We both looked on as the light grew stronger, as the text started to unfasten itself from the ceiling and sprinkle down on us. He read aloud to me, "I had heard You with my ears, but now I see You with my eyes; therefore I recant and relent, being but dust and ashes." At that moment, for the first time, I felt a mad desire for him—and he for me. We tore off each other's clothes, pressing our naked bodies together. He found his way to me, and I pulled him deep inside myself.

[Page 72]

He read from the ceiling, "Hul was a farmer and a herder, the single descendant who could trace his lineage back to both Cain and Abel—the maternal line to Abel, the paternal line to Cain. One day, after tending to his flock, Hul lay down to sleep. In his dream, he saw a man at Beth El who slept with his head resting on a pillow of rock. Above the man, a ladder rose from the earth all the way to the heavens. Hul saw angels rising and falling along the ladder. Then he saw God come down from heaven to stand at the head of the sleeping man. Hul heard the words God spoke. Then suddenly the man, Jacob, was gone from Hul's dream. God had also vanished. Nothing but the ladder remained, rising from the now bare rock to pierce the sky. Hul started to climb. Day after day and night after night, Hul climbed the ladder, until he reached heaven's gate. There he saw a legion of angels guarding the entrance to heaven. Hul approach the group and spoke to the leader of the guards. 'I am Hul,' he said, 'descendent of Cain and Abel. I would like to speak with God.' The leader of the guard stood firm and refused Hul's request. 'No man,' he said, 'may enter God's abode.' Hul grew angry and spoke stridently, 'Then tell God I will return here with an army, and I will break through these gates and lay waste to what lies beyond them. At that time, man will reign supreme in heaven as on earth. God's glory is soon coming to an end.' The leader of the guards responded, 'Any man who attacks these gates will be defeated and cast down to the depths of the deep to be food for the Leviathan. There will be no mercy for you or your brothers. Your line will be blotted out for eternity. Those who follow you will die. Their lines will be blotted out.' Hul turned away in anger and descended the ladder. He returned to his camp and his flock, confused and enflamed by the vision of heaven. For months, every time Hul closed his eyes he saw the ladder, the gates of heaven, and the faces of the guards. He saw through the gates and into the heavenly domain. After a while, he stormed against his visions—'be gone with this ladder, vanish you angels. Away with the heavenly gates and even heaven itself!' Nothing worked. The vision remained. One day, Hul went through his camp and began to raise an army. He rode to neighboring camps and convinced others to join. He sent his sons and the sons of his allies to distant camps in the highlands, along the desert, by the river, on the sea, and soon the army had

swelled to an enormous size. When the army was brought together, Hul led it to the base of the ladder and began to climb.
Wild, raging, ravenous, Hul's army assaulted the heavenly gate
and attacked the guards. Though the guards resisted for a full
day and night, they finally succumbed. Hul's army killed every
angel among them. Then the army broke through the gates.
Like an angry, hungry swarm of locusts, the army destroyed
the fruit trees, smashed the marble archways, ripped apart the
silken tents, and burned everything in sight with fires lit from
their torches, torches carried up the ladder from the earth. The
heavens groaned. The heavens burned. God's angels, caught by
surprise, tried desperately to repulse the invasion. They were cut
down by the steel blade of the sword. When everything was destroyed, when the last resisting angel fell, Hul approached God,
who sat alone on his divine throne. 'I have conquered your domain,' Hul proclaimed. 'I have defeated and slaughtered your
angels. You, God, are at my mercy. I reign supreme. I rule the
heavens. I am king here.' 'You might control the heavens,' God
replied, 'but nobody can control both the heavens and the earth
at the same time. If you are here, you are not there. If you are
there, you are not here. You must choose which realm you desire most.' Hul thought for a moment and then said to God,
'I will leave you then in this wasteland. You will be alone here
for eternity—as alone and debased as the dirtiest desert hermit.
I will return to earth and rule over my fellow man. I will sur-
round myself with luxury of every kind.' Hul directed his army
out of the gates and back down the ladder. When he returned
to earth, Hul led his forces into battle, expanding his territory
far and wide. He seized and razed village after village, town after
town, until they called him king. God, in heaven, spoke to himself thusly, 'Heaven, my home, has been destroyed. The earth
has been consumed by evil. War rages there incessantly. There is

no peace. When they finally set down their weapons and search for me, they will not find me. When they call out for me, I will not hear them and will not answer. When they need me, I will pay them no heed. The earth will be ruled by wickedness. At some time, distant from now, another man will climb the ladder and see this devastation. He will return to earth and tell the people, 'I have been to heaven, and it is abandoned. God has withdrawn from there.' He will implore them, 'It is our task to call Him back to us, to again live in harmony with the divine. The man will say this, and nobody will listen. They will call him a madman, call him a fool.' "

[Page 73]

He read from the ceiling, "Hul looked on as Jacob returned to Beth-El and rested his head on the same rock as he had many years before, when he was still a young man. Again, Hul merged his dream with Jacob's and saw Jacob climb the ladder to heaven. He saw Jacob enter through the open gates that swung back and forth in the gusty wind. Hul watched as Jacob took in the devastation of the heavens. He looked on as Jacob descended the ladder and lifted his head from sleep. In the years since he had seen Jacob, Hul had gone from a farmer and a shepherd to a warrior and a king. He had grown rich and powerful, had expanded his kingdom north, south, east and west—north to the mountains, south to the desert, east to the river, west to the sea. But as Hul's power waxed, those around him became envious and ambitious. Hul grew older and weaker, his body became frailer, his passions dulled, his rage dissipated. At first occasionally, then more frequently, Hul lamented his plundering of heaven, his choice of earth over the divine, his becoming king. At last, sensing the time had come, Hul's neighbors invaded his kingdom, destroyed his army, plundered his capital, and razed his palace. Luck alone saved King Hul from death as he escaped and set out for his ancestral lands on the edge of the empire. He gathered a small flock on a plot of land. On his first night there, Hul fell into a reverie on the border of sleep—and in this moment, everything that had happened seemed as if it had taken place in mere seconds, all of history unfolding from one moment to the next—the climbing of the ladder, the destruction of heaven, the conquering of empire, the coronation as king, the treachery of his neighbors, the attack of his enemies, the fall of his empire, his escape to the land of his youth. It was nothing more than the shutting and opening of his eyes. Hul approached Jacob. Jacob told the old man what he had seen: the heavens destroyed, God withdrawn. Hul spoke to Jacob. He told him about the forces of chaos, the power of the watery deep, told him about the winds of creation and the raw edge of the world. When Jacob departed, Hul climbed the hillside where his flock was grazing. A boy from a nearby encampment approached Hul and asked, "What did you tell that man, the man who dreams of heaven?"

"I told him," Hul said to the boy, "that to find divine harmony one mustn't look up and down, as the ladder invites us to do, but to the side—to the farthest horizon, the edges of the unknown."

[Page 74]

One spring day a woman named Fo came into the theater looking for Tania. Tania hadn't been at the theater since late fall. The woman was a poet and performance artist from Iran, had come to Berlin from Amsterdam. She was looking for somewhere to stage a piece. She didn't speak German but had written it in English. It was called *Persian Song, Revisited*, after, she told me, a poem by Hafez called "Persian Song." She was thin, had long black hair, a long, thick nose, rich eyebrows, big lips. She held her body perfectly straight, which made her look tall, even though she wasn't particularly tall. I told her I was the acting director of the theater in Tania's absence. She asked, as acting director, if I could decide whether Der Blaue Punkt would host her piece. Yes.

[Page 75]

Frowning zealots—tell them! Tell them!

[Page 76]

Fo stood naked in my workroom as I draped fabrics over her shoulders, as I wound fabrics around her chest, hips, and legs. I could see nothing but bones—shoulder bones and hipbones and ribs and cheekbones and knee bones and shinbones and elbows and ankles. I closed my eyes and imagined her body in the bathtub, a body that was nothing but a heap of bones, the body in the bathtub being pulled out by Walt. Which body was it? Was it my body—or was it this body, this darker image of me?

[Page 77]

Rosa Fuchsbein: "This is it—imagine it: there is a young poet from Tehran named Fo. She arrives at a theater in Kreuzberg and wants to perform a piece based on the famous poem by Hafez. It's called *Persian Song, Revisited.*"

[Page 78]

I run the tape measure down the side of her body, my fingertips gliding over her skin. I reach the sudden horizontal plane of her hipbone, pause there before continuing down her thigh, past the knee, to the bone of her ankle. A world full of "frowning zealots," I think to myself as I consider her work, as I close my eyes and imagine this body wrapped in fabric. In my imagination, I can see a veil that reaches from her head down to the ground, something like a reverse wedding train. I see her bony arms rise and her bony fingers grasp the lacework. I see as she lifts it off, revealing her sharp face with its massive nose, those thick lips, those bulging cheeks, those thick, perfect, crescent moon eyebrows. I look on as the veil falls to the ground—as her body reveals itself, as she becomes fully exposed to the gaze.

[Page 79]

The clinic's library is a place of secrets, with secrets on every page of text. You are in the armchair, he across from you in another. Neither of you could say the name Mila, because the name Mila came from Rosa Fuchsbein. You still imagine her chasing you, chasing you to erase your lies, to grab the pen from your fingers and to write words over your pages, just as I write mine here, taking away your world, as you took away mine. This is a story of revenge.

[Page 80]

Walt said to me, "I have a friend here. He lives close by. His name is Daniel Cohen." There was something about the way he said it—the way he said it made me feel it as a tremor in my hands. It wasn't like an ordinary tremor that would make my hands shake—what I call an external tremor. This was a deep, core, internal tremor—a tremor of terror as powerful as an earthquake, though, somehow, from the outside, my hands remained perfectly still.

[Page 81]

I pull on the sweatpants and the sweatshirt Walt had bought for me around the corner on Kottbusser Damm. I see his packed suitcases in the hallway. He says he has a plane to catch in a couple of hours, though it's obvious that there is no plane to catch. There might have been a plane to catch months or years before, and there might be a plane to catch months or years from now—but not now. He can't leave. His will falters. Out there, beyond the apartment, beyond the city, is an abyss of delusion. Here is where Walt exists. And he only began to exist here at the very moment when I stumbled from the building on Chamiso Platz wearing Tania's clothes.

[Page 82]

I almost laughed when Hruška said to me one day in our session: "Cohen told me that you were also at the party in Berlin when he met Sy Kirschbaum." I knew if I laughed at this moment, it would have been a big mistake. Despite what Sy maintains, it is clear Hruška is on his side, arrayed with him against me.

[Page 83]

Walt must have been waiting for me on Chamiso Platz. There is no question of coincidence or accident. He'd followed me to the building earlier in the evening. He spent long hours shivering, freezing on that park bench as, inside the apartment, Rosa Fuchsbein played God.

[Page 84]

Rosa Fuchsbein led me to Room 277 of the Hotel des Bains to meet Theo Gutman and left me in front of the closed door. She didn't say, "Open the door," or, "Go inside." She just walked away in silence as I stood gazing at the wooden door with the number 277 etched into a small bronze shield. "Go ahead," I said to myself, but my body didn't move. I thought again about what he had told me after that night at the Charité. He said he'd read more as I slept and learned that after Hul had died, the boy who'd questioned him, Nathan, concluded that God was not permanently withdrawn but was only biding time and gathering forces in a higher realm. With a new legion of angels, God was preparing to attack and reclaim the heavenly domain. This Army of the Distant Heavens would not stop with heaven. It would hurl itself down the ladder toward earth—it would annihilate all that lives, all that breathes "the stolen breath of God." From town to town, Nathan spread his message, crying in the marketplace, "The army of a vengeful God is coming. The angelic legions will bathe the world in blood. The time has come to burn the ladder to heaven, to seal off the heavens once and for all from the earth. To renounce all belief in the divine."

[Page 85]

"Just as Nathan spoke these words in the marketplace," he told me, "a raven appeared in the sky and flew in circles above his head. A harbinger, Nathan believed, that the day of reckoning drew near."

[Page 86]

Tijl Howleglas was from Dutch Sint Maarten. Amazingly, I had met him in New York years before (I wonder if you knew this?) when I was a student at the Fashion Institute and he was studying literature. He was tall, thin, had black curly hair, a narrow face, big glasses. He appeared with Fo that day at Der Blaue Punkt.

[Page 87]

Tania returned to Berlin. Her skin was as gray as ash. Eyes dim, distant, lusterless. She moved slowly around the theater—spoke in a voice below a whisper or just remained silent. When I asked her what she thought of Fo's performance, the first performance at the space that she'd had no part in putting on, she said, "Fo is beautiful."

[Page 88]

Rosa Fuchsbein called me in the middle of the night. Tania was at her place. She said I needed to come there.

[Page 89]

The doctors and nurses had stabilized Tania. I asked a nurse if it had been an attempted suicide, but she said she didn't know. I asked Rosa Fuchsbein if Tania had tried to kill herself and she just shrugged her shoulders like it didn't matter. "On some level," she said, "when you use like Tania does, it's always an attempted suicide." I ran into Tijl when I finally left the hospital. There, in the darkness, Tijl took me in his arms, and I sobbed with my face pressed against his chest, smearing his clean white button-down shirt with mascara.

[Page 90]

This shadow-structure haunts your pages. You should imagine it in the shape of a Jewish star—three male points: Cohen, Kirschbaum, Myerson. Three female points: Fuchsbein, Fo, Milena. Then there are six points of intersection: Tania, Tijl, Anton Grassfeld, Ingrid Müller, Dr. Hruška, and Isaac Mondschein. Finally, we have six sides, each twice bisected to create eighteen segments—edges, surfaces, lengths—which imply duration. The three sides of the downward pointing triangle: Slatky, Horak, and Sidney Keter. The upward pointing triangle: Pepi Kafková, Jackie K., and, of course, Ida Fields.

[Page 91]

He offered me orange juice, but my stomach was too weak to take it. I drank two large glasses of water and ate a couple of plain rolls—no jelly donut! Flashes of nocturnal scenes came in and out of focus as we ate together in silence at the table. The bruises on my arms and legs, over my thighs, buttocks, and back, the slash of red welt on my stomach were aching like hell. Who was it, I wondered, who cracked that proverbial whip?

[Page 92]

I can see it coming now—coming from the blurry distance— the death around which this story revolves. It could have been Tania who died—and Tania would have formed the gravitational force here—but you've left her out. You left Tania out because you can't confront it, just as you can't confront, even if you've included it, the death that's coming, the death you're clumsily foreshadowing here.

[Page 93]

The train crosses the border somewhere between Bad Schandau and Děčín. The Elbe bends away in the distance, carving its way between sandstone cliffs. I change trains in Prague, again in Brno, on my way to Zelená Hora.

[Page 94]

The "all-clear" or *Entwarnung*—that long, steady tone—how often is this sounding a prelude to catastrophe?

[Page 95]

Walt didn't see me watching him as he took down the bottle of bourbon. I watched as he hesitated, sighed, sniffed at the bottle- neck. He put the bottle down, picked it back up, spilled a few drops into the sink. His hands were shaking, and as I watched him, I wondered if in fact my shaking had nothing to do with me but was connected to some deeper collective tremor, and just as this thought came to me, I noticed that my hands were shaking, too. But this shaking wasn't my normal shaking, or at least I didn't think of it that way. It felt like the shaking of a normal nervousness, anxiety caused by watching someone one loves do something utterly stupid and self-destructive, yet inevitable. He picked up the bottle and took a long swig, then another, and another, until a quarter of the bottle was gone. "Fuck," he said—a kind of whisper-shout. He screwed the cap back on the bottle, sat down at the table. His head fell into his hands.

[Page 96]

You and I—points on opposite sides of the star, meeting only through the mediation or interaction of other segments and points. That's precisely how you showed up at Walt's place that night, called there by whom? Fo? I opened the door and let you in. You quickly moved by me. You said something with a voice so soft I couldn't hear it. You went to the kitchen, where Walt was passed out on the sofa. You shut the door, and though I tried to hear what you said, I could make out only muffled sound.

[Page 97]

Kirschbaum returns to Berlin in search of *The Book of Moonlight*. This story starts to turn into fiction. And that requires a stripping of me layer after layer, until—nearly naked, nearly dead—I can emerge from a house on Chamiso Platz—and in this way I exit your story and enter Walt's. You had two choices at that point—to destroy Walt or to destroy me.

[Page 98]

Fo is on stage at Der Blaue Punkt. I sit next to Tijl as Fo appears out of the darkness in a yellow robe. Yellow—the color of the hoopoe bird.

[Page 99]

An ultramarine feather drifts from the rafters to her feet. She looks down at it, ponders. Then she turns her gaze upward and begins.

[Page 100]

Der Blaue Punkt—The Blue Spot, The Blue Point. "The locus coeruleus," Theo Gutman told me when I met him in room 277 of the Hotel des Bains, "the locus coeruleus, the blue place, is located in the pons of the brainstem, produces the neurotransmitter norepinephrine, and is primarily associated with arousal in the sleep-wake cycle, the body's response to stress, and the functioning of attention, memory, and motivation."

[Page 101]

What is the meaning of this "I" that appears on every page of the manuscript? It never evolves or dissolves—it simply asserts itself time after time—hundreds, thousands of times—until under this metamorphic pressure it becomes as hard as a precious stone. This "I" watches as Milena (Mila) enters the Volksbühne's Roter Salon. The Grassfeld Reading! Nothing but a Trojan horse. This is the real opening scene: Fo is on stage. I sit in the audience next to Rosa Fuchsbein. Tijl, Fo's lover, is there. Daniel Cohen is across the way. Kirschbaum lingers in the shadows beyond the beam of the stage light. And Walt? Back at the apartment, of course, writing himself into oblivion.

I'll have to pick this up next time, next week. I'm sure you heard those footsteps. They belong to the dean and the dean's assistant as they walk in lockstep from the administrative wing to ambush me on my way out of the lecture hall. Don't worry. I'll slip out the back door and sneak around the corner, then down the stairs and out into the glorious autumnal darkness. In the meantime, you'll file out of the lecture hall, blocking their way. Don't hesitate to make noise—speak loudly, ask them questions, or engage them in conversation—distract them! We can't let them have their way—we can't let the dean and the dean's assistant control what goes on here, no matter how suspect, no matter how misguided, no matter how dubious the pedagogy. Introduction to Literature! If I learned anything from Jan Horak, it is that there is no such thing as an "introduction." It is all just a spinning around of a wheel, everything forming and dissolving, falling apart, ripping at the seams. "In the beginning"—but there was no beginning. "When the earth was unformed and void"—an infinite amount of time casts back from that point—or down, down into a watery nothingness, into the deep, into chaos. This is why the dean and the dean's assistant wait by the door. They cannot tolerate chaos. They are the guardians of order. They want their words back: introduction, literature, course, college, teacher, and student—the list could go on forever. They can't condone such a shifting of definitions. What should we call this enforcing of the "correct" definitions? It is nothing less than authoritarianism in its purest form. Trust me—I've seen it before, I've read about it; I've lived it through Horak's eyes: the fascist impulse. We need to band together to shatter this structure when we see it. Relationships as chaos, power as a void—a void as infinite and primal as the watery deep. Storm the door!

Waylay them—I'm heading out the back. Go! Go! Go before
they check their watches and break through these gates, before
they haul me away to the dean's office, that lion's den!

Milena's Marginalia (Part 3)

[Page 102]

OU POSSESS Fo—or at least this is what you imply, or the "I" in the story possesses the "her." And it could be that this is a way of saying "you" possess "me," despite the implication that I could be trapped or "walled in" by Walt's prose or Sy's translation—in other words, in those pages of Grassfeld's scattered on the floor, everything out of order. Those years, those utterly banal years of existing in that strange gap in time and space until, suddenly, the world shifted ever so slightly, and the gap closed and everything we created got crushed and disfigured—or it (we) rushed out from the edges into the wilderness, which was nothing more than a collective nightmare. You capture it. You do. I can't deny it, even if you try to harness and control what should be allowed to become what it became: a ruthless, violent, destructive landscape of greed, domination, egotism, ambition, and, above all, hate. Hate.

[Page 103]

I sat drinking beer with Tijl, even though I hate beer. He was watching Fo talking with you on the other side of the room. You stroked your beard, touched her arm in one of those pathetically obvious gestures of "seduction." She cupped her elbow in her hand and ran a finger slowly back and forth across her lower lip. At some point, you took out a pouch of tobacco and rolled a cigarette. Tijl couldn't stop looking. Fo had performed magnificently—her *Persian Song, Revisited.* It didn't seem like jealousy, though I can't imagine Tijl wasn't jealous. And it didn't seem like curiosity, though I have to believe he wanted to know. His face, eyes, skin seemed to transform into some impenetrable substance, resisting my emotion, my longing.

[Page 104]

I sat across the table and looked at Tijl as he gazed across the room watching you watching Fo. How in the world could you write, "I slid off her blouse and put my hands on her tender breasts"? It is all a lie.

[Page 105]

I can imagine the rest of that night—the night you descended those stairs in the building on Grunewaldstrasse, the night you first took the vial of cloudy yellow liquid from the chemist Kaesbohrer, the night you claim to first have heard the distant noise, the noise that, you told me, forms the sonic foundation of what is expressed in the trembling of my hands. Before the Grassfeld reading, before what you call the seduction of Fo, before the scene on Chamiso Platz, before your novel *Stuck,* before the first trip to the Hotel des Bains—there, then—that perception, or apperception—no! That wrecking ball of apperception, there, then: Kirschbaum smashing his computer, trying to destroy ev-

erything that represents the modern world, his wife Beata fleeing the apartment; Kirschbaum slicing his foot open on a shard
of plastic, waking up in that cheap Kreuzberg hotel—there you
are, Daniel Cohen: you move through the city at night, tracing
the paths of the underground tunnels, that network of arteries
conveying the vibrations of history, which, you say, penetrate
my body, agitate my soul, and cause my hands to shake until
my mind spins out of control and I collapse in a heap of nothingness, which, later, Fo would call the prelude to rebirth—my
being freed from the straightjacket of the self. I see you as you
make your way down to the river to the crumbling buildings still
bombed out from the war. The sound is not the steady drone of
the "all-clear," it's the pulsing beat of the swarm—the movement
closer and closer, the tremor of the earth. Time pulsates, time
shakes the soil and cracks the foundations of these shallow ruins,
these mountains of folly, as you pass through the unlocked doors,
through the dark entryway and into a yard strewn with rubble,
trash, and broken glass. What burns in your gaze, what kind
of rheumy film covers your eyes, those swollen, bloodshot, sick
eyes? You lie down to sleep—and as you fall into the dreamscape
you are no longer Daniel Cohen but Hazo, son of Hul. I lurk
there in the shadow at the edge of the dreamscape as a ladder
appears beside you. It rises from that trash-strewn yard above
the building and then stretches out toward the night sky over
Berlin. How could it be, I thought, that a path to heaven could
open in this most demonic of places, this city that has been the
center of evil, these streets through which evil pulsated and still
vibrates and trembles with the reverberations of history—how?
Hazo, son of Hul, rose from the ground and began to climb the
ladder. Rung by rung, he moved upward until he approached
the first layer of cloud. He hesitated, stopped, and then started
to come back down. I could see the strange look in his eyes when

his feet found the ground again—a look of total abandonment, a desperate look, something related to a process of detaching himself from what had come before. He started to gather debris: newspaper pages, scraps of boxes, splintered planks of wood. He set the debris in a pile at the base of the ladder. He struck a match and lit the pile on fire. It burned quickly, first the paper and the cardboard, then the wooden planks, and finally the very bottom of the ladder itself—those sides and rungs made of ancient Lebanese cedar. Then it happened: the fire shot up the ladder like a lightning bolt in reverse, a fiery streak that cut through the clouds on its way to heaven—a missile of fire projected toward the abandoned abode of God. You spoke, "Let the path to heaven be closed. Those who seek the divine must imagine a new way. The old way has been destroyed." As you spoke, and continuing long afterwards, ash from the charred cedar wood came sprinkling down from the sky and began to gather at your feet. The dream faded. It was getting cold—and there you were, asleep in the courtyard, looking barely alive. I moved closer, put my hand on your cheek, which felt as cold as ice. For a moment, I thought maybe the dissipation of the dream had taken the life from you, allowed your soul to escape, to mix with the wind and ash, leaving this lifeless body. It was dark. I couldn't see much, but I sensed your lips had turned blue. I bent over you and placed my hand directly above your mouth. Thank God, I could feel the ever-so-slight pulse of your breath against my palm. I gently slapped your cheeks, trying to rouse you. It didn't work. There was no other option—I had to pull your limp body onto my back and drag you from that yard to the street like a corpse. The street was abandoned, but after a while a van came by, and I flagged it down by basically throwing myself in front of it. It was a bread delivery truck of Grossbäcker Siegfried making the early rounds. The driver, Ahmed, seemed like a gentle man. He didn't say much, looked nervously at your body, at me, drove to my apartment and helped me carry you upstairs, where Tania prepared two hot water bottles, which we tucked under your eiderdown. After an hour, your skin had regained some color, your breathing had strengthened—and we were pretty sure you would live.

[Page 106]

She was fifteen, Tijl told me, when those frowning zealots grabbed her from the street and locked her in a windowless room. They shouted insults at her, struck her, threatened to rape her. She'd written an essay on Attar's *The Conference of the Birds*, focusing on the poet's disdain for authority and his dedication to the equality of all beings, beings as equal "shadows" cast by the divine light. *Do not again, dear God, I pray, create such powerful kings; my eyes have seen the blight their glory brings.* This was the beginning of the campaign to shame and humiliate her—and if that didn't work, to kill her. But she refused to yield. She became wilder, more radical—a swirling storm—until the time came for her escape.

[Page 107]

Fo made it to Paris, from Paris to Amsterdam. Her father had died when she was seven. Her three older brothers lorded over the house as tyrants. If her mother defied them, she'd pay the price. Fo always thought they'd hunt her down—that's why she left Paris, that's why she left Amsterdam, that's how she found her way, with a descendent of sugar plantation slaves, Tijl Howleglas, to Berlin.

[Page 108]

Pathways—lines of migration cut into the cartographic fabric—converging in that strange city, Berlin—a desolate, half-abandoned place. I felt this convergence, the bringing together of disparate energies, as I sat in the workroom and prepared for the premier of Fo's *Persian Song, Revisited*. The robe—hoopoe yellow—draped over her body. She tells me that the feeling of wearing the robe reminds her of a passage in the Qur'an, when Eve, before she eats of the tree of knowledge, is clothed with garments of faith in God. I can feel the bones of her shoulders beneath the silk.

[Page 109]

Fo looked toward the sky and had a vision of the gates of heaven. There was no ladder. To reach them would require a spreading of one's wings—a flight, a launching of one's body and soul into the oblivion of the blue. But first, before one's wings could be spread, a stripping away was required. It was there, in that windowless closet, after the final beating by her eldest brother, where she put her lips together and sounded her new name: Fo. A syllable, a partial name, a propulsive sound. Fo. "Why not Foe with an e" I asked her, "as in enemy, opponent, antagonist?" She shook her head, smiled. "No," she said. "No."

[Page 110]

Fo: "The self and faith must both be tossed away." Yes, yes, yes!

[Page 111]

Hruška said to me, "I see that you like to walk along the edge of the clinic's garden, close to the garden wall. It's as if you're tracing the border between confinement and freedom, trying to understand what prevents you from trading one for the other, what holds you here, what cages you. You are, of course, quite free to pass through the clinic's gate and into the fields beyond."

[Page 112]

I gaze out the window at the wounded cedar. Near the bottom, its trunk flares out into what look like an octopus' legs, driving the tree's roots into the brown, thirsty grass. A golden ball of fossilized resin bubbles from the "scar," as they call it, reflecting the play of light and shadow.

[Page 113]

From my window, I can see you down there, notebook in your lap, pencil in your hand. What difference is there between your notebook and Hruška's pad of paper? You have a chewed-on nub of pencil, while he has a fancy fountain pen—that's true. What is the nature of real authority, real power? Is it the changing of her name to Fo? Is it the replacing of Milena with Mila? Flesh and blood with ink or graphite, blood with gray smudges? Bodiless, weightless smudges, immortalized (or immobilized?) in that resinous ball of collective memory we call "history"?

[Page 114]

"You need to become a nomad," Rosa Fuchsbein said to me one long, dark night shortly after Tania had died. "Don't move on those cut pathways of modernity—asphalt roads, highways, groomed trails, vectors in the sky, vectors on the seas. There are other, older, more complex pathways, which might not be apparent. They are not directly in front of you; they are to your right and to your left. Don't fight to remain in one place, to root yourself—struggle instead to unfasten your body from this ground."

[Page 115]

"I'm starting a theater in Venice, on the Lido," Rosa Fuchsbein said to me after Tania died. "It's in the abandoned Hotel des Bains. Each room contains a scene, which will change depending on who opens the door. I've found an actor to play a character named Theo Gutman, who fled Berlin in 1934 after the Hereditary Health Court ordered his forced sterilization. And I've found an actor for the role of the novelist Anton Grassfeld. Grassfeld doesn't have a particular room. Rather, he wanders the halls searching for his fictional double, a character also named Anton Grassfeld, though he, the novelist, is unaware this double is a monster of his own creation, the body to his shadow. There are others, too, like a young girl named Diya—but you'll see everything for yourself when you come to Venice and take the boat out to the Lido. We'll need costumes, of course, but don't bring anything with you. Just come. I'll have the sewing machine and fabrics ready."

[Page 116]

Rosa Fuchsbein: "Invert reality and journey south to the Hotel des Bains. To get there, you'll need to leap off the rails of consciousness, career away from the highway of selfhood and into the ravine of the unself."

[Page 117]

Each day, Walt sat at the kitchen table in silence and drank straight from the bottle. He would look out for long stretches of time at the courtyard where the building's inhabitants kept their bikes chained up, where they sorted their trash into glass, plastic, paper, and compostable biomass. I would speak to him— or at least I think I did (was it all in my head?)—but my words didn't register. His arm rose and fell with the bottle. In his right hand, he held a pen, which in fits and starts would move across the page. One day, I spotted what seemed to me a title: *The Exilarch*. A couple of weeks later, it was crossed out. Some months after that, a new title appeared below it: *Black Fire, White Fire*. I wondered: did this book begin or end with the death of Amos, the death of his son?

[Page 118]

Fo said to me: "His body is lanky, gawky, his ribcage bony and arms long. He moves awkwardly through the bar to a table in the front row. He's with two other guys—white, Dutch. He's wearing a white shirt with a wide collar, a pair of olive-green pants that are tight over his thin legs. Glasses, curly hair cut short, furrowed forehead, ample nose—he's right in front of me, and when I start to perform, he takes out a notebook and begins to jot things down. After my first short piece, his friends whisper something to him and move away to the bar to order drinks. The tables around him are mostly empty. Between pieces, I watch as his eyes squint and widen, as his mouth silently forms the words he seems to be writing. I think to myself that these next pieces will be just for him. I will perform so he continues to gaze at me, so he continues to jot down notes. I start to perform, and as I do, I can feel my soul lifting from me, moving up and away from the dais, moving beyond the pale light and the marijuana smoke. And then his soul, too, seems to be lifting into the air, to meet mine in a realm beyond our bodies. Where do you live? He asks me later. Nowhere, I say to him. How do you live? He asks. Between things, I say. He: Why between? I: Because there's less violence between. He: But isn't there violence even there? I: Yes, even there. He: And even if there's less violence in between, isn't there also less protection? I: Less, protection, yes, but more pathways for escape, more lines of flight—and a soaring through these airy channels is the only means of preserving truth, of shedding the shell of selfhood, molting the skin of identity. He: But isn't this shedding and molting, isn't this flight, leaving behind all that you are and, thus, all you should be trying to preserve? I: I soar to be free—only to be free—to be free of selfhood, to be liberated from identity. *Noises in the hallway—shouting in the street. Drunks and addicts.* He: Tell me everything about you so I can fall in love with you. I: You are in love already. I saw you write it down in your notebook in the club while I was up on stage. He: Then I have no choice but to fall into the cracks with you. I: Isn't this the life you've always led? *Muffled noise, the blur of color, the grayness of pencil marks, blue and black ink smudges— black skin, red blood—night, or the blinding brightness of the desert sun, the power of tropical wind, rain falling in torrents. He places his lips on my breast—that is it, all of it—a blur of sensation, raging with power, unmaking order, setting us free."*

[Page 119]

"There must be a scar in my head, running straight through the locus coeruleus," I told Hruška, "as thin as a single hair split into a thousand strands. When electricity flows over this thinnest of scars, the signals get blocked, the energy concentrates. This concentrated energy seeks to find its way out of my brain, eventually flowing into the brainstem and then to the spiral cord, where it emanates out to the right and left, causing shaking, vibrations, and tremors in my hands."

[Page 120]

There was a knock. I opened the door, and you were standing there. I'm sure you remember your shock upon seeing me dressed in Walt's old sweatpants and sweatshirt while Walt was passed out drunk on the sofa in the kitchen. "How's Walt?" You asked in a pathetic way. "He's drinking himself to death," I told you, "and there's nothing you or I can do about it."

[Page 121]

Fo: "In that windowless room, day turned into night, night into day. I could hear footsteps patrolling beyond the locked door. Out there, beyond my prison, shame burned hot like a forest fire. Inside, I could sense the ceiling lifting from the room to reveal the night sky. I rose my arms above my head so high that my fingertips could stroke the skin of heaven."

[Page 122]

I stood in the kitchen. Walt sat at the table next to me. It had been over three weeks since I'd left the apartment. I closed my eyes and thought about the last time I'd left. I was riding my bike down Gneisenaustrasse to Mehringdamm, the wind breaking cold against my cheeks, freezing the tears that streamed hot from my eyes. Rosa Fuchsbein had called with the news. Tania had died.

[Page 123]

Tijl said to me that Fo's closet of nightmares became a portal into the garden of transcendence. She descended deep into herself only to unmake that self, to metamorphose into a bird, a hoopoe, which could spread its wings and soar to heaven. But then her mind would falter, and the hoopoe bird would come crashing down into that nightmare closet and become a human body again, her body—frail, cold, hungry, terrified of footsteps and voices on the other side of the door.

[Page 124]

Your novel, this novel, is a prison disguised as a closet. Or more accurately, it is a set of closets within closets, with the outermost framing being the city of Berlin itself. You've placed one door to escape the whole structure. It leads to the clinic Zelená Hora and the authority of Dr. Hruška.

[Page 125]

You talk about resistance seeping in from the periphery or edges—but the truth is that power is radiating out from the center, pushing all else to the margins. But this, too, you might say, is a creative act, even if it is at the same time authoritarian and tyrannical.

[Page 126]

You have called Rosa Fuchsbein devious—and she is devious. How could she be anything but devious as a pioneer of the blending of life and theater?

[Page 127]

How could I know, you once asked me, if that room in the Charité's Nervenklinik was real or staged, if Rosa Fuchsbein had not herself painstakingly written those hundreds of thousands of tiny luminescent characters under whose wan, shimmering light we first made love?

[Page 128]

I discover it in Room 277 of the Hotel des Bains: *Black Fire, White Fire*, by Walt Myerson. It's an unfinished novel about a man named Nathan Friedl. Friedl came to Berlin from the east. His father had a silk shop in a village near Kyiv, traded with the Armenians, who brought the silk from Persia. Nathan's father dyed it himself, cut it, and sold it as far away as Moscow (until the revolution), Vienna, and Warsaw. The elder Friedl wasn't rich, but he did quite well. Nathan was away in Kyiv when the pogroms began after the First World War. During the violence his father's shop was plundered, and his father and sister were killed. Nathan's mother was caught by the mob walking through the town square. The mob locked her inside the synagogue with fifty others and burned it to the ground.

When news of the pogrom reached him in Kyiv, Nathan immediately left for home. He found his family's house, surprisingly, untouched—its thick wooden door secure between the stones. He slid the key into the lock, turned it, and the door swung open. Everything was just as it had always been—a pause in life midstream—and yet life and spirit had been drained away. He found his father's best leather suitcase, the one he'd take to the markets on the Black Sea to place his orders and to settle his debts with the Armenians. As he opened the suitcase, he closed his eyes and imagined his father drawing out those pieces of silk—examples of the wares—silks already dyed in workshops to the south and east—deep blue, regal purple, rose red, saffron yellow. At one point, when he was seventeen, his father had trained him to be a bookkeeper in the shop, and Nathan was a talented and natural bookkeeper. Six months later, though, he left the shop for Kyiv to be an artist, a poet. Now, he loaded things into the suitcase: two of his father's suits, shirts, socks, a photograph of his parents with his younger sister. In his father's study, he found the safe box, unlocked it with the key he knew to be under the false bottom of his bottom-left desk drawer, and removed the bars of gold. It was safest, the elder Friedl would say to his son, to pay the Armenians in gold.

Nathan knew he couldn't linger, couldn't delay. On his long walk from Kyiv, he'd heard that bands of peasants were moving like unpredictable swarms. They could arrive suddenly—even in places they'd already been. They were cutting down Jews, torching villages, plundering towns, burning synagogues, looting homes and shops, raping women and girls—killing, killing so that the blood of the Jews was turning the waters of the Dneiper red.

[Page 128 Reverse]

Nathan found a room on Auguststrasse in Berlin, the same address from which his friend Bergelson had written to him months before. But Bergelson was long gone—had disappeared into the depths of the city. It had been Bergelson's letter that inspired Nathan to come, those vague but lurid descriptions of the city veiled by dusk, a kind of desperate vividness that seemed to beckon toward a type of freedom unknown for a Jew in the east. Bergelson had left Kyiv while the Germans occupied the city, before the Red Army moved in, before the mobs came to power, before the massacres in the city and throughout the countryside. By the time Nathan made it to Berlin, food and jobs were scarce, money was worthless, the war was lost, bodies flowed back from the front in lifeless waves, an army of zombies, people shocked and maimed. Bands of ex-soldiers roamed the streets, looking for a fight, looking for new enemies—communists, socialists, anarchists, and Jews.

[Page 129]

A month or two later, or maybe it was six months, or a year— Walt's timing hadn't yet become clear. Let's just say it was at some point later that Avram Daud arrived in Berlin and occupied the room next to Nathan's in the building on Auguststrasse. Daud was a bookseller, a purveyor of rare—even singular— books and manuscripts, which he'd gather by traveling throughout Europe, the Balkans, the areas around the Black and Caspian Seas, the Levant, the Caucuses, Mesopotamia, and Persia. The most lucrative trade was in bringing the eastern books to the great collectors in the west, especially in Paris and London, where the appetite was insatiable—nearly fanatical. When he arrived in Berlin, Daud was coming from the legendary book fair in Baghdad. He was on his way to show his newest acquisitions in London when he fell ill and needed to stop for an extended stay in Berlin. This trip was of special importance, as over the previous years the war had blocked the migration of books and thus had sent Daud into abject poverty, which led to a deterioration of his physical condition. This trip would set things right again, and one work above all had already attracted vigorous interest in London. It was an esoteric assemblage of a certain previously unknown school of biblical commentary, the Mondschein School. The entries, spanning as many as a thousand years, centered on Jacob's dream of the ladder.

On his fourth night in Berlin, Avram Daud's fever spiked, sending him into wild fits of delusion. Armies of demons massed around him, their swords dripping with the blood of angels. These demons were coming down a tall ladder, seemingly after a great victory, and were led by a man they called "The Exilarch"—a shepherd-warrior named Hul. In Daud's fever dream, Hul had captured Jacob and was preparing an execution. When all was ready, he lifted his sword and was about to bring it down on Jacob's neck when he was stilled by Avram Daud's scream. Nathan had never heard such a sound of terror. He came rushing into the room and found a tall, thin man with thick gray hair and a short gray beard lying on the bed with his bedclothes drenched with sweat.

[Page 130]

As Nathan tends to Avram Daud each day, he discovers among the bookseller's papers copies of a newspaper called *The Rising*. He knows it from back home. Its main agenda was to combat what its editors saw as oppressive foreign influences and powers aimed at subjugating the folk. It was a diverse set of forces, the paper argued—capitalism, Bolshevism, liberalism—but these forces centered on what the paper called the 'social plague of Jewry,' which had as its goal the eradication of the peasantry (by way of land expropriation) and the creation of a socialist-capitalist Jewish state dominated by an alliance of the labor Bund and the Rothschilds. The mastermind of this theory was the journalist and philosopher V. Shulgin. It was Shulgin who'd called out the mob during those weeks of slaughter.

Why did he have so many copies of *The Rising*? Nathan asked Daud. The bookseller told him he was taking the papers to Paris and London. They were warnings that violent words led to the shedding of blood, to catastrophe. They were warnings that catastrophe was coming.

[Page 131]

Nathan read from Shulgin's articles as Daud rested beside him: "There is no peace in a nation, a nation either newly created or centuries old, when another, foreign nation exists within its borders and seeks to undermine the will of the people. The tens of thousands of Jews in Kyiv and elsewhere are a direct threat to the nation. Bolshevism might be the greatest social virus of the age, but a virus is only a carrier of a deeper malignancy. Judaism is the malignancy within the virus of Bolshevism. Therefore, the Jews will never stand against the Red Menace. Therefore, the Rada must stand against the Jews." From another article: "If the Bolsheviks conquer us, our women and children will be like sheep to the wolves. The Jews have chosen sides in this war. It is time for our battalions to have their way." Another: "The Jews have their ears in the Rada and their hands on the throat of the nation." Another: "It was a Bolshevik plan to encourage massive immigration of Jews into Kyiv in order to undermine the government and to pave the way for the Bolshevik advance." Another: "The Black Hundreds stand ready to answer the nation's call." Another: "Ancient Russia—Kyiv—will liberate modern Russia from its inner imperialists, and once again tradition and order will be restored."

[Page 132]

Now, Nathan believed, V. Shulgin was in Berlin. He was in exile from the Bolsheviks. Nathan was shocked to discover this when at the train station on Potsdamer Platz he'd picked up a copy of *The German Worker* and read the following lines—lines that absolutely must have come from Shulgin's pen: "The German nation is at a turning point. Bolshevism is threatening to spread from the east—from Russia—to Germany. Bolshevism is more than a political idea. It is a disease that infects a nation's citizens one by one until it has spread throughout the country. Jews are the principal carriers of the Bolshevik virus. Unless the Germans act, the Jewish-Bolshevik virus will consume Germany, as it did Russia and beyond. In my country, when the infant nation was at its most vulnerable, the Jewish disease fell upon it and smothered it. The situation in Germany is even more severe. Here, the Jews are hidden among the people. They own industry and control vast commercial empires. They have newspapers; they sit in the halls of government. Together, these magnates form the tip of the spear—ready to lead the hundreds of thousands of Jewish Bolsheviks across the nation when the call to revolt comes from

Lenin and Trotsky. Like all diseases, the Jewish-Bolshevik virus, the Red Plague, requires quarantine and vigilant eradication."

[Page 133]

Revenge. Walt's novel was a story about revenge, but a strange type of revenge against an enemy who consisted only of words on paper.

[Page 134]

Nathan became consumed by the hunt for Shulgin, as if killing Shulgin would balance the scales of justice, would settle the score for the deaths of his father, mother, and sister. A report by the Red Cross had been published in the Jewish press. It cataloged the disaster: dozens drowned in Chernobyl, in Gornostaipol; in Ziadkovsky, fifteen thrown in a well; north of Kyiv, one hundred Jews thrown overboard from a riverboat; thousands slaughtered in Uman—families massacred in broad daylight, wives raped in front of husbands, children watching parents die; two hundred killed in Pechanka; one hundred in Belaya Tserkov; two thousand burned to death in Tetviev on a single night, four thousand altogether. On and on the report went— pages of death, words of death. One hundred and fifty thousand, Nathan read, one hundred and fifty thousand Jews died in the pogroms following the war. These words were now driving Nathan to hate; it was hate to combat hate, violence to confront violence.

[Page 135]

Nathan sat down on his bed and put his head in his hands. He tried to clear his mind. Easier would be to let go of the whole Shulgin affair, as Avram Daud had implored him to do. Better would be to turn to other things in that atmosphere of freedom, or at least in an atmosphere he'd imagined, albeit briefly, was free. Now, in Berlin, he took up his pen to try to write poetry as he had in Kyiv. He held the pen over the empty page. No words. Shulgin had seized control of words—Russian words, German words, Yiddish words—bending the words of poetry into words of propaganda, ink into blood, the words of life into death. He sat there, staring out into the courtyard. Thoughts of violence surged through him. This iron-rich substance was making its way from the outer reaches of his being deep into his heart; violence was hardening this softest of human hearts.

[Page 136]

The dawn broke into Nathan's room. He went out into the cool, misty morning air. He walked toward Rosenthaler Platz. A pawnbroker's shop was just opening for the day. Nathan went inside. The woman behind the desk was old and wrinkled. Nathan scanned the display case, pointed to a dagger with a reddish wooden handle and a double-edged blade. The woman removed it from the case and placed it on a piece of green oilcloth in front of Nathan. He picked up the dagger. The grip was comfortable, both smooth and textured. He was about to put the tip to his finger when the old woman stopped him. Her husband, she said, had sharpened the blade thoroughly before putting it into the case. There wasn't, she said, a sharper, sturdier blade in all Berlin. He paid her and left the shop.

As he entered the building on Auguststrasse, he passed by two drunks, both struggling to make it upstairs to their rooms. He entered his room and locked the door. He sat down on his bed and rolled up his sleeve. Nervous, trembling, he moved the blade to his arm. Before he confronted Shulgin, he needed to know how the blade cut through human flesh, how easily it pierced the skin—how much pressure was needed. Nathan closed his eyes and thought about his lover, Miriam, who he'd left behind in Kyiv, never telling her about his parents or about leaving for Berlin. There she was, or the image of her, or the ghost of her (had the mob of demons found her, too?). She hovered there in the thin morning light. Nathan reached out and pushed the nightgown from her shoulders. He moved toward her naked body, feeling her breasts on his chest, her heart, her breath, her fingers on his arm. As her lips fell onto his neck, the dagger's blade fell into the skin of his forearm. Blood rushed to the surface, blood as thick as these memories, as the musty air in his room. Miriam vanished. Nathan took an old handkerchief and wrapped it tightly around the wound. He went to the window and watched as the light slowly banished the shadow from the opposite wall.

[Page 137]

V. Shulgin wrote: "Nothing can be done to stem the tide of cultural and civilizational decay. There is only one possible way: we must undertake one last and greatest stand in the defense of our Christian way of life. There must be one final effort to reverse the Bolshevik advance. It is too bad this weak and decayed society has no will, no strength to do it! Our enemies grow more powerful. Grayness eclipses the whole of Christendom. Will Christendom succumb to primitivism, to the great Jewish regression? Have all of Europe's warriors fled abroad?"

[Page 138]

V. Shulgin wrote: "The goal of Bolshevism is Jewish control of the grain trade—and when this happens a Christian will either have to pay the master or starve on the street."

[Page 139]

Nathan bought a large Sanwald map of Berlin and hung it on the wall of his room. Standing before it with a thick pencil, he could trace the echoes of Shulgin's footsteps through the city. Route one: beginning on Pestalozzistrasse in Charlottenburg, moving down Leibzigerstrasse, across Kurfürstendamm to Düsseldorferstrasse, onto Emserstrasse to Ludwigkirchplatz. Route two: Hochmeisterplatz, down Welffälischerstrasse to Fehrbellinerplatz, through Preussen Park to Bayerischestrasse, over to Olivaerplatz, left on Xantenerstrasse, cross Brandenburgischestrasse, down Paulsborner and back to the beginning, Hochmeister. Route three: Pragerplatz, down Motzstrasse, right onto Landshuterstrasse, left on Barbarosa to Giedischstrasse. Route four: Hansaplatz, up Lessingstrasse and across the river to Allee Alt Moabit, east on Invalidenstrasse, right on Borsig, left on Tieck, right on Gartenstrasse, left on Elsässerstrasse, ending near Nathan at Rosenthalerplatz. One day a series of jagged vectors, the next a rectangle, the next a wide arcing movement. Nathan traced these geometries, imagined them, walked them in his dreams.

[Page 140]

The idea was simple: Nathan would pinpoint the intersections, the places where Shulgin crossed and re-crossed, those dark spots on the lines that raced over the Sanwald map. In these places, Nathan would lie in wait to ambush Shulgin. Here, at these intersection points, Shulgin would transform from words into body, and with that shift, Shulgin would be ready to move from life to death.

[Page 141]

One February night, out a dreamlike darkness, Shulgin appears in front of him on a gas-lit path. He is alone—and alone and isolated, Shulgin seems small, helpless, almost like a child. Nathan moves from the shadows onto the path, starts to close in on him. Shulgin senses he's being followed. He looks over his shoulder as his breathing gets heavier, as he picks up his pace. Nathan is a few steps behind Shulgin now, who feels the danger, attempts to make a quick move up the sloping embankment, loses his footing, and falls to his knees. It is a Sabbath night. Nathan glides the dagger from its leather sheath. His arm thrusts down toward Shulgin's abdomen, and at that very moment Nathan is seized by a total amnesia. It could be that in this moment, Walt writes, he forgets all of Shulgin's words, all of Shulgin's crimes, forgets who Shulgin is—even the very name, Shulgin. Yes, if Nathan forgets even that name, Shulgin, then all that remains on the gas-lit path is blood and the echoes of a ghastly scream. Again and again, the knife rises and falls, until memory comes flooding back, and Shulgin has vanished, and only Nathan remains there—there, lying on the floor of his room on Auguststrasse in a pool of his own blood.

[Page 142]

They took him to the hospital, but he'd already lost consciousness. A doctor was able to stanch the flow of blood and sew up the wound before it was too late. After they attended to him, the nurses brought him into a room with another patient, a man named Theo Gutman.

As Nathan slept, a tall, thin man with gray hair and a gray beard arrived in the hospital room. He placed a leather-bound book on the small table at the head of Friedl's bed. After the man left, Gutman moved over to look at Friedl, to see this young, beautiful man. He was pale, thin—nearly insubstantial, more ghost than human. Gutman picked up the book the old man had left and saw that it was full of hand-copied pages with perfect characters—characters that seemed to radiate a strange blue-green light. It was called *The Book of Moonlight*. When Nathan Friedl awoke the next day, Gutman asked him his name. Nathan leaned over, opened the book, and read the first name that appeared there: Isaac Mondschein. He dipped his finger into the book's blue-green light and caught its glow. Once he was strong enough, he placed a chair on the top of the room's table and climbed up to reach the ceiling. Standing there, balancing, he moved his finger across the ceiling's surface and saw the first words of *The Book of Moonlight* appear above him: *And he dreamed, and behold a ladder was set on the ground and its top reached the sky.*

[Page 143]

I rushed from the room and slammed the door behind me, closing the door to the world of Room 277 of the Hotel des Bains. Alone again in the hallway, I heard Anton Grassfeld's footsteps in the distance. I fled in the opposite direction.

[Page 144]

The stealing of this manuscript as ludic act. Rebellion as comedy. I ran from the clinic—raced away in fits of laughter, gorgeous laughter. Ha! Ha!

[Page 145]

I made it to Vienna on the first night. I knew I had to keep moving, because Kirschbaum would discover what I'd done, and he'd be after me, his path would lead, as mine was leading, to the Hotel des Bains.

[Page 146]

This is what Kirschbaum feared the most: in Vienna I'd come across the precise moment when, in Jan Horak's *Blue, Red, Gray*, Josef Solomon changed his name to Josef Kostel—in other words, I would exit one world and enter another, I would slip through Kostel's fractured, diffuse memory, and once this transition was accomplished, I'd be able to roll up the story like rolling up a carpet on the floor, making room for the laying out of another—or simply for the sake of the exposure, the bareness underneath.

[Page 147]

"Name?"

"Milena," I tell the clerk at the Hotel Riva in Vienna. The hotel is shabby, the room surface-clean: bedspread smells of mildew, carpet of some faint pesticide. Furnishings are ugly Biedermeier pieces. Everything an oppressive crimson with gold embroidery, gesturing toward opulence, evoking cheapness. I sit at the desk and switch on the lamp, but the light is weak, barely enough to read by. No matter, I tell myself, none of it matters. I need to block it all out, focus on the manuscript, which I have brought here as a sacrificial offering, as part of this ritual performance. I set it down and run my finger over the title page, somehow afraid to turn it over and begin. I push it away and instead move a sheet of hotel stationary in front of me. Hotel Riva, Vienna, Austria. Wien. Österreich. The hotel pen is heavy and surprisingly good quality. I start to write.

[Page 148]

Dear Daniel,

The first thing you should know is that I have no name. I am not Mila or Milena. At most, I could be M., as your Kaesbohrer becomes K., a "variable," as you say, "in his own equation." And it could be that we should add another initial to this M. to make it more concrete, or more "relational." Let's take a J. And we'll have M.J., then, a bodiless symbol—and how much time did you spend trying to do the opposite—trying to build a body, a human body—a female body—around those names? We have Mila—a poor girl barely alive, bruised, beaten, addled, possibly raped, pale skin, shaven pubis, rail-thin arms and legs. And Milena—smoking a cigarette outside the Bar Internationale, cutting fabrics for the songbirds' robes, her fingers running down Fo's waist. There she is in the Volksbühne's Roter Salon, sipping a vodka and tonic, talking about (or listening to him talk about?) theories of radical performativity? Because she is radical. Or he is? Or they both are—together. She is "intoxicating," as you say, and "sexy," and "smart," yes, she is an "insatiable fire." There is the walk in the forest—first Milena is above you, then you are above her. Fear? There is only fear—even as you wrote those words: "touch" and "lips" and "breasts" and "skin" and "fire." These words form into sentences, into paragraphs and pages, fill the white pages with black ink, and yet you're still afraid—afraid of the smoke, the burning, the flames, the freedom—afraid of the laugh. This is why Milena can't exist and becomes the bodiless M.J.—confined by not one but two periods: one period divides her; the other prevents her becoming. Still, Milena persists, the same Milena, who, on the night of Ingrid Müller's party, dragged you from the courtyard when you were nearly dead. She was there, in your apartment, as you set out to destroy yourself, half trying to finish this book, half trying to escape it. Milena, defined by her tremor, a tremor, as you write, which worsened year after year such that in the end she had to leave Berlin for the clinic at Zelená Hora after what you describe as a "nervous breakdown." She could barely pick up a pair of scissors and couldn't for the life of her draw a straight line or hold a measuring tape flush against a human body. You remember the Hotel Riva? How could you forget it? Those days in late June, early July when even the bedbugs were stilled by the heat, when you lay there, naked, happy, talking about your love of swimming.

M.J.

[Page 148]

Tomorrow to Merano, where we both know what decision was made—two vectors presented themselves, one of love, one of fear—it was an awful dream of merging selves.

Again, I must break off; we're at the end of the session—or well over time. I apologize for keeping you past the designated hour; there was no other way. For God's sake, I'm stuck in these marginalia and can barely carry out basic tasks like grooming, laundry, eating properly and at appointed times, sleeping—to say nothing of finding the elusive "balance" everyone keeps talking about. Everything, rather, is unbalanced, off-kilter. Over the weekend, for example, I took a long, slow walk with my father. Ever since his decline in health—or perhaps more accurately, his decline in wellness—he hasn't said much, and I couldn't tell whether this was a way of keeping his thoughts to himself or whether these thoughts had become jumbled to the point that he couldn't find a way of expressing them. Surely, he had thoughts, even if of the most mundane nature. Over the past months, in any case, I'd tried to shield him from anything he might find unpleasant—including, or especially, my deteriorating status at the college and my increasingly tense relationship with the dean and the dean's assistant. After my bold escape from the lecture hall following last week's lecture, however, I received the following note from the dean, written on his behalf, of course, by his assistant. I know our time has run out—but please stay for a few minutes longer. Here's the letter:

Dear Sy Kirschbaum,

Some irregularities have come to our attention concerning your course (EN 102: Introduction to Literature—Section 3) and related matters. In the interest of clarity, we will enumerate the most relevant issues:

1) *The course syllabus has been taken from the department's syllabus archive, specifically from Professor Rosinky's 1997 version, without alteration of anything but the name of the instructor—and this alteration consisted only of you crossing out "Rosinky" and penning in "Kirschbaum" next to it.*

2) *You have not made available, either on the college's reserve system or through the bookstore, any of the readings on the Rosinky syllabus.*

3) *Despite teaching a literature class, you have not discussed a single piece of literature that has been assigned on the syllabus for the students to read.*

4) *Our investigations have conclusively found that your students have not read a single page of any text for your course.*

5) *Students claim they have not participated in any way in any session of your course. We remind you that we cap the course at 20 students to ensure participation. The school's policy of encouraging "active learning" was described to you during your initial meeting with the dean and in the teaching packet you received with your course registration list.*

6) *Students in your course admit to regularly using your course to a) sleep, b) engage in social media, c) "zone out," d) doodle.*

7) *You have not collected a single essay or other assignment. Students admit to having done no written work in your course.*

8) *Most students in your course describe your lectures as "pointless."*

9) *25% of your students describe your lectures as "disturbed" or "disturbing."*

10) *We know you are using class time to disparage the dean.*

11) *You have failed to make yourself available for office hours for students to discuss their concerns directly with you. Our email of September 10, insisting that you hold regular weekly office hours, has not been answered.*

12) *By our count, you have received 76 emails from students in your class. You have not responded to one, and the Technology Office (TO) has informed us that you have not opened or read any of them. According to the TO, you have not logged into your college email account ever.*

13) *You are said to lose your composure in class—at times laughing hysterically, at others crying or pounding your fist on the lectern. Students have referred to these moments as "unsettling" displays of emotion.*

14) *You failed to post midterm grades and have not responded to 10 separate requests that you do so immediately. Furthermore, you have no apparent plan to calculate and report final semester grades.*

15) *Finally (for now), you have failed to show up to a single mandatory faculty or committee meeting, in violation of the terms of your contract.*

There's no point addressing the dean's ridiculous letter. I have to believe those so-called "investigations" are nothing but an attempt to coerce me. Proof of this—not that I need any— is that I am standing here in front of you, standing in front of all of you, for not even one of you has missed a single lecture.

My college ID still triggers the outer door. My paychecks continue to arrive. I continue successfully to cash them. Despite this counterevidence, during my walk with my father I divulged to him that the dean was building a case against me, that his enforcer (the dean's assistant) had struck the initial blow. I guess I'd expected some sympathy or commiseration about my ill treatment at the hands of executive power, but what I got from my father was something else. "It's a shame," he said to me, "that you couldn't have turned this into something. You could have built on this, a building block for the future—an accomplishment. I'd hoped that at some point you would have discovered some entrepreneurial spirit, a will or desire to succeed."

LECTURE TEN

Milena's Marginalia (Part 4)

'VE BEEN UNABLE to break away from Milena's words for the entire week since I last saw you—reading the marginalia over and over, searching—no, chasing—no, interrogating—no, scrutinizing—every word—beyond words, every mark that falls in that one-inch border zone between the text and the edge of the world, that snow-covered landscape, that frame of perfect emptiness.

[Page 150]

"It occurs to me," you wrote, "that I can't remember your face in any precise detail. Only how you finally walked away between the tables of the coffeehouse, your figure, your dress, these I can still see." It was from this room in Meran, from this room in the Pension Ottoburg, that you wrote these words. I sit at the same spot, occupying your place at the desk.

[Page 151]

"The whole Milena"—how could you forget that you claimed, after that night, to have grasped the whole of me? I can think of only this as I read about the death of "her" mother, the funeral, a truly sorry affair as you describe it, with the icy gazes from the two sisters, the priest's empty words, the cold space, the abominably cold day (this was true), the ground as hard as rock—and you hear her talk to Pawel in her native Polish—and despite the scene, you feel the language's sensuousness, and you are set on fire by it, a fire that quickly burns itself out in the drab, ugly hotel room that evening. I can think of only this interplay of ice and fire while I sit at this desk in Meran. Where else could I allow these memories to obliterate me?

[Page 152]

Not long after we arrived at the clinic, you told me to lie down in the garden and to try to "extract" from the disease as much "sweetness" as possible. But you were the one extracting—sapping me of memory, of strength, of sanity—draining me to prop yourself up against the trunk of the Siberian cedar, with your notebook in your lap and your pencil in your hand, while I lay in the grass a mere body's length away. And while we were out there in the garden, we were both being watched. Up in the window on the second floor was Kirschbaum, looking down on us, waiting anxiously for our embrace. There he was—didn't you see him? Did you see him with a pencil in *his* hand—writing this scene, writing us?

[Page 153]

You write, "Hardly a moment of time remains for writing to the real Milena since the even more real one was here all day long, in this room, on this balcony, in the clouds." This statement alone, beyond everything else I have added in these margins, is sufficient proof.

[Page 154]

"Not for its own sake but as a signpost on the road toward her person, on a road along which he continued to walk with increasing happiness until realizing in a bright moment that he was making no progress but simply running around in his own labyrinth, only more excited, more confused than before." Tijl read this to me.

[Page 155]

"Words," Tijl read to me, "cut their way through the body."

I can think about only these words and your presence while at the desk in this room in the Pension Ottoburg, alone with this stack of pages, as lifeless as a corpse, in front of me.

[Page 156]

Tijl read: "I have the sensation of leading you by the hand behind me along the subterranean, dark, low, ugly corridors of the story, almost endlessly in order to have, I hope, the good sense to disappear on reaching the bright light at the exit."

[Page 157]

Regarding the Sanwald map—I quote you something Walt wrote in his notebook during those melodramatic years: "I bought a new map of Berlin, a Falk Plan, hung it on my wall, stared up at it for a long time, and for an instant it seemed incomprehensible to me that they built such a big city when you need only one room."

[Page 158]

A few days ago, at the Hotel Riva in Vienna, when the appointed hour came (Wednesday 10:00 A.M.), I looked out the window and saw a tall, skinny man passing in front of the hotel's entrance. He was anxious, agitated. It was Kirschbaum. He caught up with me. I thought naively that it would have taken him longer, but he knows how to locate these tracks, how to find those traces, those wan lines penned on old maps—those "corridors" of stories told long ago, long since forgotten and gathering dust on shelves, in boxes. What a boxed-up life! Boxed up and packed away, boxes of stories buried in closets and attics and basements, coffins of countless characters. One must be a necromancer to find the breath of these deceased words.

[Page 159]

Finally, we come to the night. Night—that's the word, the word that resonates again and again in her poetry, as if all poetry swirls around this darkness, exists only there: *Night suddenly flooded the window / with darkness, brimming vacant voices. / Night, infecting with venomous breaths. / Night.*

It's after Tania died. I'm in charge of the theater. I have Rosa with me, though you leave her out. It's her you want—her, Fo, and you can't have Fo, of course, if Rosa is around. You call her by a different name. I refuse that name completely. With every part of me, with every particle of myself, I reject it. You say in this "story," for dramatic effect, that it's the night of the premiere of the fifth piece of her planned seven-part cycle, a piece called *The Rebellious God*. But it isn't opening night, it's the night of the third performance, a Saturday night following the Thursday premiere and the Friday show. This is important, because even in this world of spectacle and saturation, of the commercialization of everything, the piece causes a major stir.

The Rebellious God has the following basic story, though maybe the story itself isn't the key thing. The God in the piece is named Allah, and he's become fixated on what is going on in the underworld. Allah decides he'd rather rule there and proposes to the king of the dead that the two of them exchange realms. Satan rejects this proposal, as the realm of the underworld, the realm of "The Fire," is ten times—a hundred times—the size of heaven or "The Garden." Allah and Satan communicate through messengers; they never meet directly. Still, Allah knows that Satan often takes the form of a man, leaves The Fire, and goes to earth. There is one tavern Satan frequents. It is an underground tavern called the Auerbach Cellar. There, Satan sits at a large table in the far corner and drinks beer and laughs and makes deals for people's souls.

The quest is to kill Satan while he's vulnerable in his human form, his mortal human body. To get to him, one also must be in human form, and thus vulnerable and mortal. The angels, even the strongest of the legionaries, are not nearly powerful enough to subdue Satan and kill him. Only Allah can do it. Allah knows that behind Satan's table in the Auerbach Cellar is a hidden door that leads to a passage that goes straight down into The Fire. Allah will need to lure Satan away from the table to another room where he can't escape, to distract or weaken him, and then to kill him without hesitation. Any hesitation would be fatal, because Satan is likely to be stronger in his earthly form than Allah. What's more, Allah suspects that other demons lurk in the Auerbach Cellar as a force of personal guards. Finally, Allah knows that if Satan kills him, Satan will invade The Garden, bringing total darkness to heaven and earth.

Allah takes the form of a woman. For each of Fo's performances, she'd worn a costume of a single color, and for *The Rebellious God* she has something as close as possible to the color of pale moonlight, white silver with the faintest shade of blue. For this piece, it is not a robe or a tight suit, but a simple party dress, thin straps over the shoulders, clean classic cut that ends in the middle of the thigh. The dress makes her brown skin and black hair look luscious—and the effect is just as seductive as one would imagine.

She enters the Auerbach Cellar as the piece begins, comes down the stairs into the dimly lit space. Satan sits at his table. Others in the tavern move around silently, slowly exiting the space to the right and left as she descends. He drinks his beer, watches as she approaches him. He gestures for her to sit. She sits. They talk. At some point, he touches her arm. She touches his arm. The tension rises. It's the tension of the anticipated violence, sure, but there's another key element. As Allah seduces or lights the fires of Satan's passion, her passion also becomes enflamed, and she no longer just wants to lure him away to kill him, she wants to lure him away to make love to him, to have him enter her body:

> *Tired of being a prude, I'd seek Satan's bed at midnight and find refuge in the declivity of breaking laws. I'd happily exchange the golden crown of divinity for the dark, aching embrace of sin.*

[Page 159 Reverse]

Allah and Satan are somersaulting toward the act. Allah plans to kill him, but will she first have him? And if she has him, if he enters her, isn't this risking death? And if she suspects, as the audience does, that Satan is on to her ruse, that he knows this woman is Allah, despite the danger—or maybe because of it—does this make her want him even more? Mutual seduction, self-seduction, spiraling to the moment when Allah invites him to leave the table, to follow her to the bathroom. He hesitates, and in this moment, she knows he's on to her. He agrees to come. The set shifts. A wall descends from the ceiling, the floor opens, and a bathroom stall rises out of it with an adjacent sink. She, Allah, moves into the space, opens the stall door, closes the toilet lid, flushes the toilet—seemingly a call for him. Satan chugs the remains of his beer and walks into the bathroom.

The space in the stall is cramped. Satan is big, muscular, and you know very well the nuances of Fo's body, as do I. They embrace, a wolfish embrace full of a diffuse violence, a surge of energy that's been contained for too long. He rips the moonlight dress from her body as if it's made of paper. He does the same with her bra, underwear. In an instant, she's naked. She's moving, too, to strip off his shirt, to undo his pants. As his pants fall to the ground, she hears a clang; of course, she doesn't know he's brought a knife with him to slit her throat. Behind the toilet there's another knife, placed there by her for his throat. As if to set the stage for the throat cutting, his hand finds her throat and her hand finds his throat as their naked bodies press together, move awkwardly in the narrow space of the bathroom stall. He lifts her, presses her against the wall, enters her (or so we suspect) as she wraps her legs around his waist, thrusting her pelvis toward him, taking him in. This is a raw, even gruesome scene— a sex act, a performance of a tawdry embrace in a dirty bathroom stall, so real, so authentically acted that I, the director of Der Blaue Punkt, can't tell if the intercourse is real or staged.

She makes a move to shift, unlocks her legs, and slides them to the ground. She climbs onto the toilet, faces the wall, and offers herself for him to take her from behind. This is his chance. He reaches down into the pocket of his pants and pulls out his knife. She reaches behind the toilet where her knife is fastened and slides it out of the sheath.

How could it have ended in any other way? The lights cut at the precise moment the knives are poised for slaughter. The darkness of the theater combines with silence.

As you'd expect, news of a performance featuring Allah fucking Satan in a dirty bathroom stall spread like wildfire through Berlin's sizable Muslim community. On Friday, after the Thursday night opening, the police called the theater and told me to shut the performance down. The German counter-terrorism force sent a representative over, Rotkopf, who told me the "chatter" about the play was "feverish" in the intercepts, a level that almost always means immanent threat. I told this to Fo and the others, but everyone agreed to do the Friday show—and on Friday the theater was absolutely packed, more people than at any other single performance in the decade of the theater's existence. On Saturday, Rotkopf called again: shut it down, useless risk, chatter high, full of violence, etc., but again we made the collective decision to continue. Fo was especially adamant that the same forces that had locked her up in Iran would not "devour" her in Berlin, where the spirit was one of artistic freedom and unfettered self-expression.

The Saturday performance came. It was the best show of the three—beautiful, raw, sensuous, shocking, appalling, sad, grotesque. There was no incident from Berlin's Muslims, but something else had been brewing beyond the attention of the security state. A group of neo-Nazis in the eastern suburbs had heard about a performance that was taking place in Kreuzberg in which Allah, the God of Islam, was meeting the devil in the Auerbach Cellar—in other words, that Allah was taking the place of the German Faust. In other words, for these men, there was in Kreuzberg an intolerable Islamization of the bedrock of German culture, the Faust legend, and a direct assault on the cultural foundation of German society.

Twenty members of the so-called "white wolves" gathered in a nearby pub in Neukölln. The police, after the fact, "discovered" that they had clear records of what had been going on with the wolves from various informants. The task force assigned to monitoring the wolves had also picked up increasingly violent chatter, but it was dismissed as business as usual. In any case, the wolves drank their beer in the pub. Around the time the show was coming to an end, they took up their positions on the street. Five pairs of men were scattered throughout the neighborhood to hunt down specific "cultural criminals." Foremost among them, of course, were Fo and the German man, Otto Pech, who played the role of Satan. The other ten wolves massed for an attack on the building.

You had a secret plan to meet her at a bar on Graefestrasse. She left me at the theater only minutes before it happened. She was exhausted from three straight days of performing the most devastating role she'd ever written for herself. I can close my eyes as I sit at this desk at the Hotel Ottoburg in Meran and see her slowly dressing, slowly wiping the makeup away. She said some soft words to me, I can't remember what, and then to Rosa Fuchsbein, to Otto Pech. Tijl had asked for her, but she must have told him she was meeting you because he left in a rush without saying goodbye to me. I can only imagine him, angry and desperate, as he walked away from the theater, took a turn along the canal, passed the hospital, and was met there, in the darkness, under a thicket of branches, by a pair of wolves. "The black boyfriend," they called him—the "black boyfriend of a Muslim whore." They beat him until he was unconscious— three broken ribs, broken jaw, six broken fingers, broken nose, concussion.

I was sitting with Rosa Fuchsbein as the door to the theater crashed open. We went out to see what was going on, and they grabbed us. They tied us to the chairs with ropes they'd brought with them, called us mongrels, sluts, cunts as they unleashed their tornado of destruction on the space. With crowbars, knives, pipes, and axes they slashed and smashed and chopped everything possible: furniture, floors, walls, stage sets, costumes, lights. In no more than a few minutes—at least that's how it seemed to me—the entire theater was made into a heap of shards and splinters. When done, they told us that if we ever staged another play, they'd be back for us, to do to us what they were doing to the "Muslim bitch."

Was this the end of it? The end of Berlin? The night the wolves took Fo as she passed by the fountain on the corner of Grimmstrasse and Urbanstrasse on her way to meet you at the bar? Later, she arrived by ambulance at the Charité Hospital, barely alive. The end of Berlin. The end of Berlin even if Berlin continued to exist, even if we—you and I—continued to exist there, continued to exist in a space that had vanished into the past, in a space that never was.

[Page 160]

Rosa Fuchsbein handed me a vial of cloudy yellow liquid. I drank it. There I was, sitting at my desk in the theater, finishing the costume for *Silence*. It was black—a sharp, rectangular cut, like a box. She was there, and I slipped it over her shoulders. Her cheeks were dusted with a powder mixed with charcoal. Her hair had been cut away down to a couple of centimeters. I'd requested police to guard the theater, and they'd sent a patrol of four, which somehow made me even more nervous that the wolves would be back, that the police themselves *were* the wolves. Fo went on stage. The thinnest, weakest light fell on her, pulling her just the slightest bit out of the darkness. She walked to the center of the stage and stopped, turned to face the audience, and for exactly one hour she didn't move, not a twitch, barely a blink, nothing. Total stillness, total silence, until she became nothing more than a shadow, a play of light, a specter.

[Page 161]

Tijl came to see me at Walt's place. Walt was in the kitchen, drunk, trying to write—flailing. I took Tijl into the bedroom. He was healing slowly, he said. Luckily the concussion wasn't too severe, and the fractures were clean breaks. Nothing, he said, compared to what they did to Fo. He told me he had to leave Berlin, he had to go somewhere else to try to dull the memory of that night, otherwise the night and its darkness would become all of him, eclipsing everything else. Is she going with you? I asked. For her, it's the opposite, he said. She has to stay. She has to stay until the totality of that night reveals itself to her, pushes beyond all blockages, all attempts to force it away. When she can feel the raw terror again, feel it coursing through her blood, feel it destroying her, she can be whole. In other words, Tijl said, he is going and she is staying, and I, as her friend, should help her through.

[Page 162]

My last note from Meran. He's caught up with me. First at the Hotel Riva and now at the Pension Ottoburg. He knows where I'm going but has decided to try to ambush me on the way rather than to lie in wait for me on the Lido. He doesn't want me to write precisely what I need to write: about the attic apartment on Forsterstrasse, about the snow, about the cold, about the small room next to the kitchen where he sat day after day, page after page, writing a prison around himself.

[Page 163]

Rosa Fuchsbein: "There will be a man from Dutch St. Maarten in a room on the third floor of the Hotel des Bains, a scholar, a literary critic. He'll be writing about an Iranian performance artist whom he met in Amsterdam and accompanied to Berlin. She had planned a seven-part series, but it ended after six parts. It began with song and ended with silence. Don't open that door, Mila, unless you're ready to hear the whole story from him, the story you've been trying to outrun for a decade, running (without taking a step in any direction) from the story of a single night. Of course, you'll open that door! It'll be the first one you come to, the first room you enter. It contains traces of the violence that has been swirling around you, not directly touching you, but present, there, possible, a shattering violence. Where on earth could this man find refuge but at the Hotel des Bains? It's a refuge from his memory, from his history, and yet at the Hotel des Bains all memory is preserved. It is a place of past, of stories and their ghosts, the pale shape of ghosts fading in and out of view."

[Page 164]

The tremor strikes Milena when she leaves the Nervenklinik after seeing her friend Fo, who's been admitted for attempting to take her life by drinking a mysterious cloudy yellow liquid. The tremor strikes as she tries to reach into her pocket for some coins to buy a subway ticket. The shaking starts to intensify. Then it spirals, and for the first time in her life the shaking turns into an unraveling of her whole existence. She needs to get it out of her body, and to get it out of her body, you write, she needs to get out of Berlin. That's the only way she can survive. To be away from it—away from being written, away from the performance, from performers, from narrators and narrations and counternarrations, away from her life, this life, a life of lines on a Falk Plan, lines connecting Der Blaue Punkt with Walt's apartment, Walt's apartment to Chamiso Platz, Chamiso Platz to a yard of a building on the Spree, a yard to the secret room in the Nervenklinik, the Nervenklinik, through an underground tunnel, to Grunewaldstrasse. She needs to get out of it, out of it all, out, out, out!

[Page 165]

I sat beside her as she slept. Her skin had faded into the palest shade of brown. Her black hair was speckled with white, bleached, I suspect, by terror. After a long time, she opened her eyes and gazed at me. "I'm still here," she said, "inside the nightmare."

"I'm sorry," I said to her. Then I added, "I wish I could take you somewhere else."

"Take me there," she said, "right now. I'll close my eyes and you can take me anywhere you'd like to go."

I thought about it. Where would I go if I could go anywhere and take her with me? Not to Poland, not after my mother died, and nowhere in Germany, and not to the Netherlands or to New York. What had happened to the world, a world which had seemed to open up to me as a teenager with the fall of the Iron Curtain, when Hannah came and I followed her to New York and found my way to Berlin, where the energy of this newly unified "East" and "West" pulsed through me day and night? She must have sensed, as I sat there in silence, that I couldn't find an exit, that there was no pathway out for me and therefore none for her, that we were trapped in this room in the Nervenklinik, trapped in this unrelenting reality. Then, as she seemed to grow despondent, an idea came to me.

"I know a place. Let's get you up, come on, I'll help you. Don't worry, it's not far from here. It's in the same building."

She was weak and unsure on her feet, but I put my arm around her waist and draped her arm over my neck. Slowly, we made our way down the hall to the stairs and descended into the basement. The movement up the shaft and into the room was difficult. She went first, I came behind her and helped her climb up the makeshift ladder. We were in the room. She was cold. I could feel her shivering as she leaned against me for support. I took off my sweater and wrapped it around her. Then I helped her to the ground, lay beside her, and told her to keep her eyes fixed on the ceiling. The darkness soaked in, our eyes widened and widened until she said, "I see it, I see the words. Read them to me." I took a breath and began, "Jacob laid his head down on the rock to sleep and a ladder appeared above him."

[Page 166]

It's really very difficult for human beings to play 'tag' with ghosts.

"There is an unresolved scene," Rosa Fuchsbein told me, "in room 401 of the Hotel des Bains. It is your scene, not mine."

[Page 167]

Night at the Hotel Sandwirth in Venice. The wind rips through the city. I arrive in my room with a deep chill, feel the shiver of coldness merging with the shaking, the tremor. "This tremor of yours is a tangled knot that can't be undone," said Hruška. "It's a knot that must be cut." A very useful observation, coming from the man holding the knife.

[Page 168]

I take the taxi boat to the Lido, find my way to the Hotel des Bains. It's just as you write: *Milena's footsteps echo through the corridors.*

[Page 169]

December—early darkness—not summer as you claim! How could it have been summer in Venice, on the Lido, with this manuscript in my hands? The electricity in the hotel is out, the heating system has long since failed, mice and rats scurry about in the darkness, feral cats prowl the perimeter or hunt in the hallways. One fears that, in some dim corner, a homeless man will light a fire using the thousands of old newspapers packed away in the storage closets on the ground floor and the whole place will burn to the ground. I climb the stairs to the fourth floor and find room 401. I knock. No answer. I slowly turn the knob, the door unlatches, I push it open. A faint glow from the city's lights in the distance filters into the room, shifting the space ever so slightly away from total darkness. I step inside the room, feel surrounded by a strange energy, or maybe by the pulsation of my internal energy into this confined space. "An unresolved scene"—but a scene of what? What is happening here? I move toward the window, struggle to open it, and when I do I hear the faint sounds of a gypsy band playing in the distance. And the sound of a rotary telephone ringing, and the clacking of typewriter keys striking letters into the page. Mila, Milena—which name issues out of this darkness? Who should be the lover waiting in this bug-infested bed, infested like the bed in the Hotel Riva on those sultry nights in June and July. Opposites—contrasts—pushing, as you say, toward a resolution *in situ*—in sickness, death, triumph, heroism, tragedy, failure, collapse, irony, farce. What resolution? What scene? I am alone. There is no light to read this by. No light to write this, but I still scrawl these words into the grayness. Memory swarms, a loose concatenation of haptic memories: fingers, breasts, penises, skin, nipples, hair, mouths, ears, and vaginas. The tremor as memory, moving through solid matter like Hruška's *Entwarnung*, like the scream that resounds forever below the ground at Prinz-Albert Strasse 8.

I close the window. The sounds of the night are gone, replaced by a muffled cacophony of internal noises, sounds that indicate disintegration, the collapse of the hotel into the earth, this Tower of Babel struck down. The bed is made. I pull the dusty bedspread back and climb under the feather blanket, allow my head to fall into the down pillow. I close my eyes and it occurs to me (unless I'm dreaming) that I've been tricked into coming here. The manuscript was a decoy, meant only to precipitate my flight south through Vienna and Meran and Venice to the Lido. A trap. Set by whom? Rosa Fuchsbein? Dr. Hruška? Kirschbaum? I hear the door lock, then I hear voices in the hallway, a harsh hospital light coming through the crack beneath the door. I rush to the door, try to open it, pound my fists against it, scream for someone to unlock me, scream that I'm trapped, I never wanted this, never agreed to be here, that this was your idea, your plot to dominate me. Let me the fuck out! A steady voice responds, "Please calm down, Mila, everything is alright. You've had a nightmare. Nothing is happening. Go back to sleep."

A place on the edge of nightmare—the Hotel des Bains.

[Page 170]

Nightmares of confinement . . . days roaming the hallways . . . chasing distant footsteps.

[Page 171]

Old newspapers litter the tables in the dining room. I pick one up. It's called *Venkov*. On the third page there's a piece condemning a woman named Milena for being a traitor to the nation, claiming she's scheming with Bolsheviks and Jews. She should leave the country, the unnamed author opines, she is no longer welcome in the homeland.

[Page 172]

You write that you saw the two wolves who took her. You walked by them on your way to the bar. They were smoking cigarettes on the sidewalk. It was an explosion, you say, of dormant hatreds. Why now—so long after we thought wolves had gone nearly extinct in Europe? They have returned to roam the streets in dense packs, to rip and tear at flesh, to feed. The world is full of wolves again.

[Page 173]

How odd (do you remember?) that when he gave me the section of Grassfeld's novel in English the pages contained no words. Empty pages. Pages ripped from a notebook and folded in half to conceal their emptiness. Was it madness? Does he believe in this "translation"? Or maybe there's some philosophical meaning in this blankness or emptiness, a crushing and existential statement about the vacuity of stories, the emptiness of language, the uselessness of striving for truth.

[Page 174]

I'm walking along the canal one night after leaving the theater. It's late June, a warm and pleasant night. Tania is still alive, and we'd done one of our favorite works, a lyrical cycle by Pepi Kafková, a spare but monumental work about the burning of a communist-era apartment block on the outskirts of Prague, *Night of Fire*. I'm passing by the small park across the canal from the hospital when I notice a figure emerge from the thicket and start to walk in front of me. After a few steps, his foot catches on a root or a rock or an uneven patch and he falls. I move over to him and offer to help, but he waves me away, gets up, takes a few more steps, and falls again. When I come up to him a second time, I can see that the falls have torn away his pants at the knees and the skin underneath is scraped and bloody. There are other wounds on his arms and a thick, bloody stain on his chest. He is thin, smells bad. I speak to him in German; he responds in English: "No, nothing, no." He can't get up, can barely move. With all the strength I have, I somehow help him to the street. I hail a taxi and ask the driver to take us to the nearest hospital, but when he sees the blood, he refuses, calls an ambulance instead. We're cutting through the streets with the sirens whirling, with the medics working. "He's lost a lot of blood," one says.

The next day, I'm back at the hospital to see him. He's sitting up in his bed when I enter the room. Color has returned to his face. He's been washed and is wearing a clean hospital gown. "Did you get me here?" he asks. "They told me a young woman brought me in."

"Yes."

Two days later he's released from the hospital. He says, without deeper explanation, that he can't return to his place, so I take him to my small apartment in Kreuzberg. Could it be that I have fallen in love with him after three hospital visits? Did I start to love him when he started to call me "Mila" on the second day? I ask his name. First, he tells me it is Sy Kirschbaum, then he changes it to Daniel Cohen, then to Walter Meyerson, adds that I can call him Walt. This is absurd, of course, but I

don't want to agitate him. Let him be called whatever he wants
to be called.

[Page 175]

About a year ago, Walt told me, he'd been sorting through the
archive of New York's Workmen's Circle and had come across
the journals of a man named Sidney Keter, an American writer
who'd lived in Europe in the 1930s and translated into English a book called *The Book of Moonlight*. Keter had been all
over Europe, Walt said, but spent many years in Prague, where
he'd done his translation while working in the studio of the
painter Josef Kostel. There have always been at least two dis-
tinct possibilities for how Keter got his hands on *The Book of
Moonlight*, Walt said. One way was from Josef Kostel (via Horak, via Kirschbaum) and the second was from the nexus of
Avram Daud-Nathan Friedl-Isaac Mondschein-Theo Gutman,
in other words, from a secret room in the Charité Hospital's Nervenklinik. The journals, Walt said, support at times one path,
at times the other, which lead him to believe that neither was
true, that Keter had written the text himself, that there was no
"original," that someone, possibly Kirschbaum, had planted the
library card (despite its existence only on microfiche) in Berlin's
Staatsbibiothek, which read "Kriegsverlust möglich." Further,
it could be—Walt said—that even the English version, Keter's
version, never existed and that the other library card, the one
from the New York Public Library indicating that the Workmen's Circle edition was checked out on May 10, 1946, and
never returned, was a plant—a forgery, a fabrication of someone named Osterhase, an agent (perhaps an enemy?) of Keter.
But if this were true, said Walt, the whole lineage would start to
fray and unravel. This unraveling, this coming loose of the binding, according to Walt, also tore his "binding" loose, scattering

the fragments of his life. "You might think I can put the pieces back together," he told me, "but it's a brutal task."

[Page 176]

Ludic—ludicrous, delicious, and luminous, theft as play, as theater, as performance. As I careen toward the end of this stolen manuscript, I laugh. The cage, the prison—the laugh obliterating its bars and walls.

[Page 177]

As I close my eyes, I hear the door to the room lock. I call out that I'm inside, that I don't want to be locked in, that I'll soon need to get out. A steady voice tells me to "calm down" and "you're safe" and "nothing bad is going to happen to you here." I ask where I am. "At the clinic," he tells me. I say I'm not at any clinic, I'm in the Hotel des Bains. After a hesitation, he says, "You're at the clinic, Milena, where you've been for some time." "Who are you?" I ask. "You know who I am, Milena." I start to shake. Fighting my way out of it, fighting my way back to the surface of consciousness. An empty page becoming full of old traces—soaring above the Atlantic Ocean.

[Page 178]

I move through the hallways searching for Anton Grassfeld, for Anita, for Diya. Yes, it's Diya I need to find, and if I find her I can fix the center point and from this center point I can establish a radius and fix relationships between points on the curve, points on the edge of the circle of my selfhood, and through these relationships I can build a story, a life, a life that can replace one defined by randomness and chaos—lines twisted into knots, bent into spirals, broken into a million pieces. This circle, once it's inscribed, will shut you out, and that's why Kirschbaum is on his way to stop me, to block these tracings, to block this figure from finding form.

[Page 179]

When K. arrives, one of us will have to play Allah and the other Satan. A seduction unto death will commence. Or more likely, a pack of wolves will breach the doors of the Hotel des Bains and devour both of us as we press naked against each other.

[Page 180]

The nightmare returns. The door unlocks and in comes a doctor with a clipboard. I can tell it is Doctor Max de Crinis. "What is the status," he coldly asks the nurse, "of patient #401?"

[Page 181]

On one of my daily explorations, I hear a child crying in some remote part of the hotel. I search for the source of the noise for hours, until I finally discover her in the coatroom, hidden beneath a pile of old furs. She complains of being hungry and thirsty, appears not to have eaten anything substantial in days. I bring her some water, search for food in the hotel's kitchen but don't find anything edible. We leave the hotel and walk until we find a restaurant that's stayed open out of season. The girl speaks a beautiful Italian, tells me her name is Diya, that she's been looking for her mother, that her mother is in the hotel somewhere, but she (Diya) can't find her. "How long have you been looking for her?" I ask. She can't remember, but she says it feels like a very long time. She's been wandering the hallways, sleeping in empty rooms, eating the remains of food from plates in the dining room. We order a huge amount of food. Bread, pasta, seafood—she eats it all. I feel joyous as I watch her eat, joyous to be with her. After dinner, I take her up to my room

on the fourth floor and she falls asleep in my bed. She is asleep
in seconds. The bed isn't large, but the girl is small, and I am
exhausted. I climb in next to her, take this sleeping child into
my arms, and vanish into the blissful emptiness of slumber.

[Page 182]

The next day, as I woke up in the morning darkness while Diya
continued to sleep beside me, I remembered the story that was
on those pages Grassfeld had read at his reading on the night
in the Roter Salon, those pages I hadn't understood at the time
but that he, Kirschbaum, had given me in English translation
some weeks later, when we met at the bar Der Rabe. There was
a young woman in the story, with two children, a girl around
five or six years old and a boy of three. She'd paid a smuggler
with money given to her by her brother to get her and the kids
from Senegal to Milan, and eventually to a job the smuggler
had helped to arrange in Liguria. The plan was the usual one:
Senegal to Libya, Libya to Sicily, Sicily to the mainland. The
route was desperate, east through the Sahara into Libya, where
a network of smugglers moved hundreds or even thousands of
people at a time from compound to compound, house to house,
until they arrived (if they arrived) at the coast. There, the people were crammed into small, old fishing boats. If someone dis-
obeyed the smuggler, if a baby was crying too loudly or a child
or elderly person too slow, the punishment was a beating, or
being abandoned in a desert camp, in one of the sprawling concrete towns on the side of the road, abandoned into a state of
being where death was more likely than a return home, where a
return home, for many of the travelers, also meant death. She'd
made it to the coast with the children, made it onto one of the
four boats that were launched that night. The waters were calm
at first, the people around her relieved to be out of Libya and

finally, after so long, on their way. Then the boat turned out of the harbor. The wind and the waves intensified. The ship rolled from side to side, scrambling and mashing the human cargo. It seemed like the boat would start to come apart at any moment and take on water, and those in the cargo hold would drown. But somehow, hour after hour, the boat held together. It listed, it creaked, but the smugglers pushed on through the night toward port, where the Italians waited for their goods—these bodies— to move them still elsewhere and to take their cut of the profits. When the boat arrived in Sicily, the smugglers hauled them out and loaded them on trucks. The boy was sick, the girl cold and frightened. From the trucks, they were taken into a building, down a flight of stairs and into a cold, dank cellar. Bread and water were distributed. A few bags of oranges were thrown from the stairs into the space, as if the people above were feeding dangerous animals. The mother, despite the money from her brother, had crossed in debt; now she was owned by the Italians. Two days later, she and the kids were loaded onto another truck and taken to another boat. They were moved to the mainland, where yet another truck took them north, where they were passed on to a man named Ricardo, who worked for the boss, Renzo Romano. At least this is what he imagined, he, Anton Grassfeld, as he sat in the Bar Garibaldi and drank scotch, first one, then another, then another, watching his wife, Susan, lying on a beach chair reading below him, watching his daughter, Cassie, applying sunscreen to her thighs, watching his son, Rolf, trace the edge of the sea in search of shells, watching a woman he called Anita walking back and forth on the beach selling dresses and shawls.

[Page 183]

When Diya wakes up, she tells me about her dream. In it, she's on the beach, running from the edge of the sea to where her mother sits on the sand. She's not her current age but herself from years ago, maybe from when she's five or six. As she moves up the sand, she's bringing shells and sea glass, forming a pile. Her mother is getting cold, tells her it's time to go home, to have dinner, that it's late and time for bed. Even though she doesn't show it, Diya knows her mother is nervous, she sees her mother gazing into the darkness. Then Diya feels it—those eyes on her, those eyes watching her, those eyes hidden in the shadows.

[Page 184]

"He's here," Diya tells me one day. "Who?" "The man. Grassfeld. He's searching for me and mama. He doesn't know mama's gone." I want to tell her I'll protect her, I won't let anything happen to her, I'll never let him get her, but I can't, because I don't know if it's true (and I want to preserve something like truth) and I don't know what kind of threat Grassfeld represents. I remain silent, stroke her hair, and wipe the tears from her face.

[Page 185]

She picks up a pile of newspapers from one of the dining room tables and brings it over to me. She wants me to read them to her. I scan the headlines, pick one in Italian. It reports of great speeches by the dictator, the unveiling of new military technology, disgrace in Istria and Dalmatia, war in Ethiopia. I pick up a German paper: fire in the Reichstag, emergency measures declared, book burnings, mass arrests. I take a Russian paper: enemies of the state on trial, conspiracies against the people. Paper after paper, dictators in Yugoslavia, Poland, Hungary, Russia, Germany, Italy. Financial collapse. Migrations. Ethnic cleansing. Borders hardening. Nations ready for war. "What's happening to the world?" the girl asks me. "It's the first spasm of violence," I tell her. "It's the tremor before the crisis, before the breakdown, before the collapse of all that's good." I feel it creeping into my hands. The papers shake loose and fall to the floor.

[Page 186]

Very early one morning, while it's still dark, the door opens, and a different doctor comes into the room. I feel with my hand and can't find her. "Where's Diya?" I shout as I sit up on the bed and into a defensive position. "What have you done with my girl?" "She's fine," the doctor says, "she's with her father. He came and took her for a walk." "What his name?" "Tijl," he says to me. I don't have the strength at this moment to tell the doctor that Tijl is not her father. That is Walt's version, Walt fantasizing that Tijl and I were lovers, Walt fabricating that I got pregnant with Tijl's child and left Berlin to have the baby, left Berlin to be away from Walt, his drinking, his violence directed against his own body, against his own mind. But no—I was not pregnant when I left Berlin. Tijl and I were not lovers, and I did not give birth to that child. And this doctor, I realize as I crouch there in terror, is nothing but a projection of Walt Myerson's sick, besotted mind.

[Page 187]

Kirschbaum has arrived. I feel his presence in the building. I hear his footsteps.

[Page 188]

Pile after pile of newspapers. Day after day and year after year the same unending story pours from the pages: enemies on the borders, enemies hidden in the nation, enemies undermining the people, communists, socialists, Jews, racial inferiors tearing apart the cultural, economic, and racial fabric of society. Diya asks me to read it to her, to continue, and on and on this story goes, crossing borders and rivers and seas and oceans and deserts and mountain ranges, crossing languages from English to French to German to Polish to Russian to Japanese, swirling around the globe. But I can't read this story anymore. I can't look into her eyes and read this story, this truth about the world beyond the walls of the Hotel des Bains. And what, after all, are these walls made of? Nothing but the flimsiest memory, walls crumbling, full of holes, barely solid enough to stand.

[Page 189]

I sit at the table in the dining room reading this, nearing the end. She sits across from me dropping sea glass into a bowl, fishing it out, dropping it in again. I can tell she loves the noise it makes, glass on glass. I am happy for her pleasure.

[Page 190]

"If the scene in room 401 is unresolved," I ask Rosa Fuchsbein, "what should I do there?"

"Turn the terror back toward itself. That's the truest form of art: terror turned back to face itself."

[Page 191]

He's in room 276—Mondschein's room. He's staring at the ceiling. Nothing appears there. He's waiting for the ladder to emerge. It will not come.

[Page 192]

I hold her tight, this child, this orphan, this daughter of mine. I press her head to my chest, her warm body against mine. I decide I must make the trade—this manuscript for her, this manuscript to be able to leave this place with Diya, this manuscript for a future, however bleak. I will take an exit toward the future in exchange for every possible past contained here, which is to say, simply, in exchange for every possible past.

[Page 193]

The sea glass crashes into the glass bowl. I can barely think, can barely read these words—can only whisper to myself, over and over, "Mila, Milena, Mila, Milena."

[Page 194]

Might it not be better, I think, as I wait in the dining room for Kirschbaum, to set fire to these stacks of old newspapers, to set fire to this manuscript, to burn the Hotel des Bains to the ground?

[Page 195]

Better to laugh, I think—to know and yet to laugh, to suffer and yet to laugh, to turn terror back on itself and to laugh. It is the laugh of anarchy, an imagining away of words, and with the erasure of words, the falling of walls. With the erasure of words, the opening of blank fields, fields of all sizes, fields without borders, fields pushing toward the limits of imagination, into spaces beyond imagination, and further, and deeper, into the cloudy regions of selflessness and faith.

[Page 196]

There he is, walking across the room. Diya doesn't see him. She's engrossed in the game with the sea glass. She doesn't remember the nightmares. She's forgotten about the locked door, about the doctor's voice in the hallway; she's forgotten about Grassfeld; she's forgotten the words "mama" and "papa," she sees only the smooth edges of things, the dulled colors of things, the randomness of size and shape. She closes her eyes and hears a symphony of glass on glass.

[Page 197]
The tremor begins in the hand which holds the pen. I can barely keep holding it as the tremor climbs up my arm and into my shoulder, moves into my neck, shoots across the hemisphere of my body into my other arm, down the arm to the other hand and fingers, down both legs, up into my brain. Turn the terror back toward itself, let it erase itself, let the page be blank again, let chaos come and the watery deep rise and wash the world clean. Let me climb the ladder to heaven and pass through those open gates and into that ruined landscape. Let me call on God to return.

Let's go back to the night at Sladkovsky's. Cohen and I were on our second or third round of beers when I reached down into my backpack and pulled out the pages with Milena's marginalia. Slowly, Cohen leafed through them, studying the alterations, the frantic scrawling of Milena's words around and (at times) over his. Did he see her words as a scarring or a defacing of his work? Or was it something else he felt, something like the appreciation of an inspired piece of graffiti art that emerges from the insipid urban landscape and transforms not only the object that hosts it but the whole of the surrounding space—in other words, the marginalia as occupation, as rebellion?

I watched as Cohen flipped through page after page—the margins "devoured," as Milena might say, by those intruders, those trespassers, those words which crossed the boundary and staked their claim on the frontier of the text. It had been merely days since Cohen had left the clinic. He hadn't showered, and I doubted whether he'd changed his clothes. He was so anxious to get the pages back he'd barely slept. Not that I'd slept much, busy as I'd been copying down the marginalia, sensing that to destroy them—the marginalia—Cohen might be tempted to destroy the single copy of his own book. What would be left? Smoke? Ash?

Literature as smoke, literature as ash—a memory of what was, or could have been.

A Fragment of an Analysis

OME DAYS AGO, a large envelope arrived at the college for me. There was no return address. The envelope contained the following document:

Case #276: Neurotic Anarchism, A Defiance Disorder

I. Introduction

In the late spring of the previous year, a patient in his mid-forties whom I'll call "K." came to the clinic. K. was given a room in the so-called "cabin" on the southern edge of the grounds, a pleasant room on the edge of the pond with a panoramic view of the mountain ridge in the distance. Over the course of our first sessions, he told me the following basic story, and since it's against my practice, as is widely known, to interrogate such stories for a *verifiable* truth, I present it without accompanying notes or qualifications. K. grew up not far from the clinic (about a three-hour drive) in a town of reasonable size, though by no means a major city. His father, whom I'll call the Professor Emeritus, taught American literature at a branch of the state university.

The idea that the father's academic career fell into mediocrity after a promising beginning—Columbia, Harvard—was proposed by K. in one of our initial sessions. Though he spoke little about his early childhood, I could draw out the basic contours: an erratic and excitable and ultimately distant father, a conformist and controlling mother, seemingly the family's authority in all practical matters, and an older brother driven by ambition and a desire for wealth and power.

In the early 1990s, having finished college, K. left the country for Berlin, Germany. His stated reason for this flight abroad was that he'd become excluded from a certain love triangle, a geometry that seemed to exist, even to him, mostly in his imagination. Upon setting himself up in Berlin, K. started to get jobs as a translator of poetry and prose, mainly through the intercession of his roommate. Through the roommate, he became acquainted with a group of writers from a neighborhood called Kreuzberg. One of the poets among the group gave him the contract to translate her book. The apparent "success" (his term) of the collection led to other jobs, including work translating a novel by a "major Berlin writer." In other words, K. had very quickly developed what seemed to be a promising career and a strong reputation as a translator of challenging literary works.

Beyond work, K. describes a Berlin life of youthful chaos with all the dynamics of intimacy that one can imagine existing in the "post–Cold War landscape" (his phrase). The closest circle of friends and intimates included two American writers, D. and W., a costume designer and theater director from Warsaw, M., who ran a "radical" performance space in Kreuzberg, and an Afro-Caribbean literary critic, T., who'd come to Berlin from Amsterdam with his girlfriend, F., an Iranian performance artist and poet living in exile as a political refugee.

Though the object of the original "love triangle" remained the focal point of K.'s amorous desires, it faded over the years into a kind of abstraction, which could be channeled into affairs of a mimetic quality. Characteristics of the various affairs were thus remarkably consistent: consuming, total, destructive, leading to predictable breakdowns and divisions. This pattern was both interrupted and reinforced when the abstraction suddenly became real, with the archetypal woman, I., arriving in Berlin. The short-lived, adulterous affair ended in one of two ways—it was never clear which (if either) was the truth. Either the woman left K. in Berlin and went back home to her husband, K.'s closest childhood friend, or K. left her and fled to Prague, where he'd live, as he tells it, for seventeen years, the whole time translating an epic novel and a masterpiece of Czech dissent.

The patient's account of these seventeen years defies easy description and was full of countervailing tendencies (one of the reasons he was at the clinic) revealing deeper fissures in his persona, which pointed to the utterly fragmentary nature of his selfhood. It could be that K. had, in fact, given up, albeit unconsciously, on the notion of the existence of the self, taking refuge in the various crags and crevasses of his being—the particular crag or crevasse seeming to depend on a rather inscrutable combination of internal and external factors. In light of this, I've decided to try to establish some fixed points rather than to draw a seemingly unbroken timeline from point A to point B. The following points can be established: he left Berlin for Prague in the winter of 1997 on a train from Zoo Station; he acquired an antique writing desk that once belonged, he said, to a cousin of Rainer Marie Rilke; now and then he returned to Berlin, once in search of a book of mystical theology called *The Book of Moonlight*, which was referenced in the novel he was translating; he had a falling-out with his former Berlin roommate, the one who got him the job translating for the Kreuzberg scene and who then introduced K. to the Czech writer; he struggled to make enough money to get by, especially as the dollar continued to depreciate; he had multiple significant affairs with poets, historians, etc.; he met each day with the Czech writer to work on the translation; he had a contract for the translation with a major New York publishing house; he had ongoing, if sporadic, dialogue with his editor; on the verge of finishing the translation he was called back to his hometown by I., who'd had a breakdown of an undefined sort; while "home," he met with his old friend, G.—I.'s husband—in a basement bar; he returned to Prague on the edge of despair only to find the Czech writer incapable of work; he pushed the translation to the end through innumerable conflicts, overcoming himself, the writer's daughter, and the writer; he wrote a "preface" to this massive translation, as specified by his contract, but it was prevented, by the writer's daughter, from appearing in the published book; he found a publisher for the preface, who brought it out as a separate volume; he won a PEN translation award for the work; he checked himself into a private clinic near a small Czech village; after a couple of weeks at the clinic, he realized that two former intimates from his Berlin years—D. and M.—were also there; he stayed at the clinic from the spring through the summer, when he left abruptly to try to retrieve a manuscript of D.'s that M. had stolen; he caught up with her on the Lido in Venice, at a hotel called the Hotel des Bains; he gained possession of the manuscript; he stayed three weeks in Venice hand-copying M.'s marginalia; he returned to Prague to give D. the manuscript back at a bar called Sladkovsky's; he left the bar and walked to a nearby park and sat on a stone wall; he imagined shutting the door to his Prague apartment and leaving it behind forever.

Then, at this point in the story, nothing more remained of K.'s memory and his ability to narrate. Time ran full speed into the wall of the present, and he found himself out of time, in the emptiness or darkness or the void of non-existence. Non-existence, despite the immovable fact that he came to my office on the first floor of the East Building of the Mountain View Clinic each day at 11:30 A.M. and sat across from me in a leather armchair.

I should mention, before I get into the specific analysis of the case, that the following report is incomplete. It is only a fragment, as K. abruptly terminated his treatment at the end of the summer so that he could—at least he later claimed, in a letter to me—give a course called Introduction to Literature at a small college in his hometown. It's not my role to play detective, to track down every discrepancy between K.'s story and objective reality. Still, it must be said that the letter, like the rest of his narration, was dubious at best. At the same time, such dubiousness is the force that creates those beautiful fissures which allow the possibility of probing the depths of the self. As an analyst, one must slip through these narrow cracks in the surface, like entering the mouth of the cave, to glimpse the caverns that, when taken together, form the labyrinth of being.

I don't intend to dwell on K.'s letter to me. It's important from an analytical perspective, however, to say that the letter was an attack on me, the "me" of authority, the figure (or figurehead) of authority at the clinic. One could dismiss this moment of rage at authority, and others like it, as a juvenile tantrum against anything and anyone that limits the fulfillment of egoistic desire. In this way, the attack on me could be seen as a displaced attack on the figure of the father, which of course would align with K.'s claim to have come back "home" to play nurse to the ailing Professor Emeritus, while at the same time somehow taking on a job teaching college literature, his father's lifelong profession and passion. The reader of this case will immediately see the stage set, curtain, and props of K.'s amateurish theater play. In any case, it's necessary to expand beyond the father-son conflict, and I think there is strong justification to move beyond the nuclear family unit, beyond, in other words, the constellation of older brother-mother-father-patient. The attack on "authority" in the letter was, after all, not against them but against me. He railed specifically against my "authoritarian discursive style and strategies," against the "dehumanizing daily schedule, especially the fixed times for the daily meals," against the "fascist architectural planning of the clinic's building and grounds, complete with its prison-like outer wall," against "the placement of the clock tower that rises over the West Building, creating a means and atmosphere of constant surveillance," against the "voyeuristic attempts to pit patients against each other in mundane contests for simple gratifications," against the "suppression of Eros through the unspoken but stringent rules against intimate contacts," against the "discouragement of and, at times, hostility toward the meeting of guests in pairs or small groups," against the "control over information flows in the form of an elitist distribution of library keys," against the "denial of basic material goods like pencils and paper," against the "manipulation of the internal temperatures of buildings and rooms to cause creeping discomfort," and so on for many pages. This was not only a challenge to my position of authority at the clinic; it was what could be called a *scream against the structures of the world*. The patient saw abuses of power everywhere he turned—hierarchies, oppression, suppression, mechanisms of control—and in his imagination these abuses of power defined all human relationships. In opposition to these structures, he yearned for, as he said, "real freedom."

I coined a term for his condition: *neurotic anarchism*. K. is the first diagnosed case in the world. The condition of *neurotic anarchism* differs significantly from other recognized and symptomatized defiance disorders, as the latter are not only usually focused on children but are recognizable by the primacy of acute emotional responses to discipline and control and the embodiment or agent of that discipline in the form of an intimate: a parent, teacher, coach, grandparents, an older sibling, etc. *Neurotic anarchism*, while having emotional content, can be better described as an intellectual or even rational/creative act of systems-building, despite these systems being about as real as figures in the clouds. In addition, it is not the individual antagonisms that matter most, though this is not to say that these antagonisms don't matter—they do. What matters is the neurotic anarchist's understanding of what K. would call, "the total mechanism of control." The most powerful elements of this mechanism, K. believes, were embedded, through a kind of socio-cultural conditioning, in our brains, our nerves, and our blood.

II. Symbols and Power

There is no direct approach, unfortunately, that would enable me to confront what I'll call the "ecology" of power in K.'s case. I purposefully refrain from calling it K.'s "understanding" of power or his "conception" of power, because he didn't understand it in any real sense and certainly had no discernible *concept* of it. Rather, it was there, a looming mass, an entity, a feeling, a sensation. Over the months of our sessions, however, a certain set of coordinates emerged that, when mapped, could constitute something recognizable as a psychological territory. It was a map that started off as mostly empty space, but through a deeper exploration of these various coordinates, more information (I hesitate to use this term) about the hinterlands emerged, and in such a way, the known territory expanded, and the map slowly was filled in. In this case, the coordinates are what I'd call symbols or motifs, symbols in that they signify not a single thing but a complex of things, a realm, perhaps, or what we might call an imagined zone.

Sea glass

During our first session, I asked K. to focus on one memory, any memory, it didn't matter what it was about, and to share it with me as fully as possible. He was quiet for a long time before he started to tell me about a time when, as a boy, his father had taken him to the beach. His father didn't like the beach, K. said, and it surprised him that his father brought up the idea. It was fall and rather cold (his father hated the heat), and they would be going in the afternoon of a gloomy day.

They drove out to the beach, parked the car in the almost empty parking lot, and walked down the path through the dunes. K. was cold. He hadn't dressed properly, and his father hadn't paid much attention to his preparations. His mother had been away for a few days. Maybe it was longer, K. couldn't remember. And he couldn't recall where his brother might have been that day, just that he and his father had been alone in the house, that his father had spent the better part of the previous few days moving from his bed to his desk, barely eating, barely recognizing K., who survived by consuming four or five bowls of cereal per day.

Whether something had been wrong with his father, he couldn't say. Whether his mother had been gone for some special reason, he did not know. When they arrived at the beach, his father set up a beach chair and wrapped himself in a wool blanket. He took a book and pencil out of his canvas bag. K. had on a pair of dark-green sweatpants, a gray sweatshirt, and a pair of sneakers, but he could still feel the chill of the autumn air. He didn't know quite what to do. The tide seemed to be coming in, and the waves bubbled up and slid across the dark sand. The light was thinning, coming in at sharper angles, stretching shadows. K. turned away from his father, who in any case was now engrossed in the book, and slowly made his way down to the edge of the ocean. At first, he thought he'd play in the sand, dig something, build something, but for some reason couldn't begin. He took off his sneakers and socks. The sand was cold, the water absolutely freezing.

He stood for a while, ankle-deep in the water, burrowing his feet into the muddy sand, which shifted around him with every push and pull of the tide. He gazed to the right, to the left, tracing the edge of the ocean as far as it went until it bent out of view. There were only a few other people on the beach, a small group over by a wall of rust-colored rock in the distance, a man with a golden retriever bounding in and out of the surf. He turned back to look at his father. He felt a sense of estrangement from him, K. told me, an estrangement from an intimacy, he added, that in this moment seemed to exist completely outside himself, as if separated from him by a window or a wall of glass.

K. bent his head and peered down at the dark sand. There was something black near his left foot, a rock, or a fragment of shell, he thought. He reached down and pinched it between his fingers. It was oblong, about the size of a marble. It was as black as charcoal, smooth, with a slight whitish frosting on its surface. K. rubbed it between his fingers to clear the sand away, following its curves, learning its shape, feeling its density. It was sea glass, he thought, but black, and he'd never seen black sea glass before. To have a better look, K. held it up to the sky, and as the rays of light passed through it, the whole sphere transformed into a deep olive green. Something about this trick or play of light delighted K. He moved the glass to the shadow, and it was as black as the night, then he lifted it up into the light and again that milky green hue. It was a wondrous thing, K. said to me, a small miracle, a splendor. He unzipped a pocket of his sweatpants and deposited the piece of sea glass inside.

The discovery of this unusual specimen provoked him to search for other pieces of sea glass to add to it. He moved along the edge of the water, where the surf thinned to the greatest extent possible. Every few steps, when the wave would draw back that thin film of sand, he'd spy a speck of color. Light green, yellow, brown, red, blue, some deep, some lighter hues of pink, purple, and so on, some frosted white. Before he knew it, he'd gone a good distance away from his father, who now appeared as nothing more than a swatch of red from the beach chair with a long gray shadow trailing behind him. K.'s pocket was now drooping down his leg. He was getting cold.

Careful not to spill his treasure, K. hustled back to where his father was reading. He took a towel from his father's bag and spread it out on the sand. He climbed on and emptied his collection of sea glass to inspect it. Seen together against the white cotton of the towel, the colorful sea glass looked even more enchanting and magical to K., like a collection of precious gems. Except for the one piece of black sea glass. But this made that piece all the better, more valuable.

After K. arranged the pieces of sea glass on the towel by color, starting with the lightest, ending with that oblong sphere of black, he called out to his father to look at the collection. His father gazed down from his chair at the pieces arranged in a line across the towel. "Fine," he said to his son and then turned back to his book. K. waited a moment and then interrupted his father's reading a second time. "Look at this one," he said, holding up the piece of black sea glass. His father reached down and took it from K.'s hand, inspected it on his palm, and was about to hand it back when K. told him to hold it up to the sky so the rays of light could pass through it. His father did it, and K. watched from the towel as that magic occurred again, the charcoal black becoming a viscous green, as if the whole chunk were made of pure fossilized olive oil.

When they got home, K. washed the pieces one by one and put them into a glass bowl he found tucked away in the corner of one of the lower cabinet drawers in the kitchen. For a long time, well into the night, he played with his pieces of glass, scooping them out of the bowl, letting them fall back in. His whole sensorium felt alive with this: the haptic pleasure of the smooth but irregular shapes and surfaces, the visual kaleidoscope of colors, the always different sounds of the glass pieces striking each other and the sides of the bowl, bouncing up again, sliding into silent stasis.

It came time to go to sleep. K. took his bowl of sea glass and placed it on his desk across the room. Then he paused, thought for a moment, reached into the bowl, and retrieved the piece of black sea glass. It was part charcoal, he thought, part meteorite, part volcanic rock, and yet despite what must have been explosive, traumatic origins, it was as smooth as polished marble. He switched off his overhead light and turned on the lamp beside his bed. He held the black object to the light bulb to make sure it still had its power to transform from pure black to olive green. It occurred to him, K. told me, that there was more to it than just a change of color. The black was ashen, lifeless, and the green was the color of growth, of life, and the light streaming through changed the substance from something dead to something alive, or at least revealed the inner life of what appeared to lack it. This thought pleased him. He turned off the lamp and held the piece of sea glass in his closed fist. It felt warm.

Transmutation, K. thought as he lay there in the dark, a transformation of color, form, essence, indicating a related topic: the instability or the shapelessness, as he said, of the present— the quivering of reality. Was this transformative power, K. wondered, purposeful, predictable, or even controllable? Or rather, was it random, chaotic, beyond anyone's ability to guide or shape? Thoughts tumbled through his mind. He held a stone that could come to life, a stone that contained the essential secret of nature, the green of nature's birth, the green of flourishing. This force was caught and stored inside this stone, waiting only to be activated by the light of the sun. If only he could harness this force somehow, he thought, he could change so many things; he could make things right again, make them better— but what specifically? He couldn't think of anything, couldn't think even of the smallest possible thing to do with his magic stone. Thoughts spun like leaves in the wind, and in his dreams, he could see the edge of the tide as it pushed and pulled the sand, first covering then unveiling those specks of colored glass.

The Aviary

He couldn't remember where he'd seen it, this wide, tall aviary with its art nouveau latticework of flowers and vines in pale verdigris, a color that evoked the memory (even if a lost memory) of a vanished grace. He was alone, he said, when he encountered the structure. "How else," I nearly burst out when I heard this piece of the puzzle, "could it have been?" He approached it, he said, and found it in sorry shape—the metal was rusty, the paint chipping off, the stone foundation was cracked, the interior full of scattered branches, leaves, and forest debris. He put his hand on one of the spirals of twisted metal and felt its surface crumble against his palm, and once this green crust was peeled away what remained was an austere, ugly piece of iron. He slowly walked around the periphery of the aviary's base, a perfect circle spanning some twenty feet, "a calm, inviting space, like all effective prisons," he added. When he'd made it around, he came back about a third of the way to the aviary's door, which was neatly concealed by the twists and turns of the floral motifs. He tried the bolt, but it had been fused with rust and couldn't be budged. He went to the edge of the clearing and searched until he found a stone, a gray one about the size of a grapefruit, and brought it back to the door. After striking the bolt with the stone three or four times, it slid free of the lock, allowing K. to push open the door.

He entered the aviary. His feet slid against the floor—a smooth surface of polished stone. As his strides cleared away the mess, he saw that the floor, like the latticework, contained an intricate design. He spent some time clearing the entire floor with his hands and feet. The central images of the mosaic were two trees, the tree of life and the tree of the knowledge of good and evil, the branches of which were intertwined with each other, forming an interlocking, even unified, crown. He bent down and pressed his palms to the surface, moving them up the trunk of one tree into the thicket of branches, out to the extremity of the crown, sliding down another twisted branch, down the other trunk to the forest floor. He wanted, he said, to feel what kind of life this foundation contained, what kind of energy pulsed through it, but he could feel nothing, nothing alive, nothing that could be unfrozen by a momentary touch. The effort seemed to tire him, and he had the urge to lie down there, to observe the space by lying flat, to gaze up at the phantom birds that sat on illusory branches and now and then spread out their fiery or regal or rather ordinary plumage to signal to the timid observer, who stood, snack in hand, beyond those bars, that they were alive and still had the ability to soar. K. took off his jacket and formed a pillow. He slid it under his head. The early evening light slanted through the space, creating a dizzying interplay of metal bars and shadows, such that, from his perspective, he couldn't tell one from the other.

In the midst of this shadow theater, as if summoned by the observer, that man lying motionless (corpse-like, K. said) on the cage's mosaic floor, a pair of wings fluttered through the open door and whirled around the aviary's dome until they came to rest on the narrow sill that joined the copper roof with the maze of bars. At first, K. said, he thought it was an ordinary pigeon or sparrow, which would have been enough of a treat, but he soon realized this creature was a raven. The raven, at rest, turned its head from side to side, as if assessing the new surroundings, perhaps looking for a way out. There was no doubt, K. added, that the raven had already forgotten about the door. It's field of vision was mostly horizontal, even if now and then it seemed to cast its gaze down on the body lying motionless, trying to puzzle out, K. imagined, the nature of the threat or opportunity this entity represented.

As he lay there watching the raven, he felt the space become infused with a kind of energy or spirit—a wildness, an untamable quality, a creative force that was also a destructive force, like the ebb and flow of the tides, he thought, like the surging of a river and the overflowing of its banks and its flooding of the world. A certain sense of evil mixed with its opposite, a type of "good" that had nothing to do with values or morals or law or obedience— it was the "good" of becoming, of finding form. This good, K. said, ultimately started to slide toward its opposite, evil, thereby unmaking, collapsing, or simply obliterating the binary opposition of good/evil. This good/evil was replaced with a new pair— becoming/solidifying—or to put it another way, an arresting of the verbs "to open," "to unfurl," "to spread," at which point the created and formed thing became as lifeless as a taxidermist's owl or hawk or eagle perched on a makeshift log or a branch protruding from some sportsman's wall.

Nighttime crept in. The cold intensified. The wind picked up. The latticework of bars and shadows faded into an invisible boundary, the ceiling empty, endless, a chasm. For a while, even as the darkness descended, the raven's movements could be discerned or sensed, then intuited as one shade of black against another, as if the blackness had texture, a fabric swept here and there in the breeze.

Silent, still, blending into the darkness, the raven was becoming the space of the cage, K. said to me. Then, after a while, he pulled out a notebook and quoted some text, claiming, when asked, that he was not its author, but refusing to divulge to me who wrote the lines: *I don't believe people exist whose inner plight resembles mine; still, it is possible for me to imagine such people—but that the secret raven forever flaps about their heads as it does about mine, even to imagine that is impossible.*

Campfire

How old he was, K. didn't say. He'd come back to his hometown after a long time away. It was late in the fall, and he caught a bus to the north. His friend G. met him at the end station. They drove for an hour into the forest, mostly on old fire roads, some paved, others dirt and gravel. At some point, G. pulled the small blue pickup over to the side of the road and turned off the engine.

They got out, strapped on their backpacks, and started into the forest along a narrow path. G. led the way, seemed to know the land, to know how the path curved and moved even at points when it seemed to K. to vanish into an undifferentiated forest. Though it was late in the fall, the temperature was mild. After descending a gradual slope and crossing over a small stream, they were on G.'s land; the stream, G. told K., marked its eastern border. The trail, meanwhile, had bent to the south at the stream, and on the other side, on G.'s land, there was nothing but unbroken forest. They continued, first climbing up a hill, then down, moving across a stretch of level ground, then up another hill, on the other side of which a lake appeared in front of them. It was a vast, branching, wild lake that sat in a valley between the mountains. At the distant edge of the lake, along the opposite horizon, K. could trace the top of the mountain ridge, silhouetted now by the setting sun.

There was a clearing by the lake, and within it was a square of sticks connected by ropes, the outline, G. said, of where he planned to build a cabin. He was marking it out and planning it this year, he said to K., and would start to build in the spring. K. wandered across the clearing, looked around, and gazed out at the lake. From this point on the lake, K. could make out no other structures, not a sign of human life anywhere. He turned and peered into the forest. A sense of wilderness came to him, overwhelmed him, even tempted him, but K. didn't want to let on to his friend that he was frightened or unsettled. Instead, he took a few steps away from the clearing into the forest and started to gather an armload of wood for a fire.

The fire pit, a circular structure lined with stones, was set up near the edge of the lake. Around the fire pit were makeshift seats, nothing but disinterred tree stumps, roughly hewn. G. came and sat down on one, took out a small notebook, and began to jot something down. K., in the meantime, built the structure for the fire: scraps of birch bark at the bottom mixed with small twigs and dry pine needles, some larger kindling formed into a conical shape encasing this mixture, a few bigger logs, taken from G.'s stash, leaning against the kindling. The lit match caused the birch bark to curl and burn, the start of the chain reaction that would lead to the blazing campfire. K. was surprised by how fast the wood was burning. As G. continued to work in the notebook, K. went into the forest and brought back two more armloads of branches. By the time these were added to the fire, the big logs had caught, and the fire started to settle down into a slow burn.

They hadn't talked much during the drive and even less as they walked the trail from the road to the clearing by the lake. G. had set the pace along the trail, with K. following behind. Again, now, around the fire, silence seemed to consume them, until K. said, as he told it to me, "It's amazing to be in such untouched, pure nature. I can't imagine there are many places like this, places remote and yet close to civilization."

"There's not an inch of untouched land here or anywhere around," G. said. "These forests have been cleared and replanted more than once, and before that, before they were made into charcoal and sent by railroad south to heat the cities, they were being slashed and burned for hundreds of years."

"How can you tell?" K. asked.

"You can tell by looking at concentrations and dispersions."

"You can perceive those with the naked eye? From that observation you can judge the strategies of forest management by people centuries ago? By the placement of oaks and pines, by the growth of wildflowers in the clearings?"

"Of course not," G. said. "It has nothing to do with the eye. One can sense dispersions at the extremity of the soul, and one can feel concentrations at its center."

"At least it's fought its way back. The forest is resilient," K. said.

"Or it appears to be," said G. "If primitive wilderness had truly returned, we would both be sitting here shaking in terror, nothing but prey for bears and wolves. And before they came for us, the insects would feast on our flesh."

At that, G. set the grill on the rocks and opened two vacuum-sealed steaks. He placed them down on the fire and they immediately started to smoke and char. After a few minutes, he lifted them off and put them on two metal camping plates, passing one of them to K. with a fork and a serrated knife. The meat was rare and tender, and they consumed the steaks unencumbered by an accompanying grain or vegetable. When the meal was over, they sat around the fire, now and then adding another log, a stray stick, a pinecone. K. gazed into the coals, those glowing, pulsating balls of pure energy, and thought that they truly had something in common with the center of the soul. Energy concentrated, he thought, energy burning, energy seeking release into the air, dissipating.

Gradually, the fire burned down into a glowing red mash. G., sitting across the way on his tree stump, was barely visible against the darkness. K. leaned in toward the heat of the coals and asked G. what he'd been writing in his notebook. G. told him he was jotting down some notes for a play he'd been working on, a play about two friends who meet in a basement bar during a snowstorm after having not seen each other in nearly twenty years. They are meeting to discuss the condition of a woman, the wife of one of the friends, the former lover of the other. The woman has had a breakdown and has called her former lover back from Prague, where he'd been living since the conclusion of their brief affair. "And what has happened to her, to the wife, the lover?" K. asked. "That's what I'm trying to figure out," G. told him as the light of the coals dimmed between them, "that's what I'm hoping to discover, but the more I work on the play, the more unknowable she becomes."

Snowfall

He'd come home, he said, after being away for a very long time. It was one of K.'s timeless stories, stories removed from any discernible chronology. When I asked him whether this return was from Berlin or Prague, or somewhere else, he shook his head, seeming to reproach me for this question, and gruffly said it didn't matter. When I followed up by asking if this "doesn't matter" actually meant "was key, central, or vital," he bent his head toward his chest for a minute or two, hiding his expression from me. When his chin rose from his chest, he began talking about the memory, if it was truly a memory, ignoring what I'd asked.

"We planned to meet at the cabin. I hadn't been there in years, and I had no desire to ever go there again. I could very well have gone there and pulled the entire cabin apart board by board, or I could have burned it to the ground, as I had burned it to the ground countless times already in my mind. And this mental burning of the cabin had succeeded in erasing it, erasing the memory it held, the passions it evoked, what it symbolized.

"She had wanted to meet me at the cabin; it was her idea. It was wintertime, and in fact it had been snowing practically nonstop for days. I arrived early in the morning and found the place in sorry shape. Nobody had been there for years. Even though my brother should have tended to it, he'd long since moved on from the cabin, from what he calls 'cabin memories,' which is shorthand, in a sense, for childhood memories—or childhood itself. He didn't want to hear about the cabin anymore, didn't want to see it. My brother had buried the cabin with neglect long before it was buried this time by snow. Still, it stood, battered by life in the woods, airless, its doors and windows boarded up for many years. There it was, emerging out of the dawn light as I approached it from the dirt driveway, which sloped down from the road toward the lake. I looked on as the light fell on the water like a sheet of rippled silver. It was a sight so jarringly other from any sight I'd seen in years, and yet core, fundamental, a sight imprinted on my innermost being. This was my lake.

"I removed the board from the door using the special trick he'd taught me. The door otherwise had no lock. There was not much to steal inside besides some dusty books, mostly the remnants of my grandfather's great books subscription from the 1950s. I'd read them all over the years—Fenimore Cooper, Defoe, Beecher Stowe, George Elliot, Cather, Steinbeck, Proust.

"Inside, the space was caught in the past, fossilized. The cast iron pans hung from their hooks, the metal stove still contained ash, traces of a distant fire, beside it stood a stack of wood for burning, a green and gray hooked rug lay between the sofa, a leather armchair, and the stove. I opened the stove, checked to make sure everything was in order, and lit a fire. It would have to be warm, I thought, for her arrival.

"The propane tank that fueled the electric generator was out, of course, which meant that I couldn't get the pump running from the well to the house. It meant that nobody had been here for a very long time. For a few days, it didn't matter much— I could manually pump water from the well for drinking and cooking, and maybe, after a few days, a few pots to heat on the stove for a bath. I went out and filled all the jugs I could find and the bigger pots.

"I looked at my watch; it was just after nine in the morning. She had said she'd get there around noon, maybe sooner, depending on how early she could get away. But away from what? Away from her life, from civilization, away from all of it, away from herself? Just as I wanted to get away, but there was no 'away' in the cabin for me. Here, it was a burrowing.

"The stove was working fine, quickly heating the small space. I thought about climbing the narrow staircase to the loft where the two mattresses lay on the floor. Each mattress was large enough for two, two adults on one, two children on the other. I could have slept for hours, but I didn't want to be asleep when she arrived. That would have been a disaster. I moved over to the bookcase and scanned the volumes, picked up a few objects: a stone from a mountain stream, a piece of wood carved into the shape of a duck, another carving of an owl. A painting hung on the opposite wall: an autumnal forest scene with leaves of orange, red, and yellow littering the forest floor, the trees ablaze with their shedding colors. Ducks, autumn leaves—a menacing quaintness or kitsch, an unfulfilled promise. I turned back to the books and slid one from the shelf. It was a novel by Martin Dellman, a writer who lived in the cottage around the bend in the lake. As a child, I would paddle a canoe over to his dock, tie it up, and find him on his front porch scribbling away. He'd pause when I'd come up the steps and invite me for a bowl of ice cream, always vanilla, which I could have with chocolate sauce or without. When I'd ask for the ice cream without the chocolate sauce, Dellman would always say, 'The boy's a purist,' and would put two large scoops into a brown ceramic bowl. He'd fix himself a drink and say, 'It's time for a break,' and the two of us would head back out to the porch to eat, drink, and talk until he announced that he needed to 'get back to it,' and I'd run down the hill to the dock, untie my canoe and paddle home. There was no other moment, I think, when I felt as human, as real, as *there*, as when I ate my ice cream, 'pure,' while sitting on one of Dellman's weathered Adirondack chairs.

"The book was called *The Man Who Disappeared*, a thin volume in navy blue hardback that had long ago lost its dust jacket. The blue color of the book's spine was etched in my memory, a solid line of color that drew the eye from just about everywhere in the room. For decades, it sat on the shelf; for decades, nobody touched it. The cracking sound the book made when I slowly pulled open the front cover touched some deep reservoir of nostalgia, and I felt it as an aching in my chest, a hollowness of the gut. Dellman—this book outlived him, as it would outlive me, perhaps, unless the whole library in the cabin were to be used as kindling for a bonfire or to feed the wood-burning oven, its millions of words used to bake the daily bread.

"I took Dellman's book and sat down in the armchair. I started to read, first lazily, dreamily, distracted by her pending arrival, then with more focus and intensity. The story is set in a cabin on a lake. A writer, like Dellman, is living there. He is in his mid-forties, alone, trying to escape a previous life. Then one day, out of the blue, another man shows up at the cabin. It's Nahum Griggs, one of the former leaders of the Black anarchist movement. The writer had gotten to know Griggs when they were members of the same reading circle in the mid-1960s.

"By now, it's the 1980s, the Reagan years. One afternoon, as dusk settles over the newly fallen snow, Griggs knocks on the door. The writer welcomes Griggs into the house. Griggs had always been a lean man, and now he's thinned even more. His face seems sunken, his legs nothing but two narrow poles. The extent of his thinness couldn't be concealed, even by his bulky woolen coat and his thick beard, which Griggs had grown even as a young man in the 1960s.

"Griggs takes off his coat. The writer takes it, feels that it's soaked through, and hangs it above the stove to dry. Griggs takes off his hat, boots, socks. The writer can see that his other clothes are also soaked. He goes to the bedroom and returns with some sweatpants, an undershirt, and a sweatshirt, which Griggs puts on. His clothes hang loosely from Griggs's body. The writer brings Griggs a plate of food, which Griggs picks at slowly but leaves basically uneaten. He's thirsty, drinks four glasses of water. Then he falls back into the sofa, curls up his legs, and falls asleep.

"The writer remembers Griggs. He'd always worn the same brown suit to meetings of the reading circle. He knew the texts as well as anyone the writer had ever met, in college or out. The great socialists—Proudhon, Fourier, Marx, Herzl, Tolstoy. The anarchists—Bakunin, Kropotkin, Goldman, Landauer. Others like Hegel, Nietzsche, Schopenhauer, Rousseau, Vladimir Lenin. During meetings of the circle, the writer remembers, Griggs would close his eyes and speak about Marx's materialist dialectics, surplus value, the Nietzschean *Übermensch*. Griggs was no politician. He could talk to the group but would never bring it to the street, would never shout to the crowd. He was no academic either. No university degree, no interest in knowledge for its own sake. Humanism, he'd say, was the ideological veneer of capitalist exploitation and violence. They speak of racial equality, equality before the law, Griggs would say, so long as this equality never makes it to the bank, where there would never be equality, not for Black people, not for women. Equality was a joke of the white patriarchy, those who drew the lines of the urban frontier zones, those who busted up the unions, robbed the city schools, those who unleashed the police to protect the powerful.

"For Griggs, the writer recalls, the common answers were dead ends in the maze: MLK's dream nothing but airy Christian humanism; Malcolm X.'s teaching a mirror reflection of white patriarchy—self-abnegating, suicidal, laced with hate; Marcus Garvey's Pan-African nationalism a fairytale; Franz Fanon's war, a cataclysm. What was left? Or was their nothing left, no solution other than to wait for capitalism and the state to destroy themselves?

"Griggs had a following, probably fifty people from various reading circles. The group settled on a name: BAM—the Black Anarchist Movement. BAM attracted some of the most experimental artists and writers in the city, not to join BAM, which officially had no membership, no organizational structure, and no funds, but to participate, to act with others in a political relationship of choice, a relationship based on total equality and non-coercion. By the late 1960s, Griggs had turned his focus to the war, became a powerful critic of Johnson, then Nixon. The assembly of BAM swelled, pushing Griggs into the center of the city's resistance movement. The writer remembered when he heard that Griggs had been drafted, while he, the writer, had missed the draft lottery by being born in 1943, one year before the eligibility interval began. 1969. It was the year the writer got the job as the writer-in-residence at the college, the same year he got his first book contract, the same year he met his late wife, Livia, the same year Griggs went to Vietnam.

"It is late afternoon and dark when Griggs stirs and wakes up. The writer is at the table, drinking coffee, jotting notes down in a notebook, one of his self-designated 'sketchbooks,' plans for a future novel or just creative debris. He has filled hundreds of sketchbooks over the years, thousands of pages of notes, most remaining raw, fragmentary, without hope of developing into something larger, something that could strive for completion. What is it, he often wonders, that allows a fragment of prose or a set of notes to coalesce and move toward a novel? The one thing he'd like more than anything to understand, this, he knows, is what will always elude him.

"Griggs sits down at the table across from the writer. A single weak light bulb casts its light through an orangey glass globe. The writer pours a cup of coffee from the pot and waits for Griggs to tell him why he's there at the cabin on the lake, how he found him, and why him, him of all people, and why now, after many years without contact. Griggs offers no explanation, just asks a bunch of seemingly random questions. How big is the lake? The writer doesn't know; the lake has an irregular shape. How far is it from the cabin to the nearest grocery store? Thirteen miles. When does the lake freeze over? Depends on the year. How did the writer find this cabin? Belonged to his late uncle, his father's brother. How deep is the lake at its maximum depth? Around seventy meters. How high are the surrounding peaks? Between 1800 and 2300 feet. Why does the writer use the metric system for depth and the imperial system for height? The writer demurs. Griggs falls silent for a while. The writer turns back to his sketchbook. Then Griggs asks, 'Do you remember a woman named Esther Bird?'

"I closed the book and gazed down at its blue cover. The blue of the book, the blue of the sea, the blue of a late-afternoon sky. Outside, the gray afternoon, thick clouds, white snow. Inside, the fire glowed in the stove—red, orange, hints of green and blue, reflecting the painting of the autumnal forest scene across the way. It occurred to me when I read Nahum Griggs's question to the writer—the question about Esther Bird—that she wouldn't come, that she, in fact, could never come, that it would be impossible for her even to start out toward the cabin, let alone arrive. Yet I waited. All afternoon, I sat there in that armchair and gazed out at the spot in the forest where the path opened into what was, in summer, the cabin's kitchen garden. When I tired of this, I moved to the other side of the house and looked out at the lake, which at this time of day was nothing but a pool of emptiness, or, to see it another way, a total saturation, an ungraspable fullness—both—both empty and full, the black lake—the face of God.

"Do you remember a woman named Esther Bird? Do I remember Esther Bird? How could the writer or I, the reader of *The Man Who Disappeared*, forget that unforgettable character whose flight caused the rupture, the breaking apart, a breaking that produced the first spark, which caught this paper and grew into a flame—and burned and burned and burned?"

Cedar Resin

There was a certain tree, K. told me, that had been struck by a shard of Soviet shrapnel as the Red Army's artillery fired on the retreating Germans in the late fall of 1944. The amazing thing about this tree, he said, was that every so many years—and never at a predictable interval—its resin would ooze from its shrapnel wound and gather into a hard teardrop about twice the size of an adult human's fist. At first, locals called it the weeping cedar, but this didn't seem to fit. It wasn't "weeping," K. told me, it was wounded, the wounded cedar. It had a wound, he told me, which, for reasons even the most expert arborist couldn't figure out, wouldn't close.

Early one morning, at daybreak, as the light, still bluish black, was filled with nighttime shadows, K. made his way through the forest to visit the cedar. For a long time after the war, he told me, the tree had been widely known throughout the region, but by the 1970s everyone seemed to have forgotten about it. By the 1990s, memories of the wounded cedar had rekindled, though only among a small circle of enthusiasts, one of which was K.'s girlfriend at the time. The tree captivated him, K. said to me, for some unclear reason. Or perhaps there was no reason—perhaps, he said, simply because when the sunlight passed through that golden amber orb it produced a sight of true magnificence, an awesome, unlikely, euphoric beauty.

It took a combination of two trams and a long bus ride to reach the trail and then an hour's walk into the forest to find the wounded cedar. As he approached the cedar, K. saw someone moving in the shadows. He paused and looked on as a man went up to the cedar and pulled out a knife. The man proceeded to cut the resin bulb from the trunk. After depositing the amber teardrop in a leather sack, he turned back to the tree and spent a few minutes inspecting its wound, feeling inside it with his fingers. After that, he took his index finger, now covered in resin, K. presumed, and put it in his mouth, churning it around as one would a lollipop.

K. followed the man until the latter reached a tiny forest dwelling, a hut about the size of a garden shed. The man went inside and shut the door. There were several thin windows just below the roof, but the glass caught the glare and blocked any view into the interior of the space. Feeling unusually bold, K. went up to the hut and knocked on the door. The man answered and with surprising warmth ushered K. inside.

"What can I do for you?" He asked K. in a strangely accented German.

"I saw you steal the resin, the bulb of resin from the cedar," K. said, "the wounded cedar."

"Steal? How could I steal what doesn't belong to anyone? It's part of the commons, and by ancient right, people can glean the forest. For decades, nobody besides me has harvested the cedar's resin. Only I have done it. Only I have dressed the wound."

"Why does it still ooze? Why hasn't the wound closed? Is this because of what you're doing there?"

"That is a most compelling set of questions. There are many ways to answer them—but it's best, I think, not to answer them at all."

At this point, K. looked around. The hut was immaculately maintained, especially the area of the hut that contained what appeared to be the man's laboratory bench. Shelves held glass jars filled with what seemed to K. to be products of the resin—powders, small amber cubes, liquids in various hues, opacities, and viscosities. "What's all this?" K. asked him.

"Everything you see here is made from cedar resin. These jars are for incense—mostly admixtures, but some of them are pure resins from specific accretions. Each bulb of resin a tree produces is unique, has a certain set of properties that must be considered when using it to make an incense or anything else. If I didn't take these properties into account, the results could be very bad. The resin is the life force of the tree—its blood—and the resin in the bulbs is a concentrate of this force, and the denser and purer the concentration, the more power it holds. At the same time, it's not only about density, no, that would be a big mistake to assume it was all about density. The flow of the resin within trees is important to understand, as we have resin that can originate in the wood, the outer and inner rings, in the root systems, the bark, etc. All of this is medicinally important. Over here, you can see various salves, lozenges, and powders that work against any number of pathogens, some by attacking the microbes, others by supporting, boosting, or triggering a natural immune response. There is incredible power in this particular tree, the so-called wounded cedar. Because of the nature of its wound, which must be quite deep (it is impossible to tell how deep), it offers something I have found in no other tree resin. It is truly singular. I call it 'the counterforce,' and it could even be described not as a flow of resin, but as a reversal, an ebbing of the resin, perhaps one that pulls all the way back to the tree's roots. I know it's hard to grasp, but whatever it is, this ebbing or reversing resin, it occurs once, perhaps twice a decade in a concentration that can be medically distilled, certainly no more, perhaps less, and it could be that such a concentration will never occur again. In any case, the wounded cedar's counter-resin, when concentrated in a particular way to guarantee certain chemical characteristics, has a psychedelic quality, and when processed properly (and only I know how to do it), it yields access to parallel veins of history, what I call branch lines, and these branch lines depart from what I call intersecting stations, meaning that these points of divergence from the main line to the branch lines are accumulations or concentrations of energy, a certain type of blockage, perhaps, a vessel that has been filled too much and is now at the point of overflow or even of bursting apart. It's a rare substance, given the rarity of an adequate counter-resin and the amount of this resin required in the distillation process. Since you are my first visitor in many years, I will share it with you, as long as you understand that by taking one of these branch lines, the main line of your life might never be found again, or, at the very least, even if it is found, you will no longer think that the main line is the only possible route of travel, the only way from beginning to end."

"I understand," K. said.

"That, I doubt," said the man as he opened a small drawer in his apothecary's chest and drew out a small glass vial containing a cloudy yellow liquid. "Here you go," he said, passing the vial over to K. "Drink it down in one go."

K. drank, he told me, and what emerged, he said, was an existence stunningly other and yet still, without a doubt, his—his life, his reality, his unknown and unknowable existence.

Jacob's Ladder

Behind his apartment building in Berlin, K. told me, was an inner courtyard between three other buildings, all of which were crumbling and abandoned. The patch of grass between these structures was littered with debris, mostly, it seemed, broken pieces of the buildings themselves: old piping, rusted steel beams, hundreds of fragments of brick, broken chunks of concrete. K. would often gaze down at the space from his window six stories above, especially as the sun was setting and its beams found their way through the urban matrix to shine directly into the yard along a sharp vector of pinkish golden light. For ten or fifteen minutes each day, this mix of wild growth and decaying junk took on an aura of Roman ruins, a feeling that, for K., mixed hope with gloom. One day, as he gazed down into the space, K. saw a pale structure rising out of the yard. From his perspective high above, it seemed like a kind of projection. It was airy, nearly transparent, but definitely there—a ladder rising to the sky.

Throughout his years living there, he'd never been into this courtyard, access to which required exiting his building through the back and then climbing over an old brick wall that separated a narrow, overgrown patch behind his building from the adjacent space. Thinking that the ladder could very well be nothing more than a play of light—like a rainbow—he rushed to get on his shoes and jacket and scrambled as quickly as he could down the stairs. He pushed open the back door and found a place on the wall that provided some good grips for hands and feet. He surmounted it without much trouble. By now, the light was beginning to fade, the sunbeams soon to be cut off by the corner of a neighboring building. Once in the yard, it took K. a moment to gather himself before he found the ladder. He was relieved it was still there, even if impossibly pale, almost invisible. He approached it, hesitated, reached out, and ran his fingers along one of its side poles. It was made of no substance he could recognize by touch: not metal, not wood. It was something else, something unknown. He grabbed one of the rungs and felt a strange energy, a kind of heat that wasn't hot. The energy seemed to enter his body, to charge him, to find its way directly into his bloodstream, a feeling which intensified as he grabbed the ladder with his other hand, then intensified more as he placed first one foot, then the other, on a lower rung.

K. began to climb, first slowly, hesitantly. He rose to the height of the third story of his building, then to the level of his attic window, and finally above it and into the open sky. He kept climbing until he was high above Berlin, and on he went into the low-hanging clouds. In no time, he was through this gossamer whiteness and into a space lit only by the stars. The climb continued, and it seemed to K. that, infused with such energy, he could climb forever. On it went—it could have been hours or days or weeks or years or decades (he'd lost all sense of time)—until he reached the end of the ladder and stepped into the heavenly domain.

There were gates, K. said, with bars as thick as tree trunks. The gates were impossibly high, and on either side was a tower for the guards. Strangely, though, the towers were empty, and the massive gates unlocked. There they were, K. told me, swinging back and forth in the wind like the gates of an ordinary garden fence. He passed through them, moving slowly, worried what reaction this intrusion might bring. But there was no reaction, and as far as he could see, K. said, there was nothing but a desolate landscape, windswept, with the ruins of buildings sitting atop an ashen, barren ground that was devoid life. Life! Why, he asked himself, did he expect any life in this realm of death, a realm far beyond anything known to him? He continued, walking between the crumbled structures, peering into their inner chambers—chambers full of nothing but wind and shadow. Then as he turned a corner and gazed into the distance, he saw (or sensed) something move to his left. He turned that way, moved toward it, followed the imagined path, and when he came around the next corner, he saw a haggard being holding something like a processional horn or trumpet. The being, an angel, K. assumed, shrunk back in horror as he moved toward it, eventually even crouching down like a threatened animal.

"Who are you?" K. asked.

"A survivor," the angel said, "one of the survivors of the razing of heaven and its abandonment by God."

"There is no God here?"

"God has withdrawn from here."

"How could it be that the heavens have been razed and God has fled from his domain? What is the story of this destruction?"

"I know nothing about it; memory of the events has scattered with the ashes. There is only one angel who knows the story, the one we call the scribe."

The angel stood up and brushed the gray ash from his old robe. Pale, thin, the angel seemed to move over the ground without really touching it—moved gracefully, effortlessly, while for some reason K. found the way exhausting; lifting his feet seemed like pulling them out of ankle-deep mud. At some point, they turned into a small courtyard of a ruined structure and crossed over to the base of what must have once been a raised garden terrace. Plain columns still stood at its corners, holding up, somehow, the remains of the roof. Under the roof sat another figure, an angel, a woman, at a large desk, the surface of which was inlaid with an intricate marble mosaic.

"This is Esdras," the angel said to K., "the scribe, the historian of the heavens."

K. climbed the stairs that led from the ashen ground to the terrace. Esdras didn't look up, remained bent over a long scroll with a writing device in her hand. Scattered around her on the table were stacks of other scrolls and pages, which, it seemed to K., she was using to compile her account.

"Can you tell me what happened here?" K. asked Esdras.

She lifted her head and pushed back her long black hair. There was no indication of surprise on her face. "What happened here?" Esdras repeated the question. "That's what I've spent all the time since I can remember trying to figure out. We've gathered every piece of information, reports from survivors, hundreds of them, physical evidence from the landscape, analyses of the ladder that connects the heavens and the earth. I've sent researchers down the ladder to earth to try to answer key questions. They go in secret, finding pieces, asking questions, gathering parts of the story, talking to people who've seen the visions, like your friend from Grunewaldstrasse. Consider this, K., after all my work trying to write the history of the razing of heaven and the disappearance of God from the divine realm, we still don't know how it was that a ladder came to connect the heavens and the earth. There is not a single scrap of evidence to prove that God ordered this ladder to be built. How could this be? Someone must have recalled God giving the order, or someone would have at least heard second or third hand about this most unusual project. One can use a bit of reason. Not that God is limited by reason—but still, using a bit of reason, we should ask why, if in fact God did order the ladder to be built, he would have had it built in such a way as to enable the earth beings to find it, climb it unhindered, and, in this one case, to come in massive numbers, bringing terror and destruction to paradise. There are plenty of theories. Some could be considered plausible, that is, in and of themselves they make sense, but they quickly lose coherence when set against the basic conditions of existence here, not to mention when they are held up to one of the other theories. Is there a single angel with memory of the actual building of the ladder, the forming of the rails, the insertion of the rungs? No. Not even our friend here, this survivor, who is certainly old enough to have witnessed the construction and to have seen the bustle and excitement generated by such an enormous endeavor. Ask this survivor about the construction of the ladder and he won't be able to tell you a single detail. For sure, you'll hear other things from him. He can say something about the feeling of seeing the hordes of humans barreling down on his dwelling when he was but a neophyte angel, a child if we translate it into human terms, and as such it is no surprise that terror is the primary thing he recalls. But what, exactly, can I, as a historian, do with this terror? What does terror, and the terror of a neophyte on top of that, tell us about anything? Yes, it does tell us something—but not a story. This terror cannot hold pieces together, or it can hold pieces together, but it cannot order or sculpt them. As you can see, though, I have pieces, but each piece is like the terror of a neophyte—and what I lack is the thread that can string these pieces into a story, a story with a beginning and an end. Hundreds of human years have passed, thousands even, and the stacks of evidence grow larger. With this passing of time and the growing of piles, one forgets entirely about any specific piece, or a piece gets caught in the wind—there are strong winds here, you've felt them—and vanishes into the swirling realm. Or a page or scroll gets buried under the next in this incessant process of accumulation, never to be looked upon again. Despite having no order, no form, the structure, if we can use this word, begins to erode. There's an idea here, especially among the survivors, that only when the *true history* is written, only when the story is finally told in its totality, when it can spread from angel to angel throughout the realm—only then will the angels call out in unison with such strength that God will turn to face the heavens and contemplate the possibility of his return to the heavenly domain. I can tell you this will never happen—the only chance we had has come and gone. I sit here and work without pause, even though I know I will never get closer to the goal. You would think that the nature of this work would frustrate me, embitter or depress me, drive me into despair. Strangely, the more I work, the more I gather, even the more I forget, the happier I become. Today, just as you entered the courtyard with our friend, I was looking at a description of the ladder as it falls away from the heavenly gate through the clouds and felt a surge of the purest joy I've ever experienced. How can I explain it? I can't explain it, just as you, K., will never be able to explain what brought you here, or what will bring you back down to earth. Some time ago, despite these difficulties, the council of angels demanded I submit my report, the first history—even if it could never be the *true history*—of the razing of the heavens and the flight of God, or God's withdrawal, that unparalleled catastrophe. I worked on it, as you humans would say, day and night, barely taking a break to stand up from the table. I read through the evidence again: the survivor narratives, the interviews, the reports. I cut. I stitched. When I encountered a gap, I closed my eyes and imagined what might have been. I saw angels designing and building the ladder, I saw the humans who climbed, I saw their leader, Hul, and the other one, Jacob—and I even saw God—yes, to complete the story I had to thrust myself into the mind of God, because all of this must have been, on some level, according to God's will. Bit by bit, my story came together; the gaps closed. Once the story was written in the language of the heavens, the angels gathered around, and I read it aloud to them. What a scene! A combination of an outpouring of grief and a kind of euphoria—finally, many said, an idea of what had happened here! Meaning had finally come! The angels wanted to hear it again and again, and copies of the story were made and soon every angel had one, and they would gather in small or larger circles and take turns reading aloud. For a long time, this is how it was, and heaven was again united, and again the angels spoke with a single voice, and the thought spread that this unity would attract God, that he would turn to face us, that he would eventually return. We organized a festival. Every angel came from far and wide. Collectively, we turned our voices upwards and issued our call. But God didn't return. Slowly, as the days passed after the festival, small discrepancies—one might even call them mistakes— were discovered in the text. Or perhaps 'discovered' isn't right. Let's just say different views were advanced, inconsistencies and ambiguities interpreted in diverse ways. In short, a revisionist mood gripped the heavens. Factions emerged. The reading circles, which had been defined by harmony, turned into sites of vociferous debate. Conflicts grew—all hope that the initial consensus could spur God's return faded, and, if you can believe it, one small group of the most zealous proposed that a legion of angels should form and somehow invade the higher sphere, depose God—kill him—and then rule both the heavens and the earth by the blade of the sword. Luckily, the council of angels interceded and quelled the drive for violence. To calm the angels, a deal was struck that the story of the razing of the heavens and the flight of God would be revised, that I, Esdras the Scribe, would 'correct' my story to include each of the various lines of interpretation, however fragmentary, however nonsensical. This is what I've done. Here it is—the revision of the story of heaven's destruction and God's withdrawal, written in the language of the heavens."

With that, Esdras pushed a thick volume across the table. K. picked it up and opened it, gazed down at the wondrous script that seemed to glow with a blue-green luminescence, as if backlit by a bioluminescent force. K. ran his finger along the lines, tracing the flow of the characters. These words were not words in an ordinary sense; they were but shells of an inner radiance. How long, he wondered, would it take if he chose to translate this story? Could he somehow render this radiance, this inner force, this material breath of God, into ordinary pencil graphite or plain black ink?

III. Imprisonment and Escape

The history of political anarchism is full of imprisonments and escapes, escape both in the literal sense of breaking out of institutions of confinement and in the figurative sense of the breaking of those invisible chains. "Man is born free," Rousseau writes, "and everywhere is in chains." K. imagined chains (the aviary, the cabin in the snow, etc.) and the breaking of those chains (the forester's potion, the arrival of Nahum Griggs, the flight of Esther Bird). Other elements hovered between confinement and escape, like the writer Dellman and, most significantly, the liminal figure who in some sense animated each of our sessions: Ida Fields.

There are certain trajectories: northbound into the woods to the cabin on the lake, southbound from Berlin to Prague, north from Senegal to Liguria, south from Zelená Hora to Vienna to Meran to Venice, east to the Hotel des Bains. And others: east to the Baghdad book fair, west to Paris and London—vectors of movement between the lines of history, crisscrossing into a snowstorm of identity, forming a pattern as unique as a snowflake, as delicate, melting into nothingness upon touch, upon contact with any solid surface warmed by the sun. Such is the identity of K.

When I suggested to K. that the wounded cedar was his wounded selfhood, he strongly rejected the idea. When I posited that the resin that flowed from the cedar's interior was memory, *his memory*, he became sullen and withdrawn and told me that I didn't understand a thing. When I indicated that the writer Dellman was his father, he angrily got up and left the room halfway through our session. When I floated the idea that Esther Bird was none other than Ida Fields, he placed his head in his hands and issued a dark, desperate laugh. When I mentioned his parents, he'd tell me he didn't have any parents, that he was alone in the world. When I'd ask him about his brother, he'd claim to have no brother. When I inquired who, if not his brother, was paying his bill, he fell silent.

"Refuge—" I said to him one day toward the end of the summer, "you are seeking a refuge, a refuge that is at the same time not a trap or a cage. But finding a refuge," I continued, "means a cessation of movement, a desire to put things in order—to sort, classify, name, and believe. When things are unstable, one can find no refuge, no peace, and one is stuck in a whirl of confusion."

"No," K. said, "this isn't right. You've got it all wrong, backward, inverted. But this is the principal aim of a professional like you: to invert and distort the truth."

"You believe in truth?"

"Why else would I have climbed the ladder? Why else would I have spent seventeen years translating the work of Esdras the Scribe, the history of the heavens, *The Book of Moonlight*?"

When I asked him if he felt imprisoned by life, he said the clinic was his prison. I went over and opened the door to my office when he said this and gestured into the hallway. "You are always free to leave," I said. "Nothing is keeping you here."

He considered this for a moment and then said, "There is only one way Sidney Keter's journals could have ended up here."

"How is that?"

"Her flight ended in this valley, beneath these mountain peaks, in the Mountain View Clinic."

"Aren't you just reversing M.'s course?" I said to him. "Two thefts, two flights, always a doubling." K. ignored this. I went on, "In your mind, I am your jailor and the keeper of the secrets you hope to discover. But there are no secrets. What you take to be secrets are only places where your imagination has run aground."

"You have just confirmed what I had hoped to discover," K. said, "namely that Esther Bird was here, and here she was destroyed."

IV. Interruption

K. announced he was leaving the clinic during what was to be our final session. When I asked him when he planned to go, he said he was leaving that very day—by the early evening bus. I expressed strong resistance to this idea, saying he only wanted to go now that we were starting to make real progress in untangling his knotted web of thoughts. He countered that such a "web" could never be untangled and that I actually had no interest in untangling, that I was preparing to "cut the knot instead." People like you, he told me, have no patience for untangling and even less for tracing the complex twists and turns, the beauty, of the knot. You only think about, he said, a solution, and this solution means slicing through the unknowable, destroying what cannot be understood. The unknowable, he told me, has no place at the clinic and perhaps no place left in this life. I countered with a question: what if what you describe as unknowable is quite open to being discovered? Sometimes, I continued, what appears most mysterious to us is that which we don't want to see; the secret, in other words, is hiding in plain sight. At that, K. got up from the chair and left my office. I never saw him again.

There can be no other author of this piece of fiction than Dr. L. Hruška. It is one of his "unorthodox methods," no doubt, advertised on the clinic's brochure. That the document has followed me overseas shows Hruška's reach, his vigilance, the scope of his networks around the world. The postmark, as you can see from this envelope, is from Mountain View, Vermont. From the peak of Zelená Hora to the valley of the Mountain View Clinic. No doubt Hruška would say, "From mind to soul—the landscape of the self."

A Report to an Academy, Revisited

'M SORRY I'M LATE to our final lecture. I've invited the dean and the dean's assistant to attend and have been waiting by the water fountain to see if they'd come. I have nothing to hide from them, contrary to what they say in official letters and other memoranda. You know it—you've known all along that the powers here would not tolerate this pebble in the shoe. Without thought, annoyed only that they have to stop, to pause what they consider to be "forward motion," they want to draw the pebble out and flick it to the side. But this is precisely it—the pause, the cessation of movement. In this interval, everything that matters takes place. The pebble is our blessing, our gift, and let me be as bold as to say, and I'd say this loudly and clearly in front of the dean and the dean's assistant: literature itself takes place in that pause, in the attempt to remove the irritation so we can stand again on level ground without the stabbing of the pebble's raw edge turning and tumbling from heel to toe.

As you can see, the dean has not come. His assistant is absent. My colleagues in the department, all of whom I've invited, have avoided this auditorium like a house shut-in with plague.

That the dean will hear about what I say, I have no doubt. His eyes and ears are here, despite his absence. Every regime of power must rely on its foot soldiers, recruits, who, for whatever reason—malice, a lust for power, naïve trust—do its bidding and go where it cannot go without risking too much. Risking what? Dissent. Rebellion. Risking the crumbling of its paper-thin legitimacy, the legitimacy of its authority, as thin as that newly spackled drywall that separates the dean's office from his assistant's cubicle, purposefully built, I suspect, to allow her to listen to and record his conversations. That the dean would never, could never, come to this lecture is clear. He's afraid, of course, but not of me, or even of what I symbolize: a class, as he puts it, that's "out of control." What does he fear? Does he suspect what is plain to see, that he's pushed and pulled the variables of the equation around until they are hopelessly scrambled? No, I don't think so. He'll say he's created order here and others will agree. Nobody will dare to stand up and tell him that while he has achieved order, the order itself is entirely wrong. Let's say it directly: the dean fears what all tyrants fear, a loss of power, which at the same time means a loss of life. When tyrants fall, they fall hard. Underlings might survive, sliding between regimes of power—the dean's assistant has, I gather, done it before—but the one at the top must be cleared out of the way, one statue replaced by another on the pedestal. Societies of control operate with one rule: fall in line or you're gone, simple as that, even if it's a line as shaky as the one drawn by the dean; the shakier the line, the closer the guillotine's blade. It's a universal truth. There is always a fine rationale for destroying lives.

You might think, given the prelude, this final lecture will be a counterpunch to the dean. That's not the case. What a waste of time it would be to step into the ring with him, especially now as winter is closing in on us. Instead, I'll choose what some might call the coward's option. I'll say what I came here to say, pack my papers into my backpack, take my small suitcase from the storage closet by the door, and once out on the street will hail a taxi for the airport. My flight to New York leaves later this afternoon, the one for Prague tonight.

It was a strange realization that my father's undiagnosed ailment, his ebbing force, the slowing of his blood, was not an acute crisis. It was not the beginning of the problem either. It was, or is, the long-term effect of a life lived between the lines. He has asked me (told me) to go away, pointing out that he never asked me to come in the first place. Hruška would say how fitting it is that I end with this two-pronged attack, one prong curving west and south toward the "father" and the other a straight shot toward the "capital"—the dean. Alas, he'd say, my own private Schlieffen Plan has stalled out within range of canon fire of its goal, my "army" doomed to years in the muddy trenches with no hope of victory.

This lecture could begin with a list of grievances, like that most famous list of grievances called the Declaration of Independence. If it did begin this way, it would ultimately fall into the same trap, the assertion of one paradigm of power over another, the coward Jefferson erasing the only true line from the whole document, the line that recognized slavery as antithetical to the purported spirit of the movement, even though the real spirit was not about freedom but about power, the power to take land to the west of the 1763 demarcation line. The dean would love it if I were to begin with grievances. He'd then say, "Kirschbaum only complains because he wants something," or, "Kirschbaum just can't handle the role he's in," or, "Kirschbaum is throwing his usual temper tantrum, blaming everything, blaming the so-called 'system,' to avoid taking responsibility himself." One cannot fight the dean's authority with lists of grievances.

As you know, I caught up with Milena at the Hotel des Bains. She was in the dining room, sitting at a table in the opposite corner from the entrance. I slowly approached. She seemed to be, and the marginalia supports this, reading and writing as quickly as possible. When I reached the table, she looked up at me and stilled her pen. The look in her eyes seemed both totally foreign and uncannily familiar. This was it! Her eyes at that moment were glimmering like Ida's eyes, those fantastic orbs, those planets around which the moon of my existence had circled for all those years. "Ida," I said to her, naming her, and her mouth bent into a smile. "It won't be that easy for you to pull me in," she said. Then she slid the pages toward me and said, "Here, I'm done with them." I gathered them in. I could see they'd been labored over. Coffee stains, bent corners, they'd been packed and unpacked and repacked countless times with little regard for preserving their condition. Yet here they were, Cohen's pages, his novel, and hers, her story—or anti-story—whatever it was she felt compelled to tell alongside his, or around it. Though I had nothing more to say and would have liked, at that moment, to get out of there as quickly as I could, I hesitated. It could have been the long journey, the whole time not knowing what the outcome would be. It could have been the oppressive thought of this manuscript being lost forever, whatever it was, I felt exhausted and couldn't take another step.

Milena, I'd guess, sensed this, and said, "There's someone here you'd be interested in meeting. She's staying the night at the hotel. She's in room 401." I turned and started to walk away. "Just one more thing," she said.

"What's that?" I asked, facing her again. She stood.

"What will you do with it, with the novel?"

"Return it to Cohen. What else?"

She didn't answer. She leaned against the table and seemed to be gazing past me into the far corners of the empty dining room, as if other guests could be seen busily eating their meals.

I made my way out of the dining room. The elevator wasn't working. I took the main staircase to the second floor and then found the stairwell in the corner of the building that continued to the upper levels. The hallway was dark, lit only by the dull yellowy spheres every twenty feet. In such a light, I could barely make out the numbers on the doors, but at the far end of the hallway, there it was, the door to room 401. Another wave of weariness washed over me. Perhaps, I thought, there would be a spare bed in the room for me to have a rest on. I knocked.

A woman—old, short, thick curly black hair, black silk dress, round glasses—stood there, gazed at me for a few seconds, then said, "Come in," waving me inside the small space. As I entered, a strange feeling came over me, as if I were stepping back through time, into a time when the Hotel des Bains was full of guests from every European country and beyond, those years before and between the world wars. I looked around. A Persian carpet with a bird motif covered most of the floor. The bed was neatly made and covered by a spread of Indian fabric. The desk was simple, elegant, and reminded me of my desk back in Prague. On its surface was a typewriter, an Underwood, in which was loaded a half-typed page. Beside it, on the left, was a small stack of empty paper. On the right sat a large stack of typed pages. Beyond that, the room was sparsely furnished: a plain armoire, a long mirror, a desk chair, an upholstered armchair by the window, a book with a blue cover on the side table, a desk lamp, a bedside standing lamp, curtains.

"Come, sit," she said, gesturing toward the armchair. I sat down and she took a seat on the edge of the narrow bed.

"Who are you?" I asked.

"I'm Esther Bird," she said.

"I've been searching for you for many years. How long have you been here, here at the Hotel des Bains?"

"Quite a while."

"And you're here to write this?" I asked, pointing over to the large stack of pages next to the Underwood.

"You could say that. Allow me, please, to tell you what it's about. I think the story will interest you. You can sit back in the chair. Here, put your feet up on this one. I'll get something to cover you up," she said, sliding the desk chair under my feet and then going to the closet to fetch a down blanket, spreading it over my body. "Just close your eyes and listen. Rest. Calm your mind and try to find the center of the story."

"I'm ready to hear it."

"Good. Now, then, the first thing I'll ask of you is to give up the idea that what I'm telling you is the same as what's written on those pages. The pages contain the story, or stories, stories both identical to the one I'm going to tell you and, at the same time, fundamentally different."

This point struck me as nonsense, but I was too tired to debate it with her. "Sure," I uttered, "identical but also fundamentally different. I get it." My eyes were closed now, and I could feel sleep creeping beneath my eyelids. I longed for it. It had been a long, tiring journey to the Hotel des Bains.

Her voice cut in. "Joseph, son of Jacob, was out in the field when he saw an unfamiliar sight—an eagle was circling in the sky above him. As he gazed at it, the eagle slowly made its way to the east, always curving back toward Joseph as if pulling him away from his father's lands. Joseph was still a young man, but he'd heard his father and others in the camp talk about the eagle many times. An eagle like this one, large and regal, could only be the earthly form of a more powerful being, like an angel, or one of the gods worshipped by the neighboring peoples, the idol-worshippers. On the other hand, if there is only one all-powerful, almighty God, Joseph thought, then those gods would not exist, and this eagle must be a messenger sent by the Lord.

"By nightfall, Joseph had followed the eagle far to the east, well past the family's lands, beyond the neighboring peoples and into the wilderness. At last, the eagle descended into the branches of a cedar and Joseph stopped for the night. He sat down on an old pile of stones, some sort of abandoned shrine, and drank water from a skin. Then, as night fell, he took the largest of the stones and set it down for his head. The moment his head rested upon it, Joseph fell into the deepest possible sleep. A darkness as dark as death overcame him and blotted out everything. He was terrified—terrified of the abysmal darkness, of the nothingness, of the fragile layer of existence quickly giving way beneath his feet. He fell into a bottomless well, toward the center of the earth, toward the pit of his innermost despair, toward his own erasure and the erasure of the universe—toward the end of God, the undoing of creation, the emptiness of God's sleep on the seventh day. Joseph cried out, waking himself out of one dream, falling directly into another.

"It was dusk. The bluish hue of the gloaming hung in the air above him. From this position on the rock, he could see a ladder next to him, rising from the earth toward the heavens. Angels were ascending and descending on it, visible as a whirl of light, colorless, radiant. Joseph focused on trying to find the point where the ladder ended. It seemed to reach higher and higher into the rarified distance. Then he saw his eagle, his guide, wheeling around the ladder just below the clouds. This was surely, Joseph thought, the call from the heavens to climb.

"Slowly, still exhausted from the hours of walking, he approached the ladder. He set his hand on the side rail and felt a bolt of energy course through his body. This ladder contained the vital fire. It was made of a dark substance with an unrecognizable texture. Engraved between the rungs were pictures of heroes of long-past wars, the descendants of the coupling of the divine beings with human women, the *Nephilim*. As Joseph climbed, he felt infused with their energy and power, as if their power flowed from the ladder into his blood.

"With each step, Joseph came closer to the eagle, but when he reached the bottom of the clouds, the eagle, which was now quite near, soared upwards through them, directing him still higher, and again became nothing more than a speck of darkness circling in the distant sky. On and on this went, Joseph climbing, the eagle ascending, Joseph following its path, until he reached the end of the ladder where there was no rung, where everything vanished into a foggy mist. The eagle now reversed course, dove down, and seized Joseph in its talons, lifting him up with such incredible speed and force that he lost consciousness. When he woke, he found himself in front of the heavenly gates. In the distance, he could see the magnificent Fortress of Heaven, built of ice crystal. It was a sight that filled Joseph with awe. He fell to his knees.

" 'Rise,' a voice called out. Joseph stood and saw two angels in front of the gate. They approached him. 'Who brought you here?' one of the angels asked. 'I brought him,' replied the eagle. As the eagle spoke, he transformed into an angel of heaven. 'The One, the Only, the I-Am has instructed me to bring him.'

'What would the I-Am want with this creature, whose stench is so vile that it pollutes the entire heavenly domain?'

'Open the gates, Aza,' the eagle-angel said, 'and we shall see.'

"Aza undid the lock, and he and the other guardian pulled open the heavenly gate. As they entered, the eagle-angel said to Joseph, 'I am Metatron, servant of the Lord. I will bring you to the I-Am.' Metatron led Joseph to the fortress, where God's legions were gathered. All were adorned with jewels and gold. The vast army split in half as the two approached, allowing Joseph, with Metatron as his guide, to pass through the space and to climb the hundred stairs to the door of the fortress. The door opened in front of them. While the outside of the fortress was made of ice, the inner chambers and altars were made of fire—a substance burning but somehow still solid. Metatron led Joseph up the stairs and past altar after altar, seven in total, ending at the top of the fortress, where a mountain loomed above them. The mountain was dark, austere, surrounded by wind and lightning. Toward the peak of the mountain was a palace, built entirely of ruby, which glowed blood-red with each lightning strike. 'You should lower your eyes as we approach the palace of the I-Am,' Metatron said to Joseph. 'The raw vision of the I-Am, even at great distance, is too much for a pair of human eyes. The power of the I-Am will strike through your eyes and turn your soul to ash.' Joseph did as Metatron advised. He closed his eyes, bent his head down toward the ground, and locked arms with his guide. Slowly, the two made their way up the steep slope toward the palace. At the palace gates, they were met by another legion of guards, all of whom had six wings and swords of fire. The gatekeeper opened the way and Metatron pulled Joseph along. Inside the palace, the energy intensified. Joseph felt his skin and hair burning with the fires of heaven, a fire surrounding him, becoming him, and yet remaining on the surface. This is the life force, he thought, the source of creation—flowing from the I-Am to everything else, to all living things: plants, animals, angels, and human beings.

"More stairs led to the majestic throne, which shimmered in the light of the divine fire. To either side, the grand legions of the innermost sanctum were bent down on one knee, their swords pressed with the tips to the ground. When they arrived in front of the throne, Metatron instructed Joseph to slowly remove the shield from his eyes, saying, "The I-Am has prepared himself to be seen by you." Joseph obeyed and saw that sitting on the throne was the I-Am, the Lord on high, neither angel nor human but something else, something that seemed to Joseph to combine indescribable beauty with unspeakable horror, such that Joseph felt himself both lurching forward and shrinking back, terrified at its impossible form. Metatron called out, 'Lord, the One and Only, Almighty, King of Heaven, Ruler of All that Is, Joseph has come to you as you requested. He followed the path of the eagle and now stands before you, ready to hear your words. I, Metatron, scribe of heaven, will write them down for the world to remember the message you deliver here.'

"At Metatron's prompting, Joseph moved closer to the I-Am, the whole time feeling the energy increase, feeling his own power grow. It was as if by approaching God, Joseph, too, took within himself some of God's power, the power of creation, the power of bringing forth form out of the primordial chaos. Joseph was now directly before the I-Am. Next to him stood the head of the legion of angels, charged with protecting the innermost sanctum. His sword was twice the size of the others and glowed red, as if it had just been lifted from the forge. The angel, a massive, twelve-winged being, had closed his eyes. Might he have fallen asleep? What absurdity, Joseph thought, to sleep in the presence of this awesomeness, to fall into oblivion before everything imaginable and unimaginable!

"A thought came to Joseph—or not a thought but an impulse, a desire. The Lord began to speak, but Joseph did not hear him. He was overcome by a great struggle within himself, a struggle to suppress, to banish, the strongest surge of desire he had ever felt in his life. His father's words rushed through his mind, words which, Joseph knew, had been passed down through the generations: *Sin crouches at the door; its urge is toward you, yet you can be its master.* There was no mastering this desire. Its power overwhelmed him, filling him with courage, with visions of future glory. In a flash, Joseph grabbed the sword from the sleeping guard and plunged it deep into the chest of the I-Am. The Lord was dead in an instant, his spirit, some say, escaping from his body and flying away toward a far-off region, a wilderness beyond the wilderness, a wilderness inaccessible even to the twelve-winged angels, a wilderness of wind and darkness, a churning watery realm, as deep as it is high, stretching out like a nighttime horizon.

"Joseph, shocked at what he'd done, turned around with the sword still in his hand, expecting the legions would overtake him. But the angels, one and all, were bent over in grief, their wings drooped, their swords set next to them on the ground, swords now empty of the divine fire. All mourned the death of the I-Am. Silence. Even the wind beyond the palace was stilled. Metatron led Joseph away, back to the mountain, down its slope, through the levels of the fortress, past the altars, which, like the angels' swords, were now extinguished, the everlasting flames snuffed out by Joseph's act. Beyond the fortress of ice, Joseph and Metatron saw the two angels of the gates of heaven. Aza spoke to Joseph: 'You, Joseph, have done what no angel could ever do. You have rid the heavens of the Lord. This is the reason we brought you here, we, the angels of the resistance to the authority of the I-Am. With the death of the Lord, we, the rebel angels, now reign. Metatron, archangel and scribe of the I-Am, will be the chronicler of this new age, this glorious history.' As soon as these words were spoken, Metatron turned again into an eagle, grabbed Joseph by his hips and shoulders and dove down through the clouds toward earth.

"Joseph woke. He lifted his head from the pillow of stone. He kneeled in prayer, trying to discover, as he had before he fell asleep, the presence of the Lord. It was gone. What, he wondered, would become of this world without the creative force of the I-Am? What would become of it without the Lord's presence, without the divine spirit comingling with the human spirit? And what would Jacob say to his son—his son who had murdered God? Slowly, Joseph started back to camp. On his way, he found his brothers in the field harvesting the wheat. The youngest, Benjamin, put down his scythe and ran over to Joseph. 'Where have you been, brother?' Benjamin asked, adding, 'Can you feel it? Something awful has happened. Father says to gather in the flocks. He says war is coming to the land.'

"Joseph left Benjamin and continued toward Jacob's tent. He found his father sitting on the carpet with his legs crossed. 'Come sit,' Jacob said to Joseph. Joseph took his seat on the carpet across from his father. 'You found the ladder,' Jacob said. Joseph nodded. 'You climbed to the unreachable domain.'

'Yes,' said Joseph, 'I did what you were unwilling to do. You ignored the Lord's invitation; you turned your back on the heavens. I, your son, was forced to do your duty.' Jacob listened to Joseph and remained silent for a long time after he'd finished. 'Speak, father, and tell me why you refused to climb. Was it because there was no eagle soaring there? Was Metatron not with you?'

'The eagle was there,' Jacob said, 'soaring above me just as he was soaring above you. I recognized this as the archangel, and I, too, approached the ladder with the intent to climb. Then I saw those thousand faces carved between the rungs.'

'The heroes of old,' Joseph shouted, 'the warriors of God!'

'Warriors, yes,' Jacob told his son, 'though not of God. These were the faces of the angels fallen in the Great Battle of Heaven, the angels who rebelled against God's rule. These angels, led by Aza and his brother, defeated God's legion, took the Lord prisoner, and placed him under guard in the palace on the dark mountain. The throne you saw was no seat of glory. It was the seat to which the Lord was chained. Even though the rebels had defeated, captured, and imprisoned the Lord, they could not kill him. A force prevented them, and without the Lord's death, they knew he would eventually regain control, in fact, his strength was growing. They needed a man—a human being—to do it, to murder God, and I could tell from the faces on the ladder, which you also must have seen, Joseph, that the path upwards was but a path downwards, that the relationship of the above and the below had become inverted, that the ascent to heaven was the descent to *sheol*, the realm of evil. For a long time, the capture of the I-Am by the army of *sheol* created something like a balance between good and evil in the world. Now, your murder of God has destroyed this balance. Goodness seeps out and evil rushes to replace it. You can feel it in the air. It is the tension of the coming war, the advance of tyranny, the wreckage of the world.'

'What of the archangel Metatron, then?' Joseph asked. 'How could the scribe of heaven be part of the conspiracy against the Lord?'

'What Metatron writes is fiction,' Jacob said. 'What he writes is lie.'

"Joseph steadied himself and said to his father, 'If war is upon us, we must prepare for the fight.'

'And how will we fight?' Jacob asked. 'My brother, Esau, is already on the march with a thousand Edomites to have his vengeance. The Ishmaelites rise in the east. We are lost.'

'No,' said Joseph. 'When I took the sword of fire from the twelve-winged angel I was flooded with knowledge of things to come. I saw myself leading a massive army; I saw myself sitting on the right-hand side of a great ruler, the most powerful man on earth. And you, father, and my brothers were there. Everyone was bowing down to me.'

'Then you are truly the prince of *sheol*,' said Jacob, 'as it was inscribed on the ladder to the underworld, as it was written by the Scribe of the Bottomless Pit, the twin of Metatron. Through my son, through you, Joseph, the evil of *sheol* has come to the world.'"

Esther Bird stopped talking and lay back on the bed. Images flickered through my mind: ladders crisscrossing through a stormy sky, dark masses looming above me, canyons opening up below where I stood, and I was standing, suddenly, on the edge of a vast chasm, as flashes of lightning cut through the gathering darkness—lightning, bursts of fire, the roar of thunder, feathered creatures swooping down on me, menacing me, words and more words forming out of Hebrew characters, roots of words growing into ideas, collapsing into disorder, falling apart into lines and dots, curves leading nowhere. Another story gathered in the distance like a thunderstorm. No, I thought, I couldn't take it anymore. I had to get out of the room before it was too late, before the storm arrived. Jacob and Joseph, that was enough, too much, way too much, and now as one passed, another was already gathering. Hurricane winds of narration tearing apart everything, the rooftops of houses torn away and scattered like autumn leaves. In my desperation, my mind lurched in two opposite directions. The first was toward sleep, and in truth I was already halfway there. The second was toward the door, the hallway, the windswept streets, toward the ferry, which crossed the harbor to Venice, away from the Lido, away from the Hotel des Bains. I had the manuscript in my bag, I'd done it, retrieved it for Cohen, and there was nothing more keeping me, nothing holding me back, nothing besides tiredness, the over-whelming lassitude—that and her voice, a voice sonorous and perfect. Her voice cut through time; it penetrated my dream, racing through the liminal territory of hypnagogia to the borders of my dreamscape.

"There is another story in these pages; that is to say, there's one more story that's meant for you. You can keep your eyes closed, Sy," Esther Bird said to me. "You can fade away into it. That's the best way of listening to a story like this. Allow everything else to fall into the depths and find the crack through which you can pull and push your being, and don't worry if it tears and scratches your skin, don't worry about the suffering—a person can't find the way through a narrow crack like this without suffering.

"Imagine it, Sy, a cold February day, a gray sky, a dreary combination of ice and snow. She is leaving him after months of tension, stress, and conflict. He's begging her to stay as she packs a suitcase. She refuses. She needs some distance, she tells him, space—time to gather the pieces. He feels everything falling apart—pieces, yes, hers, his, pieces ripping into fragments, and for what reason? No reason, nothing but stubbornness and pride, nothing but ambition, nothing but the chasing after success. They'd had success, plenty of it, more than most, but it still didn't measure up. Along the way, they had turned on each other. At some point they faced each other and each saw in the other an obstacle, saw the other as an amalgam of flaws, not of unrealized potential but of an absence of genius, lacking the fundamental drive to bend the world, to shape it, to truly create. Ida packs. Gabe implores. Ida remains silent; Gabe becomes enraged, shouts, slams down a mug of coffee. It shatters. Coffee flows over the countertop, drips to the floor. Bits of ceramic are strewn over the counter like pebbles in a stream.

"Youth, Sy, just youth—a story about the unchecked passion of the young. Gabe and Ida were full of passion, but this passion couldn't find a way to flow. It got dammed up somewhere along the way, the pressure built, and it burst with enough force to propel Ida to Berlin. She had no plan, nowhere to go. She moved into your room in Kreuzberg. You'd finished Ingrid Müller's *Forest Poems* and Grassfeld's *Trending Toward Zero*. It was around the time you got the offer from the woman who had two names— Milena, Mila—to translate a notebook she'd discovered hidden under the floorboards of a secret room in the Charité's Nerven- klinik, a notebook which had belonged to patient #276 of the Hereditary Health Courts, a man named Isaac Mondschein. You knew the woman from the Kreuzberg scene around Grassfeld, had met her at a reading of Grassfeld's *Tendenz Gegen Null* in the Volksbühne's Roter Salon. You bought her a drink, but she didn't seem interested in you, kept looking around, seemed nervous, distracted, out of sorts, perhaps, you thought, on drugs. You saw that tremor in her hands. When she came with the notebook, she was together with another phantom of the Kreuzberg night, one who led you down into Kaesbohrer's laboratory. He was a phantom who you thought had disappeared into thin air as soon as you drank the chemist's cloudy yellow liquid—disappeared so quickly and totally that upon waking you thought he might have somehow merged with you, two characters becoming one. Now here they were at your door, the woman with two names and him, Daniel Cohen. They told you they wanted to turn the text into a play about Jacob's ladder. They had lined up a director named Rosa Fuchsbein and a lead actress named Fo. It would be the story of the final ascent of the ladder by a human being, the story of the ascent of Jacob's daughter, Joseph's sister, Di- nah. When they asked you to translate it, you agreed. You took the notebook from her. It was called *The Book of Moonlight*. And then, days later, Ida arrived at your door and broke your world apart.

"Two poles of existence: *The Book of Moonlight* and Ida Fields. One could draw an ever-curving line and hope to connect these points, to bring them into relationship, maybe even into harmony, but this was a hopeless task. Days of *Moonlight* eclipsed Ida, and those with Ida erased *Moonlight* from the face of the earth. How could you love her, love her to the point of losing yourself inside of her, only to forget about her the next day—or even later that night, as you sat down with the leather notebook, undid its string, and plunged into a world so unrelentingly other that you felt you might lose your mind?

"Your story, Sy, is here in this stack of pages, pages of ecstatic lovemaking and unbridled carnality. The pages contain a fury, an impatience that indicates a hopelessness, that foreshadows an endpoint, a burning into ash. And Ida? She is there and not there. Her thoughts fail to come to life—it is only when she is gone, when she returns to her former existence, when she is again with Gabe, that she can speak with a fully embodied voice, especially when she reveals to Gabe that she is pregnant with your child. Who but Daniel Cohen would have known that when you boarded the train to Prague from Zoologischer Garten you were leaving behind two beings instead of one? Or did she leave you? Did she leave one day as you were lost among the ruins of the heavens abandoned, searching for the pathway to the withdrawn God? She might have called out to you. She might have put a hand on your shoulder to say goodbye, only for you to shake it off; she might have done these things and more before she turned and walked out the door, left the apartment, and vanished from your life.

"There's a cabin in the woods. There's a cabin on the edge of a lake. There's a cabin that exists at times of crisis, times when there is no difference between advance and retreat. It's a play with two characters: a husband and a wife. Outside the cabin, the snow gathers, inch upon inch, foot after foot. Inside, the wood stove blazes. He, the husband, stares into the fire. Everything beyond this place, he senses, is off-kilter, wobbling; the stitches holding it together are coming apart. It's Ida's performance; it's her story, not his, not Gabe's, and certainly not yours, Sy. It is the story of loss, the death of Amos, the son you never met, the son you never knew existed.

"The sound of sea glass hitting against the glass bowl propels you into childhood, into the memory of a day at the beach with your father, into the chasm of your father's silence, into the sound of the tides, into the discovery of the black pearl of sea glass shaped as a teardrop, a tear of mourning, mourning tumbled and polished by years of ebbs and flows. You arrive at the Hotel des Bains. You make your way to the dining room. You find Milena sitting there with the manuscript. You ask her a simple question: 'What is it about?' But you know what it's about, you know it better than anyone, or perhaps, truly, you don't know at all. Milena tells you something, pushes the manuscript across the table. The whole time you're there in the dining room, you hear that sound that transports you back to your childhood bedroom—the bang, bang, bang of sea glass against the curves of a glass bowl. You take the manuscript from the table and turn away. With all your will, you try to block out the sound, you try to walk away without turning back to look at its source—the girl, Diya, lifting and dropping the pieces of sea glass into the bowl. The slightest glance, you think, will cost you everything, all will be lost, reality will crack, the fissure will widen and become large enough for your body to slip through, and the painful journey will begin—the journey through the jagged tunnel to the other side, the flip-side-reality that was partially revealed to you when you drank that cloudy yellow liquid either in the forest hut or in Kaesbohrer's basement laboratory. But this will be a darker space, much darker than a scene of a failed family life in an attic apartment in Kreuzberg. That scene had hope for reconciliation, a hope that the story could be patched up, spackled and smoothed—the mind set right again. But this one, this tunnel, leads into a forgotten space, a space like a hotel lost in the past, the abandoned Hotel des Bains, a tomb of memory on the Lido.

"You look back and see the small girl. You know her from your translation. You know her from those long days working in the Grassfelds' apartment—Susan milling around the kitchen preparing coffee, Cassie reading on the sofa, Rolf in his room playing video games. Diya is listening as you search for the right words. You look at her as she scoops the sea glass into her hands, as she lets the pieces fall through her fingers—again and again. Then, at last, she stops. She searches the bowl and fishes out a single piece—a black teardrop—and holds it between her thumb and forefinger. She looks over at you. At that moment you know; she could never have been Grassfeld's child. Diya is your child. She is the second child you've orphaned, a second story interrupted at the beginning, its paper yellowing and brittle, pencil marks fading into a ghostly gray.

"Paths bifurcate. You are on the train, not knowing (or did you know?) whether Ida has stayed or if she's gone. Daniel Cohen begins work on a novel, which ends with the death of a son named Amos. The path intersects with that of Walt Myerson, and both vectors—the Cohen vector, the Myerson vector—crash headlong into Milena's path. Divergence, intersection—it's the geometry of lives. A tangent—Ida Fields leaves Berlin. She returns to Gabe, her husband. He takes her back. He doesn't want to know too much. He's cautious with her, gentle, even though Ida might have preferred something more direct, a clearing of the air, a fresh start. There is no chance of a fresh start here.

"Her belly grows. Her breasts swell. Amos kicks against her. She drives to the cabin on the lake to give birth to Amos. Deborah, her midwife, is there and sees her through the long hours of labor, the pain, the spilling of fluids, until Amos, the fatherless child, arrives in the world. How, at that moment, could anyone possibly imagine that two years later Ida would come back to the cabin to bury him?

"One day, you pick up a novel about a man who gets stuck in a large closet and decides to go for a jog there. Amid the endless revolutions, this man remembers the death of a child named Amos. You read the novel, and again, and over and over, finding one piece of the puzzle, then another. You are gathering pieces even though there is no puzzle, until you have assembled a story hidden in the shadows of the other story, and you realize this novelist, Daniel Cohen, is writing about your life, or rather, he is writing about the alternative life you could have lived. You feel the tremor, the internal quake—it is a fault line running over a pit of truth. You cast the tremor, the shaking of the truth, into her hands—Milena, Mila.

"Then, and here I'll conclude, comes a series of convergence points. I'll name some of them: the meeting at the bar between you and Gabe; the simultaneous stays at the Mountain View Clinic of Ida Fields and Isaac Mondschein; the coming together of you, Daniel Cohen, and Milena at the clinic Zelená Hora; you and Milena at the Hotel des Bains. Such convergences, the smashing together of variables, result in the release of energy, and these spheres of energy pulsate out from the convergence points, turning the points themselves—the barroom, the clinic, the hotel—into nothing but bursts of force, force that ruptures one version of reality to make way for another."

Esther Bird fell silent. I struggled to open my eyes, to gaze at this being who, I imagined at that moment, was such a force, an energy strong enough to rupture any possible notion of the real. I was too tired. My eyelids remained stubbornly closed, sealing her off from me. The only thing I managed to say was, "Where will Milena go? What will she do now?" I heard murmurs, sounds, soft, delicate noises, but only noises, not speech. Could it be, I dreamed, that Esther Bird really was a bird and that she'd flown away from me after chirping these stories in my ear? Could it be she spread her wings and disappeared into the night, black feathers against black sky, a raven? I tried to call out after the winged creature, but it was no use. I couldn't hold anything together. My mind was pulled into the darkness beyond the window, the last dregs of consciousness falling back into the sea of oblivion, into a mountain-sized teardrop of black sea glass, which, when lifted to the moonlight, transformed into the olive-green world.

It was morning when I woke, shivering from the cold (the window had been left open), stiff and aching from a night sleeping in the armchair. I looked around for her, for signs of her presence in room 401, but there was nothing that indicated she'd been there. It was impossible that I'd imagined the whole thing, I thought, after these many years of trying to track her down, trying to recover what she stole from the New York Public Library more than half a century ago: Keter's translation of *The Book of Moonlight*. How could it be, I thought, that I forgot to mention it the previous night, forgot to ask if the stories she was telling were part of that book? It could be that Esther herself had added to it, becoming another in the long line of writers, editors, translators, and interpolators of this endless assemblage. The stack of papers on the desk was gone. The Underwood typewriter was gone. A panic hit me: was Cohen's manuscript gone, too? I unbuckled my bag and looked inside. There it was—Cohen's book with Milena's marginalia, still there, still safe, still with me.

I closed the bag, stood up, and looked out the window. The beach, the sea, the sky—a view, I thought, from room 401 of the Hotel des Bains. I closed the window, gathered my bag, and left the room, shutting the door behind me. I moved quickly down the hallway to the stairs, down to the ground floor, thought about looking in the dining room for Milena and Diya but then decided against it. I walked along the road to the pier where the ferries docked. Minutes later, a taxi boat pulled in and its passengers disembarked on the Lido. How many of these lost souls, I wondered, were heading for the Hotel des Bains? How many other scenes were unfolding behind those hundreds of doors or along the long, dark hallways, in the lobby, the dining room, the bar, the ballroom, spilling out onto the terrace or to the stretch of beach below?

I wandered through the streets of Venice, half present in that peculiar city, half lost in a tangle of memories, if such dubious cerebrations could still be called memories. Maybe fantasy is a more appropriate concept—and it could be that all memory is fantasy anyway, as unreal as language is unreal; that is to say, it is both unreal and the only approximation of reality I know. We speak, we write, I thought, as I crossed bridges and peered down lonely, narrow canals; we speak and write and are, thereby, human. We are released from our animal cages, permitted to walk free, to join society, to participate in culture. Is there another way out of this cage? Could we not squeeze through the cage's bars and win freedom on our own terms? Who would we be, what would we be, who would I be in a realm without words?

I pictured an ape in the jungle, swinging from branches, picking and eating wild fruits, grunting, picking fleas off his body— freedom, for sure, the freedom of a brute! There must be a way,

I thought, to speak and write and at the same time to be truly free—to imagine words and stories that blast through the cage, that bend the bars, that allow both ape and man—preverbal and verbal—to exist in the same being, in an "I" that is no "I," that is not one character but multiple, not one but all—an "I" that contains everything and everyone while still, somehow, remaining singular, requiring only the verb "am."

I'll end this lecture and this course called Introduction to Literature with an epilogue of sorts, maybe a postscript. It doesn't matter what we call it, simply a section appended to give the whole pursuit its final shape.

At the end of Jackie K.'s story "Dress Shop Window," as you may recall, there was a note stuck to the window, inviting the narrator, the live mannequin, to meet a man at the fairytale fountain that evening in the Volkspark Friedrichshain. The narrator doesn't show up, but she meets the man sometime later at a rooftop party; it is the beginning of a doomed love affair.

One evening, about a year before Ida Fields appeared in Berlin, I was sitting by this very same fairytale fountain in the Volkspark Friedrichshain waiting for a woman to arrive. I'd invited her to meet me there but didn't know if she would show up. I'd arrived at dusk, found a seat on one of the benches that surrounded the fountain, and taken out a copy of Grassfeld's *Tendenz Gegen Null*. I read a few pages, marking words, scribbling notes in the margins, preparing my work for the following day. The light faded as I worked; the lamps in the park began to glow brighter.

I gazed around at the sculptures representing various fairytales—Snow White, Little Red Riding Hood, The Seven

Ravens—until my eyes found their way to a statue of a girl with a deer. The story "Brother and Sister" came to me in its gothic strangeness, a piece reaching its way back into medieval times. As I thought about this, a woman appeared out of the shadows and took a seat on a bench two away from where I sat. For a moment, I thought it must be her, the woman I was waiting for, but a quick glance proved me wrong. I knew the face and body of the expected woman in perfect detail. I'd spent months tracing every bit of her, etching her inch by inch into the stubborn surface of my imagination.

It wasn't a cold night, but still, the way she was dressed was totally inadequate: a black miniskirt, black stockings with a long tear running up her thigh, a thin white blouse. Not that I could see much in the pale light of the park's lamps, but she didn't look well, and this sickly appearance was accentuated when she took out a cigarette and tried to light it, only to find that her hands shook too much to hold the match to the cigarette's tip. After a while, she got up, started walking in the opposite direction from where I was sitting. She moved awkwardly on a pair of high-heeled shoes. With each step, it seemed like she would fall. She managed to take ten or fifteen wobbly steps before the tip of one of her heels caught in a crack between the paving stones. She fell forward onto her knees with a thud and a scream of pain.

I rushed over to her and tried to help her up, only for her to push me away. I asked if I could help. She refused, got up, and made a few quick strides to get away from me before falling again. Again, I approached her. I saw that her knees were scraped and bloody. Her face was drawn, her body sickly thin. "Let me help you," I said to her. "Let me bring you to the hospital," I said in both English and German. "It's not a problem for me," I said, "there's a hospital not far from here." She shook her head, and I could see the word "no" on her lips, even though she didn't say a thing. "Can I at least give you some money for food? For anything you need?" I reached into my pocket and took out some bills. Without speaking, she rose, her legs shaking, to her feet. "Let me get you a cab. I can pay for it, it'll take you home, or wherever you want to go. I'm not trying to bother you, just to help. You don't seem well." But this woman didn't want any help from me. She removed her high-heeled shoes and walked away from the fairytale fountain and into the Berlin night.

I stood there for a long time, alone, listening to the water bubbling through the fountain. It seemed to me that something important, something meaningful had just happened—but what? I didn't know how to explain it, how to think about it. I went back to my bench, took my bag, and left the park. Once back on the street, I caught a tram and rode down to Warschauer Strasse, where the tram tracks ended—where East met West. I made my way on foot over the Oberbaumbrücke into Kreuzberg. I found a bar near Schlesisches Tor and ordered a beer. Then I took out my notebook and a mechanical pencil and wrote, "Her name was Milena." I thought for a second and added, "I called her Mila." I thought again, took a drink, and wrote, "She came from Warsaw and had a tremor in her hands."

Also by Seth Rogoff

The Education of Kendrick Perkins (with Kendrick Perkins—2023)
The Politics of the Dreamscape (2021)
Thin Rising Vapors (2018)
First, the Raven: A Preface (2017)

www.ingramcontent.com/pod-product-compliance
Lightning Source LLC
Chambersburg PA
CBHW011346010726
47493CB00011B/2976